The stirring story of the lld
in Alexander Kent's bests

Also by Alexander Kent

To Glory We Steer
Form Line of Battle!
Enemy in Sight
The Flag Captain
Sloop of War
Command a King's Ship
Midshipman Bolitho
Passage to Mutiny
In Gallant Company
The Inshore Squadron
Stand Into Danger
A Tradition of Victory
Success to the Brave
Colours Aloft!
Honour This Day
With All Despatch
The Only Victor
Beyond the Reef
The Darkening Sea
For my Country's Freedom
Cross of St George
Sword of Honour

SIGNAL – CLOSE ACTION!

Alexander Kent

ARROW

For Winifred, with my love

First published in Arrow 1976

11 13 15 14 12 10

© Bolitho Maritime Productions Ltd 1974

First published by Hutchinson 1974

Arrow Books Limited
Random House UK Ltd, 20 Vauxhall Bridge Road, London SW1V 2SA

Random House Australia (Pty) Limited
20 Alfred Street, Milsons Point, Sydney
New South Wales 2061, Australia

Random House New Zealand Limited
18 Poland Road, Glenfield, Auckland 10, New Zealand

Random House South Africa (Pty) Limited
Endulini, 5a Jubilee Road, Parktown 2193, South Africa

Random House UK Limited Reg. No. 954009

A CIP catalogue record for this book
is available from the British Library

Papers used by Random House UK Limited
are natural, recyclable products made from wood grown in
sustainable forests. The manufacturing processes conform to
the environmental regulations of the country of origin

ISBN 0 09 912940 X

Printed and bound in Great Britain by
Cox & Wyman Ltd, Reading, Berkshire

Contents

Like leviathans afloat
Lay their bulwarks on the brine;
While the sign of battle flew
On the lofty British line.

CAMPBELL

I

The Squadron

BENEATH Gibraltar's towering and craggy protection, the mixed collection of anchored shipping tugged at their cables and waited for the sudden squall to abate. Despite streaks of pale blue which showed themselves occasionally between the brisk clouds, the air was cold, with a bite in it more common in the Bay of Biscay than the Mediterranean.

Considering its strategic importance, Gibraltar's anchorage was unusually deserted. A few storeships, some brigs and schooners finding shelter or awaiting orders made up the bulk of vessels there, and of major men-of-war there were but three. Anchored well apart from the other hotchpotch of local craft were three ships of the line, *seventy-fours*, which in this month of January 1798 were still the most popular, and the most adaptable, vessels in any plan of battle.

The one anchored nearest to the land bore the name *Lysander* across her broad counter, a name to match the figurehead which stared angrily from beneath her bowsprit. It was a fine figurehead, with the black-bearded Spartan general adorned in crested helmet and breastplate, originally carved by Henry Callaway of Deptford. Like the rest of the big two-decker, it was well painted, with a look of newness which belied the ship's eleven long years in the King's service.

Back and forth, up and down her wide quarterdeck her captain, Thomas Herrick, walked with barely a pause to peer towards the shore. If he considered his ship's appearance and condition, it was more from anxiety than pride. The months of work in England to get *Lysander* ready for sea, the whole wearing business of re-commissioning and gathering what amounted to practically a raw company had gone on without a pause. Stores and powder, water and provisions, weapons and the men to handle them. Herrick had more than once questioned the fates which had given him his new command.

And yet, despite the delays and infuriating slackness amongst dockyard men and chandlers, he had seen his ship grow from a disorganised chaos to a living, vital creature.

Frightened men brought aboard by the unrelenting press-gangs, and others gathered by motives as varied as patriotism or merely fleeing into the Navy to avoid a hangman's halter, had been slowly and painstakingly moulded into something which, if still far from perfect, could offer hope for the future. The first squall in the Bay as *Lysander* had crawled south towards Portugal had brought some weakness to light. Too many seasoned hands in one watch, too many landsmen in another. But under Herrick's careful watch, and the efforts of *Lysander*'s remaining backbone of professional warrant officers, they had at least come to terms with the awesome maze of rigging, the rebellious and treacherous folds of canvas which made up their daily lives at sea.

Once at anchor below the Rock, Herrick had waited with growing apprehension for this particular day. More ships had arrived and anchored nearby. The other two seventy-fours, *Osiris* and *Nicator*, the frigate *Buzzard* and the little sloop of war *Harebell* were no longer separate entities but part of a whole. By order of the Admiralty in London they had become one. The squadron, in which Herrick's ship would hoist the broad pendant of commodore, and over which and through all imaginable circumstances Richard Bolitho would at any moment now be exercising his right of command.

It was strange when Herrick hesitated to consider the matter. It was only four months since he and Bolitho had returned to England from this same sea. After a bloody battle in which Herrick's own ship had been destroyed and a complete French squadron routed or taken, they had gone to the Admiralty together. It still seemed like a dream, a memory of long past.

The result of that visit had been far-reaching. For Richard Bolitho an immediate promotion to commodore, and for Herrick the post of flag captain. Their admiral had been less fortunate. Packed off to govern a penal colony in New South Wales, the very swiftness of his fall from grace had somehow measured the step between authority and oblivion.

Herrick's first overwhelming pleasure of being appointed

flag captain to Bolitho had been slightly marred by another of the Admiralty's changes of heart. Instead of Bolitho's own ship, *Euryalus*, the great one hundred gun three-decker which he had originally seized as a prize from the French, they had been given the *Lysander*. Easier to handle than a great first-rate, possibly, but Herrick suspected that another officer more senior than Bolitho had claimed the ex-Frenchman for himself.

He paused in his pacing and ran his eyes along the busy decks. Seamen were working on the gangways and boat tier. Others swayed high overhead amongst the black criss-cross of shrouds and stays, halliards and braces, making sure that no frayed lines, no broken wisps of hemp would greet the new commodore as he stepped through the entry port. The marines were already in position. No need to worry about their Major Leroux. He was speaking with his lieutenant, a rather vacant young man called Nepean, while a sergeant checked each marine's musket and appearance.

The midshipman of the watch must have an aching arm, Herrick thought. He was very conscious of his captain's presence, and was holding a heavy telescope to his eye, obeying the last order, to report immediately when the commodore's boat shoved off from the jetty.

Herrick shifted his gaze outboard towards the other vessels of the small squadron. He had had little to do with them so far, but already knew quite a lot about their various captains. From the little sloop which regularly bared her copper as she rolled uncomfortably in the squall to the nearest two-decker, *Osiris*, they all seemed to have some sort of link. *Nicator*'s captain, for instance. Herrick had discovered that he had served with Bolitho during the American Revolution when they had both been lieutenants. Their reunion might present pleasure or otherwise, he thought. Commander Inch of the dizzily swaying *Harebell* had commanded a bomb vessel with the old squadron, here in the Mediterranean. Of *Buzzard*'s captain, Raymond Javal, he had learned little but gossip. Hasty temper. Hungry for prize money. He had all the makings of a typical if awkward frigate captain.

He let his gaze rest on the *Osiris* once again and tried to conceal his irritation. She was almost a twin to the *Lysander*, and her destiny was firmly in the hands of Captain Charles

Farquhar. All those years ago. It was like another fate which had somehow drawn them together once more, to serve under the same Richard Bolitho. Then it had been in the frigate *Phalarope* in the West Indies during the Americans' fight for independence. Bolitho had been her captain, Herrick his first lieutenant and Farquhar one of the midshipmen. Arrogant, high-born, Farquhar never failed to prick Herrick's resentment. Even looking at his *Osiris* did nothing to help. Her ornate gingerbread and other carving at poop and beak-head displayed a lavish use of real gilt paint as an outward sign of her captain's status and prosperity. So far they had avoided meeting each other, except when Farquhar had reported his arrival at Gibraltar.

Any sort of fresh beginning had faded as Farquhar had drawled, 'I say, you don't seem to have spent much on the old ship, eh?' That same maddening smile. 'Our new lord and master won't like *that*, y'know!'

Suddenly, the lower line of black gunports opened along *Osiris*'s sloping side, and with perfect precision the whole battery of thirty-two pounders trundled into the weak sunlight. *As one*.

Something like panic ran through Herrick's mind. Farquhar would never allow his ambitious brain to be fogged by some stupid memory or dislike. He had kept his eye on what mattered most to him. Which at this particular minute was to impress the commodore. It happened to be Richard Bolitho, a man more dear to Herrick than any other living being. But if it had been Satan himself Farquhar would have been ready.

As if to make the final stab the midshipman of the watch shouted excitedly, 'Barge shoving off from the jetty, sir!'

Herrick licked his lips. They felt like dry ashes.

'Very well, Mr. Saxby. My compliments to the first lieutenant. He may muster the hands now.'

*

Richard Bolitho walked to the quarter windows of the broad cabin and looked towards the other ships. Despite the importance of the moment, the solemnity of being received aboard his own flagship for the first time in his life, he could not contain his excitement. It was like wine and laughter all bubbling up inside him, held in check by some last reserve.

He turned and saw Herrick watching him from beside the
screen door. Some seamen were carefully arranging chests
and boxes which had been swayed up from the barge, and he
could hear his coxswain, Allday, bawling angrily at someone
to take care.

'Well, Thomas, that was a fine welcome.'

He strode across the deck with its neat covering of black
and white chequered canvas and took Herrick's hand. Overhead he could hear the thump of boots as the marine guard
departed, the returning familiar sounds of normal routine.

Herrick smiled awkwardly. 'Thank you, sir.' He gestured
at the baggage. 'I hope you've brought all you need. It seems
we may be a while from home.'

Bolitho studied him gravely. Herrick's stocky figure, his
round, homely face and those bright blue eyes were almost as
familiar as Allday's. But he seemed different somehow. It was
only four months, and yet . . .

He thought of all that had happened since that visit to
the Admiralty. The discussions with men so senior and
powerful that he still could not grasp that promotion could
mean so much. Whenever he had mentioned his anxiety over
the progress being made with his new flagship he had seen
that amused look in their eyes.

The admiral who had given him his appointment, Sir
George Beauchamp, had put it into words. 'You'll have to
forget that sort of thing now, Bolitho. The captain must deal
with the running of a ship. Yours is a more exacting task.'

Eventually he had taken passage to Gibraltar in a fast
frigate, pausing in the Tagus with despatches for the flagship
of the fleet employed on blockade duty. There he had been
given an audience with the admiral, the Earl of St. Vincent, so
titled because of his great victory eleven months back. The
admiral, still affectionately known as 'Old Jarvy' by many of
his subordinates, but only when he was well out of earshot,
had greeted him briskly.

'You've got your orders. See you carry 'em out. It's been
months since we knew what the French were up to. Our spies
in the channel ports reported that Bonaparte visited the coast
many times to lay plans for invading England.' He had given
his dry chuckle. 'I think my medicine off Cape St. Vincent
taught 'em to tread warily where the sea is concerned.

Bonaparte is a land animal. A planner. Unfortunately, we have nobody to match him yet. Not on land, that is.'

Looking back it was hard to measure how much the admiral had managed to explain and describe in that brief interview. He had been on active duty with hardly a break, and yet he had been able to sum up the situation in home waters and the Mediterranean better than any Admiralty official.

The admiral had walked with him to his quarterdeck and had said quietly, 'Beauchamp is the man to plan this sort of mission. But it needs seagoing officers to push those ideas to reality. Your squadron's efforts last year in the Mediterranean told us a great deal about French intentions. Your admiral, Broughton, did not perhaps understand their true significance until it was all too late. For him, that is.' He had given Bolitho a grim stare. 'We must know the worth of putting a fleet into these waters again. If we divide our squadrons for a bad purpose, the French will soon explore our weakness. But your orders will tell you what you must do. Only *you* can decide how you are going to do it.' Again that dry chuckle. 'I wanted Nelson for the task, but he is still sorely weakened by the loss of his arm. Beauchamp chose you for this tickle at Bonaparte's underbelly. I hope for all our sakes it was a wise choice.'

And now, after all the discussions, the searching through reports to discover the value of countless ideas of the enemy's motives and objectives, he was here in his own flagship. Beyond the thick glass windows were other ships, all linked by the dovetailed broad pendant which had broken at the masthead as he had climbed aboard to the slap of muskets and the din of fifes and drums.

And he still could not believe it. He felt the same as before. As eager to get to sea as he had been in the past whenever he had joined a new ship.

But the difference would soon display itself in all manner of ways. When Herrick had been his first lieutenant he had stood between his captain and company. The link and the barrier. Now Herrick, as flag captain, would stand between him and his other officers, his little squadron and every man-jack aboard each individual ship. Five vessels in all, with over two thousand souls divided amongst them. It was that kind of assessment which brought home the reality of his command.

He asked, 'How is young Adam? I did not see him when I came aboard.' As he said it he saw the stiffness come to Herrick's face.

'I was about to tell you, sir. He is with the surgeon.' He looked at the deck. 'A slight accident, but, thank God, no real harm done.'

Bolitho replied, 'The truth, Thomas. Is my nephew ill?'

Herrick looked up, his blue eyes suddenly angry. 'A stupid argument with his opposite number in the *Osiris*, sir. Her sixth lieutenant gave some sort of insult. They went ashore on their separate duties but arranged to meet and settle the matter.'

Bolitho made himself walk slowly to the stern windows and stare down at the swirling water around the rudder.

'A duel?'

Just the sound of the word made him feel sick. Despairing. Like father like son? It was not possible.

'High spirits more like.' Herrick sounded unconvinced. 'Neither was badly hurt, though I gather Adam nicked the other fellow the worse.'

Bolitho turned and regarded him calmly. 'I will see him directly.'

Herrick swallowed. 'With your permission, sir, I should like to deal with the matter myself.'

Bolitho nodded slowly, feeling a great gap yawning between him and his friend.

He said quietly, 'Of course, Thomas. Adam Pascoe is my nephew. But he is one of *your* officers now.'

Herrick tried to relax. 'I am deeply sorry to trouble you in your first hour, sir. Not for the whole world would I wish that.'

'I know.' He smiled gravely. 'It was foolish of me to interfere. I was a flag captain and often resented my superior's hand in my own affairs.'

Herrick looked around the big cabin, eager to change the subject.

'I hope everything is to your liking, sir. Your servant is preparing a meal, and I have had some hands detailed to stow your chests for you.'

'Thank you. It seems most satisfactory.'

He stopped. It was happening again. The formal tones. The offering and an acceptance. When they had always been used to sharing. Understanding.

Herrick asked suddenly, 'Will we be putting to sea soon, sir?'

'Aye, Thomas. Tomorrow forenoon if the wind stays favourable.' He pulled the watch from his pocket and snapped open the guard. 'I would wish to see my officers —' He faltered. Even that was changed. He added, 'To see the other captains as soon as is convenient. I received some more despatches from the governor here, but after I have read them I should like to tell the squadron what we are about.' He smiled. 'Don't look so troubled, Thomas. It is as hard for me as for you.'

For a brief moment Bolitho saw the old light in Herrick's eyes. The warmth and trust which could so easily turn to hurt.

Herrick replied, 'I feel like an old foot in a new shoe.' He smiled, too. 'I'll not let you down.'

He turned and left the cabin, and after a discreet pause Allday and two seamen carrying a large case strode through the door. Allday glanced swiftly round the cabin and seemed to approve.

Bolitho relaxed very slowly. Allday was always the same, and for that he was suddenly grateful. Even his new blue jacket with the large gilt buttons, the nankeen trousers and buckled shoes which Bolitho had purchased for him to reveal his new status as a commodore's own coxswain did little to hide his thickset, rugged individuality.

Bolitho unfastened his sword and gave it to him.

'Well, Allday, what do you make of her, eh?'

The man eyed him calmly. 'A well-found ship,' he hesitated over the word, 'sir'.

Even Allday had been made to alter his ways. Never in the past had he called him anything but 'Captain'. It was their own unrehearsed arrangement. The new rank had changed that, too.

Allday read his thoughts and grinned ruefully. 'Sorry about that, sir.' He glared at the two seamen who were watching them curiously, the case balanced between them. 'But I can wait. It'll be *Sir* Richard afore long, and that's no error!'

Allday waited until the seamen had gone and said quietly, 'I reckon you'd like to be left alone now, sir. I'll see that your servant is warned about your customs.'

Bolitho nodded. 'You know me too well.'

Allday closed the door behind him and glanced coldly at the ramrod-stiff marine sentry outside the cabin. To himself he murmured, 'Better'n you'll ever know.'

On the quarterdeck once more, Herrick walked slowly to the nettings and stared at the other ships. It had been a bad beginning. For both of them. Perhaps it was all in his own mind, like his dislike for Farquhar. The latter obviously did not give a damn for him, so why should he get so easily ruffled?

Bolitho had looked exactly as he had known he would. The same gravity which could alter in an instant to a youthful exuberance. His hair was as black as ever, his slim figure no different, apart from the obvious stiffness in his right shoulder. He counted the months. Nearly seven it must be now, when Bolitho had been marked down by a musket ball. The lines at the corners of his mouth were a little deeper. Pain, responsibility? Parts of each, he decided.

He saw the officer of the watch eyeing him cautiously and called, 'We will signal the squadron, Mr. Kipling. All captains repair on board when I so order.'

He pictured them putting on their best uniforms. Inch in his tiny cabin, Farquhar in his lavish quarters. But each and all would be wondering, as he was. Where bound? What to expect? The price for both.

Alone in his cabin Bolitho heard feet thudding along the deck overhead, and after a momentary hesitation threw off his dress coat with its solitary gold stripe and seated himself at his desk. He slit open the large canvas envelope but still hesitated over reading the neatly written despatches.

He kept seeing Herrick's anxious face. They were almost the same age, and yet Herrick seemed to have grown much older, his brown hair marked here and there like hoar frost. It was hard not to see him as his best friend. He had to think of him as a strength, the flag captain of a squadron which had never acted as a single unit before. A rough task for any man, and for Thomas Herrick . . . he tried to hold back the sudden doubts. Herrick's poor beginnings, the son of a clerk, his very honesty which had marked him out as a man who could be trusted under any known circumstances, could hinder his overall judgement. Herrick was a man who would obey any lawful order without question, with no consideration for his own life or ruin. But to assume control of the squadron if its commodore should die in battle?

It was strange to realise that *Lysander's* original masters had fallen at St. Vincent. Her commodore, George Twyford, had been killed in the first broadsides, and her captain, John Dyke, was even now enduring a living hell in the naval hospital at Haslar, too cruelly maimed even to feed himself. The same ship had survived them and many more. He looked around the neat cabin with its well-carved chairs and dark mahogany table. He could almost feel them watching him.

He sighed and began to read the despatches.

*

Bolitho nodded to the five officers who stood around the cabin table and said, 'Please be seated, gentlemen.'

He watched them as they eased their chairs towards him, their mixed expressions of pleasure, excitement and curiosity.

It was a very special moment, and he guessed they were all sharing it with him, if for varied reasons.

Farquhar had not changed. Slim and elegant, with the self-assu.ance he had carried even as a midshipman. Now a post-captain of thirty-two, his ambition shone in his eyes to match his gleaming epaulettes.

Francis Inch, bobbing and horse-faced, could barely restrain his great beam of welcome. As commander of the sloop he would be vital for inshore work and sweeping ahead of the squadron.

Raymond Javal, the frigate's captain, looked more like a Frenchman than an English sea officer. Very dark and swarthy, with thick greasy hair, he had features so narrow that his deepset eyes seemed to dominate his whole appearance.

He looked at Captain George Probyn of the *Nicator* and gave a brief smile. They had served together in the old *Trojan* when the American Revolution had erupted to change the face of the whole world. Yet it was almost impossible to see him in those times. He sat hunched against the table like a large, shabby innkeeper. A year or so older than Bolitho, he had left the *Trojan* in much the same manner as himself. To take command of a captured blockade runner and sail her as a prize to the nearest friendly port. Unlike Bolitho, however, whose chance had led directly to his first command, Probyn had been captured by an American privateer and had fretted out most of the war as a prisoner until an exchange had been made with a French officer. Those vital years in his early service had obviously cost him dearly. He looked uneasy, with a sly, darting way of examining his fellow captains and then looking down into his clasped hands.

Herrick said formally, 'All present, sir.'

Bolitho looked at the table. In his mind's eye he was seeing his written orders. *You are hereby authorised and directed to proceed with your squadron to ascertain by every means in your power the presence and destination of considerable armaments . . .*

He began quietly, 'As you will know, the enemy has spent much time in seeking out some flaw in our defences. Apart from our successes at sea, we have been able to do little to stop the spread of French progress and influence. In my view, Bonaparte has never changed from his original tack, which was and still must be to reach India and seize our trade routes. The French admiral, Suffren, almost succeeded during the last war.' He saw Herrick's eyes flicker towards him, no doubt remembering when they had sailed together in the East Indies, seeing for themselves the determination of their old enemy to regain ground lost in that uneasy peace. 'Today Bonaparte must know that any delay in his preparations can only give us time to gain strength.'

They all looked round as Inch exclaimed cheerfully, 'We'll show them, sir!' He grinned at the others. 'Like we did before!'

Bolitho smiled. Glad that Inch, if ignorant of the facts, had not changed. Thankful that his excited comment had broken some of the distance between himself and the others.

'Thank you, Commander Inch. Your optimism does you credit.'

Inch bobbed and flushed with pleasure.

'However, we have no real intelligence of which way the French will move first. The bulk of our fleet is operating from the Tagus, to keep a wedge between the French and their Spanish allies. But the enemy may attack Portugal because of our presence there, or indeed he may attempt to invade Ireland again.' He could not conceal his bitterness. 'As they intended when our own Navy was beset with misfortune which broke last year in the great mutinies at the Nore and Spithead.'

Farquhar looked at his cuff. 'Should have hanged a thousand of the devils, not a mere handful!'

Bolitho eyed him coldly. 'Perhaps if a little more thought had been given to our sailors' wants in the first place, no punishment would have been needed at all!'

Farquhar smiled up at him. 'I take the point, sir.'

Bolitho looked at his scattered papers, giving himself time. He had risen too easily to Farquhar's intolerance.

He continued, 'Our duty will be first to examine the progress of French preparations in the Gulf of Lions. At Toulon, Marseilles and any other port about which we can discover enemy activity.' He looked at each of them gravely. 'Our fleet is stretched to the limit. We cannot afford to allow the enemy to scatter it to the extent it can be devoured piece by piece. Likewise, we must not have a large fleet at one end of the ocean while the enemy is at the other. Seek, find and bring 'em to battle, it is the only way!'

Javal said harshly, 'And mine is the only frigate, sir.'

'Is that an observation or a complaint?'

Javal shrugged. 'A malady, sir.'

Probyn darted him a quick glance. 'It is a vast responsibility.' He looked at Farquhar. 'If we meet with superior forces we will be without support.'

Farquhar eyed him coolly. 'But at least we will know they are nearby, my dear George!'

Herrick said, 'It is a *serious* matter!'

'Apparently.' Farquhar's eyes flashed. 'So let us tackle it *seriously.*'

Bolitho made them all turn towards him. 'One thing is certain. We must work together. I do not care what you may think of the value of these orders. We must interpret them into deeds. Drive them to a rightful and profitable end.'

Farquhar nodded. 'I agree, sir.'

The others remained silent.

'Now, if you will return to your commands and relay my wishes to your people, I will be pleased to have you aboard to dine with me tonight.'

They all stood up, already planning how they would rephrase his words to their own subordinates. Like Bolitho, each one of them, except Inch, would probably wish to be alone in his own ship to prepare himself and his ideas for whatever lay ahead. But they would have little enough time together, Bolitho thought. He needed to know each of them better, just as when a signal broke from *Lysander*'s yards his captains would read the mind of the man who made it.

One by one they made their farewells. Probyn was the last to leave, as Bolitho knew he would.

He said awkwardly, 'Good to see you again, sir. They were great times we once shared. I always knew you would be successful, famous even.' His eyes moved hurriedly round the cabin. 'I have been less fortunate. Through no fault of mine. But without influence . . .' He did not finish it.

Bolitho smiled. 'It makes my appointment all the easier to have old friends in company.'

The door closed and he walked slowly to the heavy mahogany wine cabinet which he had brought from London. It was beautifully worked, every join and surface the mark of a craftsman.

He was still looking at it when Herrick returned from seeing the other captains over the side into their various boats.

He sighed. 'Went well, I thought, sir.' He saw the cabinet and gave a low whistle. 'Now *there* is a thing of beauty!'

Bolitho smiled. 'It was a gift. More useful than some, I'd say, Thomas.'

Herrick was examining it carefully and said, 'I have your nephew outside, sir. I have dealt with his foolishness. Some extra duties to entertain his busy mind. I thought you'd like to see him.'

He touched the cabinet, adding, 'May I enquire who gave you this fine piece, sir?'

Bolitho replied, 'Mrs. Pareja. You will recall her, of course.'

He checked himself as something like a shutter dropped behind Herrick's eyes.

Herrick said flatly, 'Yes, sir. I remember her well.'

'What is it, man?'

Herrick faced him. 'With ships coming fresh from England, sir, there is always rumour, scandal if you like. There was some talk about your meeting with that lady in London.'

Bolitho stared at him. 'In God's name, Thomas, this doesn't sound like you.'

Herrick persisted, 'Because of it, your nephew crossed swords with another lieutenant.' He added stubbornly, 'A matter of *honour* they call it.'

Bolitho looked away. And he had been imagining it was because of Pascoe's background, his dead father. Traitor and renegade.

He said, 'Thank you for telling me.'

'Somebody had to, sir.' The blue eyes were pleading. 'You've done so much, for all of us, I'd not wish to see it thrown away because of a – '

'I thanked you for *telling* me, Thomas. Not for your opinion of the lady.'

Herrick opened the door. 'I will call him in, sir.' He did not look back.

Bolitho sat down on the bench seat below the stern windows and watched a fishing boat sculling below the two-decker's counter. The fisherman glanced up at him without expression. Probably in the pay of the Spanish commandant across the water in Algeciras, he thought. Taking the names of the ships. Tit-bits of information which might convey something in return for a few coins.

The door opened and Adam Pascoe stood inside the cabin, his hat tucked under his arm.

Bolitho stood up and walked towards him, feeling something like pain as he saw the way the youth was holding his arm away from his ribs. Even in his lieutenant's uniform he looked the same lean boy who had first been sent to him as a midshipman.

He said, 'Welcome aboard, sir.'

Bolitho forgot the weight of his new responsibility, his unwanted clash with Herrick, everything but the youth who had come to mean so much.

He embraced him and said, 'You've been in trouble, Adam. I am sorry it was of my doing.'

Pascoe watched him gravely. 'I would not have killed him, Uncle.'

Bolitho stood back from him and smiled sadly. 'No, Adam, but he might have finished you. Eighteen years is a beginning, not an end.'

Pascoe pushed the black hair from his forehead and shrugged. 'The captain has given me enough extra duties for my pains.' He looked at Bolitho's shoulder. 'How is the wound, Uncle?'

'Forgotten.' He led him to a chair. 'Like your own, eh?'

They smiled like conspirators as Bolitho poured two glasses

of claret. He noticed that Pascoe's hair was cut in the new style, without any queue at the nape of his neck like most sea officers. He wondered what sort of a navy it would be when his nephew's broad pendant flew one day.

Pascoe sipped the wine. 'They are saying in the squadron that this command would have been Nelson's had he not lost his arm.' He watched him questioningly.

Bolitho smiled. There were few secrets in the fleet. 'Perhaps.'

Pascoe nodded, his eyes distant. 'A great honour, Uncle, but – '

'But what?'

'A great responsibility also.'

Herrick reappeared at the door. 'May I ask what time you would wish the other captains to return aboard, sir?'

He looked from one to the other and felt strangely moved. About twenty years between them, yet they looked like brothers.

Bolitho replied, 'I will leave it to you.'

When Herrick had gone Pascoe asked simply, 'Is anything between you and Captain Herrick, Uncle?'

Bolitho touched his arm. 'Nothing that can harm our friendship, Adam.'

Pascoe appeared satisfied. 'I'm glad.'

Bolitho reached for the decanter. 'Now, tell me what you have been doing since I last saw you.'

2

Small Beginning

BOLITHO moved restlessly around his day cabin, one hand reaching out to touch objects not yet familiar. Around and above him the *Lysander*'s seventeen hundred tons of timbers and spars, artillery and men creaked and groaned to the pressure of a rising north-westerly wind.

He had to forcibly restrain himself from peering from one or other of the quarter windows to see how the rest of his squadron were getting on with preparations for weighing. He heard occasional shouts and the thump of bare feet as seamen raced in all directions to complete last minute tasks, and he could picture Herrick as he, too, fretted over each delay. It was all Bolitho could do to leave Herrick alone on the quarterdeck.

As a captain, Bolitho had been made to take his ships to sea in every sort of condition. From a lively sloop to the towering three-decker *Euryalus* in which he had been flag captain he had experienced the anxious moments before the anchor broke from the sea bed.

For Herrick it would be much the same, if not worse. To look at a captain on his own quarterdeck, remote and aloof from the bustle and confusion all around him, protected from criticism by his authority and his gleaming epaulettes, any idler might think he was beyond ordinary fears and feelings.

Bolitho had thought much in that way when he had been a junior lieutenant, or for that matter a midshipman. A captain had been a sort of god. He had lived an unreachable existence beyond his cabin bulkhead, and had but to scowl to have every officer and seaman quaking.

But now, like Herrick, he knew differently. The greater the responsibility the greater the honour. Equally, you had further to fall from grace if things went badly.

Allday came into the cabin and rubbed his large hands.
There were droplets of spray on his blue jacket, and he had
a kind of wildness in his eyes. He too, was feeling it. Eager
to quit the land again. Like a hunter who goes to pit his
strength against the unknown. Needing to do it, but never
knowing if each time was the last.

The coxswain grinned. 'They're doing well, sir. I've just
been up to the boat tier to watch over your barge. There's
a fair breeze from the nor'-west. The squadron will make a
goodly sight when we beat clear of the Rock.'

Bolitho tensed, his head to one side as something clattered
and dragged along the deck above. A voice bellowed harshly,
'Belay that line, you bugger!'

He bit his lip, imagining all manner of things going wrong.

Allday watched him thoughtfully. 'Cap'n Herrick will
see us clear, sir.'

'I know.' He nodded as if to seal the conviction.' *I know*.'

'He'll not be wanting to let you down.'

Allday removed the sword from its rack on the bulkhead
and waited for Bolitho to lift his arms while he buckled it
round his waist.

He said softly, 'Same old sword, sir.' He touched the worn
hilt. 'We've come a few leagues together.'

Bolitho looked at him gravely. 'Aye.' He let his fingers
run over the sword's guard. 'And I dare say it will outlast
the both of us.'

Allday grinned hugely. 'That's better, sir! You sound just
like a flag officer!'

The door opened silently and Herrick stepped into the
cabin, his hat under one arm.

'The squadron is ready to weigh, sir.' He sounded very
calm. 'Anchors hove short.'

'Very well, Captain Herrick.' He kept his tone formal.
'I will come up directly.'

Herrick hurried out and his footsteps could be heard
clattering quickly up the ladder to the poop above the stern
cabin. He would be taking into account the position of other
shipping, which mercifully was sparse. The strength of the
wind and the nearness of shoals. He would be aware that
there were more eyes than Bolitho's on him this forenoon.
The other captains who had appeared so relaxed and jovial

around the cabin table last night at dinner would be gauging his skill as a sailor, measuring it in *Lysander*'s sail drill, the smartness of getting under way. There would be glasses trained on the ships from the garrison, too, and from the enemy defences at Algeciras.

Bolitho said quietly, 'I am ready, Allday.'

Allday hung back below the cabin skylight and gestured above him. 'Up there, sir.'

Bolitho stood beside him and stared up towards the black mass of rigging, and beyond it to the towering main mast with its whipping broad pendant at the truck.

'Yes, I see it.'

Allday studied him gravely. 'That pendant is yours by *right,* sir. There's many watching it this day who'd have it off you if they had the chance. But while it flies, they will obey. So leave the worrying to others, sir. You've got fatter fish to cook.'

Bolitho faced him with surprise. 'Admiral Beauchamp said much the same. If not in the same words, then in the same sense.' He slapped Allday's arm. 'And thank you.'

As he strode beneath the poop and out past the big double wheel he was very conscious of the watching men all around him. Once on the quarterdeck, with the wind throwing beads of spray above the nettings and gangway, he saw the press of figures at halliards and braces, the scarlet coats of the marines in the afterguard where they waited to add their weight to that of the seamen.

'Attention on the quarterdeck!'

That would be Gilchrist, the first lieutenant, and Herrick's right hand man. Tall and lean like a bean pole, with a permanent frown, he looked much like a disapproving schoolmaster.

Beyond him were some of the lieutenants, the midshipman of the watch and numerous other nameless faces.

Bolitho touched his hat to the deck at large, comparing, despite his determination to avoid it, all this with what he had known and loved as a captain. He would have made certain that he had met and memorised the features and name of every officer aboard just as soon as was possible. The first lieutenant especially. He glanced at Herrick's stocky figure by the quarterdeck rail and wondered if he, too, was making a comparison.

A voice at Bolitho's elbow said thickly, 'A fine day, sir, if I may make so bold.'

Bolitho turned and saw a broad, red-faced lump of a man who seemed to fill the space of three. Not so much in height but in beam and depth, he stood with his fat legs straddled as if for a sudden gale, his heavy, mournful features studying Bolitho with unmasked curiosity.

He added, 'I'm Grubb, sir. Sailing master.'

Bolitho smiled. 'Thank you, Mr. Grubb.'

He should have known. There had been many tales lingering in the ship about Ben Grubb, *Lysander*'s master at St. Vincent. He had, it was said, played on a tin whistle as the seventy-four had nudged through the enemy formation and after the marine drummer boys had been cut down by grape-shot.

He looked over Grubb's vast untidy shape and decided it was probably true. He was an odd mixture. His features were like the rest of him. Wrecked by countless winds and storms, the damage well aided by heavy drinking. There was something rather fearsome about him, too. And from now on he would be one of the most valuable men in the squadron.

Grubb took a watch the size of an apple from one pocket and examined it before saying, ' 'Bout now, I'd suggest, sir.'

Bolitho nodded and turned towards Herrick. He saw Pascoe and one of the midshipmen ready and waiting with the signal party, a petty officer writing on his slate.

'Very well, Captain. We will get the squadron under way, if you please.'

He made himself walk slowly across the littered deck, trying not to look down at the various blocks and tackles which the quarterdeck division had been preparing since dawn. It would be a splendid sight for the *Lysander*'s people to see him catch his toe and pitch headlong amongst them. Strangely enough, the dreadful picture helped to steady him, and he was able to concentrate on the other ships as one by one the flags soared up to the yards to acknowledge Herrick's signal 'Up anchor'.

He heard a midshipman call, 'All acknowledged, sir!'

Then Pascoe's voice, quivering slightly to betray his own excitement. 'Stand by on the quarterdeck!'

Gilchrist's feet thudded across the planking, and even through his speaking trumpet his tone was disapproving.

'Mr. Yeo, have more hands put to the capstan bars! I want no delays!'

Bolitho did not turn. Yeo was the boatswain. He would meet him in due course. He saw the little *Harebell* rolling drunkenly, her yards alive with busy seamen. Her cable was up and down, and he thought he saw Inch's scarecrow figure by the quarterdeck rail, one arm pointing across the countless white cat's-paws which moved down with the wind and turned the anchorage into a miniature sea.

Bolitho took a telescope from the midshipman of the watch. As he trained it towards the other two-deckers he asked, 'And what is *your* name?'

The midshipman was staring at him, almost transfixed.

'Saxby, sir.'

Bolitho watched the seamen dashing aft along *Nicator*'s gangways. Saxby was about thirteen. Round-faced and innocent looking. His otherwise pleasant appearance was spoiled when he opened his mouth as both his front teeth were missing.

He steadied the glass and shut Gilchrist's metallic voice from his mind. It was all taking far too long. Caution was one thing. This amounted to a nervous crawl.

He snapped, 'There is some delay, Captain Herrick.'

'Sir?' Herrick sounded off guard.

'Execute the signal, if you please.' He hated doing it, but there was more at stake than personal feelings.

He heard the bark of orders, the muffled shouts of the topmen as they clawed along the vibrating yards.

Then, as the signal was hauled down at the rush, the cry echoed aft from the forecastle, 'Anchor's aweigh!'

Lysander's broad hull dipped heavily to one side, as with her anchor swinging free and the wind already banging and thundering in her released topsails she started to swing down across the choppy wavelets.

'Man the braces there!'

Feet skidded on damp planking, and more men ran wildly from the capstan to lend a hand.

One by one, the three ships of the line went about like ponderous beasts, while further to seaward the frigate *Buzzard* and Inch's sloop were already spreading more sail to stand clear of their big consorts.

Somebody cried out sharply, and Bolitho heard the crack of a starter across a man's naked back.

High above the deck the topmen were racing each other in their efforts to beat the rest of the squadron as Herrick shouted, 'Get the forecourse on her, Mr. Gilchrist!' He added sternly, 'And tell that bosun's mate to be less free with his rope's-end, or I will know the reason!'

Bolitho walked to the opposite side and watched as *Osiris* tacked heavily astern of the *Nicator*. She made a fine sight. Her topsails set and hard-bellied to the wind, she was heeling so steeply that her bow wave was almost up to the lower gun ports. Her forecourse and then mainsail flapped and then filled as one, so that in the hard sunlight they looked like white metal.

He said, '*Nicator* is falling astern. Signal her to make more sail.'

It might be that Captain Probyn was too busy to notice that his ship was already badly out of line with the other seventy-fours. Equally, he could be testing his commodore's mettle and powers of observation.

The signal midshipman called, '*Nicator*'s acknowledged, sir.'

Probyn's topmen were already setting the fore topgallant sail. It was just a bit too quick, Bolitho decided. Probyn *was* testing him.

Grubb was peering at the sails overhead, the compass and his helmsmen, and all without apparently shifting a muscle. Only his eyes moved, swivelling up and down, forward and abeam, like lanterns in a rough scarlet cliff.

Within an hour the squadron was free of the approaches, the three ships of the line making a proud sight under reduced canvas as they stood clear of the land. To leeward, their pyramids of pale canvas already blurred in haze, *Buzzard* and *Harebell* tacked busily under all possible sail to take station well ahead of their commodore.

Herrick called, 'Very well, Mr. Grubb. Steer east-sou'-east.'

Then he crossed to the nettings where Bolitho stood with one foot on the truck of a quarterdeck nine-pounder.

Bolitho looked at him and gave a quiet smile. 'Well, Thomas, how does it feel now?'

Herrick's face lost some of its lines. It was like seeing a cloud moving away, Bolitho thought.

Herrick replied, 'Better, sir.' He let out a deep breath. 'A whole span better!'

Bolitho shaded his eyes to look towards the land. There were probably couriers already galloping along a coast road even at this very minute. But there was no point in slipping like poachers through the Gibraltar Strait under cover of darkness. He had his orders, but the Earl of St. Vincent had made it very clear it was up to him how he interpreted and executed them. It would do no harm for the enemy to know a British force was once more abroad in the Mediterranean.

He let his gaze move up to the masthead, to the big dovetailed flag which was now as stiff as a plank in the steady wind. *His flag.*

He looked along the crowded decks at the scurrying seamen, the great coils of rope and lashings which to any landsman would seem like a hopeless tangle. And still further to the beakhead, beneath which he could just see one of the Spartan general's massive shoulders, Inch's sloop was a mere sliver of white against the horizon haze, leading the squadron. He smiled to himself. As he had once done in his own first command at the Chesapeake. Another ship. Another war.

Herrick asked, 'Do you have any instructions, sir?'

He looked at him, seeing Pascoe watching from the lee rail, one hand on his hip.

'The ship is yours, Thomas.' He made to turn away and added, 'What did you have in mind?'

'I should like to exercise the gun crews.' Herrick tried to relax. 'I am satisfied with the sail drill at present.'

Bolitho smiled. 'So be it.'

He realised that Gilchrist was hovering close by and added, 'I will be in my cabin.'

As he walked towards the wheel he heard Gilchrist say coldly, 'I have two men for punishment. Slackness on duty, and insolent to a bosun's mate.'

Bolitho hesitated. Floggings at this early stage would be bad enough under any conditions. With the little squadron standing out to sea where almost any sail might be a Frenchman or a Spaniard, it was hardly in keeping with their proud mission.

He heard Herrick say something and Gilchrist's quick retort, 'His word is good enough for *me*, sir!'

Bolitho strode aft beneath the thick deck beams. *He must not interfere.*

He passed the marine sentry by his cabin door and frowned. Not yet, anyway.

*

A full day after leaving Gibraltar the promise of a fast passage to the Gulf of Lions received a setback. Perverse as ever, the wind dropped away to a faint breeze, so that even with all available canvas set to her yards the *Lysander* was barely able to command three knots.

The squadron was scattered from its original formation, and each of the two-deckers moved with little enthusiasm above her own perfect reflection.

Bolitho had sent the frigate to scout far ahead of the main force, and as he paced restlessly back and forth across the poop deck he was thankful for taking that one small precaution. Captain Javal would be able to take advantage of the inshore winds, and it was to be hoped he would use them to some purpose. He smiled despite his impatience. Both he and Farquhar were still frigate captains at heart, and the thought of Javal's freedom, out of reach from any signal, was enough to rouse the envy of a man tied to a ponderous seventy-four.

He heard Herrick speaking with his first lieutenant and thought suddenly of the flogging on the previous afternoon. The usual brutal ritual of administering punishment had aroused little excitement amongst the assembled company. But as Bolitho had watched from the poop as Herrick had read briefly from the Articles of War he had imagined he had seen something like triumph on Lieutenant Gilchrist's narrow face.

He had expected Herrick to take Gilchrist aside and warn him of the dangers of unnecessary punishment. God alone knew that the penalties for thoughtless hardship could be harsher than the actual event. The mutinies at Spithead and the Nore should have been warning enough even for a blind man.

But as he paused to glance down at the quarterdeck he could see little between the two officers other than what you might expect under normal circumstances.

Gilchrist touched his hat and then walked forward along

the weather gangway, his shoes clicking on the planking as he strode in the strange bouncing manner which Bolitho had already noticed.

After a moment he ran lightly down the larboard ladder and joined Herrick at the weather nettings.

He said, 'A snail's pace. I wish to heaven we could find that wind again.'

Herrick watched him warily. '*Lysander*'s copper is clean, sir. And I have checked each sail myself and there is nothing we could do to gain even half a knot.'

Bolitho turned, surprised at his tone. 'That was not a criticism, Thomas. I know a captain can do many things, but controlling the elements is not one of them.'

Herrick forced a smile. 'I am sorry, sir. But I have been feeling it badly. So much is expected of us. If we fail before we have begun . . .' He shrugged. 'A whole fleet may suffer later.'

Bolitho stood up on some bollards and steadied himself against the nettings while he peered across the quarter to where *Nicator* was steering lethargically on the same larboard tack. Her topsails were barely filling, and her masthead pendant lifted only occasionally against the empty sky.

Of the land there was no sign, although the lookouts, clinging like tiny monkeys high above the deck, would be able to see it as a purple blur. The southern shore of Spain. He shivered in spite of the clammy heat, remembering the other times he had come this way. He wondered why Herrick was being so evasive. It was so unlike him to concern himself with what might happen because of 'maybes'. Again that nagging doubt. Was it because he was feeling his responsibility as too heavy a burden?

He said without turning, 'Your senior, Thomas. What do you know of him?'

Herrick sounded guarded. 'Mr. Gilchrist? He's competent in his duties. He was in *Lysander* as second lieutenant when she fought at St. Vincent.'

Bolitho bit his lip. He was angry with himself for being unable to hold his silence for more than a day at sea. More than that, he was hurt in a way he could not explain. Thomas Herrick was a friend, and over the years when they had fought and almost died in one battle after another, had endured thirst and fever, fear and despair, he had never felt such a gulf between them.

He said, 'I did not ask about his appointments!' He had not meant it to sound so blunt. 'I want to know about the *man*!'

'I have no complaints, sir. He is a good seaman.'

'And that is enough?'

'It has to be, sir.' Herrick was watching him with something like desperation. 'It's all I know.'

Bolitho stepped down and took out his watch. 'I see.'

'Look here, sir.' Herrick moved his hands vaguely. 'Things change. As change they must. I feel so marooned from my ship and people. Whenever I try to rouse the old style of things I become entangled with the affairs of the squadron. Most of my wardroom are young lieutenants, and some have never heard a gun fired in anger. Young Pascoe, the most junior lieutenant aboard, has seen more action than they have.' He was speaking quickly, unable to check the sudden flow of words. 'I've excellent warrant officers, some of the best I've sailed with. But you know how it is, sir, the word has to come from aft, it *must*!'

Bolitho studied him impassively. He wanted to take Herrick aside. To the cabin or a place beyond the scope of watching eyes. To tell him he understood. But then their roles would be as before. Bolitho thinking of a ship's routine and crowded world between decks and Herrick waiting to put his thoughts into deeds like the excellent subordinate he had always been.

He made himself say, 'Yes, it *must* be so. A ship relies on her captain. As I do.'

Herrick sighed. 'I had to speak – '

Bolitho added slowly, 'I did not agree to your appointment because of our friendship. But because I thought you were the most fitting man for the task.' He saw his words hitting Herrick's face like blows and continued, 'I have not changed my mind about that.'

From the corner of his eye he saw the master's vast bulk surrounded by serious-faced midshipmen as they gathered for the noon ritual of using their sextants to estimate the ship's position. By the rail Lieutenant Fitz-Clarence, the officer of the watch, was making a convincing show of studying the men working above on the main yard, but the stiffness of his shoulders betrayed that he was also trying to hear what his two superiors were discussing.

Bolitho said, 'So let's have no more gloom, eh? There'll be enough to fret about if we close with an enemy. That has not changed either.'

Herrick stepped back a pace. 'Aye, sir.' His face was grim. 'I am sorry if I disappoint you.' He watched as Bolitho returned to the poop ladder before saying quietly, 'I will endeavour not to do so again.'

Bolitho strode right aft to the taffrail and clasped the gilded scrollwork with sudden despair. Try as he might he seemed unable to meet Herrick, to cross the bridge between them.

'Deck thar!' The lookout's hoarse cry made him start. '*Harebell*'s signallin'!'

Bolitho hurried to the poop rail and checked himself, fretting until Fitz-Clarence, *Lysander*'s second lieutenant, came out of his thoughts to shout, 'Aloft with your glass, Mr. Faulkner! I want that signal, and I want it *now*!'

The midshipman of the watch, who seconds earlier had been drowsing by the nettings, congratulating himself on being spared Mr. Grubb's formidable instruction in the intricacies of navigation, fled to the lee shrouds and began to climb rapidly towards the maintop.

Fitz-Clarence surveyed his progress, hands on hips, his elegant head thrown back as if he expected the midshipman to slip and fall. The lieutenant seemed to like striking poses. He was very smart, even dapper, and what he lacked in height he obviously tried to replace with a constant show of authority.

Herrick stood by his elbow, hands behind him. Bolitho noticed that the hands were clasping and unclasping, making a lie of his outward calm.

Eventually the boy's shrill voice floated down to them. 'From *Harebell*, sir! *Buzzard* in sight to the nor'-east!'

Bolitho thrust his hands into his pockets, his fingers gripping his watch to steady his sudden anxiety.

Captain Javal was retracing his course to rejoin the squadron. He must have sighted something either too powerful to deal with or to warn his commodore that the enemy were even now giving chase.

He saw Herrick hurry to the ladder, and seconds later he joined him at the rail.

Bolitho said, 'Signal the squadron to close on the flagship. We will shorten sail directly to make their task easier.'

Herrick stared astern, his gaze very clear in the reflected glare. He said with surprising bitterness, '*Osiris* is already gaining, sir. Captain Farquhar must have eyes like a cat.'

Bolitho watched him in silence. Reading Herrick's mind as if he had shouted it aloud. He knew that if Farquhar was here as flag captain there would have been no hesitation. No need for the commodore to suggest the obvious.

Herrick touched his hat and returned to the ladder. But Gilchrist was already on the quarterdeck, his speaking trumpet in his hand as he snapped, 'Bosun's mate! Pipe all hands to shorten sail! Take the name of the last man aloft!'

He turned to look at Herrick, adding, 'Council of war, sir?' It sounded like a challenge.

Herrick nodded. 'Aye, Mr. Gilchrist.' He hesitated. 'Captains repair on board.'

Bolitho looked away, realising that he had been willing Herrick to speak out. To silence Gilchrist's arrogance once and for all.

The hands came hurrying from their work above and below in answer to the shrill of calls, barely glancing round as they ran to their stations for shortening sail. Bolitho saw Pascoe buttoning his coat as he followed his own men to the quarterdeck, touching his hat to Gilchrist, who responded with, 'Take a *firm* hand of your people, Mr. Pascoe.'

Pascoe looked at him questioningly, his eyes flashing in the sunlight. Then he nodded. 'I will, sir.'

'By heaven you *will* indeed!' Gilchrist's voice made several seamen pause to stare. 'I'll have no favourites in my ship!'

Pascoe glanced briefly at Bolitho on the poop and then turned on his heel, his seamen closing around him like a protective barrier. Bolitho looked at Herrick. But he was on the weather side, withdrawn from all of them.

He relaxed very slowly. Gilchrist had made his play openly but too soon. He had displayed to his commodore that he would expect to be upheld by him even against his own nephew. Gilchrist was a remarkable man. There was a lot more to him than Herrick recognised or understood. No mere lieutenant would dare to speak as he had done at such short acquaintance. No amount of personal influence could save a lieutenant from a flag officer, even a mere commodore, should the latter choose to use his authority to his own ends. He had never sailed with Gilchrist before, nor had he even met him. But *Lysander*'s first lieutenant knew a great deal about him, nonetheless. Knew enough to understand that Bolitho would never use personal ties to show favouritism. But for what purpose?

He walked to the opposite side of the deck, feeling the sudden heat on his face as the great maincourse was brailed up to the yard, allowing the glare to enfold the deck like a dying fire.

And from whom was Gilchrist drawing such confidence? He turned to watch the other two-deckers, overhauling steadily, and moving into a short, uneven line. Farquhar? Was he so eager for promotion that he had gained an ally for just that reason? He certainly had both influence and the funds to tempt a man. Or was it Probyn? From what he had seen of that one it seemed unlikely. He was lucky to hold a command in this squadron at all, let alone risk his good name for spite. He thought of Herrick. *Impossible.*

Allday appeared on the poop deck and touched his forehead.

'It'll be an hour or so afore *Buzzard*'s up to the squadron, sir.' He looked meaningly at the open skylight. 'Your servant has cooled some wine in the bilge for you.'

Bolitho hardly heard him.

'I hope Javal brings us good news.'

Allday studied him, momentarily taken aback. It was not like Bolitho to speak so openly about his thoughts. He must be worried about something. To Allday it seemed impossible that Bolitho should be troubled about the squadron's affairs, for in his eyes he could do almost anything. Nor about the dark-eyed Catherine Pareja back there in London. There had been talk in plenty, but that had probably been born of envy, he thought. God knows she was a fine looking woman and did not give a damn for what people might say about such 'goings-on'. One thing was certain, she was responsible for Bolitho's recovery from his wound after their last visit to this sea. But that was over and past. It was unlikely they would meet again.

So what then? Lieutenant Pascoe? He grinned. He was a lively young devil. Very like his uncle, and the same as some of the faces in the portraits Allday had seen at the old house in Falmouth.

He started as Bolitho said sharply, 'The wine will be red-hot by the time you have decided to stand clear of the companion way!'

Allday stood aside feeling slightly better. He waited until he heard Bolitho speaking with Ozzard, the cabin servant, through the open skylight, and then sauntered down to the quarterdeck where the afterguard were still busily making up halliards and securing the braces after trimming the sails.

Pascoe looked up as he passed. 'You look like a dog with two tails!'

Allday grinned. 'Now then, Mr. Pascoe, it's not fair to take advantage of a poor sailorman!'

Pascoe shook his head. 'Advantage of *you*? When that day comes Bonaparte will be crowned King of England!'

Gilchrist's shadow fell between them.

'I believe that you have been given extra duties, Mr. Pascoe?' He stared at him flatly. 'By the captain?'

'Yes, sir.' Pascoe regarded him without expression.

'Then be so good as to get on with your tasks, *Mr.* Pascoe.' He glanced at Allday. 'And not waste time with the commodore's coxswain.' He tapped one foot gently on the deck. 'A good seaman no doubt, but hardly fitting company for a King's officer, eh?'

Allday saw the sudden flash of anger in the youth's eyes and said hastily, 'My fault, sir.'

Gilchrist's mouth twisted very slightly. 'Really. I do not recall asking for the opinion of a common seaman. I am not accustomed to passing the time with – '

They all turned as Bolitho appeared beside the wheel.

He said harshly, 'In that case, Mr. Gilchrist, I would be obliged if you would take a glance at the weather forebrace and attend to it, instead of, what was it you said? Passing the time in idle gossip!'

Gilchrist opened and shut his mouth like a landed fish. Then he said, 'At once, sir.'

Herrick appeared by the rail. 'Is something wrong, sir?'

Bolitho looked past them, his eyes angry. '*Very*, Captain. And when I discover what it is I will be glad to let you know.' He glared at the others. '*All* of you!'

*

'Show me again on the chart.'

Bolitho stood beside the cabin table as Javal leaned across it. The other captains waited in silence, their bodies swaying while *Lysander* lifted and dipped heavily in irregular troughs.

Javal explained, 'Sighted her at first light, sir.' His tanned fingers cradled the Spanish coastline as if to trap what he had seen. 'Small vessel. Schooner most like.' He glanced calmly at Bolitho, his greasy hair still showing droplets of spray as evidence of the haste with which he had been pulled to the flagship by his boat's crew. 'I expect her master took sight of *Buzzard* and thought prudence to be more use than valour.'

Farquhar did not try to hide his disappointment. 'A schooner, you say? God damn it, Javal, I'd hardly think it proper to run for the squadron because of a mere toy!'

Javal ignored him, his dark eyes still on Bolitho. 'I have good men for lookouts. I reward 'em from my pocket if they do their work to my satisfaction. I find that more profitable than flogging 'em for failing in their vigilance.' His eyes seemed to flicker towards *Osiris*'s captain. 'Unlike some.'

Herrick stepped nearer, as if to stop a flare-up of tempers. 'Then tell us, Javal. My sailing master assures me that a wind is close by, and I've little room for passengers. Especially the squadron's captains.'

Javal showed his teeth. Like the man, they were jagged. 'She was running with the wind and had all canvas spread. Yet she was making precious little headway.' He looked at Bolitho. 'Strange for a Mediterranean schooner, I'd have thought, sir?'

Bolitho leaned above the chart, his mind going back and forth over Javal's report. With *Buzzard* and *Harebell* sweeping ahead and to windward of the squadron it was unlikely they would have failed to sight the schooner had she overreached them along the coast.

He saw Javal's strong fingers touch a point on the chart. Almost to himself he said, 'Out of Malaga, you think?'

Javal nodded. 'Almost certain, sir. And heading to the east'rd. In my opinion she'll remain at anchor *here*,' he tapped the chart again, 'until nightfall, or such time as she believes her way is safe.'

Bolitho walked quickly to the stern windows and watched the slow caress of wind over the blue water. Here and there, just the merest dab of white foam. Grubb was right. The wind was returning as he had prophesied.

Captain Probyn said thickly, 'This damn schooner might be anything at all. Or nothing. I agree with Farquhar, there's no point in – '

He turned as Farquhar strode to Bolitho's side, his handsome features suddenly eager.

'I think there is a point after all.' Farquhar watched Bolitho's profile. 'The Dons have an arsenal at Malaga, I believe? A great foundry for artillery?'

Bolitho smiled slightly, his eyes searching. 'Yes. I could be mistaken, as could Captain Javal's lookouts, but a coastal schooner makes good speed, unless well laden.'

He returned to the table, the others crowding on either side of him.

'The Dons will wish to show their ally they can help in any future campaign against us. Bonaparte needs armaments of every kind, and the waters around Malaga dictate that small ships be used to carry just such weapons.' He straightened his shoulders, feeling the wound beneath his coat like a burn. 'It is a small beginning, but it is sooner than I had hoped. We will close the land at dusk and cut her out. At best we may gain information. At worst we will seize another vessel for the squadron, eh?' He could not contain his smile of excitement. It was like a tonic. 'Does anyone not agree?'

Probyn shook his head, his features still brooding over Farquhar's change of heart.

Javal said, 'I know the bay where she is anchored.' He was thinking aloud. 'After dark we should be able to take her with little trouble.'

Bolitho could sense them waiting for his next words.

He said, 'You will take charge, Captain Javal. I will make a signal to *Harebell* to assume your duties until this affair is settled.' He looked at Herrick. 'I will transfer to *Buzzard* with some of our own people, say twenty or so good hands. Seamen, *not* marines. I want no boots and bayonets for this venture.' He smiled at Javal. 'I trust you will agree to that?'

Javal gave a wolfish grin. *'Willingly!'*

Herrick asked quietly, 'And the squadron, sir?'

'I will give you your orders.' He said it deliberately, excluding the others. Showing Probyn and Farquhar where his trust lay. 'You can stand closer inshore tomorrow, if you feel it prudent. If not, we will make a rendezvous to fit in with Captain Javal's plan of attack.'

He glanced quickly around their faces. Farquhar, cool and expressionless. But his fingers tapping a little tattoo on the table betrayed his true feelings. Thinking perhaps that he could do the work better than Javal. Better than Herrick.

Probyn, his heavy face lined with doubt, watching Javal as if to discover something. Considering maybe the extent of Javal's prize money if he succeeded in taking the schooner, or what would become of the squadron if *Buzzard* and the commodore came to grief.

And Herrick? He was never any use at hiding his doubts. His face was set with worry, his eyes almost hidden in a frown as he peered at the chart, seeing perhaps the whole venture laid in bloody ruins.

There was no such anxiety troubling Javal.

'Then I suggest we make a start, sir.' He rubbed his hands. 'Or the bird may quit the coop.'

If he was feeling any dismay at being accompanied by his commodore he was concealing it admirably, Bolitho thought.

He replied, 'Yes. Return to your ships. My flag captain will make known the final orders by signal.' He lowered his voice. 'I wish to make one thing clear. The squadron will stay together. I want no foolhardy risks taken, but if an opportunity presents itself I want no hesitation either.'

They hurried from the cabin and he added slowly, 'Pass the word, Thomas. Some volunteers and a boat to ferry them to *Buzzard* without delay. Send Allday to manage it, if you will.' He looked up, seeing the same wretchedness on Herrick's face. 'Well?'

Herrick said, 'Must you go, sir? Let me take charge of the attack.'

Bolitho watched him. He was more afraid of controlling the squadron than he was of the raid. Of being killed even.

'No. Javal is a hard man. And two captains in one ship are never close to success. Rest easy, man, I have no wish to end up dead, or rotting in a Spanish prison. But we must make a beginning. Show our people that we can lead as well as we can command their daily lives.' He reached out impetuously

and touched his arm. It was as stiff as a teak rail. 'It applies to
the pair of us, as well you know.'

Herrick gave a deep sigh. 'I tell myself that I must never be
surprised at your ideas. Ever since I can recall – ' He shook
himself. 'I will pass the word to Allday at once.' He swung
round, his sudden determination making him appear almost
pathetic. 'But I'll be greatly pleased to see you back inboard
again!'

Bolitho smiled and walked to his sleeping compartment and
the big chest in which he kept a pair of pistols. As he knelt
over the lid he felt the ship tilting more readily to the wind,
the urgent clatter of blocks and rigging to betray its growing
power. He looked up, seeing himself in the small cabin mirror,
the unruly lock of black hair above his right eye. He grimaced
sadly, touching the deep scar which was partly hidden beneath
the lock. An early reminder of what could happen in a split
second. Like the dull ache in his shoulder. The small step
between life and oblivion.

Allday clattered into the adjoining cabin, the hilt of his
cutlass glinting under his blue jacket.

'Party ready, sir.' He was already reaching up for Bolitho's
sword. 'All fighting Jacks!' He grinned. 'Picked 'em myself.'

Bolitho let him buckle his sword around his waist. He asked
mildly, 'Were they not *volunteers*?'

The big coxswain grinned all the broader. 'Of course, sir.
After I told 'em my point of view, so to speak.'

Bolitho shook his head and strode out of the cabin without
looking back.

A cutter was pitching and creaking at the main chains, and
the picked seamen were crowded amongst their weapons and
the hands at the oars in an untidy mass.

Bolitho glanced around the quarterdeck and at the men who
were already at the braces and along the yards overhead preparing to make more sail once the cutter had returned.

Herrick stood with the side party at the entry port, his
features composed again.

Bolitho was about to reassure him, to tell him to take good
care of the ship in his absence. But *Lysander* was Herrick's
ship, not his.

Instead he said lightly, 'Until we meet again, Captain
Herrick.'

Then he swung himself out of the port towards the waiting boat.

By the time he had reached the sternsheets and regained his breath the cutter was clear of the ship's side, the oars losing their confusion and falling into a slow rhythm across the choppy water.

It was then Bolitho realised that Pascoe was also in the boat, his dark eyes alight with excitement as he waved to someone on the two-decker's gangway.

Allday hissed angrily, 'I knew you'd want him left on board, sir. No sense in putting all the eggs in one basket, so to speak.' He hid his face from the oarsmen. 'It was Mr. Gilchrist who gave the order.'

Bolitho nodded. If he had harboured any doubts about Herrick's first lieutenant, they were gone now. By ordering Pascoe into the cutting-out party he had achieved two things. He could say that Bolitho was taking his nephew as an act of favouritism. He would share fully in any glory if the attack was successful. And if it was not? He looked at the youth, seeing his excitement as he had once known it at eighteen years. If that happened, then Allday's comment would be only too true.

He stared across Pascoe's shoulder and watched the frigate's masts spiralling and swaying in the wind.

Pascoe said brightly, 'By God, I'd like to command a ship like *Buzzard*!' He saw Bolitho's expression and added, 'One day, sir.'

Bolitho said, 'We will deal with this business first, Mr. Pascoe.' He smiled. 'But I understand your feelings.'

Allday fingered his cutlass and looked from one to the other. Now he had two to watch over. He frowned as the boat's coxswain failed in his first attempt to steer under the frigate's lee chains. And if anything happened to either of them he would settle Lieutenant bloody Gilchrist's hash for him no matter what.

The last seaman had barely scrambled aboard when Javal shouted, 'Hands aloft and get the ship under way, Mr. Mears! We've a lot of distance to cover before nightfall!'

He looked at Bolitho and doffed his hat. 'You are most welcome, sir. Though I fear you may find my quarters a mite cramped.'

Bolitho returned his smile and replied evenly, 'I have commanded *three* such vessels in my time, Captain Javal, but thank you for the reminder.'

Allday glanced down as Pascoe nudged him in the ribs.

Pascoe murmured quietly, 'I think my uncle made his point very well, don't you?'

Allday grinned, suddenly reassured.

'And that's no error, Mr. Pascoe!'

3

Alone

UNDER topsails and jib the thirty-two gun frigate *Buzzard* stood close-hauled on the larboard tack, her yards braced round so tightly that from the deck they appeared almost fore and aft.

Bolitho gripped the hammock nettings and strained his eyes through the gloom. The light had gone suddenly, as was natural in these waters, and he was conscious of the muttering between *Buzzard*'s master and her first lieutenant as they peered at the compass or inspected the set of each flapping sail.

Javal seemed confident enough and content to leave the navigation to his subordinates. Like him they were well-used, a trained and self-reliant team. There was nothing false about Javal, and no trimmings in his quarters, which for a successful frigate captain were spartan. The cabin furniture consisted mostly of heavy chests, scattered about and within easy reach when required.

Javal joined him, his eyes screwed up against the spray which spattered above the nettings with each steep roll.

He said, 'The coast is about a mile or so on the larboard bow, sir. If I am to weather the headland I'll have to stand clear very soon or come about for another approach. I wanted a wind, but this one blows too merrily for my liking.' He pulled a stone bottle from his coat. 'A drink, sir? A warming swallow of Hollands will do you good.'

There was no offer of cup or goblet, so Bolitho held the fat bottle to his lips, feeling the gin running down his tongue like fire.

Javal remarked offhandedly, 'Took quite a few bottles off a blockade-runner last August in the Channel. Better than nothing.' He swung round, his voice harsh. 'Watch your helm, damn your eyes! You'll have us in irons before the next hour!'

He became calm again. 'I'd suggest we make our play soon now, sir.'

Bolitho smiled. That sudden spark of anxious rage had shown that Javal was more human than he wished him to believe. It was never easy to close a little known shore in the dark. Harder still with a senior officer breathing down your neck.

He replied, 'I agree.'

Javal said, 'I'm putting my first lieutenant in charge. The launch and the cutter should suffice, but in case there is a chance of a hue and cry being carried inshore to some Spanish garrison, I'd suggest a small landing party below the headland.' He hesitated. 'Your lieutenant perhaps?'

'Very well.' Bolitho looked across the blurred procession of white-capped waves. 'Mr. Pascoe is young, but has seen action enough.'

Javal studied him curiously. 'I will attend to it.'

He hurried away barking out orders to the already assembled seamen. Blocks squeaked noisily and the boats began to move above the tier, the hands guiding them without effort, as if it was all in broad daylight.

Bolitho tried not to listen to the clatter of weapons, the occasional hesitation as a man failed to answer his name on a check list.

Allday loomed out of the darkness and said, 'It'll be a hard pull in this wind, sir.' He seemed to sense something. 'Can I help?'

Javal strode past. 'We will heave-to, if you please!' In a louder tone he called, 'Mr. Mears! Stand by to lower boats!'

Bolitho said swiftly, 'Go with Mr. Pascoe. He will take the jolly boat.'

Allday understood but replied awkwardly, 'But my place is with — ' He grinned. 'But you are right, sir.'

Bolitho saw the gleam of white breeches against the opposite bulwark and heard Pascoe say, 'I'm going now, sir.'

Bolitho moved to his side. 'See you take care, Adam.' He tried to make light of it. 'Your aunt would never forgive me if anything happened.'

Pascoe turned his head as some seamen dashed past, their chequered shirts very pale and stark.

'I *must* go, sir.'

Bolitho stood aside. 'Good luck.'

Moments after the frigate had laboured round into the wind, her remaining sails booming in confusion, the three boats were in the water alongside, and then soon pulling away towards the land.

Javal rubbed his hands. 'Bring her about and steer sou'-east by east, Mr. Ellis. And put two good hands in the chains just to be sure we do not gut the keel out of her!'

He crossed to Bolitho's side and waited in silence until his ship was once more under command of wind and rudder. Then he said cheerfully, 'This is always the worst part. The waiting.'

Bolitho nodded, his ears trying to hold on to the swish and creak of oars. But they had gone, swallowed in the other sea noises.

He said, 'Aye. I'd prefer to be going with them.'

Javal laughed. 'God's teeth, sir! I wish to make the Navy my career for many years yet. What chance would there be of that if I allowed my commodore to be taken?' It seemed to amuse him greatly.

Bolitho snapped, 'I dare say.'

Javal cleared his throat and said in a more sober tone, 'It will be all of four hours before we know anything, sir. My first lieutenant is very experienced. He has been with me for some eighteen months. He has cut out several such vessels without many losses to us.'

Bolitho nodded. 'I will use your cabin again, if I may. A short sleep will refresh me for tomorrow.'

He could almost hear the lie being thrown back in his face. *Sleep?* It would be easier to walk on water.

Javal watched him grope towards the cabin hatch and shrugged. Bolitho was probably worried about this first action under his overall command. Surely he would not be troubled at the thought of a man or two being killed? He reached for the stone bottle and shook it against his ear. It would help the hours to pass more quickly, he decided.

*

Bolitho felt his way to the glowing compass bowl and peered at the steeply tilting card. *Buzzard*'s head was almost north-east.

The master said helpfully, 'Beg pardon, sir, but the wind 'as backed two points or so. An' some rain 'as bin fallin'.'

Bolitho nodded and walked forward, his body angled against the deck and the wet pressure of wind across the quarter. It would be dawn soon, and already he could see the nine-pounders on the gun deck standing out like black bars below the weather gangway.

Javal was by the quarterdeck rail, hatless, and with his hair whipping in the wind.

He said shortly, 'Nothing yet.' He looked at him briefly. 'Did you sleep well, sir?'

Bolitho rested his hands on the rail, feeling the hull shivering and straining like a living thing. He had been unable to remain in the cabin a moment longer. The hours had been an eternity, and Javal's quarters like a damp, unsteady prison.

'A little, thank you.'

'Deck there! Land on th' weather bow!'

Javal snapped, 'Leadsmen to the chains again, Mr. Ellis! Lively now!' In a calmer voice he added, 'That will be the headland. We have clawed round in a mad circle during the night. With the damned wind backing on us, I feared we might be blown hard aground.'

Bolitho said, 'I see.'

He looked away, hiding his feelings from the other man. What had happened? Where was a signal? Any sign that the raid had been completed?

Javal remarked, 'Mears should have fired a gun or a rocket.' Even he sounded uneasy. 'God damn it, we'll be too close inshore within the hour.'

Bolitho ignored him and tried to imagine what it was like beyond the dim shadow which the lookout had reported as land. If Lieutenant Mears and his boats had failed to take the schooner, or for some reason had been unable even to grapple with her, they would have to pull back to the *Buzzard* as best they could. In a stiff wind, and after a night at the oars, they would be in need of help, and quickly.

From forward came the cry, 'By th' mark seven!'

Javal said quietly, 'Jesus!'

The master called anxiously, 'It shallows fast hereabouts, sir!'

'I am aware of that fact, thank you!' Javal glared at him. 'Watch your helm!'

'By th' mark five!' The leadsman's chant sounded like a dirge.

Javal muttered, 'I will have to alter course to starboard, sir.' The words were being dragged from his throat.

Bolitho looked at him, noticing how the people and objects around the quarterdeck had assumed shape and reality in the first dull light.

He said briskly, 'Do your duty, Captain Javal.'

He turned away, sharing the other man's despair.

'Deep four!'

Bolitho thrust his hands behind his back and walked aft. The frigate was sailing in about twenty-four feet of water. It was only minutes before she ran her full length ashore. Over his shoulder he saw the land reaching out towards the bowsprit. Mocking him.

'Man the lee braces!' Feet scampered across the decks. 'Put up the helm!'

With a squeal of blocks the yards creaked ponderously above the decks, and as the wheel was hauled over and over *Buzzard* started to swing once again towards the open sea.

Javal said harshly, 'Steer due east. Lay her as close as you dare to the headland.'

'By th' mark ten!'

Bolitho watched the land as it started to slip past the forecastle, the faint marks of white at its foot where the wind drove the sea into beaches and small coves.

'Deck there! Sail on the weather bow! Comin' round the point!'

Javal sucked in air. 'Run out the larboard battery, Mr. Ellis!' He added sharply, '*Belay that order!*' His face glowed faintly in a bright red flare which had just burst clear of the land. 'Stand by to shorten sail!' To Bolitho he exclaimed, 'The schooner, by God! Mears has taken her!'

Even without a glass Bolitho could see the low-hulled vessel thrusting away from the encroaching land, her great sails rising like wings above the choppy wavecrests. At her counter he saw the darker shapes of *Buzzard*'s boats being towed astern, a lantern rising and dipping at her foremast to confirm the capture. Perhaps Mears feared that because of the delay, his failure to signal earlier, he might be met with a broadside rather than cheers.

Javal snapped, 'We will come about. Lay her on the starboard tack and steer sou' by west until we have more sea room.' He glanced at Bolitho by the nettings. 'You will wish to rejoin the squadron, sir?'

'Yes.'

He walked clear of the busy seamen and marines as they ran to obey the pipe. It was over, and as far as he could tell, without a shot being fired. He found he was shaking badly. As if he had been there with them.

When *Buzzard* leaned steeply on her new tack Bolitho saw the schooner following suit, her lee bulwark almost awash. She was certainly deep laden.

He said abruptly, 'Heave-to at your discretion, Captain. Signal your lieutenant to close within hailing distance.'

Javal eyed him doubtfully. 'Aye, sir. If you say so.' He saw Bolitho's expression and said no more.

Bolitho walked slowly to the nettings, shutting out the sounds of the unexpected preparations to heave-to once again. He did not even hear the squeak of halliards as the signal flags ran up the yards and broke to the wind. He was watching the boats surging along under the schooner's stern. The jolly boat was not one of them.

*

Lieutenant Mears had no intention of shouting his news from the captured schooner's deck. While *Buzzard* rolled heavily in short, steep waves he crossed the narrow gap between the two ships in his cutter, its sleek hull lifting and rearing like a dolphin until it was made fast to the frigate's chains.

In the stern cabin the sea's noises were muted, like surf booming in a long cave.

Bolitho kept his hands clasped behind him, his head lowered between the deck beams as Mears, still panting, told his story.

'We pulled under the headland as planned, sir. Then we separated. I took my boat direct for the schooner's seaward side, and Mr. Booth headed his around and under her bowsprit. There is no doubt that the schooner's master was expecting the weather to worsen and was anchoring for the night. Our suspicion he had sighted *Buzzard* was ill-founded.'

Bolitho asked quietly, 'And the jolly boat?'

Mears rubbed his eyes. 'Your lieutenant was ordered to take it to the western side of the headland and beach it. If the Dons had tried to send for help from the land, Mr. Pascoe's party would have been able to intercept them.'

Javal snapped, 'You took your damn time, Toby.'

The lieutenant shrugged limply. 'The first part went well. There was only an anchor watch, and they didn't even raise a shout until our fellows were amongst 'em. No boarding nets, no swivel guns, they almost died of fear.' He hesitated, sensing the tension around him for the first time. 'We waited for the jolly boat to come around the point and join us again. When it failed to appear I sent Mr. Booth in the cutter.' He spread his hands helplessly. 'With dawn close by, and every minute adding to the chance of discovery, I dared not fire a signal until I had received news of the landing party.'

Javal nodded grimly. 'That was well said, Mr. Mears. Some would have left the few to save the many.'

Bolitho asked, 'What did your people discover?'

'It had been raining, sir.' Mears looked at the stern windows, streaked with salt and droplets of spray. 'As it is now. Booth found the beached jolly boat with its hull stove in and two seamen dead nearby. Another was lying in some dunes. They had all been killed by sword thrust, sir.' He fumbled inside his stained coat. 'Mr. Booth found this in the sand. I could not understand it. It is surely an admiral's sword –'

He broke off as Bolitho snatched the glittering hilt from him and held it to the windows. The blade was snapped like a carrot halfway from the ornate guard. It was like yesterday. Vice Admiral Sir Lucius Broughton on the splintered quarter-deck of his flagship. Handing his beautiful sword to an astonished Adam Pascoe and saying gruffly, 'Any damn midshipman who tackles the enemy with a dirk deserves it! Besides, a *lieutenant* must look the part, eh?'

He heard himself say, 'It *was* an admiral's once. It belongs to Mr. Pascoe.' He touched the stain on the hilt. Blood and wet sand. He added quietly, 'He would not part willingly with it.'

The others stared at him.

Then Mears said, 'Mr. Booth searched as long as he could, sir. There were many hoofmarks in the beach, leading from inland. He feared that his own party might be challenged at any moment, and I had given him a direct order to return to me if – '

'He did not find the lieutenant *anywhere*?'

Mears shook his head. 'Nor your man either.'

'No.' Bolitho stared out of the streaked windows. 'Allday would not leave him.'

'Sir?'

Bolitho turned towards them. 'What of the schooner?'

Mears collected his wits. 'You were right, sir, She is filled to the deck beams with powder and shot. And –' he looked at Javal's grim face, ' – two of the finest cannon I have ever laid eyes on. Siege artillery, if I'm any judge, and only newly tested.'

'I see.'

Bolitho tried to concentrate his mind on what their capture could mean. Adam was gone. Allday, too. Probably out there dying. Waiting for a rescue which could never come.

Mears said, 'I am afraid the schooner's master was killed when he tried to jump overboard. But I found papers and charts in his cabin. Enough to show that he had orders for Toulon.'

Javal exclaimed, 'By God, you were right about that, too, sir. The Dons are working like fiends to help their powerful ally at Toulon!' He dragged a bottle from one of his sea chests. 'You did well, Toby. Take a drink while we decide what to do.' He looked at Bolitho. 'The wind is rising, sir. We had best get under way again.'

'Yes.' Bolitho felt the deck lurching unsteadily as the wind hissed against the hull. 'Detail a prize crew to take the schooner direct to Gibraltar. Fetch your clerk and dictate a despatch for the admiral there. He will know what best to do about the cannon.'

Mears grinned wearily. 'She is a fair little prize, sir. Worth a penny or two.'

Javal glared at him and said quickly, 'I am sorry about your lieutenant, sir. Had you known him long?'

'He is my nephew.'

The two officers looked at each other, appalled.

Javal said, 'By God, if I'd only known, sir, I would have sent one of my other officers.'

Bolitho looked at him gravely. 'You did what was right. You were short-handed. But in any case, honour and danger must be shared as equally as possible.'

Mears suggested, 'If I took one of the boats under sail, sir?'

'No.' Bolitho looked past him. 'In daylight you would stand less than a dog's chance.' He turned his back. 'Carry on with your duties, Captain Javal. There is nothing we can do here.'

The screen door slammed shut and Bolitho sat down heavily on the bench seat below the windows. He turned the broken sword over several times in his hands, seeing the boy's pleasure at receiving it, his pitiful pride when they had met for the first time.

He looked up, startled, as if he expected to see Allday nearby, as he always was when he sensed he was needed. Now there was not even him. There was nobody.

Somewhere beyond the bulkhead he heard a sailor singing some strange song which he did not recognise. Probably dreaming of his tiny share of the prize money, or of some girl back in England.

Feet clattered overhead, and he heard someone bawl, 'Bring the boats alongside and man the tackles!' The recovered boats were thudding against the hull, and he thought he heard someone give a cheer as the schooner made ready to part company.

Javal opened the door, his face wet with rain. 'Schooner's about to leave, sir. Are you sure you do not wish to send a separate despatch to the admiral?'

'No, thank you. You were in charge of the cutting-out. It is right that your name should be on the despatch.'

Javal licked his lips. 'Well, thank you indeed, sir. I just wish there was something I could do about –' He broke off as voices shouted across the upper deck and the hull dipped more heavily in the wind. 'I'd better go, sir. Get her under way before we lose a spar or two.'

He hurried out, and moments later Bolitho heard his voice through the partly open skylight.

'Set the forecourse, Mr. Mears, though I fear we will have to take in a reef or so before long. We are rejoining the squadron.'

'By God, I'd not have his conscience on a matter like this, sir.'

Javal's reply was swift and sad. 'Conscience does not come into it, Toby. *Responsibility* sweeps it out of the window.'

*

Allday sat with his shoulders against a slab of broken rock and watched the horses which were picketed at the foot of a slope. Across his lap Pascoe lay quite still, his eyes shut in a tight frown as if he were dead. Squatting or lying dejectedly nearby, six other sailors were waiting like Allday to see what was going to happen next.

He squinted up at the sky, wishing the rain would return to ease his raging thirst. By the set of the sun it must be about noon, he decided. Around him the rough, winding track appeared to turn inland. He sighed. Away from the sea.

He felt Pascoe stir on his cramped legs and placed one hand across his mouth.

'*Easy*, Mr. Pascoe!'

He saw his dark eyes staring up at him, the pain and the memory of what had happened flooding back.

'We are resting a while.' He nodded carefully towards the soldiers by the horses. 'Or *they* are any rate.'

As Pascoe made to move he pressed one hand on his chest. It felt cool despite the sun overhead. He brushed a fly away from the livid scar on Pascoe's ribs, the mark which had been left by the duel at Gibraltar.

'What . . . what *happened*?'

Pascoe felt his body as if to seek out his limbs one by one. Like the rest of them he was without shoes or belt, and wore only breeches and the remains of his shirt.

Allday murmured, 'The bastards took everything they could. I think they killed two of our lads back on the road because they were wounded and couldn't keep pace with the horses.'

He thought of the pitiful screams and then the silence, and was glad Pascoe had been unconscious.

'Then how did I –' Pascoe's eyes clouded over. 'You carried me this far?'

Allday tried to grin. 'The soldiers are not Dons but native troops. Moors most likely. But even these bastards recognise an officer.'

He watched the soldiers warily, wondering where they were

being taken. And it had all happened so suddenly. The sound of horses' hoofs squeaking in the wet sand just a few yards from the beach where they had dragged the boat. A patrol, some soldiers returning to camp, he still did not know or care.

In minutes the horsemen would have passed them by, too busy with idle chatter to notice the inert shapes along the beach.

But Pascoe had said, 'They will see Lieutenant Mears and the two boats, Allday.' There had not even been a slight hesitation. 'If they warn the schooner our people will be cut down whatever they try to do.'

And so while Mears and his men had taken the schooner intact, on the other side of the headland Pascoe had made his stand.

With drawn sword he had run up the beach shouting, 'At 'em, lads!'

It had ended just as swiftly. The clash of steel, men cursing and slashing in the darkness while the horses wheeled like great shadows from all sides.

Pascoe had been knocked senseless by a sabre, and the seamen had thrown down their weapons. The soldiers had stripped them of their possessions and had beaten them systematically without emotion or any sign of pleasure. Then, kicking and punching the dazed men they had driven them ahead of the horses, on to the road, away from the sea.

Pascoe licked his dry lips and then touched the bruise on his head. 'It feels like hammers on an anvil.'

'Aye.'

Allday tensed as the senior horseman shouted something to his companions. They were well armed. A dozen in all. He glanced at the surviving sailors. They looked beaten. Frightened.

The horseman walked slowly towards the little group and stood looking down at Pascoe. He was tall and very dark, and wore a pale-coloured fez with a dangling cloth to protect his neck from the glare. He pointed with his whip and nodded at Pascoe.

'*Teniente! Teniente!*'

He gave a slow smile, displaying some very yellow teeth, then spat deliberately on Pascoe's leg.

Allday struggled free of Pascoe's body and lurched to his feet.

'You mind your manners, you bloody hound, when you're talking to a King's officer!'

The man stepped back, the smile vanishing as he yelled to his men.

Allday felt his arms pinioned by at least three soldiers before he was thrown face down on the wet sand, his wrists wedged to the ground by the boots of his captors. He kept his eyes on Pascoe's pale face, willing him to remain still.

The biting slash of a whip across his spine was like a hot iron. He clamped his jaws together, holding his breath as the shadow of the man's arm rose and fell again. And again.

He concentrated his stare on two small insects which were moving by his face, shutting out the voices above him, the swish of the whip, the searing pain on his bare skin.

Then it stopped, and he rolled to one side as one of them kicked him savagely in the ribs. Half blinded with sweat and sand he staggered to his feet, seeing Pascoe's face and knowing that the soldiers wanted just one excuse to kill all of them.

But they were mounting their horses, calling to each other as if nothing out of the ordinary had occurred.

Pascoe gripped his arm. 'Let me help.' He tore off his shirt and dabbed at Allday's scarred back. 'It was all my fault!'

'Now don't you think like that, Mr. Pascoe. You did what was right an' proper, and well you know it. You could have lain low and we'd have got back to *Buzzard* with no bother.' He gritted his teeth as the bloodied shirt moved across his skin. 'But a whole lot of our lads would have paid for it.'

The horsemen wheeled round them, and a sailor cried out as one struck him with his whip. They moved off along the road again, their bare feet soon bleeding on stones and rough chippings, their tongues almost clinging to their lips with thirst.

Allday looked up briefly as the senior horseman cantered to the head of the ragged procession, and felt slightly better. He had someone to hate. Someone who would be the first to know it, if once he got the chance. He turned painfully to watch Pascoe. He was striding along at the head of the little group, his jaw set against the pain, his dark eyes fixed on some point in the far distance.

God, he thought, our Dick would be proud of him. If only he was here to see.

*

The air in *Lysander*'s cabin was oppressive and heavy. Bolitho spread the chart beneath his hands and stared at it for several minutes. He had returned aboard less than an hour back and was still wearing the same clothes, his chin rough for the want of a shave.

Over his shoulder, her hull and reduced sails bending and wavering through the thick glass windows, the *Osiris* followed obediently in *Lysander*'s wake, with the other two-decker astern of her.

Farquhar and Probyn were sitting on opposite sides of the table, while Herrick waited by Bolitho's elbow, his face anxious as he watched the brass dividers and rule moving across the chart.

Bolitho said, 'The schooner which Captain Javal took two days back carried a few other items of interest. She was en route for Toulon, but there was a letter addressed to the captain of another, and I suspect larger ship, which is now lying *here*,' he rested the points of the dividers on the coastline, 'some forty miles sou'-west of Cartagena. A small bay used by fishermen, I believe, but now probably taken for a safe anchorage by Spanish transports.' The dividers ran along and up the coast towards the Gulf of Lions. 'All the way there must be such ships waiting to carry materials of war to Bonaparte's army. He *must* be preparing for an invasion.'

Herrick asked quietly, 'What do you intend, sir?'

'Had I known the content of the letter I would have held on to the schooner and used her against her old masters.' The dividers beat a slow rhythm on the chart. 'But no matter. The Dons will not know she has been taken yet. There is still time.'

Probyn said bluntly, 'Unless some of the landing party were captured, sir. *Made* to tell what they know of our intentions.'

Herrick snapped, 'That's a bloody stupid thing to say!'

'No, Thomas.' Bolitho looked at him impassively. 'It is a possibility. We must face up to it.'

Try as he might Herrick could not drag his gaze from the broken sword which now lay on Bolitho's desk.

He said, 'I find it hard, sir.'

'I know.' He held his gaze for a few seconds. 'He is close to you also.'

He turned away, forcing himself to retain control of his

emotions. *Is, is, is.* He must not allow himself to think of Adam as gone into the past.

He looked at the other captains. 'We must obtain a new element of surprise. Attack and probe, gain all the knowledge we can of the enemy's strength, and hurt him when he least expects it.'

Farquhar nodded slowly. 'If we attack this shipping, sir, and then put out to sea in another direction, the enemy will not know what we are doing, or what our true mission might be.'

Bolitho replied, 'Exactly. It is something I learned, and learned well from the French. One determined ship can tie down a squadron. A determined squadron can hamper a whole fleet.'

They fell silent until Probyn said, 'The Dons may send a force down from Cartagena. There is little sea room for what you plan to do.'

'I will post Captain Javal to watch over our backs.' He faced him calmly, watching for an argument. 'The Dons may be prepared for a local attack, another cutting-out expedition or the like. A ship of the line is not what anyone will anticipate.'

Probyn gasped, 'No *sane* man certainly!'

Bolitho nodded grimly. '*Lysander* will make the attack.' He looked at Farquhar. 'You will stay to seaward and act as the situation dictates.'

Farquhar's eyebrows rose very slightly. '*My* decision then, sir?'

Herrick interrupted harshly, 'You'll not rate a broad pendant yet, dammit!'

Farquhar gave a cool smile, 'The idea never entered my mind.'

Bolitho tugged at his neckcloth. It seemed to be choking him. He said, 'I will send you written orders directly. So now, gentlemen . . .'

Herrick ushered them to the door and closed it behind them.

Bolitho sat down in a chair and rested his head in his hands as the calls shrilled from the gangway to mark the captains' departure. Outside the cabin the sea was deep blue, like ruffled silk, as the wind ghosted the ships gently eastward. If only it had been like this when *Buzzard*'s boats had taken the sleeping schooner. It would have halved the time. Saved lives.

Herrick returned and said, 'I have ordered the squadron to take station again sir. Your servant is waiting to attend you.'

'Thank you, Thomas.'

Herrick looked at the snapped sword. 'If he is still alive, there may be a chance to arrange an exchange – '

Bolitho stood up violently. 'Do you not think I have gone over and over what might or might not be done!' He swung away, his eyes blurred. 'Send Allday to me with – ' He broke off, and for a long moment they stared at each other like strangers.

Then Herrick said tonelessly, 'I'll attend to the details, sir.'

Bolitho opened his mouth to prevent his leaving, but no words came. When he looked again Herrick had gone.

Ozzard, the cabin servant, slipped through the door and moved diagonally towards the sleeping compartment, his eyes averted.

Bolitho sat on the bench and watched him. He knew little about Ozzard, other than he was capable and had served the previous commodore well. It was said he had been a lawyer's clerk and had volunteered for the Navy because of some crime he had committed against his employer. He was a very quiet man, and was moving now like a soft-footed poacher as he laid out a clean shirt for his commodore.

Bolitho saw the way his hands moved, the shirt shaking as he unfastened the collar.

He is terrified of me. Fearful that I will punish him merely to ease my own pain.

The realisation helped to steady him, and he was suddenly ashamed.

He said quietly, 'Thank you, Ozzard, I can manage now.'

The man regarded him nervously. 'If you're *sure*, sir?' He backed away, as if still expecting Bolitho to turn on him. By the door he hesitated and then said, 'I've had some education, sir. If you like I could come back and read to you. It might help to pass the time. And you wouldn't have to say anything.'

Bolitho turned away from him, hiding his face. 'No, not just now, Ozzard. But I appreciate the thought.' He saw the man's reflection in the sloping windows as he moved silently from the cabin. 'More than I can tell you.'

4

The Captives

RICHARD BOLITHO stood by the quarterdeck rail and watched the sunset. It painted the sky in great rust-coloured patterns and gave a sharp edge to the western horizon. *Lysander* moved comfortably under forecourse and topsails, her broad hull tilting hardly at all to the west wind which had followed her for most of the day.

He stared along the length of the ship, through stays and shrouds and beyond a greasy plume of smoke from the galley funnel. He could just make out the tiny outline of *Harebell*'s sails as she moved ahead of her flagship, her yards holding the dying sun like uplifted crosses.

The rest of his ships had disappeared to the south that afternoon, and under Farquhar's command would even now be making more sail to beat their way around and ahead of *Lysander*'s point of attack. He pictured the chart in his mind, collecting the scraps of information which had formed into a loose strategy. He could almost see the line of the shore, the hills behind the bay, the depths of the sea and places where there was no depth at all. Against that he had another list of items he did *not* know. What the enemy were doing there, or if indeed they were there for any purpose which warranted risking his ships.

The main topsail billowed and flapped noisily as the wind dropped and then gathered strength again. The master's mate of the watch relaxed and made some joke with the helmsmen, and at the lee side of the deck Lieutenant Fitz-Clarence re-adjusted his vigilant pose.

Bolitho tried not to let his mind drift from what he had to do. But with the ship so quiet, and with no questions to answer or problems to solve, he was unable to stay aloof from his anxiety.

Two days since he had returned on board, two further days since Javal's men had taken the schooner. She would be at Gibraltar by now, opposing winds or not, unless she had run foul of an enemy. She would be sold in a prize court, maybe taken into the King's service. Her few remaining crew members would either be sent to a prison hulk or offered an alternative fate, that of signing on aboard a British man o' war. After five years of conflict you heard a dozen languages and dialects in any king's ship.

And Adam ? He walked slowly to the nettings and stared hard at the sea. The land was beyond even a lookout's vision, and the sky was already so dark that it was difficult to see the horizon's division, which moments ago had glowed like hot copper.

Another lieutenant had appeared on deck and was murmuring with Fitz-Clarence, while from forward and deeper in the fat hull he heard the shrill of a call, the pad of bare feet as the next watch prepared to take over the ship until midnight.

A freak breeze fanned the stench aft from the galley, and he realised just how empty his stomach was. But the thought of oatmeal gruel and greasy lumps of boiled meat, left-overs from the midday meal, were enough to revolt him against eating anything.

Herrick appeared through the cabin hatch and crossed the deck.

'I've told Mr. Gilchrist to muster all officers and senior warrants in the wardroom after eight bells, sir.' He hesitated, seeking out Bolitho's mood in the gloom. 'They're looking forward to meeting you very much.'

'Thank you, Thomas.'

He turned slightly as a bosun's mate ran along the starboard gangway, followed by various other members of his watch.

A ship's boy was inspecting the flickering compass light, another the hour-glass nearby. Two stiff marines swayed gently at attention as they suffered a close scrutiny by their corporal. How black their red coats looked in the darkness, Bolitho thought. Made more so by their gleaming crossbelts and breeches. They were the sentries. One for Herrick's quarters. One for his own.

The master was rumbling away to a midshipman. The latter seemed bent almost double to write something on his slate, the pencil very loud in the clammy stillness.

The newly arrived lieutenant straightened himself away from the rail and touched his hat formally.

'The watch is aft, Mr. Fitz-Clarence.'

Fitz-Clarence nodded. 'Relieve the wheel, if you please, Mr. Kipling.'

More grunts and shuffles, and then a helmsman called, 'Course east-be-north, sir! Steady as she goes!'

Grubb sniffed noisily. 'And so it should be! I'll be back on deck afore the glass is turned!' It sounded like a threat.

Bolitho shivered. 'I'm ready, Thomas.'

He heard the bell chime out from forward, a gust of laughter as a topman slithered down a backstay nearly knocking another to the deck.

They walked to the cabin hatch and Herrick said, 'The fact that the wind has backed to the west'rd makes me think Mr. Grubb is right. We will have an easier task to drive inshore than I'd thought possible.'

Down the ladder and past a seaman carrying a biscuit sack from the wardroom. He pressed his shoulders against a cabin door as if afraid he might hinder or touch either commodore or captain.

Bolitho saw the lantern light playing across the breeches of the nearest guns. Some of the ship's twenty-eight eighteen-pounders, yet they managed to look at peace. It was hard to picture them enveloped in smoke and powder, bursting in-board on their tackles as their cheering, noise-crazed crews sponged-out for another broadside.

Further aft he saw the bright rectangle of the wardroom door, and beyond it the movement of *Lysander*'s officers, and every available man of warrant rank, too, who could be spared from duty on deck.

Herrick paused and said uncertainly, 'It seems a long time since a wardroom was *my* home.'

Bolitho looked at him. 'And mine. When I was twenty I thought that life became easy when you were promoted captain. I soon learned differently. And now I know that each span of authority has its snares, as well as its privilege.'

Herrick nodded. 'More the former than the latter, in my opinion.'

Bolitho tugged his coat into place, the movement involuntary and unnoticed. Herrick had not mentioned Adam or any part of the cutting-out since his return aboard. But he guessed it was rarely absent from his thoughts. He remembered when Pascoe had served with Herrick as a midshipman aboard his little two-decker, *Impulsive*. It was strange how he had felt about it. Jealous perhaps? Afraid that the boy's trust in Herrick might change to something closer than he himself could offer?

It all came surging up again, like a demon which had been biding its time.

Like the moment when he had arrived at Gibraltar, which should have been the proudest time in his service. Hearing about Adam's gesture on his behalf, risking disgrace or maiming in a forbidden duel.

There must be something deep in our family, he thought bitterly. With little training or effort, so many of them had proved unnaturally skilful with the sword. He could recall exactly standing face to face with a French lieutenant aboard a privateer in the East Indies. Face to face, both almost spent, but each holding on to that madness which only battle can sustain. He had felt something like pity for the man. Willing him to give in. Knowing, even as he parried the other's blade aside for that last fatal blow, that he could not help himself.

He said sharply, 'Well, Thomas, let us be about it then.'

The *Lysander*'s wardroom was packed with men. As Herrick led the way aft Bolitho was again reminded of his own youthful days as a junior lieutenant in a ship of the line such as this. Then, he had wondered about the men who lived and dreamed in the cabins above the wardroom. Admiral or captain, it had made little difference then.

He glanced at the expectant faces as they stood back to make a passage for him. Some he vaguely recognised from their duties about the upper deck. Others he did not know at all.

The immature expressions of the lieutenants set against the more controlled scrutiny of the warrant officers. Grubb's great shape beside Yeo, the boatswain, and against the stern-most eighteen-pounder a severe looking man who he guessed was Corbyn, the gunner.

The scarlet coats of the marines seemed to overshadow the untidy clump of midshipmen, there were about eight or nine of them present, while managing to stay slightly apart from all the rest, Edgar Mewse, the purser, and Shacklock, the surgeon, completed the gathering.

Gilchrist reported, 'All present, sir, but for the fourth lieutenant, Mr. Kipling, who has the watch. And Mr. Midshipman Blenkarne who shares it with him.'

Herrick cleared his throat and then laid his hat on a table. 'Thank you.'

Bolitho nodded. 'Be seated, gentlemen. I will be as brief as I can.'

He waited impassively as they scrambled for chairs and sea chests, the most comfortable places going to the most senior, until a mere handful of midshipmen were left nothing but the hard deck to sit upon.

Bolitho said, 'The flag captain will have told you what we are about. The bones of the plan are that we shall close the land on the day after tomorrow at first light and destroy what enemy shipping we cannot take as prizes.'

He saw two of the midshipmen nudging each other cheerfully. One he recognised as Saxby, his wide, gap-toothed grin as broad as if he had just been promised a month's leave on full pay.

'If the wind goes against us we will stand off and act accordingly.' He glanced at Grubb's battered face. 'But the master has promised full co-operation from a higher authority than mine.'

There was laughter and a good deal of humour at Grubb's expense. He remained immovable in their midst, but Bolitho could see the pleasure his comment had given him. He knew Herrick was watching him all the time. He of all people would see through his mask, his efforts to show the assembled officers that their commodore was a man beyond and above inner despair.

Bolitho had lost many good friends at sea. There was no friendship stronger than one born in the demanding hardship of a man o' war. Sea and disease, the sword or a cannon's harvest had pared away many such faces. It was no wonder that these men could accept Pascoe's absence. Hardly any of them had been together long enough to know the pain of such a loss.

He realised they had fallen silent, that he must have been standing for several seconds without speaking.

Almost harshly he continued, 'To create as much confusion as possible, we will land *Lysander's* marines under cover of darkness.'

He sought out Major Leroux who was sitting, arms folded and stiff-backed, beside his lieutenant. He had met Leroux only formally, but he had been impressed. It was always difficult to break the inbuilt contempt for the marines, the 'bullocks', which was common amongst most ships' companies. Their rigid ideas of drill and organised discipline in the worst of situations were at odds with the more casual and boisterous behaviour of the average seaman. Bolitho had come up against many marine officers, and although he had soon grown to respect their loyalty and prowess in battle, he had rarely discovered one who had displayed much initiative. Nepean, the marine lieutenant, for instance, was fairly typical. Impeccably dressed and ready to answer the call to duty at any hour, his eyes had the empty glassiness of one quite happy to obey rather than to lead.

But Major Jermyn Leroux was totally different. Tall and square-shouldered, he had the outward appearance of a scholar, despite his military bearing. Bolitho had spoken with him on the quarterdeck about the training and recruitment of his marines, but never once had Leroux made an idle boast, or suggested he could offer something beyond his means.

He said, 'I will discuss the final details with you tomorrow, Major.'

Leroux nodded. He had still, rather sad eyes, and an expression of a man who felt strangely out of place.

He replied, 'Allowing for marines who are sick and otherwise unfit for duty, sir, I can muster ninety men.'

'That will be sufficient.' Bolitho turned to Herrick. 'Swivels in the boats, and grapnels in case we need to scale any defences.' He did not wait for any comment but added, 'When Captain Javal took the schooner there was a need for stealth. This time I want our force to seem far greater than it really is.'

One of the eighteen-pounders which shared the wardroom with its occupants squeaked slightly against its lashings as *Lysander* dipped her massive bulk into a trough. Bolitho heard faint shouts from the watch on deck, the groan of the rudder beneath the counter as the helm was corrected.

He said, 'We have rare freedom to act as we choose on this mission. We must lose no opportunity to discover what the enemy is planning. Neither can we turn from the chance to damage his security.' He looked at Herrick. 'If there are any questions?'

Gilchrist stood up, his forehead partly hidden by a deck beam. 'Will there be no *seamen* in the landing party, sir?'

'A minimum.' Bolitho kept his voice calm. 'The bay which *Lysander* will have to enter and cross may be well defended. There will certainly be a battery of sorts, even if it is only light artillery. Captain Herrick will need every available hand on brace and gun tackle, I can assure you.'

The hint of action ran round the wardroom like wind through ripe corn. But Gilchrist stood his ground, his bony figure angled slightly to the deck's tilt.

He asked, 'Major Leroux will be in overall charge then?'

'No, Mr. Gilchrist.' He felt Herrick stiffen at his side. '*I* will.'

Gilchrist gave what could have been a shrug. 'A risk surely, sir.' He glanced at the other officers like someone sure of an audience. 'We were all grieved to hear of Mr. Pascoe's er – disappearance. To invite another disaster in your own family . . .'

Bolitho looked down at his hands. It was strange that he could hold them so still when he felt like seizing the man and beating him senseless.

He replied calmly, 'If Captain Herrick has no objection I am taking *you* ashore with me, Mr. Gilchrist. You will be able to see for yourself where the value of risk may lie.'

Gilchrist stared at him then at Herrick. He stammered, 'Thank you, sir, it is an honour.' He sat down without another word.

Herrick said, 'If nobody else has anything to offer?'

Lieutenant Fitz-Clarence stood up and gave Bolitho a determined stare. 'We will show them, sir! God help me, we'll pistol the vermin!' He was almost glowing with excitement. In his mind's eye he probably saw Gilchrist already dead and himself as first lieutenant.

Bolitho gave him a nod. 'Well said, Mr. Fitz-Clarence. But mark this.' He looked around the wardroom. 'All of you. Whatever you may think of the Dons, do not imagine they are like the French. When this war began the French fleet was almost in irons for want of good senior officers. Far too many were senselessly butchered in the Terror, merely to placate a mob. But that is over and done with. New men with fresh ideas are alive in their fleet. The handful of older officers who survived the guillotine are respected again, and their zeal will be all the sharper now that they know the price of failure. Armies can fight bravely under almost any conditions known to man. But without power over the sea lanes, without the life-blood of supplies and replacements they are like marooned sailors, halfway to a living death.'

Fitz-Clarence was still on his feet, but his face had lost some of its assurance.

He said lamely, 'Well, sir, I am still confident of our success.'

Herrick waited for him to be seated. His blue eyes were fixed on Bolitho. 'Perhaps you would care to join me in my cabin?'

'Thank you.' Bolitho picked up his hat. 'My throat is dry.'

He walked between the silent officers, knowing the air would explode into supposition and general excitement once the door was shut behind him.

Outside the wardroom Herrick said quietly, 'Let *me* go, sir. I asked before. Now I'm pleading.'

They walked in silence to the ladder and up again to the next group of cabins.

Herrick threw open the door of his quarters and gestured to his servant to leave. As Bolitho seated himself by the table he opened his cabinet and produced a bottle of claret.

Bolitho watched him, seeing all the arguments building up in his friend's mind as he busied himself with the glasses. If some other seventy-four was wearing the commodore's broad pendant Herrick would have the great stern cabin to himself. Strangely enough, it was hard to see him there.

'Now, Thomas.' Bolitho took a glass and held it to a deck-head lantern. 'I know what you are about to say. Let me speak first.' He sipped the claret slowly, hearing the sea sluicing along the lower hull and dashing spray against the closed port. 'You think I feel my nephew's disappearance so grievously that I am prepared to throw my life away as a gesture. To say I do *not* feel it would be a lie. Equally, it would be false of me to say that my upbringing, my very way of life, would not stop me from such a vanity. Like you, Thomas, I have seen too many good men, so many fine ships and ideals thrown to the winds because of the conceit of perhaps only one man in authority. I swore I would never allow my own feelings to make others suffer, and for the most part I have, I think, been true to that.'

He was on his feet, pacing slowly the few yards along the length of the cabin. Herrick sat on the breech of a nine-pounder, his eyes glinting in the yellow light as he followed his restless movements.

'When my wife, Cheney, died –' He broke off, aware for the first time that he was moving round the cabin. 'Enough of that. You shared it all. You brought news of her death, a burden for any man to carry, let alone a friend.'

Herrick looked at him wretchedly. 'I know.'

'I suppose that Adam has come to mean so much because of my loss. I told myself that if or when I fell in battle, or died of some other cause, he would gain the advantages of the Bolitho family, advantages which should have come his way by happier circumstances.' He shrugged helplessly. 'You never think that fate might take one and leave the other behind, Thomas.'

Herrick rolled the glass in his fingers, searching for the right words.

'That is why I ask the chance to go with the marines.' He stopped, seeing the refusal in Bolitho's grey eyes.

'No. The day after tomorrow we will land on an enemy coast. Not some rock or island, or an outpost in the Indies, but in Europe. Do you think it right to commit our people to such a venture without leadership?' He laid one hand on Herrick's shoulder. 'Come along, Thomas, be honest. Were there not many times in the past when you have maligned your senior officer for leaving you to take the cuffs and stabs while he stayed clear of danger?' He shook him gently. 'I asked for *honesty*!'

Herrick gave a half smile. 'On some occasions.'

'*Some?*' Bolitho watched him with sudden affection. 'By heaven, you took me to task enough, let alone a commodore or admiral!'

Herrick controlled the smile. 'That was different.'

'Because you are you, Thomas. And I am the same man as I was then.'

Herrick put down his glass. 'And Mr. Gilchrist?'

'I need an experienced sea officer.' His tone hardened

slightly. 'He sent young Adam into that boat. Perhaps because he has experience of battle despite his years. Or maybe for some other, less praiseworthy reason.'

Herrick looked at the deck. 'I find that hard to believe, sir.' He faced him again, his features more determined than they had been since the ship had left Gibraltar. 'But if I discover a truth in it, he will know it.' His eyes were like a stranger's. 'And pay.'

Bolitho smiled gravely. 'Easy now. Perhaps I am speaking hastily.' He moved to the door and heard the marine sentry drawing his boots together. 'But we had best concentrate on the immediate future. Otherwise we will all be made to *pay* for it!'

*

Allday thrust the hair from his eyes and said hoarsely, 'It seems we have arrived, Mr. Pascoe.' His lips were so dry from thirst that he could barely speak, and the sun across his head and shoulders burned as mercilessly as it had all day, and the one before that.

Pascoe nodded and lurched against him. Behind them the five gasping seamen staggered like drunkards, staring without comprehension at the lip of the hill track, the hard, glittering horizon beyond. *The sea once again.*

The forced march had been a nightmare, and while the mounted troopers had made a show of drinking as much as they pleased, they had made certain their prisoners were given hardly anything. When two wrinkled peasant women had offered some water by the roadside the horsemen had ridden at them threateningly, driving them away, laughing when one had gone sprawling in the dust like an untidy bundle.

They had lost one more of their number. A seaman called Stokes. He had sat watching the troopers on the previous evening as they had prepared to make camp for the night. He had been unable to drag his eyes from the great skin of coarse red wine which was being handed round amongst the troopers, his raging thirst, the pain of his lacerated feet making him a picture of misery and despair.

After a muttered conversation the troopers had beckoned him over, and to the other prisoners' astonishment and envy had offered him the skin of wine, gesturing and grinning at him to take his fill.

When they had finally realised what was happening it was already too late. As Stokes drank and drank to his capacity, his face and chest soaking in spilled wine, the soldiers urged him on, and then supporting him bodily, while others poured more into his gaping mouth.

Starved, sun-dried and already terrified as to what his fate might be, Stokes had changed in that instant into a raving madman. Capering and reeling, vomiting and falling in all directions, he was pitiful to watch. And whenever he had dropped choking on the ground they had begun all over again.

This morning, as the prisoners had been freed from their ropes and herded on to the rough track, they had seen Stokes still lying where he had last fallen, his body surrounded in a great red stain of dried wine, like blood, his face a mask of flies.

When Pascoe had tried to reach him he had been kicked back to the others. None of the troopers even went to see if Stokes was still breathing. It was as if they had tired of a game and wished only to get on towards their destination.

Allday shaded his eyes and studied the blue sea beyond the hill rise. What a barren place it was. Mountains inland, and this part all ups and downs in stony gullies. His torn feet told him he had walked every inch of it.

A whip cracked, and once more they started to shuffle forward. As they panted up the last slope Allday said breathlessly, 'Ships, by God!'

Pascoe nodded. 'Three of them!' He seized Allday's arm. 'Look at all those people!'

The track which led down to the foreshore and joined another, better-made road was alive with tiny moving figures. Like ants, which at a distance appear to move without purpose or direction, it was evident as they drew nearer that the activity was well ordered. Dotted about were armed soldiers and civilian supervisors who stood like rocks amidst the tide of human movement.

Pascoe said, 'Prisoners.'

'Slaves, more like.'

Allday saw the whips in the hands of the guards, the fearful way the ragged prisoners moved around each vigilant figure.

He turned his head towards the ships. Two brigs and one larger vessel, a transport. All three anchored close inshore, and the water between them and a newly constructed pier was an endless coming and going of oared boats and lighters. There were lines of neat tents by the hillside, and across the bay, scored out of the grass and gorse of a low headland, was what appeared to be a battery, the flag of Spain lifting and curling high above it.

Pascoe murmured, 'The ships look well laden.'

They fell silent as the senior horseman cantered towards them, his whip trailing down his leg and along the road. He pointed at the seamen and barked an order. Two troopers dismounted and gestured with drawn sabres towards the first line of tents. The whip swung round, separating Pascoe and Allday from the others and at the same time pointing to another, smaller line of tents.

Outside one Allday saw an officer watching them, shading his eyes with his arm as the horseman urged them towards him. Allday silently thanked God. The officer might be a Spaniard, but he was far better than their captors.

The horseman dismounted and reported to the officer, who after a slight hesitation walked towards them. He was very slim and wore a white tunic and scarlet breeches. As he drew closer Allday noticed that his smart uniform and gleaming cavalry boots were less so, and like the man himself, showed signs of having been out here in this terrible place for some while.

He walked around them very slowly, his dark features thoughtful, but without any sign of emotion.

He stopped in front of them again and said in careful English, 'I am *Capitan* Don Camilo San Martin, of His Most Catholic Majesty's Dragoon Guards.' He had a sensitive face, marred by a thin, even cruel mouth. 'I would be obliged if you would honour me with your er, titles?' He held up one neat hand. 'But before you begin, I must warn against lies. That fool of a man told me how his patrol discovered you and your sailors. How after a great fight he was able to overpower you and bring you to me.' He seemed to draw himself up in stature. 'I am in command of this er, enterprise at the moment.'

Allday breathed out slowly as Pascoe replied, 'I am Lieutenant Adam Pascoe of His Britannic Majesty's Navy.'

The Spaniard's sad eyes moved to Allday. 'And this? I understand he, too, is an officer.' His mouth lifted slightly. 'Of some lesser value perhaps?'

'Yes.' Pascoe swayed but kept his voice level. 'A warrant officer.'

Allday found time to marvel at Pascoe's quick thinking after what he had just endured. The Spaniard seemed content with the lie. If they were to be separated now, there was no chance of escape, if chance there was.

'Good.' *Capitan* San Martin smiled. 'You are very young, *Teniente*. I am right therefore to suppose that you were not alone? That you are from an English ship, eh?' He held up his hand in the same tired gesture. 'I know. You are an officer and bound to your oath. That I respect. In any case, the question must have an obvious answer.'

Pascoe said hoarsely, 'My men, *Capitan*. Could you order your soldiers to take care of them.'

The Spaniard seemed to consider it. 'In good time. But for the moment you and I have matters to discuss.' He pointed to his tent. 'Within. The sun is cursed hot today.'

Inside it was cool, and as Allday's eyes grew accustomed to the shaded interior he realised he was walking on a thick carpet. After the rough road it was like a gentle balm for his torn and blistered feet.

San Martin remarked, 'I see from your back that you had some rough handling on your way.' He shrugged. 'They are ignorant savages. But good fighters. My grandfather used to hunt them for sport.' It seemed to amuse him. 'But we must change with the times.'

An orderly brought some goblets and began to fill them with wine.

San Martin nodded. 'Sit down, if you wish. You are now *prisoners of war*. I suggest you make the most of my hospitality.' He smiled again. 'I was once a captive of the English, and exchanged a year back. I learned to improve my understanding of your people, as well as the language.'

Pascoe began, 'I must insist, sir – '

He got no further. San Martin stared up at the roof of the tent and shouted, '*Do not insist with me*, Teniente!' The sudden effort brought a rash of sweat across his features. 'I have but to say the word and I can make you vanish! How do you enjoy that' eh? Those animals you saw out there working on the road and defences are *criminals*, who but for the urgency of this task would be in their rightful places, chained to the oars of a galley or rotting on gibbets. I could have you flung amongst them, *Teniente*! How would you like to eke out your life chained to a great sweep, sitting in your own filth and living hour by hour to the beat of a drum, the lash of a whip, eh?' He was almost beside himself. 'You would have very little time to *insist*, that I promise you!'

Allday saw the soldier with the wine bottle shaking badly. He was obviously used to his master's violent outbursts.

He continued more calmly, 'Your ship, or ships perhaps, are in our waters to do us some harm.' He gave a slow smile. 'Your commander, do I know of him?'

He did not wait for answer but strode from the tent.

Pascoe whispered quickly, 'He does not know about the schooner.'

'To hell with the schooner, Mr. Pascoe. What will you tell him?'

Before he could reply the Spanish captain was back again. With great care he laid a loop of stout cord on the table and stood back to examine it.

'You will see that it is joined at both ends.' He sounded matter of fact. 'There are two large knots in it, here and here.' He tapped it with his finger. 'A circle of pain. Our inquisitors found it of some use for obtaining confessions of guilt in the Americas, I believe.' He looked hard at Pascoe. 'If I had this placed around your head, each of the knots would fit against an eye. By twisting the cord from behind, tighter and tighter, I am assured the agony is unbearable.' He picked up the cord and threw it to the orderly. 'And of course, the climax comes when both eyes are forced from their sockets.' He snapped an order to his orderly who almost ran from the tent. 'Like grapes.'

Allday exclaimed hoarsely, 'You'll not let those devils use it on our lads!'

'*I have told you!*' San Martin's face was working with emotion. 'You are prisoners of war. You will be treated as such while you are under my guard.' He sat down, his chest working painfully. 'Now drink your wine.'

Allday dropped his goblet as a terrible shriek echoed round

the tent. As Pascoe made for the entrance two pistols appeared in San Martin's hands as if by magic.

'Stand! It is not one of your wretched sailors! It is only a prisoner. The effect will be the same after they have watched his pain!'

San Martin's eyes remained as still as the two pistols as he studied Pascoe's horrified face. The terrible screams continued for what seemed like an hour, but when they ceased the sound remained in the tent like a curse from hell.

San Martin replaced the pistols in his belt and said, 'Sailors *talk* a great deal. I will go now. Do not try to leave the tent or I will have you killed.' He picked up his hat and banged dust from its yellow plume. 'When I have spoken to the sailors I will know about your ships, and probably much more as well.'

The tent seemed very silent after he had gone.

Pascoe sank down on to the carpet and retched uncomfortably. 'He's right.'

Allday watched his despair, the quiver of his blistered shoulders as he tried to control himself.

'No one but a fool would stay voiceless after being made to watch that torture.'

The Spanish captain, true to his promise, was back within an hour. He seated himself on one corner of a brass-bound chest and said calmly, 'One of your men was very willing to speak with me.' He smiled sadly. 'Do not look so troubled, *Teniente*. Mine would sell my very soul if they were in the same position.' He became formal. 'Your ships have been in these waters for over a week, yes? You are sailing to spy upon the French, our ally. Such matters are not my concern. My orders are to command over these dogs until the bay is properly defended.' He tapped his chin with the rim of a wine goblet. 'I did discover one piece of news which may be of use to those better placed to use it. Your ships took a Spanish vessel.' His mouth twisted with sudden fury. 'Those fools who brought you here were so drunk with their *victory* they allowed a ship to be stolen from under their noses!'

Allday thought of the knotted cord and could almost feel pity for the senior horseman with the whip.

As if to confirm his thoughts, San Martin snapped, 'It will not happen again!'

He calmed himself with an effort. 'No matter. Your war is over. I will have you transported to more er, secure quarters where you can be held in accordance with your station.' He eyed them dully. 'I will send for some food.'

He was obviously disinterested in matters relating to any ship, friend or foe, now that he had attended to his prisoners.

Two armed soldiers escorted them to a nearby tent, and a short time later the same orderly brought a basket of bread and fruit and a large earthenware jug of coarse wine.

Pascoe said bitterly, 'Then it's over, Allday. We'll not see England for a long while.' He looked away. 'If ever.'

Allday stood by the tent flap, careful not to show himself to the sentry outside.

He replied, 'Nothing's over yet.' He added grimly, 'Be thankful for one thing. That gibbering seaman who spoke with the Don was one of Cap'n Javal's men. They all were in our party.'

Pascoe looked up at him. 'What difference does it make?'

Allday walked from the flap and poured a mug of wine.

'Any *Lysander* would have known you to be the commodore's nephew.' He saw the shot go home. 'Think what the Don would have made of *that*, eh? They'd have used you as something to bargain with maybe.'

Pascoe stared at him. 'I am sorry. I did not think.'

'Not that our Dick'd – ' He broke off and grinned. 'Beg pardon, I was forgetting my place.'

'Go on. Please.'

Allday shrugged. 'I've sailed with your uncle for a long time.' His voice was far away. 'We've seen and done a lot together. I've watched him ache for the brave lads who've fallen at his bidding. Seen him walk about a deck as if in a dream, while the planks have spouted splinters from sharpshooters trying to mark him down.' He shook himself, ashamed at betraying a deeply guarded confidence. 'He would not risk his people even for you.'

Pascoe scrambled to his feet and crossed to his side. 'For *us*, you mean.'

Allday smiled. 'Ah well, it's good of you to put it like that. But cox'ns are easier to get than blood relations!'

Pascoe sighed. 'I wish I could do something for him.'

A shouted challenge made Allday peer through the flap again.

'There's a rider dashing into the camp as if the goblins of Exmoor were at his tail!'

Pascoe said, 'Let me look.'

Together they watched San Martin as he stood outside his tent, his dark head lowered as he squinted at a mounted trooper who was gasping for breath and shouting his message from the track below the tents.

Allday muttered, 'Something's afoot.'

Pascoe gripped his arm. 'I understand a little Spanish.'

Something in his tone made Allday forget the scene by the tents.

Pascoe added quietly, 'A fisherman has sighted a ship, a *big ship*.'

They stared at each other for several seconds.

Then Allday said thickly, 'If it's *one* ship on her own, we know which one she'll be, don't we, Mr. Pascoe?'

They turned back to the sunlight as San Martin yelled a stream of orders which were terminated by the urgent blare of a trumpet.

Allday thought of the headland battery, the one bitter turn of luck which had let a Spanish fisherman send a warning.

'You just said you wished you could do something?' He saw Pascoe nod with slow understanding. 'So be it then. For if *Lysander*, or any other King's ship pokes her beakhead into the bay now, it'll be the last damn thing she does on *this* earth' an' that's no error!'

San Martin's voice was suddenly very close, and Pascoe said quickly, 'We'll have some wine.' He thrust a full mug into Allday's fist. '*Say something!*'

Allday gulped on the wine and nearly choked. 'I can remember as if it was yesterday, when I was in the old *Hyperion* and–'

San Martin threw open the tent flap and strode into the shade.

'Good.' He looked at the wine and the bread. 'Good.'

Pascoe asked, 'The trumpet, sir. Does it mean danger?'

San Martin studied him searchingly. 'Of no importance. To you.' He moved round the tent like a trapped animal. 'I was going to have you put aboard a ship today. But I will have to wait until tomorrow. I am sending you to Toulon. The French admiral has more time than I to deal with such matters.'

Allday said gravely, 'It is war, sir.'

San Martin regarded him for a long moment. 'Riding a fine mount into battle is war. Commanding this miserable rabble is not.'

He paused by the entrance. 'I will probably not see you again.'

They waited until his footsteps had receded and then Allday said, 'Thank God for *that*!'

Pascoe ran his fingers through his hair, combing out grit and sand.

'He is keeping the ships here until tomorrow.' He was thinking aloud. 'So our ship must be very near.'

Allday watched the side of the tent as it pressed inwards with the hot wind.

'If the wind holds as it stands now, Mr. Pascoe, *Lysander* will be standing inshore right enough.'

'You're *sure* it will be *Lysander*?' The youth watched him gravely.

'And aren't you?'

He nodded. 'Yes.'

'Then it will be tonight or first light, I reckon.' Allday swallowed another mouthful of wine. 'So we'd best put our heads together and think of some way to warn her off.'

He remembered what Pascoe had said earlier. *We'll not see England again for a long while. If ever.* Whatever they could do to warn the ship, and whatever the result of their sacrifice might be, one thing was certain. They would both pay for it dearly.

5

The Only Way Out

BOLITHO tugged his hat firmly over his forehead as *Lysander*'s heavy, thirty-four foot launch dipped into the lively wavecrests and soaked the occupants with spray. He peered astern but the ship was already lost in darkness, while on either quarter he could see the white splashes from oars as the two cutters held their station on him. Despite the careful preparations, oak looms tied with greased rags and the tight stowage of weapons and equipment, the combined sounds seemed tremendous.

He turned his attention ahead of the launch, and could just discern the outline of the gig, the occasional splash of phosphorescence as a seaman in her bows marked their progress with a boat's lead and line.

The gig was commanded by *Lysander*'s senior master's mate, named Plowman, who had been highly recommended by the master himself. Bolitho thought that if Grubb could not take part in the raid personally, then Plowman was the next best choice. Grubb had confided in his thick, wheezing voice that Plowman had served in a Welsh trader along these shores in happier times. 'Leastways, that's what 'e says, sir. I reckon 'e was doin' a bit of blackbirdin' with the Arabs!'

Slaver or not, Plowman was taking the little procession of overcrowded boats straight inshore without the slightest show of hesitation.

It was strange that the more important the work, the lowlier the man who was most needed.

He felt Gilchrist shifting his bony figure beside him, the quick nervous breathing as he clutched his sword between his knees.

Bolitho tried not to think of the possibility of disaster. That already, out there in the blackness, muskets and blades were waiting to cut them down in the shallows. Perhaps Gilchrist was thinking much the same.

Someone lost the stroke in one of the cutters and he heard Steere, the fifth lieutenant, call anxiously 'Easy there! *Together!*'

The boats were so heavily laden with marines as well as their oarsmen that it took plenty of brawn to pull them. The resulting splashes and creaks, grunts and curses were only to be expected.

The bowman called, 'Gig's 'eaved-to, sir!'

Bolitho leaned forward, suddenly aware that the white, writhing patterns no longer came from Plowman's oars but from sea against land.

'Easy all!' The launch's coxswain tensed over his tiller bar. 'Stand by in the boat!'

Gilchrist snapped, 'I can't see a damn thing!'

The two cutters were backing water vigorously, their pale hulls gleaming in the darkness as an offshore swell swung them in a dance.

Metal rasped and boots shuffled as the marines prepared to quit the boats. It only needed one of them to loose off his musket or fall against the seaman who was holding the lanyard of a stem-mounted swivel gun and stealth would go by the board.

Bolitho held his breath, watching Plowman's gig loom from the darkness and touch the launch with barely a shudder. Hands reached out to hold them together, and after a few more fumbling thuds Plowman appeared in the sternsheets, his teeth very white as he muttered, 'There seems a fair beach up yonder, sir.' His breathing was even, as if he was actually enjoying himself. Remembering perhaps when he and his men had gone after live cargo. 'Not very big, but by the looks of the water I'd say we're safer here than gropin' to the next bay.'

'I agree.'

Bolitho tried not to think of the time. It was like a mental hour-glass, the sand running away remorselessly.

Plowman added, 'I'll lead then.'

He made to turn towards the bows but stopped as Bolitho said, 'Once we are ashore you will take charge of the boats. You have done well, Mr. Plowman, to get us this far. I'll see it's not forgotten.'

Plowman protested, 'I could put one of my lads in charge, sir.'

'No. We will need you again later. I don't want Mr. Grubb's

right-hand man getting lost in Spain! The master would never pardon me!'

Several men chuckled and Plowman sighed. 'That's true, sir.'

Fifteen minutes later the gig and then the big launch thrust into hard sand, and while seamen stumbled waist-deep in water alongside, and oars and weapons went in all directions, Bolitho ran with Gilchrist up the beach, their swords in their hands.

This would be the moment. Bolitho halted by some scattered rocks, his eyes straining in the darkness, trying to pitch his ears above wind and sea.

But no challenge came, no ripple of flashes from the higher darkness above the beach. And with each precious minute more and more men were squelching out of the shallows and hurrying to their allotted positions. The crossbelts grew in numbers, and when the cutters, which had watched warily for any sign of attack, came in also, the small cove seemed to be full of silent figures.

Major Leroux strode up the beach. 'All mustered, sir.'

'Very well. Have the boats stand off. Pass the word to Mr. Plowman to remain close inshore for one hour and then return to the ship as arranged.'

He watched Leroux beckoning to his orderly. One hour. It should be long enough to know if they had an even chance of success.

As the boats and their depleted crews splashed astern from the beach, Bolitho could sense the uncertainty around him. Despite their military code, the marines were not land animals. The thought of being left in foreign territory, denied a link with their ship and the only way of life most of them understood would be uppermost in their minds.

He said, 'Send out your scouts, Major Leroux.'

The marine nodded. 'We will need some good men to flank us, too.'

He hurried away, and in no time at all the whole landing party was on the move.

It was much as Grubb and Plowman had described, although the track which followed the high ground above the beach was rougher than expected. Men swore savagely in the darkness, and occasionally Bolitho heard Nepean or one of his sergeants demanding silence under all manner of threats.

After an hour Bolitho ordered a rest, and while the marines sat or crouched on either side of the track he called his officers together.

'It will be growing lighter in five hours.'

He saw Midshipman Luce shaking stone chippings from one shoe, and thought again of Pascoe. In the poor light he was not unlike him. They had been, no *were* good friends.

'According to my calculations we have a gully to cross and then we will be very near to the bay. The chart describes the first headland as loose and worn down by the sea. So it is my guess that any defending battery must be mounted on the opposite headland.'

Gilchrist said angrily, 'We can never march all that way before *Lysander* begins her attack.'

'Are you speaking to me, Mr. Gilchrist?' His voice was so mild that Luce jammed on his shoe and stood very still to listen.

'I'm sorry, er, sir.' Gilchrist sounded off balance. 'It was an opinion.'

'I am glad to know that.' He looked at the others. 'But we must seize any pieces which might be capable of crippling *Lysander* before the attack begins. Unprepared for our visit the Spaniards may well be. But the bay will be like a nest of hornets once the first shot is fired.'

Leroux tightened his sword-belt. 'I agree, sir. And the sooner we get to the gully, the better I'll be pleased.'

Bolitho looked round, feeling the dust and grit against his face. The wind was holding. It was to be hoped that Herrick's 'lady luck' did the same.

He said, 'Get them moving again.'

Leroux strode away, and after a few whispered commands the marines clumped on to the track. In the darkness their belts made a long, undulating snake of crosses.

And still nothing moved from the outer darkness. Not a stray dog, nor some befuddled fisherman groping his way to a boat to prepare for the dawn. It was as if the whole of the shore had been abandoned.

Stranger still, Bolitho found that he was able to think without interruption, his gait almost relaxed as he strode beside the middle section of marines. He thought of the times he had sailed past this coastline in both directions. Now he was actually walking along it. Names on the chart crossed through his mind like memories. Cartagena, which lay less than forty miles away. Alicante, Valencia, each held a place in his memory. And five years back, in this same war, Spain had been an ally of England.

He realised that a whispered command was coming back down the line, and as he hurried forward he saw Leroux and Nepean in close conference with a corporal.

Leroux did not waste words. 'This is Corporal Manners, sir. A good skirmisher by any standards.' He looked steadily at Bolitho. 'He's been leading the scouts.'

Bolitho kept his tone level, although he knew that something was very wrong. 'Your advance party has reached the gully?'

Leroux nodded. 'Tell the commodore, Manners.'

The marine's dialect was like a sound of home. Manners explained, 'The gully is there as we expected, zur. But there must have been a great cliff fall. It's almost sheer-cut, like the side of an abbey.' He hesitated. 'I was a tin miner in Cornwall afore I signed on, zur.'

'Then you will know what you are talking about.'

Bolitho looked past them, his mind grappling with the totally unexpected.

Manners added, 'I *could* try an' get down with the grapnel an' line, zur.'

Bolitho shook his head. 'Under cover of darkness it would be fatal.' He looked at Leroux. 'What do you think?'

The major replied, 'It would take hours. Even if we could do it, the men would be in poor shape for a pitched battle afterwards.'

'And *Lysander* would already be in the bay.'

He felt despair crowding in on him. He had been blind, too stupid to plan for this one real barrier which made all other preparations a waste of time. *And lives.* He had relied on the chart's sparse information and his own eagerness. His mind rebelled at the word. For vengeance?

'We will have to march them around the gully, sir.' Leroux was watching him. Sharing his anxiety. 'However –'

'Indeed, Major Leroux. That one word *however* tells all.'

Lieutenant Nepean remarked, 'We will circle whatever defences there are in the bay, sir, and storm the battery from inland.'

Leroux sighed. 'Pass the word to Sergeant Gritton. We will follow the scouts as before.' In a quieter voice he said to Bolitho, 'There is nothing else we can do now.'

It could have been a reproach, but it was not.

Gilchrist's tall figure came out of the gloom. 'I hear that we are cut off by the gully, sir.'

'That is so.' He tried to discover his reactions. 'So we will have our forced march after all.'

He saw the marines plodding past again, muskets slung, heads bowed as they watched the legs of the men in front. Most of them did not know where they were, let alone what they were doing here. *Trust.* The word came at him like a shout. It was all they had, and he had thrown it back at them.

Gilchrist said in a dull voice, 'It is what follows that troubles me, sir.' He turned to take up his position with the next file of marines.

Leroux snapped, 'That man puts an edge to my patience, sir.'

Bolitho glanced at him. 'Captain Herrick is satisfied with his competence.'

Leroux slashed at a gorse bush with his curved hanger and replied, 'It is not for me to speak of others behind their backs, sir.'

'Remember that word we were using, Major?' Bolitho heard the hanger cut angrily at another patch of gorse. '*However?*'

'I know that Captain Herrick has served with you before, sir. The whole squadron knows it. He is a fine man, and a fair one. It is hard to be either in a ship of the line, from my experience.'

'I will agree to that, Major. Thomas Herrick has been my friend since the American Revolution. He has saved my life more than once.'

'And you his, to all accounts, sir.' Leroux darted a swift glance at his panting file of marines. 'He has a sister, sir, did you know that?'

'Yes. She means a lot to Captain Herrick. The poor girl has had much to endure, that I also know.'

'Yes. She is a cripple. I met her once when I went to Kent on a mission for the captain when we were refitting *Lysander*. To see a face so fair, and so betrayed by her useless limbs, is enough to break a man's heart.' He added slowly, 'Mr. Gilchrist has asked for her hand in marriage.'

Bolitho gripped his sword hilt and stared into the darkness until his eyes hurt him. He had been so busy with his own affairs he had not once considered Herrick's other world. Herrick had begun his service as a poor man without privileges. Compared with officers like Farquhar, or himself for that matter, he still was poor. But over the years he had managed to save, to swell his meagre beginnings with prize money and the reward from his promotion to post-captain.

Leroux said, 'Captain Herrick's mother died just before we sailed from Spithead. So you see, sir, his sister is all alone now.'

'He did not tell me.' Bolitho's mind went back over those first moments when he had joined *Lysander* at Gibraltar. 'But maybe I gave him no chance.'

He fell silent, and Leroux hurried on towards his scouts, leaving him to his thoughts.

Herrick loved his sister dearly. To find her a husband would be more important than almost anything. Even his loyalty to him. He thought, too, of Gilchrist's hostility, and forced himself to ask why he should want to marry a crippled girl. He could find an explanation for neither.

He lifted his head and stared up at the stars. So cool and aloof from all their pathetic efforts on earth.

So often in the past when he had served, fretting and impatient under his superior officers, he had told himself he could do better. But they had had fleets to command, great events to consider and manipulate. He had been given just one small chance to show his ability, to prove that he could now join that élite group of men whose flags flew with pride for all to see and obey.

As he listened to the weary, dragging boots of the marines at his side he knew he had failed.

*

'What can you see now?' Pascoe kept his voice to a whisper as he watched the sentry outside the tent flap.

At the back of the tent Allday was bent almost double while he peered through a small hole cut with an improvised blade which he had fashioned from a drinking cup.

Allday held up his hand to silence him. From the rear of the tent he could see part of the beach below the camp, the glitter of stars on choppy water and a riding light from one of the ships. There was no moon, so that any small glow from fire or lantern shone out with false brightness, even from as far as the other headland.

It was past midnight, from what he could judge, but there had been plenty of activity in and around the camp with barely a pause since that trumpet call.

It was quieter now, but above the headland he could see a few pin-pricks from lanterns, and guessed that the battery was fully manned and getting ready for the dawn. Something red wavered for just a few seconds and then died as quickly. He felt sweat on his neck and chest. That was a furnace door being opened and closed. They were heating shot to welcome the ship with fire.

He ducked down, and together the two of them lay side by side on the ground, faces almost touching.

Allday whispered, 'The battery's heating shot. That must be why we've got a native trooper as a sentry. Every Don in the camp will be an artilleryman, and needed for those damned cannon.'

Pascoe's face was pale in the darkness. 'What shall we do?'

Allday gestured at the flap. 'Just one guard, is there?'

'Aye. They seem to think we're safe enough.'

Allday grinned in spite of the mounting tension. 'With good reason, Mr. Pascoe! Not much harm we can do if we start walking, is there?'

'I know.' It sounded like a sob.

'Easy.' He touched his shoulder, feeling the rawness left by the sun. 'If we can make an explosion, like the way we spoke of, we might be able to drive the ship away.'

Pascoe nodded firmly. 'How can we cross the camp? It must be all of a mile to the other side.'

Allday looked at the rear of the tent. 'If there is more than one guard, we are dead before we begin.' He let his words sink in. 'But if I take this one before he shouts for aid, one of us can wear his uniform.'

Pascoe wriggled on his stomach to the flap again. 'He's sitting down.' He came back again, moving like a poacher. 'I think he may be asleep. But take care.' He touched his wrist. 'There could be more guards close by.'

Allday examined his crude knife and said, 'If I get taken before I can do anything, you stay still and pretend to be asleep. Don't let on that we were doing it together.'

Pascoe showed his teeth. 'The *hell* with you, Allday!'

Allday smiled. 'That's more the sound of it, Mr. Pascoe!'

Pascoe stayed by the flap, shutting his ears to the steady scraping sound of Allday cutting through the tough canvas. The sentry did not move, and Pascoe was certain that someone would hear the steady thud of his heart against his ribs. The noise stopped and he took a quick glance across his shoulder.

'Are you going now?'

But he was alone.

He rose on one knee, holding his breath as Allday's shadow flitted round the side of the tent, his bare feet soundless on the sand. It was as if he had transformed himself into a great, enveloping cloak. One moment he stood there, towering above the dozing soldier. Then he was down and around him, merging the shadows into one, with little more noise than a brief yawn.

He tugged open the flap as Allday came back through the narrow entrance, dragging the inert soldier behind him.

Allday spoke through his teeth. 'Dare not light a lantern. You'll have to dress best you can. Here, pull his tunic off while I get his breeches. He stinks like a sow.' He groped quickly for a belt. 'Ah, he has a pistol, too.'

Pascoe felt the man's skin under his fingers. It was clammy and hot, but unmoving.

Allday muttered, 'I think I broke the bastard's neck.'

Pascoe stared at him and tore off his own breeches. He stood naked for a few hesitant seconds before struggling into the dead soldier's. His own breeches were almost torn to shreds, but they were part of his remaining link. He tightened his lips. There was no link any more.

Next the tunic and belt. Allday was right. He would never have been able to get his powerful bulk into this man's clothing.

He heard Allday moving across the tent, the gurgling of wine, and wondered how he could drink at a time like this. He gasped as Allday's dripping hands clamped around his face and neck and down the open collar of his tunic.

Allday said grimly, 'Got to make you as dark as possible see?

God help us if they see you in daylight. Don't reckon they'd
have seen a red-faced trooper before!'

He clapped the fez on Pascoe's head and draped the neckcloth carefully to hide as much of his face as possible.

Pascoe picked up the musket and checked it. Fortunately it
was a new one, probably French.

'I'm ready.'

Allday dragged the corpse aside and covered it with a piece
of canvas.

'Good. Now just loop some cord round my wrists behind
my back. This has got to look right an' proper.' He grinned.
'Not *too* tight, mind.'

They looked at each other in silence.

Then Pascoe said, 'If they take me alive . . .'

Allday shook his head. 'They won't. Me neither.'

Outside the tent it seemed almost cool, the deep shadows of
tents and earthworks unreal and menacing.

Allday wondered what the guards did with the slaves
and prisoners during the night. All being well they would get
a rude awakening wherever they were.

It was all so easy. They walked quickly down the slope from
the officers' tents and onto a rough, partly completed track
which Allday guessed led towards the new pier. Dying
embers from a fire glowed redly by an unlimbered wagon,
and between the big wheels he could see several sleeping
figures.

He heard Pascoe's footsteps close behind him, the regular
tapping of his musket against his hip as he carried it slung over
one shoulder.

Something moved away from a pile of timber and he hissed,
'Avast, Mr. Pascoe!'

Pascoe unslung his musket and jammed the muzzle into his
spine, pushing him along as fast as he dared. The shadow called
something and then laughed before turning away again into
the darkness.

Allday murmured, 'Well done, but I hope you're watching
your trigger finger!'

They continued in a straight line, using the dark margin
below the stars to show the way to the headland. There were
no lanterns there now. The gun crews would be resting by their
weapons. They had little to fear.

Allday halted and felt Pascoe stop immediately.

'What is it?'

Allday said quietly, 'There's someone directly ahead of us. Right in our path.'

Pascoe whispered, 'We daren't stop here. We're out in the open.'

'Aye.' Something about the figure standing in their way worried Allday. 'Just laugh if he says anything. I'll try and jump on his back as we pass.'

But the man did not challenge them, nor turn as they moved abreast of his lonely vigil.

He was tied to a post, his eyeless sockets huge and black above his bared teeth. Allday stayed silent, knowing it was the senior horseman who had beaten him with his whip.

Pascoe said it all for him. 'If they do *that* to one of their own . . .'

After a few more minutes Allday said, 'I think we'd better rest here. Take our bearings.'

They were almost on the sea's edge, the sand made uneven by the comings and goings of many feet as the anchored ships and lighters had been loaded.

The nearest one, a brig, seemed harder in outline, Allday thought. The dawn was closer than he had believed. How inviting she looked. He thought of the task they had set themselves and shuddered. *Any* ship would seem so just now.

He turned his attention to the low headland. Two humps, about a cable apart, marred the otherwise level outline. So there were two batteries. It was unlikely there would be more than one magazine. The Spanish captain had hinted that he had enough to do without adding to his work at this stage.

'We'll take the inner one, if you agree?'

Pascoe nodded. 'The one with the oven.' He nodded again. 'It's more likely that the magazine will be there. They'll not want too many delays when cradling heated shot into a primed gun!'

Allday watched his silhouette. It could have been the commodore speaking.

'I think I can see a path. We'll follow it. If we're wrong, we'll double back and try elsewhere.' Pascoe added firmly, 'It'll be a quick death.'

But their choice of direction was the right one. The path

widened as it curved around the back of the headland, and even to Allday's sore feet felt smoother.

Sheltered once more from the sea it was much quieter. They heard other sounds. Rustlings in the salt-dried grass, the distant neigh of tethered horses, a persistent whistle from some night-bird on the search for prey.

They turned yet another bend and found themselves staring straight at a tall wooden gate. It was wide open, and in the dim light of a hanging lantern they saw some crude steps leading up the hill to a point which must be directly below the first battery.

Allday asked quickly, 'Do you have that whip?'

Pascoe fumbled with the unfamiliar belt. 'Yes, why ——' He broke off as two figures moved slightly from inside the doorway.

Allday snapped, 'Use it! *Lively*, or we'll never reach that bloody gate!'

Both of the sentries were armed, Allday could see their bayonets glinting in the yellow glare. They were both Spaniards, artillerymen by the look of their boots and wide breeches.

He caught his breath as the whip passed against his shoulder. 'Harder, for God's sake!'

Pascoe gasped and struck out again, remembering with sudden clarity the way the horsemen had beaten them. Without emotion or pity.

The two sentries were watching with little curiosity. In this awful place it was a regular spectacle.

Then a musket clattered as one of them brought it up from the ground, and Allday bounded forward, dragging it from the astonished sentry's grip and driving the butt into his face in one savage thrust.

Pascoe ran to join him, but the second guard was already dashing wildly up the steps, his voice yelling like a madman's.

Allday threw up the musket and fired, seeing the man hurled round by the force of the ball before falling out of sight. They heard his body rolling down a slope in a small avalanche of loose stones and earth.

'*Come on!*' Pascoe ran up the steps and almost charged head-long into a sentry who was trying to let himself through another entrance which was guarded by a stout studded door.

Allday reached out and seized his neck, turning him easily and then smashing his head into the door.

It swung open into a narrow passageway, and as more shouts and running feet echoed overhead Pascoe said breathlessly, 'Bolt the door.' He held up a lantern. 'This must lead to the powder room.'

'It's dry enough.' Allday dragged two heavy barrels against the door. 'Be easy with the lantern.' He sniffed. 'I'll wager they're wondering what the hell is happening down here!' He cocked the second musket.

Boots and muskets hammered on the heavy door, and then just as suddenly fell silent.

Pascoe looked at his companion. 'Here goes then.'

*

Major Leroux handed Bolitho a small pocket telescope. 'I doubt if you will be able to see much yet, sir.'

Bolitho raised himself up on his knees, feeling the ache in his limbs and back from the long march overland. Scattered around the hillside gorse and dried grass he could see the belts and breeches of the marines as they lay gasping for breath in untidy clusters.

The sky was paler, as were the stars, there was no doubt about that. But horizon and land were still interlocked, and only where the shoreline was edged with pale sand could he get a true idea of their position. They were on a hillside, behind and about level with the headland. In the small glass he could see the crude gashes where the ground had been dug into earthworks and pallisades, the occasional flicker of light from a single lantern. It played on a pair of fat gun breeches, probably twenty-four pounders, he thought.

Leroux was leaning on his elbows, sucking quietly at a round pebble.

'Down this steep slope and up the next to the pallisade, sir. Even allowing for there being no other protection at the rear, we might lose half our men in a charge.' He glanced at his weary marines. 'Shipboard life takes the wind out of 'em. They're not infantry or line soldiers.'

Somewhere in the distance a dog barked with sudden vigour. It was like the beginning of another day.

Bolitho snapped, 'This morning they will have to act like soldiers, Major. We must attack without delay. Before the trumpet calls the garrison to arms.'

He felt the other officers moving closer to him. He kept his gaze directed towards the sea, the three dark shapes of the anchored ships. Perhaps they could silence the battery and then fight their way to some boats. All because of that gully. And his own blindness.

He said shortly, 'Mr. Steere, you will take what seamen remain with us and head for the beach. Mr. Luce will accompany you.' He nodded to Leroux. 'Carry on. We had best move directly.'

Leroux touched his sergeant's arm in the gloom. The man jumped as if he had been hit by a ball.

The major said curtly, 'Sergeant Gritton. Pass the word. Fix bayonets. Check each man. When I give the signal, the whole line will advance at the trot.'

The marine straightened his hat. 'Yessir.' He might just as well have been ordered to polish his boots from the little emotion he showed.

Men stirred along the hillside, and steel clicked against steel as the bayonets emerged to glint feebly in the dull light.

Bolitho drew his sword and said quietly, 'We will make as much noise as we can. It is the best weapon today.'

He swung round as a single shot echoed and re-echoed round the hills like a ricochet.

For a moment he imagined that a picket had sighted his marines, or worse still they had been outmanoeuvred even as they prepared to mount their attack on the battery.

Nepean called, 'Down there, sir! I saw a flash. A man fell, I think.'

There were muffled shouts, and the single lantern on the battery began to move across the flat ground behind the earthworks as if carried by a spirit.

Leroux muttered, 'It's no signal, by God. There must be a madman at work.' He added bitterly, 'In heaven's name, look at the confusion! There's no chance of a surprise now!'

Bolitho could see even without the major's telescope the surging figures along the battery wall. Most were very pale, as if only partly dressed, rudely awakened by that mysterious shot.

He replied harshly, 'It is our only chance, Major.' He lurched to his feet and waved his hat towards the astonished marines. 'Are you with me?' He could feel the madness rising in his throat like bile, the fierce pounding against his ribs as if his heart was trying to break free.

With something like a growl the marines stumbled from their positions and as one and then another pointed his bayoneted musket towards the battery Leroux yelled, *'Charge!'*

Down the slope, yelling and cheering like wild things, the marines soon forgot the order to keep down their speed. Faster and faster, feet kicking over grass and stones, the wavering line of bayonets brighter now as a faint glow showed above the headland.

Here and there a man fell, only to stagger upright again, find his musket and double after his yelling companions.

Bolitho heard a few shots, but who was firing and where they went he did not know. He knew it was getting harder to maintain the pace, and realised they were going up now instead of down.

He gasped out, 'Lively! Make for the pallisades!'

Some louder bangs came from above, and he heard a man gurgle and roll away down the slope.

But several marines had fallen behind and were kneeling to take aim above the heads of the others. A ball slammed past Bolitho's head and he heard a voice scream out with agony from the battery wall.

Leroux was yelling, 'A path! Sergeant Gritton, take 'em up there!'

Crack, crack, crack! Balls ripped into the pallisade from both sides, and as if from a great distance Bolitho heard the urgent clamour of a trumpet.

They had to reach that wall. Breach it before help came from the camp. They had all heard the horses. Cavalry would disperse the tired marines and destroy them piecemeal.

He almost fell across a sprawled soldier in a gateway, before he was pushed aside by a yelling marine at the head of the leading section. His mind reeled but clung to the strange fact that the gate was open, the sentry killed.

Up some steps and around a narrow bend where he saw some half dozen Spaniards beating against a broad door with weapons and fists, oblivious it seemed to the onrushing marines.

One turned, then the whole bunch of them scattered from the door, fighting each other to climb up and over a partly finished wall.

Whooping like fiends the marines charged amongst them, the bayonets lifting and stabbing, the awful cries drowned by their own excited madness.

Bolitho shouted, 'Stand fast, marines!' To Leroux he gasped, 'Stop them, for God's sake! We must get through that door!'

Shots banged down from the battery and several marines fell kicking, but as others were still hurrying up the steps it seemed likely they would soon be unable to move, to escape the hidden marksmen.

He saw Sergeant Gritton with a great axe standing framed against the door, heard the mighty clang as the blade hacked into the studded timber.

Leroux fired a pistol and handed it to his orderly as a body spilled over the rampart and pitched amongst the yelling marines.

'He'll never get it down in time!'

He fired his other pistol and cursed as the ball whimpered harmlessly towards the sky.

'Ready, lads!' Gritton was almost screaming. 'It's openin'!'

Bolitho thrust himself through the press of men, aware that the door was swinging inwards, knowing that no axe had done it, and that in the next seconds his men might be smashed down by a blast of canister.

Gritton was bawling, 'Shoot, lads! Let's be at the bastards!'

Then another voice, louder even than the sergeant's. 'Avast there, Sergeant Gritton! Hold your fire, damn you!'

Bolitho felt himself being carried bodily through the door on a tide of cursing, cheering marines, and as they burst into a roughly-hewn passage and fanned out on either side he stared at the two figures who were etched against a solitary lantern.

Leroux gasped, 'One of *us*! Shoot that soldier, Gritton!'

The 'soldier' threw down his musket, and as his arms were seized by two marines he called hoarsely, '*It's me!*'

Bolitho pushed the marines aside and gripped the youth around his shoulders. 'I must be dreaming!'

Allday shouted, 'Then so must we, sir!'

Leroux was at his side again. 'This is the main magazine, sir!' He stared at Pascoe's stained face. 'Did you . . .? I mean, were you going to . . .?'

Pascoe said huskily, 'We planned to blow the magazine. The commandant here knows a ship is nearby.' He looked at Allday, the strength suddenly gone out of him. 'And we knew she would be *Lysander*.'

Allday nodded, his filthy face split into a grin. 'What we didn't know was that we'd see the bullocks this fine morning!'

Bolitho controlled his reeling thoughts. They might still be too late to do anything. But it no longer seemed so black, so impossible as it had just moments ago.

'Major, take some men to the battery. Tell your sharp-shooters to fire with care. I doubt you'll get much opposition. They'll not be keen to shoot down here and build their own inferno.' He looked at Pascoe and Allday. 'As *you* were quite prepared to do.'

Allday said, 'One thing, sir. There's a second battery on the outboard end of the point. I think this is the only magazine, but –'

He broke off as the passageway shook to a sudden explosion. There was cheering, too, and the sporadic clatter of musket fire.

Bolitho nodded. 'That was a gun from the other battery, I'm thinking.'

Pascoe made to follow him as he ran after the marines, but he said, 'No, Adam. Yours has been the lion's share of danger. Remain here with these wounded marines until I know what to do.'

As he hurried along the dimly lighted passageway, past great vats of shot, barrels of powder and cradles for carrying the massive balls up to the furnace, he kept thinking of what had happened. Pascoe and Allday had survived. Not only that, they were here, with him, though how they had managed it he could not begin to comprehend. If he had been turned back completely by the gully, or had arrived at the camp perhaps minutes later, they would have blown up the magazine and battery, and themselves also. He felt the emotion pricking his eyes. To make that sacrifice, such a reckless gesture,

without even waiting to see if a ship was actually entering the
bay. They had *known* she was *Lysander*. It had been enough.

Another great bang brought dust filtering from the beamed
roof, but he took time to sheath his sword, to compose
himself, as Leroux, hatless with blood above his eye ran
down some steps and shouted, '*Lysander* is in sight, sir. The
other battery has opened fire on her, but this one has struck
to us.' He sighed heavily. 'Listen to my lads. Their *huzzas* are
a reward enough.'

Bolitho flinched as another bang echoed around the
magazine.

'Traverse some of the cannon to point on the other battery.
There is heated shot, I believe.'

Leroux led the way up the steps, his coat scarlet again in a
rectangle of dull light from the sky.

Bolitho felt the salt air across his face, and watched the
cheering marines as they hurried about the earthworks,
firing as they went towards the other battery. He ignored the
hiss of balls which flicked past him and stared fixedly at the
high pyramid of canvas which appeared to be rising from the
sea itself.

The seventy-four was moving very slowly into the bay,
her lower hull still in deeper shadow. Herrick was coming in,
just as he had known he would. No battery on earth would
prevent his attempt to complete the plan of attack, nor
frighten him from his attempt to rescue the landing party.

A gun crashed out from the battery, and he gritted his
teeth as a tall waterspout erupted violently alongside the
ship's hull. *Too close.*

He snapped, 'Hurry your men, Major! Tell them that the
sea is their only way out!'

6

Attack at Dawn

'COURSE nor'-east, sir!' The helmsman's voice was hushed.

'Very well.' Herrick moved restlessly to the weather side of the quarterdeck and peered towards the land.

As he turned to look along the upper gun deck he realised he could see some of the crews quite clearly, although at first glance it seemed as dark as before.

He walked aft to where Grubb stood near the wheel with Plowman, his best master's mate.

'There should have been a signal by now, Mr. Grubb.'

He ought to have held his silence and kept his anxiety to himself. But it seemed endless. *Lysander*'s slow and careful approach towards the hidden land, the nerve-stretching tension as the men stood to their guns on each deck, while others waited at braces and halliards in case he should order a sudden change of tack.

Occasionally from right forward in the chains he heard the leadsman's cry, the splash beneath the bows as he made another cast.

There was no chance of a mistake. With the wind holding steady across the larboard quarter, the sea depth checking with that shown on the chart, plus Grubb's vast local knowledge, there was no room for doubt.

The sailing master looked even more shapeless with his arms thrust deep into the folds of his heavy coat.

'Mr. Plowman repeats 'e saw the landin' party safe away, sir. No challenge, nor even a sight of a whisker from the Dons.' He shook his head and added gloomily, 'I agrees with you, sir. There ought to 'ave bin a signal long since.'

Herrick made himself walk forward again to the foot of the great main mast, where Fitz-Clarence was surveying the gun deck below the rail.

Herrick said, 'It's damn quiet.'

He tried to imagine what Bolitho and the marines were doing. Hiding, captured, perhaps already dead.

Fitz-Clarence turned and looked at him. 'It's lighter, sir. Much.' He raised one arm to point towards the land.

Herrick could see without being told that the nearest wedge of darkness had mellowed, and it was possible to see a crescent of sand, the lively movement of spray across some scattered rocks. *Lysander* was standing very close inshore, but the depth was safe. At any other time it would have been the perfect approach, the ideal conditions which were usually missing when most needed.

'By th' mark ten!'

Grubb confirmed it by muttering, 'The 'eadland must be fine on the larboard bow, sir.' He coughed throatily. 'We'll be able to spit on it within 'alf an hour!'

Below the quarterdeck rail he heard someone give a short laugh, the immediate bark from a gun captain to silence him.

The hands had been at their quarters since last night when they had dropped the boats and he had watched them pull towards the land. Down there, and deeper still on the lower gun deck, the waiting seamen were probably whispering their doubts, making jokes about their captain's caution. What would they say if he lost the ship, and them with her?

Fitz-Clarence remarked, 'Pity we are out of contact with *Harebell*, sir.'

Herrick snapped, 'Attend to your duties, Mr. Fitz-Clarence!'

It was perhaps only a casual comment. Or did the lieutenant mean that if he was too nervous to make a decision one way or the other, he should signal for the little sloop to make the first move?

He walked a few paces up the tilting deck, feeling the crews of the nine-pounders watching him as he went past. Every gun was loaded and ready behind its closed port. The cutlasses and boarding axes had been honed on a grindstone on the main deck. It seemed hours ago.

He saw Lieutenant Veitch, who was in charge of the upper deck battery of eighteen-pounders, lounging by the hatchway, chatting with his two midshipmen. Perhaps they did not even care. They were like he had once been. Content to leave it to others. When the events moved too swiftly for thought it was always too late anyway. He shifted his feet and watched the dawn light growing above the land. He had been in many sea fights. Had seen so much, and had known the mercy of survival. But this sort of work was beyond him.

High above the deeply-shadowed decks he heard the topsails and forecourse flapping and then filling hungrily to a sudden thrust of wind. Higher still the topgallant sails were set and drawing well, and he thought he saw one of the masthead lookouts kicking his legs to hold back the chill of the damp air.

He moved across to the opposite side of the deck, strangely spacious without the marines. He tried to picture each one of the officers throughout his command, from Fitz-Clarence, with his elaborate guise of complete self-confidence, to those like Lieutenant Kipling on the lower gun deck, and Veitch who was apparently so relaxed with his crews below the bulging canvas. With Gilchrist ashore, and Lieutenant Steere with him, he was short-handed enough. But those who remained were barely moulded into a team as yet, and the progress of their gunnery under fire was still to be tested.

'By th' mark seventeen!'

He heard himself say, 'Bring her up a point, Mr. Grubb.'

'Aye, aye, sir!'

Herrick ignored the sudden scuffle of bare feet as men hurried to trim the yards. He had made a small decision. There was time yet to change it.

He thought of the rest of the squadron, and mostly of Captain Farquhar. Farquhar had his instructions. With the other two-decker, and *Buzzard* to watch over their flank, he would be ready to come to his aid as soon as he received the word. When daylight made it possible to contact *Harebell* . . . Herrick shook himself with sudden desperation. It would all take time. *Too much time.* Bolitho and the landing party had not made their signal as arranged. To take *Lysander* into the bay without either support or intelligence from the shore was madness. Bolitho had made that plain enough.

'Course nor'-east by north, sir!'

'Very well.'

Herrick thought of Farquhar once again. He would love to have him ask for help. Equally, he would despise him if he failed now to make a decision. He was flag captain. How sour the title tasted at this moment.

He said slowly, 'We *will* enter the bay, Mr. Grubb.' He looked towards Fitz-Clarence's squared shoulders. 'Run out the larboard battery, if you please.'

As the pipe ran from deck to deck and the port lids were heaved open, Herrick heard a muffled cheer, as squealing like disturbed hogs the *Lysander*'s guns were trundled out. He tried to compose his thoughts, seeing Bolitho's calm face in his mind.

Fitz-Clarence reported warily, 'Larboard guns run out, sir.'

'Thank you. Pass the word forrard to the carronades. Fire only on my command. It is always hard to mark a land target – ' He broke off, sensing the lieutenant's curious stare. 'As you will discover.'

Lysander was heeling quite steeply to the press of sail, but Herrick knew from experience that it was better to hold on to as much agility as possible under these circumstances. No ship had ever got the better of a well-sited shore battery. It was like trying to kill a flea with a feather.

He crossed to the weather side and held on to the hammock nettings and watched the surge of white water below some fallen rocks. The western headland was slipping abeam, and as *Lysander*'s jib boom picked up the first thin ray of light like a lance he saw the bay and the solid land-mass beyond.

He snapped, 'Alter course two points, Mr. Grubb. Steer nor' by east.' He knew Grubb was protesting silently behind him but concentrated on the span and depth of the little bay. It might be empty. Perhaps they had all been wrong from the beginning.

As the braces were manned again, the yards trimmed to hold the wind, he made himself walk aft to the compass, feeling the eyes of the two helmsmen on him as he checked the course and then turned to examine the set of each sail.

'Nor' by east, sir.'

He nodded. 'Good.'

Grubb added, 'She's full an' bye, sir, as close 'auled as she can be.'

Herrick was peering up at the great sails, noting how they were starting to flap and shiver. The yards were braced tight round, and the ship must be losing way despite the press of canvas. But it would give him the maximum time and room to move.

'Deck there! Musket fire on the larboard bow!' A pause and then from the foremast lookout, 'Ships at anchor, sir! Three on 'em!'

The sudden crash of a large cannon made more than one man yelp with alarm.

Herrick held his breath, counting seconds, until with a whine and a loud splash the ball plummeted down well clear of the opposite side.

'Let her fall off a point, Mr. Grubb.'

Herrick listened to the squeak of steering gear, the noisy response from the topgallant sails as the *Lysander*'s jib boom edged round very slightly towards the out-thrust pointer of the other headland.

Bang. He was astonished to realise he could now see a pale beach behind the anchored vessels. And some running figures, like insects, without personality.

Bang. There was a great chorus of shouts as a ball smashed down hard alongside the bow, hurling a curtain of spray over the forecastle.

Plowman remarked, 'Good shootin'.'

Grubb said, 'Means they was waitin' for us. Must 'ave known all along.'

Fitz-Clarence shouted, 'One of the ships! She's trying to get under way!'

Herrick wiped his forehead. He felt frustrated at every turn. Sickened with the new understanding that even surprise was denied them.

'A brig, sir!' Young Saxby shouted wildly, 'She's cut her cable!'

Herrick saw the flutter of pale canvas as the brig set her foresail and jib, the way her outline was shortening as freed from her anchor she started to pay off towards the sea. The same wind which carried *Lysander* towards the tell-tale water-spouts of falling shot would take her to safety.

He drew his sword and walked briskly to the quarterdeck rail. It was a climax of bitterness and worry, of concern for Bolitho and for his own ability.

'Mr. Veitch! As you bear! I want that brig held!'

The lieutenant came out of his trance and yelled, 'Gun captains! On the uproll!' He crouched behind one of his eighteen-pounders, peering through the open port. '*Fire!*'

The whole battery belched fire and smoke in a long, ragged salvo. As the smoke came funnelling back through the ports, and the gun crews threw themselves into action with sponges and rammers, Herrick saw the sea around the brig pockmarked with great circles of white spray.

Gun trucks squealed as the eighteen-pounders were heaved and manhandled up the sloping deck to their ports. Captain by captain held up his hand, and then Veitch roared, '*Fire!*'

Again the long-drawn-out crash of cannon fire, the bright red and orange tongues spitting out from the hull, their heavy balls skipping across the water and throwing up great hoods of spray over and around the brig. When the smoke had drifted clear Herrick saw that the brig's main mast was gone and she seemed to be drifting helplessly out of command, her decks in chaos.

He shouted, 'Cease firing! Mr. Fitz-Clarence, I want both cutters ready to lower in five minutes.' He was wiping his eyes as more stinging powder-smoke breezed up over the quarterdeck. 'You take command.' He gripped the lieutenant's arm and swung him towards the nettings. 'That middle vessel is a transport of some sort. Deep hulled. Cut her out before they try to scuttle her. If you get any resistance, stand off, and I'll rake her as we pass.' He pushed him towards the ladder and yelled, 'Mr. Veitch! Shorten sail! Get the to'ga'n's'ls off her!'

Grubb peered aloft as a ball slapped through the main topsail like a great metal fist, leaving a hole as big as a man's waist.

He said, 'Gawd A'mighty.'

Herrick strode about the deck, his mind grappling with one situation to another. As the ship's angle lessened to the reduced pressure of sails the boarding nets were raised, and with a chorus of yells and cheers the two cutters were swayed up and across the gangway. Men tumbled over the side, cutlasses and muskets held high, while other hands unlashed the oars and thrust away from the ship's fat side.

More crashes came from the land, and one ball shrieked through the weather shrouds and made a seaman drop, gasping on to the nets which were spread to protect the guns from falling debris.

And how quickly the light had filtered and strengthened within the bay. Herrick turned from watching the two boats thrashing around the counter and realised he could see the hill battery, a plume of smoke above it. It would soon be time to wear ship, he thought. Beat back across the bay and cover the cutting-out party and their boats.

Bang. He turned swiftly as a ball slammed into the lower hull, shaking it to the very planks under his shoes.

Under topsails, forecourse and jib, *Lysander* was making very slow progress, and as a target she could not have looked better.

Herrick said harshly, 'We will stand off shortly, Mr. Grubb.' He shut his ears to someone screaming. 'We have done all we can.'

Two more balls skipped over the blue water like a pair of darting sharks. One whipped between the two cutters narrowly missing the frantic oar blades, the other thudded into *Lysander*'s side just below the beakhead.

He made himself watch the efforts of the two cutters. One had already grappled the heavy transport ship, the other was exchanging musket fire with darting figures along her poop.

He must recall the boats also. The whole venture was a shambles. He turned to Midshipman Saxby, who was standing with the signal party, when he heard a man yell with disbelief, '*Sir!* On t'other battery, sir!'

From the yards and the gun decks men began to cheer, and as Herrick stared fixedly at the hairline mast above the Spanish battery he saw the flag jerking to the top, the same one which was streaming from *Lysander*'s peak.

Grubb muttered, 'I can see scarlet! Them bloody bullocks got there after all!'

The rest of the voices were drowned in one tremendous explosion. It swelled out and down from the headland, hurling rocks and fragments right along the beach and scattering some soldiers who had been trying to approach the battery from there.

Herrick tried to control his grin. 'Heave-to, Mr. Veitch!' He nodded sharply. 'Yes, *you!* Promotion comes fast in a ship of war!'

He pointed at the transport. The explosion in the remaining battery had finished all resistance, and he could see Fitz-Clarence's men swarming aboard, the Spanish flag dipping to confirm the capture. The second brig was under way, her sails filling as she made all possible speed to escape destruction.

Herrick watched her calmly. '*Harebell* will catch that one.'

Sails awry and thundering, *Lysander* came up into the wind. No more shots were fired from the land, and along the foreshore only the dead and injured remained to mark the extent of the bombardment.

'Get more boats lowered.' Herrick gauged the slow drift across the bay. 'We may have to anchor, but I want every man-jack picked up.'

Saxby shouted, 'Commodore's coming along the beach now, sir!' He was hopping up and down. 'And here come the marines!'

Herrick gripped the rail and watched the untidy procession with something like awe. He saw Lieutenant Steere standing up to his waist in water beside a boat which his seamen must have unearthed somewhere. The hesitant steps of the wounded being carried aboard, the two cutters speeding from the prize ship to help the others.

Grubb ambled to his side. 'It'll give the Dons somethin' to bite on, sir.'

Herrick nodded. One ship sunk, a larger one captured, and the defences in ruins.

He stiffened. 'Mr. Saxby! Give me your glass!'

Grubb stared at him. 'What is it, might I ask, sir?'

Herrick handed him the glass and replied quietly, 'The commodore has his nephew with him.'

The master gave a low whistle. 'His cox'n, too, be God.' He snapped the glass shut. 'I don't reckon I can stand any more miracles in one day!'

Herrick walked slowly along the gangway, unable to take his eyes from the approaching boat. It had been a near thing. He had almost not made the decision. Perhaps Grubb was right about miracles.

He sought out Veitch's figure on the quarterdeck. 'Stand by to receive the commodore!'

Moments later Bolitho clambered up and through the entry port. His face was grimy with smoke and his elbows were showing through his sleeves, but he was smiling in a way which Herrick had almost forgotten.

Bolitho said, 'That was a fine piece of timing, Thomas!'

'I almost obeyed your orders, sir.' Herrick grinned awkwardly. 'Then I remembered what you would have done in my place.'

Bolitho threw back his head and took several deep breaths. It had been very close. Leroux's men had fired three heated balls into the other battery, and he had thought they might surrender. But they had been urged on and rallied again and again by a slim, fanatical officer. Allday had said he was the camp's commandant. The Spaniard had also managed to keep up an accurate bombardment with his seaward cannon, and at least two balls had hit *Lysander*, maybe more.

Then, as the ship had seemed about to tack away from the merciless cannon fire, one of Leroux's heated shots had ploughed into the battery's powder store. It had ended there, and he had seen the Spanish captain torn apart in the blast, his sword still waving in the air.

He turned and watched as Pascoe limped through the port, accompanied by cheers and laughter as some of the gun crews clustered round to slap his shoulders or point at his wine-stained uniform.

Herrick shook his head. 'And I doubted if we could do it, sir.'

Bolitho eyed him sadly. 'With men like these I could do just about anything, Thomas.'

Allday walked past, his bare feet held painfully away from ring-bolts and gun tackles.

Bolitho unbuckled his tarnished sword and handed it to him. 'Here, Allday. I'll be down directly.'

Allday looked at him, the strain coming back to his face. 'Aye, sir.'

Bolitho added quietly, 'I'll take it amiss if the level in my decanters is still high when I examine them.' He watched him fondly. 'I'm grateful for your safety.'

Herrick waited until Allday had vanished through the cabin hatch before saying, 'It is the first time I have known him robbed of a reply, sir.'

Bolitho watched the marines climbing or being hauled bodily through the port, the looks of bewilderment, pain and sheer pleasure at being safe and alive. He could feel his own wildness ebbing away, and imagined what it had been like for Pascoe and Allday.

He shook himself from his thoughts. 'Well, Captain Herrick, get the boats secured and signal our prize to up-anchor and take station to lee'rd.' He clapped him lightly on the shoulder, his smile returning. 'We will rejoin the squadron directly.'

*

Bolitho waited in silence until Herrick had completed his examination of the chart. Through the stern windows he could see the captured Spanish transport wallowing heavily in *Lysander*'s wake, and wondered for the hundredth time at his decision not to send her to Gibraltar as another prize.

Herrick straightened his back and looked at him. 'I agree, sir. According to our calculations we are standing into the channel between Spain and the island of Ibiza. Mr. Grubb assures me that Cape San Antonio is some twenty-five miles off the larboard beam.'

Bolitho leaned across the chart and studied the scattered bearings and soundings along the Spanish coastline. Two days since Herrick had sailed into the bay to rescue them before ordering Inch's *Harebell* in hot pursuit of the remaining brig. Either the brig was faster than she had appeared, or Inch had lost his sense of direction. The latter was more than likely, he decided.

Herrick said bluntly, 'I can discover no reason why we have not met with the squadron, sir.' His eyes remained steady as he added, 'Captain Farquhar knew very well that we might need support.'

Bolitho walked to the stern windows and watched the Spanish ship's foresail billowing in the uncertain wind. She was a strange catch. Filled to the deck seams with powder and shot, with fodder for horses and mules, and enough tents to shelter an army, she remained a mystery. She was named *Segura*, and once clear of the land he had sent for her master, a squat, furtive looking man who had been openly dumb-founded by Bolitho producing a letter which Javal's men had brought from the captured schooner.

The Spanish master had insisted in halting English that he did not know his ultimate destination. Indeed, there was nothing in his quarters to prove otherwise, and unless he had hurled his orders overboard at the first sign of danger, he was as much in the dark as his captors.

He did not seem like a clever liar. He had admitted that he had been told to take his cargo to a rendezvous in the Gulf of Valencia where he could expect an escort and maybe other merchant vessels under charter for the military. He had pleaded that he was a poor sailor who had no wish to become involved in war. The Spanish commandant who had been in charge of loading his vessel had given him instructions which would place him under French control. There were many vessels, the master had said, which the French were using throughout the Mediterranean to support their newly-founded outposts.

Should he ignore this unexpected catch? If some sort of rendezvous did lie ahead, it would be better to re-form the squadron before making a new intrusion into enemy waters.

But Farquhar was not here. There was little variation in wind, nothing in fact which should have prevented the other ships from making contact.

He said slowly, 'Perhaps Captain Farquhar was involved with the enemy.'

'Perhaps.' Herrick sounded doubtful. 'But the fact remains, sir, *Harebell* has not returned, with or without a prize, and we are alone. Very much so.'

Bolitho nodded. 'True. I think we will maintain the present course. Farquhar may decide for reasons of his own to rejoin us closer to our final destination.' He ran his fingers over the chart and the area marked *Golfe du Lion*. 'The French are stirring up an ants' nest, Thomas. They have more in mind than invading England, I think.' He moved his hand to the shores of Africa. 'I am certain it will be *here*.'

He thought suddenly of the vivid flash above the ramparts as Leroux's men had fired a glowing ball into the Spanish powder store. In this short while how his men had changed. They had rarely hesitated, and he had been moved by their efforts even when the attack had seemed hopeless.

The news must have reached higher authority by now. Even as far ahead as France. If the squadron was feeling its way, so, too, the enemy must be wondering at its intentions.

He walked aft yet again and stared at the prize ship. Lieutenant Fitz-Clarence was in command, no doubt relishing his unexpected promotion.

Herrick said, 'If *Harebell* doesn't return within a day, I fear we must assume her lost.' He rubbed his chin. 'And that'll mean we will be without "eyes".' He added with sudden bitterness, 'Damn that Javal! I'll wager he's away after some fat capture to line his pockets!'

Bolitho watched him thoughtfully. 'That is as may be. Or perhaps the whole squadron is destroyed?' He touched his arm and smiled. 'That was a *joke*, Thomas. But do not imagine I am untroubled.'

He turned as a tap came at the screen door. It was Pascoe, a stranger almost in his proper uniform.

'You sent for me, sir?'

'Yes.' Bolitho gestured to a chair. 'Have you had any more time to think about your ordeal?' He saw the youth's dark eyes go distant and added, 'It could be important, Adam.'

Pascoe stretched his legs. 'I had the impression that the Spaniards are so willing to aid their ally that they will do anything but fight. They were using galley slaves, felons, anyone who could lift and carry to build defences and prepare ways of loading all manner of vessels.'

Bolitho looked at them and smiled. 'With the Earl of St. Vincent's ships watching Cadiz and the Biscay ports, I think it unlikely that all this is for England's benefit.' He nodded firmly. 'This is what I intend. On to Toulon and the smaller French ports close by where, with luck, we shall meet with our other ships. Then south-east to Sicily where we can water our vessels and make discreet enquiries.' His smile broadened as he watched Herrick's doubt. 'I know, Thomas, the Kingdom of the Two Sicilies is at peace with France. It does not follow it is at war with *us*, eh?'

He looked at the open skylight as he heard the lookout's hail, 'Deck there! Sail on the larboard bow!'

Herrick stood up. 'If you will excuse me, sir.' He gave a shy grin. 'Though I fancy you still find it hard not to run on deck with the rest of us!'

Bolitho waited for him to leave and then said, 'And you, Adam, how are all the aches and pains?'

Pascoe grinned. 'I never knew a body had room for so many bruises.'

Feet padded overhead, and Bolitho could picture the midshipman of the watch being chased to the shrouds with the biggest telescope available. *Harebell* was obviously alone. No matter. One more prize might have helped their esteem with the admiral, it would not have been worth risking their only sloop.

Pascoe asked quietly, 'I would wish to ask something, sir?'

Bolitho faced him, seeing the determination, a touch of anxiety. 'You've earned the right to ask as you will.'

Pascoe did not return his smile. 'The lady, Uncle. Catherine Pareja. The one you – ' He faltered. 'You knew in London.'

'Well?' He waited. 'What of her?'

'I was wondering. Did you take her *home*, I mean, to your house in Falmouth?'

Bolitho shook his head slowly. Seeing her face. Feeling her warmth, her need of him. 'No, Adam. Not to Falmouth.'

Pascoe licked his lips. 'I did not mean to pry.'

'It is all right.' Bolitho crossed the chequered deck and gripped his shoulder. 'It is important to you, I can see that. But my feelings mean a lot to me, too.'

Pascoe tossed the hair from his eyes. 'Of course.' He smiled. 'I understand.' He hesitated again. 'I liked her. Which was why I – '

Bolitho eyed him gravely. 'Which is *why* you crossed swords. For my name.'

'Yes.'

Bolitho walked to his desk and took out the broken sword. 'Take this. It was a comfort to me when everyone else thought you were dead.' He saw him holding it as if it was red-hot. 'But save it for the enemy, not for those who try to hurt you with words.'

He looked round as feet clattered down a companion ladder and seconds later Luce, who was apparently midshipman of the watch, hurried into the cabin and reported, 'Captain Herrick's respects, sir. It is *Harebell* in sight, and she will be in signalling distance within the half-hour.' His eyes flickered towards Pascoe. 'No other sail in sight, sir.'

'Thank you, Mr. Luce.' Bolitho compared the pair of them. Pascoe was a year older than Luce, if that. He was glad they had each other's friendship in the teeming and often heartless world of a ship of the line. 'My compliments to the captain.'

He needed to go on deck, up to the foretop if necessary, despite his hatred of heights, to see what was wrong with Inch and his overdue sloop. He sighed. It was quite useless.

While his own broad pendant remained above this or any ship he was bound to stay immovable, to keep his energies for decisions beyond ship-handling.

The others were watching him, and Pascoe asked, 'May I go with Mr. Luce?'

'Of course.' He watched them leave. Nothing changed.

He had just completed writing his notes on the raid when Herrick came to the cabin again, his face relaxed into a smile.

'*Harebell* has signalled, sir. Two sail to the nor'-west. If I wronged Captain Farquhar, then this is the moment to admit it.'

Bolitho moved quickly to the chart, recalling the change of wind, the feel of sand and dust on his cheek as he had listened wretchedly to the Cornish marine's news about the impassable gully.

He said, 'Admit nothing, Thomas. Not even Farquhar could drive his ships that fast to get them to the nor'-west of us!'

He snatched up his hat. 'Inch must have lost his brig, but by God he's brought bigger fish to us today!'

Herrick hurried after him, his face working with fresh doubt and apprehension.

It was very bright on the quarterdeck, and the sun was almost directly above the main yard. Bolitho nodded to Veitch, who had the watch, and then strode to the weather side, his eyes reaching out beyond the forecastle to the glittering horizon and its attendant haze.

Herrick yelled, 'Make to *Harebell*. *Investigate. Keep station to lee'rd.*'

Bunting slipped and slithered in colourful confusion across the deck until to Luce's satisfaction it was properly bent on to the halliards and was soon breaking to the wind.

'*Harebell*'s acknowledged, sir.'

Herrick said sourly, 'Should damn well think so. Francis Inch always was too quick off the mark.' He grinned despite his anxiety. 'The idiot!'

Minutes dragged by, and groups of seamen, who moments earlier had thought of nothing but their midday meal, poor though it was, were thronging to shrouds and gangways to stare towards the sloop's small outline.

Luce had swarmed halfway up the weather shrouds and had his glass steadied against the ship's easy plunge and roll.

Below him, Pascoe was looking up, his eyes slitted against the fierce glare, hands on his hips. Remembering perhaps, Bolitho thought, when he had been a signals midshipman.

Grubb said mournfully, 'If they're to be two more prizes, we'll be 'ard put for trained 'ands to manage *this* ship.'

Luce's cry brought sudden silence to the quarterdeck gossip. 'From *Harebell*, sir! *Enemy in sight!*'

Bolitho walked slowly to the cabin hatch and leaned against the handrail. In his mind he could already see them, beating down the coast towards him. He had seen them long before the sloop's confirmation, perhaps when Luce had come to the cabin.

He said, 'Signal Inch to close on the *Segura*.' He waited, seeing their mingled expressions of doubt and excitement. 'When he draws nearer you can signal him to keep the prize under his lee. We'll not lose her if we can help it.'

Herrick asked flatly, 'And us, sir?'

Luce called again, 'From *Harebell*, sir. *Two sail of the line.*'

'*Us*, Thomas?'

Herrick moved closer, shutting out the watching officers nearby. 'Will we take on the pair of them?'

Bolitho pointed slowly along the bare horizon. 'Unless you can see anyone else, Thomas.'

Gilchrist came hurrying aft, his feet tapping in his strange bouncing gait. He looked straight at Herrick.

'Orders, sir?'

Bolitho said calmly, 'Beat to quarters, Mr. Gilchrist. And I want the ship cleared for action in ten minutes.'

Gilchrist strode away, his long arms beckoning urgently to the marine drummer boys.

Bolitho turned to Herrick again. 'And get the t'gallants on her, Thomas. I want the enemy to see how eager we are.' He held him back, adding softly, 'No matter how we feel, eh?'

He walked to the poop ladder and started to climb. At his back he heard the staccato beat of drums and the immediate stampede of hurrying men as *Lysander*'s company answered the call.

Bolitho leaned on the poop rail and shaded his eyes to watch the sloop's outline changing yet again as she heeled on another tack, trying to fight her way across the wind to rejoin her flagship. Soon now the enemy would show his face.

Bolitho examined his own feelings. It was his first sea action since last year.

He watched the haze around *Harebell*'s masts, remembering the other times. Was that why he had ordered more canvas to be set? To get it over with, if only to discover his own strength or weakness?

Below decks he heard the screens being torn down, the clatter of gear being dragged free of guns and hatchways. From the age of twelve he had been a part of this life, shared it, endured all it could offer and threaten.

He looked at the men darting around their guns on the upper deck, the marines marching stolidly along either side of the poop as if on a routine parade.

Now he was the commodore. He smiled grimly. But without a squadron.

7

One Company

'CLEARED for action, sir.' Gilchrist's face was inscrutable. 'Nine minutes exactly.'

Bolitho did not hear Herrick's reply and walked unhurriedly to the weather side of the deck. With her great mainsail brailed up and every visible gun manned and ready, the ship had taken on an air of tension and of menace.

Herrick came towards him and touched his hat. 'Apart from seven sick or injured men, sir, the ship's company is at quarters.' He watched him enquiringly. 'Shall I pass the order to load and run out?'

'Later.'

Bolitho took a telescope from its rack and trained it towards the larboard bow. The sea's face glittered painfully in the glare. Like a million tiny mirrors. More silver than blue. He stiffened as first one and then the other of the ships swam across his lens.

Herrick was still watching his face. Searching for something. Their fate, perhaps.

Bolitho said, 'Seventy-fours, at a guess. This wind is making it heavy going for them.'

He held the glass on the leading ship. She was turning away, displaying her length, the twin lines of chequered gunports. Her sails were in disarray, he could see them criss-crossing with shadows as her master tried to hold the wind until he had completed his change of course.

He said, 'She handles badly, Thomas.' He bit his lip, trying to picture his own ship from the enemy's viewpoint. It would take an hour before they were at grips. To have a chance against two powerful seventy-fours he must hold on to the wind-gage. At least until he could rake one, or pass between the pair of them. He added slowly, 'Too long in port maybe. Like us, they need all the drill they can manage.'

Bolitho watched *Harebell*'s slender hull passing across the bows on a converging tack, her officers steeply angled on the small quarterdeck. He thought he saw Inch waving his hat, but forgot him as Luce's men hoisted the signal for *Harebell* to take up her new station. As a mere spectator, at worst a survivor who would carry the news to the admiral or Farquhar.

He walked to the gangway and ran his eyes along the upper deck. The worst part. The waiting. It was a pity only half the company had found time to eat before the call to quarters.

He asked, 'Do we have any beer left, Thomas?'

Herrick nodded. 'I believe so. Though I doubt that the purser will be pleased to broach it at this moment.'

'But *he* will not be fighting.' Bolitho saw his remark rippling along the nearest group of gun crews. 'Pass the word for it to be issued directly.'

He turned away. It was a cheap way of raising their morale. But it was all he had.

He returned to the quarterdeck and stood with one foot balanced on a nine-pounder. Its captain peered up at him and knuckled his forehead. Bolitho smiled at him. The man was old, or looked it. His hard hands covered with tar, his arms entwined with fierce, blue-coloured tattoos.

He asked, 'And who are you?'

The man showed his uneven teeth. 'Mariot, sir.' He hesitated, doubtful at prolonging a conversation with his commodore. Then he said, 'Served with your father, sir, in the old *Scylla*.'

Bolitho stared at him. He wondered if Mariot would ever have told him had he been on another gun in some other part of the ship.

He asked, 'Were you there when they took off his arm?'

Mariot nodded, his faded eyes far away. 'Aye, sir. He were a fine man, I served none better.' He grinned awkwardly. 'Savin' your presence, sir.'

Herrick stopped beside him, his face questioning.

Bolitho said, 'This man served with my father, Thomas.' He shaded his eyes to look for the enemy. 'What a small world is bound up in a navy.'

Herrick nodded and asked Mariot, 'How old are you?'

The man shook his head. 'I can't rightly recall, sir.' He patted the gun's breech. 'But young enough for this little lady!'

Bolitho walked slowly back and forth across the deck, his ears deaf to the cheerful shouts which were welcoming the first of the beer. *All in one company.* A man who had been with his father in India. Allday, his trusted coxswain and friend who had first been brought to him by a press-gang. Herrick, once a junior lieutenant under him, and Adam Pascoe, his brother's only son, perhaps the link between all of them.

Herrick was saying, 'They may be handled poorly, sir, but I'd be happier if we had some support. Even a frigate to snap at their damned backsides!'

Bolitho paused at the nettings, realising that he was soaked in sweat. 'Lysander fought and defeated the Athenian fleet nearly four hundred years before our Lord was born. He captured Athens a year later, if my old tutor was to be believed.' He smiled at Herrick. 'Surely he will not let us down today?' He added in a quieter tone, 'Be easy, Thomas. Your people are watching you. Show one sign of doubt and we may well be done for.'

Herrick linked his hands behind him, his chin on his neck-cloth. 'Aye. I'm sorry. It is strange how you never get used to the one thing you've worked and trained for. The sight of an enemy's sail, the sound of his broadside. Keep going until he's struck or gone under.' He added with unusual bitterness, 'Those fancy people in England who go all weepy at the sight of a King's ship working out of harbour never spare a thought for the poor devils who have to man 'em. Who die every day just to keep *them* in comfort and safety.'

Bolitho watched him impassively. It was easier to see the old Herrick now. Quick to speak out for the underdog, no matter how much wrath he incurred from his superiors. Which was probably why he was still a junior post-captain.

He asked, 'And your sister, Thomas, how is she keeping?'

Herrick brought his thoughts under control. 'Emily?' He looked away. 'She is missing our mother, no doubt, although she took some looking-after towards the end.'

Bolitho nodded. 'And you have hired someone to take care of Emily while you are at sea?'

Herrick faced him, his eyes staring into the sun. 'May I ask, sir, are you coming to the matter of Mr. Gilchrist?'

'I had heard something, Thomas.' He was surprised at Herrick's tone. His readiness to defend an understanding.

Herrick's eyes were almost colourless in the glare. 'Emily is taken with him. He is a reliable officer, if hasty-tempered at times.' He lowered his head. 'And what he has, he has earned, sir.'

'Like you, Thomas.'

'Indeed.' Herrick sighed. 'And I care very much for what Emily wants. God knows, she has had precious little in this world!'

'Deck there!'

Gilchrist was striding across the deck, his hands cupped. 'What is it?'

'Leadin' ship is makin' more sail!'

Herrick snatched a telescope and hurried to the rail. 'Damn their eyes! They will try to divide our defences.'

Bolitho watched him, seeing his mind at work with how best to present his ship to the enemy, yet still holding on to what they had been saying.

Gilchrist said sharply, 'They'll not get too near, sir. They'll more likely use chain-shot or langridge to try and cripple us. Then rake our stern at leisure and at little risk.'

Bolitho said, 'Make a signal to *Harebell*. We will alter course. Steer sou'-east.'

Herrick asked huskily, 'Is it wise, sir? There's less than a league between us. If we hold on as we are, we might be able to outsail them. With the wind in our favour it'd be hours before the Frogs could beat round and come after us.'

Bolitho took the glass from him and trained it on the two ships. They were moving, wide apart, towards *Lysander*'s larboard bow. They were having a hard time to stay so close-hauled, and turning any more towards the wind would put them all aback. Less than three miles. Herrick had always been good at estimating distance. *Lysander* would touch the leading two-decker bow to bow almost at right angles and then the second Frenchman would act as he saw fit. Go to larboard and present a broadside as *Lysander* fought herself free from the first embrace, or luff and work round under their stern while they were actually engaging the other one.

Herrick's plan gave them and the prize an excellent chance of escaping both. It also meant running away, with a real possibility of a long stern-chase until they met up with another enemy force. He cursed Farquhar silently. With three ships facing them the enemy would soon change their tactics.

He walked aft, feeling Grubb's eyes on him as he checked the compass. North-east by north, with the friendly west wind holding across the quarter. He looked at Grubb's ruined features.

'Well? Will it hold, d'you think?'

'The wind, sir?' He wiped his watery eye. 'Aye.' He nodded his head towards the nearest gun crews and beyond to the upper deck. 'It's *them* I ain't so sure of.'

Gilchrist was striding past and halted on the other side of the wheel, his voice scornful. 'Really, Mr. Grubb! If we are to weep before we fight, I see no hope for anyone!'

Grubb stared at him stubbornly. 'You was in this ship at St. Vincent, sir. Like me an' some of the others.'

'Yes.' Gilchrist had a way of speaking to Grubb but projecting his words to Bolitho. 'I'm proud of it.'

Grubb shrugged. 'They was a trained company. Cap'n Dyke 'ad 'ad this ship in more scrapes than I can shake a stick at.' He turned to Bolitho. '*You* knows, sir.' He did not actually look at Gilchrist. 'Better'n anyone, if I'm a judge.'

Bolitho walked forward to the rail, deep in thought. 'Have *Harebell* and the prize acknowledged?'

Gilchrist followed him, his shoes tapping. 'Aye, sir.'

'Then tell me! I'm not a damned magician!' He calmed himself. 'Execute the signal.'

He looked at Grubb's reddened face. 'Lay her on the starboard tack.'

Men rushed to the braces, the afterguard's boots keeping perfect time as they hauled the mizzen yards round, letting the sails empty and then billow out again, tilting the ship on an opposite tack.

Bolitho raised his glass, his legs straddled as the deck dipped under him. He found he could shut out the bellowed orders, the flap and thunder of sails overhead, and hold on to the small, silent world in the lens.

He saw a darker shadow pass across the leading ship's foresail. She was edging slightly away, feeling a new strength

as she allowed the wind to move a few points further abaft
her beam.

'Course sou'-east, sir!'

Gilchrist snapped, 'Mr. Luce, what of the others?'

Luce was equally sharp in his reply, well aware of the
tension between his superiors. '*Harebell* and prize on station
astern, sir.'

Bolitho pursed his lips and watched his two enemies. They
were getting larger every minute, and he could see the bright
tricolours at their peaks, the flash of sunlight on raised telescopes or weapons. They would have seen the commodore's
broad pendant. A valuable capture. A suitable ending to this
impudent gesture.

Herrick was beside him. 'They're both falling off a few
points. Our change of course has aided them. They could
take the wind-gage from us if we overreach them.'

'Which is why we must make certain they don't.' He pointed
his arm at the other ships. 'I have given them more wind, as
you say, Thomas. If we continue on this tack we will be
abeam of the leading Frenchman in a half-hour. His consort
may then try to rake our disengaged side.'

'However.' He saw Major Leroux turn slightly and smile
at him. 'What they will not be able to do is steer upwind with
us so near. They would be in irons.'

Herrick was unimpressed. 'I know. But now, they don't
have to worry about that, sir.'

Bolitho looked at him. 'Consult with the master and your
first lieutenant. In ten minutes I intend that we shall wear
ship.' He saw an unspoken protest on Herrick's face but
continued, 'We will then lay her on the same tack as earlier
and steer nor'-east.'

He watched the slow understanding moving over his
features like sunlight through departing cloud.

Herrick said slowly, 'By God, we'll either collide with one
of 'em or – '

'*Or* we shall pass between them. They cannot luff without
risking damage to spars and canvas. If they turn and run
downwind we will rake their sterns. If they stay as they are,
we will engage from either battery as we sail through.' He
held on to Herrick's stare. 'After *that*, your guess is as good
as mine!'

He added, 'Now attend to it. I'm going to speak with the people.'

He strode to the quarterdeck rail and waited until most of the seamen were peering aft towards him. He saw Lieutenant Veitch, arms relaxed, standing with his back to the enemy, his hanger already unsheathed and glinting. Near him, two midshipmen and a gunner's mate. All part of the pattern. The red-coated marine at each hatch, ready to stop any terrified man from fleeing below. And along either side, half hidden by the gangways which joined forecastle to quarterdeck, were the men who would see the enemy through the ports. Would keep their heads no matter what. Or go under.

Bolitho said, 'Up yonder, lads, are two fine French gentlemen.' He saw the stiff grins of the older men, the nervous twisting of heads of the others, turning as if they expected to see the enemy right here on board. 'For most of you this is the first time. While you serve your country it will not be the last. A few days ago you did well. A prize taken, another ship sunk by these eighteen-pounders.'

He pictured two similar lines of men on the deck below, waiting in almost complete darkness for the ports to open and run out the massive thirty-two pounders. They would be trying to hear what he was saying, the word being carried by ship's boys and midshipmen, and probably distorted along the way.

'But this is no brig, lads. Nor a newly-built shore battery.' He saw the words reaching them. 'Two ships of the line, and fine vessels they are.'

He heard Grubb whisper, 'Anytime now, sir.'

Bolitho looked along the crowded deck, well sanded to save the men from slipping in battle. 'But they have a fault, nonetheless. They are crewed by Frenchmen, not Englishmen!'

He turned aft, seeing the men waving and cheering, the grins on the faces of the midshipmen, as if they were going on a Royal cruise. He felt sickened with himself. Angry that he could make it sound so simple.

He said sharply, 'Pass the order to load, if you please. Then run out the larboard guns.' He saw a flash of doubt and added, 'Yes, the larboard ones. They must be made to think we are sticking to our – ' he smiled grimly, ' – our guns!' He walked quickly to the opposite side. 'And stop them cheering. They'll need all their wind directly.'

'I'm here, sir.'

He raised his arms and allowed Allday to buckle on his sword. Allday was no better. He was doing this deliberately. Letting the seamen and marines see how calm they were.

He looked at him and said softly, 'We are a fine pair.'

Allday gave a secret smile. 'At least we *are* a pair again, sir.' He stared towards the enemy, his eyes calm. 'It'll not be easy.' He watched the ship with professional interest. 'Still, I don't suppose they're looking forward to it either!'

'*Run out!*'

The pipe was repeated to the deck below, and hesitantly at first, as if testing the quality of the air, the *Lysander*'s larboard guns trundled into the sunlight like black teeth.

'Frenchies are running out, too, sir.'

'Good.'

Bolitho pulled out his watch and flicked open the guard. It was warm from resting against his thigh. He snapped it shut. Within a short time it could be as cold as its owner.

A dull bang echoed across the choppy strip of water, and seconds later a thin spout of spray burst up alongside. It brought a baying growl of anger from *Lysander*'s gun crews, but Bolitho heard Veitch yell, 'Be ready! Starboard guns prepare to run out.' He squinted at the quarterdeck and saw Herrick nod. 'Both sides will engage independently!'

A youth at one of the nine-pounders whispered something, and Mariot, the old gun captain, replied, ' 'E means *separate*, see?' He saw Bolitho's brief smile and added, 'We'm ready for th' buggers, sir.' He moved inboard from his gun, paying out the trigger line as he went. 'Just like we done in th' old *Scylla*!'

Pascoe called, 'The enemy are shortening sail!'

Bolitho nodded, watching the leading Frenchman's topgallant sails vanishing as if by magic. Preparing to meet *Lysander*'s challenge. If they continued on this converging course either of the French captains would be well placed for the first broadsides.

He looked at Herrick. Beyond him, Gilchrist was poised by the rail, his speaking trumpet already raised.

Bolitho said, 'Very well. This is the time, Captain Herrick.'

He held his gaze. 'Put up your helm, and let's be amongst them!'

Gilchrist yelled, 'Braces there!' He was weaving from side to side, his voice like metal as he urged the seamen to greater efforts. 'Heave! *Heave!*'

Bolitho gripped the poop ladder and felt the ship shuddering, every stay and shroud humming with strain as the great yards started to creak round. He heard the helmsmen panting with exertion as they threw their weight on the spokes, hauling the wheel over and further still.

Veitch was shouting above the thunder of billowing canvas, 'Starboard battery! *Run out!*'

Bolitho looked aloft at his pendant, willing it to hold direction, while all around him seamen and marines were rushing to obey the demands from their officers and bosun's mates.

He lowered his head and watched the leading French ship. Was it imagination? He held his breath, and then as the deck under his shoes began to heave over the opposite way he saw the French ship gathering speed, swinging past *Lysander*'s bowsprit and flapping jib as if caught in a tide-race.

''Old 'er *steady*!' Grubb sounded fierce. ''Nother man on th' wheel, 'ere!'

The yards ceased their creaking and steadied on the larboard tack, the topsails hard-bellied again, thrusting the ship over until spray sluiced above the lower line of port lids where the gun captains were already shouting their readiness to fire.

Herrick tugged at his hat as the wind blew more spindrift over the hammock nettings and across the smooth planks between the guns. It dried almost as soon as it had fallen, like summer rain, Bolitho thought.

'Course nor'-east, sir!'

'Steady as you go.'

Bolitho raised his glass, feeling the wind whipping at his coat as he trained it on the enemy. His sudden alteration of course had caught the two French captains by surprise. He saw the leading ship's ornate stern slipping past *Lysander*'s starboard bow, the gap widening more and more until he could see the second seventy-four's jib boom pushing through the left side of his lens.

A ripple of orange tongues darted from the leading Frenchman's hull, and he heard some of the balls hissing overhead, the sharp crack of a stay parting somewhere in their path.

He strode across the deck and seized Herrick's arm. 'The fool fired too soon.' He gestured towards the waiting seamen. 'Starboard battery, Thomas. Give him a broadside! With luck there'll be time to reload before we cut across his stern.'

Herrick waved his arm. 'As you bear!'

The earsplitting roar of the broadside, the great spouting bank of choking smoke as it was blown towards the enemy, made several of the marines loose off their muskets. They had no hope of finding a target, and Sergeant Gritton bellowed, 'Punishment for the next bugger to fire without orders!'

Bolitho stood on a bollard to peer above the hammock nettings, his eyes smarting in smoke as he watched for some sign of damage. The enemy's sails were pockmarked with shot holes, and he saw a gap in the boat tier, an upended launch split in halves. But the tricolour was still there, and the ship was holding direction as before.

He heard his men cheering and whooping and snapped, '*Reload!* I want three rounds every two minutes.' He saw Gilchrist staring at him. 'Gunnery is all we have now.'

There was a ragged crash of cannon fire from larboard, and he realised that the second Frenchman was trying to hit *Lysander* with his forward guns, the only ones which would bear.

Veitch was yelling, 'Larboard battery!' His hanger glittered above his head. 'As you bear, lads!'

Bolitho saw one of the midshipmen scuttling to the hatch to pass the order.

The hanger cut downwards. '*Fire!*'

Once more the ship shook and bucked violently as both gun decks erupted in a slow and regular broadside. Men were already hurling themselves on the tackles and handspikes, reaching blindly for charges and fresh shot, many of them retching as smoke funnelled downwind to hide the deck from view.

Veitch shouted wildly, 'Faster! Come on, number three! *Sponge out!*'

Bolitho wiped his streaming face, his mouth like dust as he watched the Frenchman's foresail flapping in all directions like a torn sheet, the long black scars along the enemy's forecastle where some of the broadside had gone home.

The leading French ship was still on the same course, her captain probably unwilling to expose his stern until the last moment. Or hoping his consort might produce some kind of miracle.

Herrick said, 'All loaded and run out again.' His face was streaked with grime. 'Less than two minutes, by my reckoning!'

'*Fire!*'

The starboard guns hurled themselves inboard on the tackles, the orange-tinged smoke rolling downwind towards the Frenchman which now appeared to lie diagonally across the starboard bow.

Bolitho gritted his teeth, seeing *Lysander*'s drifting smoke light up again to the enemy's immediate reply. The deck jerked under him, and he saw men duck as the balls shrieked low over the quarterdeck, some dropping in the sea almost a mile away.

Bolitho shouted, '*Now*, Thomas! Pass the word to the carronade crews forrard!'

Herrick nodded, his face a stiff mask as more shots crashed into the side or sliced between the sails.

Bolitho strode down the deck to the lee side, seeing the leading French ship's stern rising like a golden horseshoe above the eddying smoke. *Lysander*'s forecastle was already passing through the gap between them. He winced, in spite of his warning, as a carronade blasted out its great grape-packed ball with an accompaniment of Veitch's foremost eighteen-pounders as they came to bear on the enemy's most vulnerable point.

Veitch was almost screaming. 'Stop your vents! Sponge out! *Load!*'

The thunder of cannon fire, the squeal and rumble of guns being run out, the endless mad chorus of yells and cheers seemed to be reaching out from another world, or from the depths of hell.

Severed rigging twisted like snakes on the protective nets across the upper deck, and as the gun crews stooped and heaved, their naked bodies running with sweat and powder, they looked like the servants and not the masters of their bellowing black charges.

'*Fire!*'

Bolitho heard a man scream, saw a body bounce down from the main top before pitching over the side.

More shots slammed through the smoke, but he heard Grubb exclaim hoarsely, 'The old smasher 'as done it, sir!' He took off his crumpled hat and waved it over his head. 'Must 'ave got 'er rudder!'

Bolitho watched narrowly, realising that although *Lysander* had sailed through the gap, the leading Frenchman's stern was still pointing straight at him. The murderous charge of grape from the carronade, accompanied by the forward guns, which by their harsher bark suggested they had been double-shotted for the purpose, must have ripped through the stern and disabled the steering. She was falling downwind, swinging her stern round, and he saw that her once ornate gallery was in ruins, her poop pitted and splintered from the onslaught.

As he watched he saw her mizzen stagger, held upright by stays and shrouds a while longer, and then begin to fall. Tiny figures were sliding down from the mizzen top, others ran like mad things to escape the great plunging mass of rigging and spars as with a crash, audible even above the thunder of guns, it swayed down into the smoke, the bright, flapping tricolour with it.

'T 'other one is tryin' to follow us round, sir.' Grubb's eyes were streaming. ' 'E'll take our wind.'

Bolitho pointed towards the second ship. 'Mr. Gilchrist! Prepare the larboard carronade!'

He saw the other ship's jib boom thrusting through the smoke like a black lance, the tiny pin-pricks of musket fire from her beakhead and foretop. With her yards hard-braced and the wheel over, she was struggling round to starboard, presenting more and more of her scarred side as the range shortened rapidly.

The larboard carronade slammed back on its slide, the ball exploding in a whirling mass of splinters and broken rigging directly abaft the enemy's beakhead.

Herrick yelled, 'By God, his fore is coming down!'

As the enemy's foremast started to totter drunkenly towards the sea his broadside rippled along his exposed side, a few of the gun ports remaining silent as a mark of Veitch's earlier success. But Bolitho knew it was the most carefully prepared attack so far. The deck bounded repeatedly, and from below he heard a metallic clang and a great chorus of shrill screams. The French marksmen were still firing, too, and as he paced restlessly about the deck Bolitho saw thin splinters flying from the planking as a sharpshooter tried to hit *Lysander*'s officers.

A sharper bang came down from the pockmarked sails which now seemed to be towering above the nettings like a cliff, and a second later the after end of the quarterdeck was filled with kicking, screaming men. The French had a swivel gun in the top, and the canister fired at close range was evidence enough of the enemy captain's anxiety.

Herrick shouted, 'The Frog's out of control! She's swinging towards us!' He peered through the smoke. 'Mr. Grubb, put up your helm!'

But the master was coughing and cursing through the smoke, dragging corpses and wounded alike from the wheel, or what was left of it. The whole charge of canister had struck the wheel like a target and had scythed away in all directions, marking deck and guns, men and fragments in a great pattern of blood. More men ran dazedly to Grubb's aid, hauling at the remaining spokes, their eyes squinting as if fearful of the mutilated bodies around them.

Bolitho said harshly, 'It's too late.'

The enemy's bowsprit, the great dragging mass of severed mast and yards was directly across *Lysander*'s bows. The enemy was still firing, as were his own men. At the most forward positions the range was down to about thirty feet.

Balls whimpered overhead or thudded into the hull with great hammer-blows. One burst through a port and ploughed into a gun crew which was sponging out for the next shot. The eighteen-pounder, freed from its tackles, careered across the tilting deck, its trucks making little bloody lines as it thrust through the remains of its crew.

Harry Yeo, the boatswain, was bawling for his men to get the gun under control, brandishing a boarding axe like some primitive warrior.

Bolitho looked at Herrick. 'We will ram her!' He sought out Gilchrist. 'Get the tops'ls off her!' He felt a musket ball zip past him. 'We must fight free before the other Frenchman recovers!'

Herrick nodded jerkily. 'Mr. Gilchrist! Pass the word! Repel boarders!'

Bolitho heard more cries, and then Leroux's voice, 'Kill those marksmen in the main top!'

He said urgently, 'No, Thomas. We must board her! They'll cut our people to fragments.'

He seized the rail as with a great groaning crunch *Lysander*'s jib boom smashed through the enemy's beakhead. The impetus carried both ships in a slow embrace, the guns falling silent and giving way to the sharper cracks of musketry.

Bolitho drew his sword. 'Work the ship clear, Thomas.' He wanted to reassure him in some way, and saw the uncertainty on Herrick's grimy face giving way to something worse as he replied, 'Let someone else go, sir!'

A great chorus of shouts and yells came from forward, and through the dangling remains of rigging and drifting smoke Bolitho saw men already trying to swarm down along the bowsprit.

He snapped, 'There's no time!' Then he ran along the starboard gangway, pointing down at every other gun on the disengaged side, shouting at their crews to follow.

When he reached the forecastle there were already a dozen or more corpses lying amidst the fighting seamen from both sides. Cutlasses rang against each other, and from the shrouds and the forechains of both ships the marksmen kept up a haphazard fire to add to the chaos.

Bolitho shouted, '*Carronade!*'

He thrust a wounded man aside and hacked a French petty officer across the neck, feeling the blow lance up his arm and bring a stab of fire to his wounded shoulder.

A wild-eyed marine seemed to understand what he wanted and threw himself on the carronade's tackles, while Midshipman Luce and some more seamen came running to his aid.

'*Fire!*'

The carronade's explosion made most of the boarders fall back in momentary confusion. When they peered at their own ship and saw the bloody remains of the men who had been about to swarm on to *Lysander*'s deck they decided to retreat.

Bolitho yelled, 'Boarders away, lads!'

He waved his sword, feeling his hat plucked from his head by a pistol ball from somewhere, and then he was leaping and half falling down on to the enemy's shattered beakhead. When he stared back to see how many of his men were following he found himself looking into the eyes of *Lysander*'s massive, unsmiling figurehead, and he felt the insane grin coming to his lips, the uncontrollable wildness which forced him on through upended ladders and broken spars, gaping corpses and great coils of fallen rigging.

Steel to steel, the men swaying back and forth locked together, feet stamping, teeth bared in curses and fear as they hacked and slashed their way aft along the forecastle deck.

From one corner of his eye Bolitho saw his flagship, nudging firmly through the enemy's torn shrouds, the smoky scarlet of Leroux's marines as they maintained a murderous fire on the Frenchman's upper deck.

From the direction of the drifting smoke he knew that both ships were standing downwind, the darkened water between the arrowhead of their embrace littered with splintered wood and a few bobbing corpses.

Sunlight lanced through the smoke, and he saw the gap widening. Herrick had succeeded in easing *Lysander*'s bulky hull round to a point where she could use sails and rudder to work clear.

He saw a man darting towards him, an upraised pistol aimed at his chest. In those split seconds he shared the moment with the unknown French sailor. He had a thin dark face, teeth bared in frantic concentration as he took aim. Bolitho was too far away to reach him with his sword, and his arm ached so much from fighting his way through the yelling press of men that he felt he could not raise it even to defend himself.

The blade of a heavy cutlass cut downwards across his vision, so fast that it made an arc of silver in the hazy sunlight.

The French sailor gave a shrill scream and lurched away, staring with agonised horror at the pistol still gripped with his own hand on the far side of the deck.

Allday ran to Bolitho's side, the cutlass edge red against his coat.

'A moment, sir!'

He ducked under two fallen spars and hacked the wounded man across the neck, felling him with no more than a sob.

He said between gasps, 'Better'n letting him live with one hand!'

Bolitho shouted, '*Fall back,* lads!'

A few more minutes and they could take the French ship. *He knew it.* Just as he knew that the other seventy-four was probably working round again to pour a broadside into *Lysander* before she was able to return the fire.

'Fall back!'

The cry ran along the bloodied decks and mingled with the cheers of Leroux's marines, some of whom were squatting in *Lysander*'s beakhead picking off their enemy like wildfowlers in a marsh.

Many hands reached out to haul the boarders back into *Lysander*'s protection, as with a splintering, jerking symphony she tore free from her opponent's fallen spars and shrouds and swung heavily downwind.

The lower gun deck erupted in one more savage broadside, the thirty-two pounders smashing into the enemy's side and making the holed and battered timbers shine with tiny tendrils of blood which ran freely from her scuppers.

Pascoe yelled, '*Huzza!* Huzza for the commodore!'

Bolitho strode aft, taking his hat from a grinning, pigtailed seaman who had somehow managed to retrieve it from the vicious fighting.

Herrick greeted him hoarsely, his eyes moving over him as if anticipating some terrible wound.

Bolitho asked, 'Where is the other one?'

Herrick pointed vaguely over the larboard quarter. 'Standing off, sir.'

'I thought she would.'

Bolitho looked from foremast to quarterdeck. The fore topgallant mast had gone, and several guns lay upended. There were plenty of shot holes along the upper deck, and the busy thuds of hammers, the dismal clank of pumps, told him that there was damage enough below the waterline also.

He said, 'Get the ship under way.'

He saw Pascoe kneeling beside a dying marine. Holding his hand and watching his face losing its understanding and recognition.

Grubb peering at his compass, and his new helmsmen staring fixedly at the flapping sails and waiting for them to respond, their bare feet slipping on blood.

The marines falling back from the hammock nettings,

checking their muskets, their faces dull now that the fight had gone out of them.

Midshipman Luce using one of his flags to staunch the terrible wound in a man's thigh. The wounded seaman peering up at him, repeating like a prayer, 'Promise you'll not send me to the orlop, Mr. Luce!'

But, like ghouls, their aprons scarlet, the surgeon's assistants came for him, carrying him bodily down to the horrors of the orlop deck.

Bolitho saw it all and more. Like so many, that seaman who had faced the terrible demands of battle was unable to accept the horrors of a surgeon's knife.

Grubb muttered, 'She's answerin', sir.'

'Steer nor'-east.' Bolitho looked up as the wind explored the holed sails. 'And signal *Harebell* to stay in close company.' He wondered briefly how Inch had felt as an impotent spectator.

Herrick came aft and touched his hat. 'We beat 'em, sir.'

Bolitho looked at him. 'It was no victory, Thomas.' He listened to a man sobbing from the deck below the rail. Like a young boy. A child, with all defences gone. He added quietly, 'But it has shown all of us what we can do.' He nodded to Leroux as he walked past with his sergeant. 'And next time we will do that bit better.'

He walked to the poop ladder and paused halfway up it to look for the enemy ships. With missing masts and spars, and their attendant snares of trailing rigging, they made a sorry sight.

Lysander's company had done well in their first battle together. But to attempt more, even though he had been tempted, would have invited disaster.

Allday climbed up beside him.

'It feels strange, sir.'

Bolitho looked at him. Allday was quite right. Before, they had been kept too busy after a sea fight to brood or to find pain in misgivings. He saw Herrick. The captain. The man who really counted just now.

Allday sighed. 'They did proudly, all the same. There's a different *air* in the ship.'

Bolitho walked slowly aft to the taffrail, letting the wind explore his stained clothes and aching limbs like a tonic.

Harebell was tacking across the larboard quarter, very clean and bright in the glare.

He pulled out his watch. The whole battle had taken less than two hours. Some corpses drifted astern, pale-faced in the clear water, and he guessed they were some of the French boarders who had fallen in the attack. And what of their own bill? How many lay dying or awaiting burial?

Two seamen ran along the poop, marlin spikes in their hands as they peered round for ropes which needed repair. For them it was over. *For now.* They chatted to each other, thankful to be whole, grateful to be alive.

Bolitho watched them in silence. Perhaps Herrick was right. About people in England who did not spare a thought for men like this.

He nodded to the two seamen as he strode to the ladder. If it were the case, he decided, then it was their loss. For men such as these were worth a thought, and much more beside.

8

Aftermath

JOSHUA MOFFITT, the commodore's personal clerk, tapped his teeth with a pen and waited as Bolitho leaned back at his desk and took another swallow of coffee.

Bolitho let the strong black coffee explore his stomach, and tried to concentrate his mind on the report he was dictating for the admiral. If it would ever be sent. If it would ever be read.

He knew Moffitt was watching him but was almost used to his strange opaque stare by now. In the sleeping cabin he could hear Ozzard, his servant, making up the cot, his feet barely audible on the deck, and wondered at the fates which had made these two men fill their present roles. It would be better for them both if they were reversed, he thought. Ozzard, who attended his daily wants, from shaving water to a clean shirt, had been, it was said, a lawyer's clerk. He certainly had education, more than some of the officers. Moffitt, on the other hand, whose duties involved the careful writing of every order and despatch, of noting down each of Bolitho's personal signals and instructions for the other captains in the squadron, was a product of the slums. He had wispy grey hair and glazed staring eyes which peered out from his parchment face like those of a man near to death. Or, as Allday had remarked unsympathetically, 'I've seen better looking rogues dangling on a gallows!'

From the little he had been able to discover, Bolitho had learned that Moffitt had been in a debtors' jail, awaiting transportation to the new penal colony at Botany Bay. A hopeful lieutenant with a court's warrant for encouraging recruitment to His Majesty's Navy as a direct substitute for transportation to the other side of the world, had arrived at the jail, and with several others Moffitt had begun a new life. His

first ship had been an eighty-gun two-decker, and in a brief
skirmish off Ushant her captain's clerk had been killed by a
stray musket ball. Moffitt had used the opportunity well, and
had made yet one more change in his affairs by assuming the
dead man's duties. Transferred to *Lysander* at Spithead, he had
been ready and willing to offer himself as commodore's clerk,
unless or until a better fitted person could be found. The rush
to get the ship ready for sea and complete all repairs in time
to receive Bolitho's broad pendant had allowed Moffitt to slip
into his new role with barely a ripple.

Bolitho looked into his cup. It was only too easy to send
Ozzard to make fresh coffee. It was one of his weaknesses.
But he would stick to his rule and try to eke out his supply
as long as possible.

He heard the insistent thud of hammers and the rasp of
saws. The work of repairing the damage was still going on
without a break. This was the morning of the fourth day after
the battle. *Lysander*, with the sloop and the prize in company,
had continued in a slow north-easterly crawl, the hands
turned-to until there was no proper light in which to work,
to get her ready to fight again when required.

In his mind's eye he could see the chart when he had
examined it before his meagre breakfast. They had been forced
to maintain a very slow progress. Tattered sails had had to be
sent down from aloft for repair or replacement from their
stocks. The jib boom had been almost entirely refashioned
after its thrusting collision with the French seventy-four, and
he could join with Herrick's report in complimenting Tuke,
the carpenter, for his energies and devotion to perfection.

Herrick quite rightly had written well of Lieutenant Veitch.
The third lieutenant had controlled the gunnery throughout
the battle, but more than that, he had decided, without calling
for permission or advice, to double-shot some of his guns to
help the carronade's attack on one of the enemy ships. Double-
shotting was a risky thing under perfect conditions and with
experienced seamen. Yet Veitch had managed to keep his head
enough to select such men from disengaged guns and use the
bombardment to maximum effect. Midshipman Luce, Yeo,
the boatswain, and Major Leroux, all had been placed on the
captain's record for Bolitho's approval.

On the other side of the coin, *Lysander* had lost thirteen dead, either in the battle or later of their wounds. The surgeon had reported another five who might die at any moment, and ten who would almost certainly be fit for duty with any kind of luck.

The enemy had probably lost far more, as well as the hurt of being driven off by a single ship. But where men were concerned it was of little comfort. They had weeks, perhaps months yet to endure without additional support. Muscle and bone were more important than hemp and oak frames, and men themselves more vital than all besides. He tried not to think of his own report, as yet unfinished at Moffitt's bony elbow.

The clerk asked, 'Will we continue, sir?' His voice, like the man, was thin and scratchy. His entry in the muster book described him as being aged thirty-eight. He looked nearer sixty.

Bolitho eyed him gravely. 'Where did we get to?'

The pen moved across the papers. '*During the action the ship was under control the whole time, and only when entangled with the second French vessel's rigging was she forced to lose way.*' The opaque eyes were level again. 'Sir?'

Bolitho stood up and walked to the quarter gallery, his hands behind his back. He could not keep Herrick's face out of his thoughts. In the battle, at the moment when a collision had shown itself unavoidable. That was the moment. It stood out even above the thunder of gunfire, the awful cries, the twisting scarlet patterns around the wheel. In those vital minutes Herrick had hesitated. Worse than that, at a time when the French had taken the initiative, and might have used it to attack the ship from either side, he had made a wrong decision. It was like hearing his voice, here in the cabin. The anguish as he had ordered Gilchrist to repel boarders. And it had been the wrong order. Defensive action at that stage could have broken *Lysander*'s morale, quenched her people's willingness to do battle, as easily as if their flag had been torn down before their eyes.

He forced himself to think of Herrick as the captain of his ship. Not as Thomas Herrick, his friend. In the past he would have despised any senior officer who had used friendship to cover up failure or incompetence. But now he knew that choice was not that easy, nor so free of prejudice. Herrick had almost pleaded with him not to leave the quarterdeck to join the fighting in the bows. Fondness for him, or a desire to keep his advice and determination close by, or both, the effect could have meant complete disaster. Bolitho had noticed, if only in hindsight, that the French captain had remained aft during the time when *Lysander*'s boarders had been carving a bloody path through his men. How would the fight have gone, he wondered, if the French captain had rallied his men in the forefront of the struggle, even at the expense of his own life, while his British counterparts had stayed clear and in comparative safety?

He leaned his hands on the sill below the salt-stained glass. Herrick was no coward, and could no more display disloyalty than he could betray his sister. But up there, on the quarter-deck, when he had been most needed, he had failed.

Bolitho said shortly, 'I'll finish it later, Moffitt.' He turned and thought he saw a quick gleam of curiosity in his eyes. 'You may copy out what we have already done.' It would keep Moffitt busy and the report at arm's length for a bit longer.

There was a tap at the screen door and Herrick stepped into the cabin.

'I thought you would like to know at once, sir. *Harebell* has signalled that she has sighted two sail to the east'rd.' His blue eyes moved briefly to Moffitt at the table. 'It will most likely be the rest of the squadron.' He added bitterly, '*This* time.'

Bolitho saw his glance fall on the pages of the report and felt something like guilt. As if Herrick had read his mind. His nagging doubt.

'Yes. What is our estimated position?'

Herrick frowned. 'At eight bells we fixed it as approximately forty miles north of the island of Majorca. With the poor progress and damage to canvas and helm, even the master will not make a stronger estimate.'

Bolitho looked at Moffitt. 'You can go.' He heard Ozzard letting himself out of the sleeping cabin.

Herrick asked, 'What are your orders, sir?'

'When we can rejoin our other ships I intend to call a captains' conference.' He walked to the windows again, seeing Herrick's reflection in the thick glass. 'After I have heard Captain Farquhar's explanation for waiting until this second rendezvous, I will say what I think we should do. As flag captain, you must ensure that each ship, from *Lysander* to

Harebell, understands my standing orders exactly. To me,
initiative is a worthwhile substitute for blind obedience. But
I'll have no selfish manoeuvres, nor will I tolerate rank
disobedience.'

Herrick said, 'I understand, sir.'

Bolitho turned to face him. 'What do you think, Thomas?'
He waited, willing him to speak out. '*Really* think?'

Herrick shrugged. 'I believe that Farquhar is petty-minded,
and eager enough for advancement, that he will act as he
thinks fit whenever possible.'

'I see.'

Bolitho crossed to his wine cabinet and touched it with his
fingertips. He could see her smiling at him, hear her infectious
laugh as she had watched his pleasure with the gift. So warm,
so generous with her love. Reckless, too, with her hostility for
anyone who had dared to show criticism of their brief affair.

'Is that all, sir?' Herrick was studying him, his face tired and
grim.

'No, Thomas.' He turned, hating the strain on Herrick's
features. He had probably not slept more than an hour or two
at a time since the battle. 'It is *not* all.'

He gestured to a chair, but Herrick remained standing, as
he had known he would. He cursed inwardly. That was the
trouble. They knew each other too well for any sort of conflict.

He said, 'I must complete my report for the admiral. Sooner
or later I will have to send a despatch to him, my personal
understanding of the situation here. Upon it might well
depend a whole new strategy. If I am wrong, there is far more
than my head at stake. If St. Vincent sends a great fleet to the
Mediterranean, and we discover too late that the French have
sailed west instead of east, maybe to join their squadrons from
the Biscay ports, England, and not merely a battle, will be
lost.'

'I realise that, sir. A heavy responsibility.'

Bolitho stared at him. 'Are you deliberately being evasive?
You know damned well what I mean! This is an important
mission, with no risk too great to complete it. When I send my
first despatch to the admiral, I must also tell him the state of my
squadron.'

Herrick faced him stubbornly. 'While the rest of the squadron
took itself elsewhere, sir, our people fought and acted better

than I'd have believed possible. I've said as much in my own report.'

Bolitho shook his head sadly. 'And what of you, Thomas? What must *I* write of your part in it?'

He watched the strain growing on Herrick's face. 'I am not speaking of your seamanship, your bearing under fire, nor would I dare to.'

Herrick looked past him. 'I did my best.'

Bolitho hesitated, but knew that this, and only this, was the moment. He said flatly, 'It was not good enough. And you know it.'

Overhead, a faint cry came from a lookout. 'Deck there! Sail on the lee bow!' So Farquhar's ships, if they were such, were in sight from *Lysander*.

Herrick replied, 'If that is what you believe, sir, I suggest you say as much in your report.'

Bolitho stared at him. 'Don't be such a *damned fool*!' He could feel the blood churning in his head, the wildness from the battle returning. 'You were *slow*, Thomas! You waited too long before each decision. You know as well as I that in a broadside battle you've no time for reflections!'

Herrick watched his rising anger with apparent calm. 'Do you think I don't realise that?' He shrugged, the movement helpless or despairing. 'When I lost *Impulsive* last year I began to feel doubts. About my strength, my nerve, if you like.' He looked away. 'I sailed *Lysander* into that bay because I had to, something drew me there, like times in the past when I just *knew* it must be done. You sent no signal, but deep inside me I felt you were there, waiting, *expecting* me to come. Perhaps I felt as you did about Adam Pascoe. It went deeper than logic.'

Bolitho asked quietly, 'And four days ago?'

Herrick faced him again. 'I watched those two ships. Hour by hour I watched them drawing nearer. Imagined their people at quarters, peering along their gun muzzles at *me*. And when you decided to attack them single-handed, and we had the second one right across our bows, I could barely speak or move. I heard my voice passing orders. But beyond it I was like stone. Something dead.' He wiped his forehead with one hand. The skin was damp with sweat. 'I can't do it. That battle last year decided it for me.'

Bolitho stood up and walked slowly to the windows. He recalled Herrick's excitement at the Admiralty when he had been appointed flag captain. A pleasure rising to match his own. They had not questioned the dangers or pitfalls of their mission. And neither of them had once considered his own ability to manage it.

He said, 'You are too tired to think properly.'

'*Please*, sir.' Herrick's voice was hoarse. 'Don't show pity, or humiliate me with understanding! You know what this is costing me, in God's name spare me further shame!'

Feet clattered in the passageway and Bolitho said, 'Leave me, I'd like to think.' He tried to find the words, despising himself for causing him such pain. 'Your value is too great for me to abuse it.'

The door opened slightly and Midshipman Saxby poked his head into the cabin.

'Captain, sir?' He smiled nervously as he saw Bolitho and showed the gap in his front teeth. 'Mr. Gilchrist's respects, and could you come on deck?'

When Herrick remained silent, Bolitho asked, 'Is something wrong?'

Saxby swallowed. 'N-no, sir. The first lieutenant wishes to turn up the hands to witness punishment.'

Herrick came out of his thoughts and said harshly, 'I am coming, Mr. Saxby.' He glanced at Bolitho. 'I am sorry, sir.'

Bolitho looked for a long while at the closed door. It had been like watching Herrick's eyes peering from a strange mask. A prisoner. What had he said? *Something dead.*

He turned as Ozzard padded silently into the cabin from the other door. Overhead and beyond the bulkhead he heard the stamp of booted feet as Leroux's men tramped aft, the more subdued movements of the company assembling to witness punishment.

Ozzard asked mildly, 'Can I do anything, sir?'

Bolitho looked up at the skylight, hearing a dull thud as the grating was rigged for the man to be seized up and flogged.

'Yes. *Close that skylight!*' He frowned. 'I did not mean to shout at you.'

He strode to the opposite side. *Damn Gilchrist and his punishments.* What was he trying or prove, and to whom?

Ozzard said warily, 'Your clerk's outside, sir.'

'Fetch him.'

Moffitt re-entered the cabin and blinked in the reflected sun-light.

He said, 'I've finished the first part, sir, and I thought – '

'Wait.' Bolitho had raised his voice, as if to drown the sound of the lash across a man's naked back. 'I wish you to write a letter.'

Overhead, the drum rolled and stopped, and the flat crack of the cat on bare skin intruded once again.

'Ready, sir ?'

Moffitt, like Ozzard who was humming quietly in the sleeping cabin, was unmoved by the slow, drawn-out ritual of punishment. While he . . .

Bolitho snapped, 'Address it to Captain Charles Farquhar, of His Brittanic Majesty's Ship *Osiris.*'

He rested his forehead against the sun-warmed glass and looked down at the frothing water below the counter. How inviting it was. Cool. Cleansing.

Behind him he heard Moffitt's nib scratching across the paper. It never faltered to the roll of the drum, the crack of the lash.

Farquhar would have a good reason for being off station. Of that he was certain.

'Sir ?'

He bunched his fists tight against his thighs until the pain steadied him.

'*Upon receipt of this order you will make all arrangements to proceed on board* Lysander, *flagship, the transfer to be effected immediately.*' He hesitated again, fighting his will. '*And there take on the duties and appointments of flag captain.*'

This time the nib did falter.

He continued, '*Your present post will be assumed by Captain Thomas Herrick.*'

He walked to the table and looked over Moffitt's narrow shoulder. 'I will want two copies directly.' He reached out and took the pen. He felt Moffitt staring at it, as if defying it to move. Almost savagely he wrote, '*Given under my hand, aboard His Majesty's Ship* Lysander. *Signed, Richard Bolitho, Commodore.*'

It was done.

*

With the hands dismissed from witnessing punishment, and the approaching ships confirmed as *Osiris* and *Nicator*, Thomas Herrick returned to the cabin to make his report.

Bolitho sat below the great span of windows, watching *Osiris*'s yards swinging smartly, her sails retaking the wind as she assumed station astern of *Lysander*.

He said quietly, 'I want both captains aboard directly.'

'Yes, sir.' Herrick looked tired. 'I have already made the signal. I will heave-to when all ships are on proper station. *Osiris* wishes to communicate immediately.'

Bolitho nodded. Farquhar would have news for him. News important enough to explain his absence from the original rendezvous. Bolitho did not look at the sealed envelope on his desk. The *news* he in turn would give Farquhar would make even him take notice.

He said, 'I have made no note in the official log, or my own report about what you told me earlier.' He saw Herrick's shoulders sag. 'But I accept your word, naturally.' He heard the clatter of blocks and the groan of cordage as the ship rolled heavily under reduced canvas, knowing that at any minute he would have to face the others. To begin again. He continued, 'I could shift my pendant to another ship, Thomas. But I recall only too clearly what happened when that was done when I held a similar command. The whole company took it as a personal slight, a lack of faith by the admiral in their ability and trust. I thought it unfair then, as I do now.'

Herrick's voice was husky. 'I understand. I don't relish the prospect of failure, and what it will mean. Equally, I'll not protest against something which I have begun.' He shrugged helplessly. 'Because of my feelings for the Navy, and for *you*, I'd kill myself rather than risk lives and a cause, to cover my faults.'

Bolitho watched him sadly. 'I am not removing you from duty.'

Herrick exclaimed, 'Then why have you agreed that – '

Bolitho stood up quickly. 'What would you have me do, eh? Give Gilchrist command and send you home? Replace you with Javal perhaps, when we have but one frigate for this whole mission?' He looked away. 'I am giving you *Osiris*. She is a well-found ship, and trained to a high standard.' He heard Herrick's intake of breath but went on remorselessly. 'You will not have to worry about the affairs of the squadron for the present, but concentrate instead on *command*. What you make of it is up to you. But I trust you, above all else, to do your duty well.' He turned slowly and was shocked to see that Herrick was as before, unnaturally calm. 'Farquhar will assume your present duties until . . .'

Herrick nodded. 'If that is your order, sir.'

'*Order?*' Bolitho made to move towards him. 'Do you think I want you faced day by day with the officers and men you have trained and commanded since you took *Lysander*? To know that every hour brings a doubt, a fear that you will let them down in some way?' He shook his head. 'That I will not do. Nor will I, *can* I, jeopardise the squadron's strength because of something which is precious to me.'

Herrick looked round the cabin. 'Very well. I will prepare to leave.'

'No slur will fall on you, Thomas. I will see to that. But I'd rather see you captain of some worn-out brig than breaking your heart on the beach, deprived of the one life you love, and for which you have given so much.'

Herrick seemed momentarily confused. He said, 'Farquhar. I never liked him. Even as a midshipman, I never really liked him.' He turned to the door. 'I little thought it would end like this.'

Bolitho crossed the cabin towards him and held out his hands. 'Not *end*, Thomas!'

But Herrick kept his hands at his sides. 'We will see, sir.' He left without looking back.

Allday entered the cabin, and after a slight hesitation took the sword from its rack and examined it.

Bolitho sat down on the bench seat again and watched him miserably.

'Cap'n Herrick's off then, sir?' Allday kept his eyes on the sword.

'Don't *you* start at me, Allday.' But there was no bite to his tone. 'I have taken enough for one day. For a thousand days.'

Allday looked at him, his eyes very clear in the reflected light. 'You did right, sir.' He smiled sadly. 'I'm just a common seaman, who but for you would be working aloft or being punished for some petty fault or other. But I'm a man, and I've notions for those I serve, an' – ' he seemed at a loss, ' – and

feel strong for.' He drew the old sword carefully and held the
blade in line with the sun, apparently studying its edge.
'Cap'n Herrick is a good man. In another ship he will find his
feet again.' The sword went into its scabbard with a sharp
click. 'But if not, then the deck of the flagship is no place for
him, sir.'

Bolitho stared at him. It had happened often in the past,
but never before had he needed Allday's support more. In his
ship, indeed the whole of his little squadron, there was no
man with whom he could really share his fears, his doubts.
When he had crossed from wardroom to cabin, and then been
given his own broad pendant, he had left such luxuries behind
him for good.

Allday added calmly, 'When I was first pressed into your
ship, I'd planned to give leg bail at the first opening. I knew
the penalty for desertion well enough, but I was that determined. Then at the Saintes, when all God's protection was
thrown aside under the cannon's bellow, I looked aft and saw
you. And it was then that I knew there were some captains
who *did* care for the likes of us, the poor buggers who were
expected to cheer for King and country when we sailed into the
enemy line.'

Bolitho replied quietly, 'I think you've said enough.'

Allday watched his lowered head with something like
despair. 'And you never sees it yourself, do you, sir? You fret
about Cap'n Herrick, or what chance we have against this foe
or that, but you never take a watch to think of yourself.' He
tensed as Ozzard padded through the other door, Bolitho's
coat and hat in his hands. 'But it's said and done now.' He
watched Bolitho stand up, his eyes blind as he held out his
arms for the coat. 'And I reckon it will be all right.'

Bolitho felt the sword-belt around his waist. Allday had
understood better than most would do. Had guessed his
intention perhaps from the moment of Herrick's admission.

He said, 'I will go on deck now and greet the others.' *And
afterwards say goodbye to Herrick.* 'And thank you for –' He
looked at Allday's homely face. '*Reminding* me.'

Allday watched him stride from the cabin and then put his
arm round Ozzard's shoulders.

'By God, I'd not have his position for a dozen wenches and a
whole ocean of rum!'

Ozzard grimaced. 'Not likely to get the offer, I'd say.'

On deck it was still clear and bright, the afternoon sea choppy with lively cat's-paws and long shallow swells. The three ships of the line, sails in flapping confusion as they hove-to to drop and receive boats, would have gladdened Bolitho's heart at any other time. Now, as he stood on the poop deck and watched the two barges speeding towards *Lysander*'s side, the marines already lined up at the entry port to receive the two other captains, he felt a deep sense of loss.

He saw Herrick at the lee rail, his hat well down over his eyes, and close by his first lieutenant, Gilchrist, arms folded, spindly legs apart to take the staggering motion. Of the action there was little to show. Brighter patches of planking where the carpenter and his mates had done their work well, fresh paint to hide other scars and replacements. Above the busy decks the sails, too, were neatly patched, and it was difficult to picture the smoke, to remember the din of war.

What Herrick was thinking at this moment he could hardly dare imagine. He must be very proud of the way his company had faced up to battle and its backbreaking aftermath. Just months ago most of these hurrying seamen had been working ashore on farms, in towns, with skills or without, life in a King's ship not even a possibility.

They would be sorry to see their captain leave. For the new men especially Herrick would be familiar, in some way a beginner like themselves. If they had displeasure to show it would be turned towards their commodore. If necessary, he would see to it himself, he thought grimly. Herrick's name was too valuable to be damaged because of his actions, right or wrong.

The first boat hooked on to the chains. It was Farquhar. *Naturally.* He came through the entry port, as elegant and as smart as if he had just left his London tailor. He doffed his hat to the quarterdeck and ran his eyes calmly along the swaying lines of marines and glittering bayonets. His hair was very fair, gathered at the nape of his neck, and it shone above his collar like pale gold.

Bolitho watched him shake hands with Herrick. How ill-matched they were. Had always been. Farquhar's uncle, Sir Henry Langford, had been Bolitho's first captain. At the age of twelve he had joined the eighty-gun *Manxman*, terrified and filled with awe. Fourteen years later, Langford, then an admiral, had given him command of a frigate. His nephew had been appointed into her as midshipman. Now, Farquhar, in his early thirties and a post-captain, was with him again. If he survived the war he would rise to high rank and position, both at home and in the fleet. Bolitho had never doubted it from the beginning, just as Herrick had never accepted it.

More shrills from the silver calls, and he saw George Probyn of the *Nicator* heaving his untidy shape through the port.

On the other side of the quarterdeck Pascoe was standing with Luce by the signal party, and Bolitho imagined that he himself must have looked like that when as a lieutenant he had witnessed comings and goings of aloof and unreachable beings.

He sighed and walked to the ladder.

Herrick said, 'If you will come to my quarters, Captain Probyn. The Commodore wishes to speak with Captain Farquhar.'

Farquhar's eyebrows rose slightly. ' 'Pon my word. Bit formal, aren't we, Captain Herrick?'

Herrick regarded him coldly. 'Yes.'

Bolitho watched Farquhar as he strode into his cabin. Watchful, wondering probably what his commodore's reactions were going to be, sensing something deeper around him, too. But confident above all.

'I have my report, sir.'

Bolitho gestured to a chair. 'In a moment. Our attack, as you will have realised, was successful. We have one good prize, and despatched another Spanish vessel in the bay. Four days ago we met with two French ships of the line and engaged them. We broke off the action after crippling both vessels. Our losses were small. Considering.'

Farquhar smiled quietly. He did not look quite so confident now. He said, 'I followed your instructions, sir. *Buzzard* reported sighting a convoy of some five sail, and we gave chase. Under the circumstances . . .'

'You acted correctly.' Bolitho watched him gravely. 'Did you catch them?'

'Captain Javal managed to damage a couple, sir, but he only succeeded in making one heave-to. Unfortunately, I was unable to reach the scene on time as I had lost my main topgallant mast in a squall. *Nicator* took the lead, and due to some, er,

misunderstanding of signals, fired a half-broadside into the
French vessel, so that she began to founder.'

'And then?'

Farquhar tugged an envelope from inside his elegant coat.
'My boarding officer managed to save this letter from the
master's safe before the vessel capsized and sank. It is addressed
to a Yves Gorse, who apparently resides in Malta. It contains
instructions for Gorse to prepare watering arrangements.'
He thrust the letter across the table. 'For merchant vessels on
their lawful occasions, or words to that effect. I believe the
letter to be in some sort of code, but the vessel's master is such
a dolt that I could get nothing from him. But the small convoy
was out of Marseilles. A French corvette was escorting them
through these waters, not because of any threat from us, but
because of Barbary pirates and the like.' He was keeping the
most important until the last. 'My first lieutenant did manage
to discover one thing, sir. I have several Frenchmen pressed
into my company, and one of them told my senior that he'd
heard one of the survivors claim that the letter had been sent
aboard their ship by order of Admiral Brueys himself!'

Bolitho looked at him. Brueys was perhaps the finest and
most capable admiral in the French navy. In any navy for that
matter.

'You did well.' Bolitho rubbed his hands on his thighs.
'This man Gorse may be a spy or agent of some kind. Perhaps
the French intend to attack Malta.'

'Or Sicily?' Farquhar frowned. 'Bonaparte is said to have
intentions towards the kingdom. They are at peace, but he
probably believes, as I do, that in war there is no such luxury
as neutrality.'

'Maybe.' Bolitho tried not to think of Herrick. 'We will make
haste to Toulon and Marseilles. Following your discovery,
we can now determine the strength of these preparations.'

Farquhar asked, 'Your prize, sir. What does she hold?'

'Powder and shot. And fodder.'

'Fodder?'

'Yes. It troubles me, too. All the French and Spanish
preparations are for a full-scale attack. They blend together
into a sort of strategy. But fodder. It does not sound like a
local attack. It sounds like cavalry and heavy artillery. And all
the men and horses to sustain them.'

Farquhar's eyes gleamed. 'This vessel, too, was carrying fodder.' He looked around the cabin. 'I am sorry, sir. But should we not wait for the others? It will save time.'

Bolitho looked at the sealed envelope. 'This is for you, Captain Farquhar.' He walked to the stern and watched the other ships, hearing the rasp of a knife as Farquhar slit open the envelope.

Farquhar said quietly, 'You have me all aback, sir.'

Bolitho turned and studied him thoughtfully. 'It was a hard decision.'

'And Captain Herrick, sir?' Farquhar's face was masklike. 'Is he ill?'

'Not ill.' He added shortly, 'Execute the arrangements directly. I want the squadron under way before dusk.'

Farquhar was still watching him, the letter in one hand. 'I cannot begin to thank you, sir.'

Bolitho nodded. 'You obviously think I made the right choice.'

Farquhar had blue eyes. But they were not like Herrick's, and in the light from the sea they were like ice.

'Well, as you have asked, sir, yes I do.'

'Then see that the squadron's affairs show some sign of this.' He looked at him evenly. 'Captain Herrick is a fine officer.'

The eyebrows moved again. 'But?'

'No *but*, Captain Farquhar. I want him to feel his strength in a well-trained ship, where he has no personal contact as yet. He will be kept fully occupied. I think it will be good for him *and* the squadron.'

Farquhar smiled. 'My first lieutenant *will* be surprised. It will do him good also.' He did not explain what he meant.

'The first lieutenant in this ship is Mr. Gilchrist. I suggest you make his acquaintance without delay.'

He waited for a sign but Farquhar merely remarked, 'Gilchrist? I don't think I know him.' He shrugged. 'But then, why should one bother to *know* these people?'

Bolitho said, 'I would appreciate it if you would keep your personal dislikes out of the meeting.'

Farquhar stood up. 'Of course, sir. You should know that I have never *disliked* Captain Herrick. Although I am well aware of his hostility towards me.' He gave his tight-lipped smile. 'I cannot imagine the reason for it.'

Bolitho saw Ozzard hovering at the door. 'Show the other captains aft, Ozzard. Then you can bring some wine.' He tried to speak lightheartedly, as if he was untroubled, unreached.

Ozzard bobbed, his eyes on Farquhar. 'Aye, aye, sir.'

Bolitho crossed to a quarter gallery and stared at the small white-horses cruising down from the horizon. Each piece of news and every thin rumour took them deeper and deeper into the Mediterranean. Each time it would be *his* decision. One captured letter had taken him into a bay where men and ships had been destroyed. Now Farquhar's chance find would send them still further north-east, to the harbours of the French navy. Pieces of a puzzle, all set against a chart and the remorseless run of sand in an hour-glass.

The door opened and he turned to see Herrick and Probyn entering the cabin. He waited until they were seated and then beckoned Ozzard to the wine cabinet.

At that moment there was a knock on the door and Gilchrist peered in at them. He saw Herrick and said, 'I am sorry to intrude, sir, but I wish to speak with the flag captain.'

Farquhar's voice made him turn.

'*I* am the flag captain, Mr. Gilchrist. I will trouble you not to forget it!' There was an uncomfortable silence and he added, 'I will also trouble you never to enter the commodore's quarters without my permission!'

The door closed and Farquhar leaned sideways in his chair to look at the cabinet.

His voice was perfectly normal again. 'A fine piece of joinery, sir. I know his work well.'

Bolitho glanced at Herrick, but he was already beyond his reach.

9

Wine and Cheese

CAPTAIN CHARLES FARQUHAR strode aft to greet Bolitho as he came on deck. In spite of being without coat or hat, Farquhar managed to retain an air of elegance, and his ruffled shirt looked as if it was freshly laundered.

He said formally, 'Course east-nor'-east, sir.'

Bolitho nodded and glanced up at his broad pendant and the set of the yards. The wind had veered slightly during the night, and there was evidence that it was weakening also.

He took a telescope from the rack and trained it over the larboard nettings. It was as if the scene stayed permanent and the sails were merely pretending to make the ship move. And yet it was three wearying weeks since he had watched Herrick pulled across to the *Osiris*, and two of those weeks had been spent along this stretch of coast. He watched the familiar shark-blue blur of land. It was maddening to realise that just out there was the busy port of Toulon, and behind its protective walls and batteries lay the answer to his speculation and doubts.

Farquhar remarked, 'Not even a sign of a sail, damn them.'

Bolitho replaced the glass and looked along *Lysander*'s upper deck. The forenoon watch had begun. One like all the others before it. Everywhere, above and along the decks, men were at work, splicing, painting, blacking-down the standing rigging, examining a hundred and one things for flaws and possible wear.

It was eerie to find the Gulf of Lions so empty. It was like being laughed at. The French must know that an enemy squadron was active in their waters. Any tiny fishing craft might have sighted it and passed the news to garrisons ashore. Perhaps they were too busy to care, or were content to let the British ships tack wearily back and forth, consuming their stores and resources, and with nothing to show for it.

He said, 'We must get some news soon, or we'll have to push closer inshore.'

Farquhar eyed him calmly. 'If we had some more frigates, sir.'

Bolitho bit back an angry retort. It was not Farquhar's fault. But in every campaign they seemed to be short of frigates, without which it was like trying to find a blind man in a dark room.

He peered astern, watching *Osiris*'s big forecourse filling and emptying in the uncertain wind, as if the ship was breathing heavily. She was a mile away, and beyond her he could just see the leeward side of the prize *Segura*. He wondered how Probyn had been getting on with his separate patrol to the east of Toulon, to seaward of the small islands which protected the approaches. He had Javal's *Buzzard* in company, while the rest of the squadron had to be content with the sloop. He could just make out *Harebell*'s cream-coloured topsails, etched against the French coastline like sea-shells. Inch would be in no doubt of his importance. It was to be hoped he did not allow his eagerness to tempt him closer inshore. There he could lose the wind, or fall foul of some well-sited artillery.

He turned to look at *Osiris* again. Three weeks, and on every single day he had wondered about Herrick.

Farquhar followed his glance and said, 'She is handling well.'

Only a casual interest. Bolitho had already noticed that about the elegant captain. Once out of a ship, and no matter how long he had served in her, or what great events she had shared, Farquhar was able to dismiss her from his thoughts. He was entirely without sentiment, and seemed to live for today, and where it would lead in the future.

Nevertheless, he had to admit that Farquhar's efficiency had showed itself throughout the ship. Gun drill and contests between batteries and decks had cut the time for loading and firing by minutes.

Although he always appeared to have time for his own leisure, Farquhar was never far away when needed. And his officers, from Gilchrist to Mr. Midshipman Saxby, had been made to realise it.

Farquhar had always borne a reputation for harshness. But as yet he had not shown himself as a tyrant. He had examined all the ship's books within hours of getting the squadron under way, from the punishment and muster books to the rarer ones about stocks of canvas and oil.

It was a new side to the man's character, and Bolitho being the man he was never considered that his own past example to Farquhar was bearing fruit at last.

He saw Lieutenant Fitz-Clarence strutting busily back and forth on the lee side of the quarterdeck. That was another thing. Farquhar had quite rightly removed the second lieutenant from the monotony of prize-duty aboard the *Segura* and had sent instead a master's mate. Whenever the weather had made it possible he had recalled the prize-master and had replaced him with another. Midshipmen, warrant officers, even a resentful Gilchrist, had had their share. It made sense, and kept them on their toes.

But Farquhar had not asked permission. As flag captain he had taken it as a right.

He had even cut the number of punishments, if not their severity. He had examined every case himself, and if the unfortunate seaman had made a genuine mistake, or one had been caused by a superior's carelessness, he had dismissed it, and to ram home his point had given the accuser an awesome pile of extra duties. If on the other hand the case had been proved, he had ordered stiffer punishment than Herrick had ever permitted. It was, it seemed, his one real failing.

Farquhar said suddenly, 'We shall have to lose *Harebell* or *Buzzard* shortly, sir.' It sounded like a question.

'Yes.'

Bolitho paced slowly along the weather side. The deck seams clung to his shoes, and he could feel the heat thrown back from the bulwark. And it was barely nine o'clock in the forenoon. Each day brought hotter weather, more tension to those who endured it. Farquhar had put his finger right on the point. He could not delay much longer. He would have to send word to the admiral. His own estimation of the French preparations and intentions. Once he had despatched one of his badly needed scouts, he would be committed. Set against the consequences if he was proved wrong, that in itself was unimportant.

If only Inch had been able to capture the Spanish brig before the two French ships had chased him away. He could have sent her to the admiral.

He paused and shaded his eyes to look for the prize. She was too slow and vulnerable. And she still might prove useful as a deception. He thought of her packed cargo. Or as a bribe.

Steel rang on steel, and he walked to the quarterdeck rail to watch as the off-watch midshipmen faced each other for practice with sword and cutlass.

Farquhar glanced at him. 'I thought Mr. Pascoe would be well employed, sir.' There was nothing in his voice to betray his thoughts. 'He has already proved his skill on one of my previous lieutenants.' He smiled briefly. 'He has a good eye.'

Bolitho watched Pascoe walking behind two of the midshipmen, speaking to each in turn. Their faces were crimson with exertion and were obviously aware their commodore and captain were looking on.

Clang, clang, clang, the blades moved in a jerky rhythm. How different in a real battle, Bolitho thought grimly. The madness, the eagerness to strike at a man before he beat you to the deck.

Gilchrist appeared below the larboard gangway.

'You'll have to do better than that, Mr. Pascoe!'

Bolitho felt Farquhar tense as he snapped, 'What ails that damned fellow?'

Fitz-Clarence was making elaborate steps along the lee side, trying to warn Gilchrist that he was not alone.

Farquhar called, 'Mr. Fitz-Clarence! I'll trouble you to stand still!'

He turned and looked at Gilchrist's uplifted face.

'You were saying, Mr. Gilchrist?'

The first lieutenant replied, 'The drill is *untidy*, sir.'

Bolitho watched the little drama in silence. The midshipmen's arms still wavering in the air, the swords in disarray. Seamen who had been working in the weather shrouds pausing to watch, their tanned bodies gold in the sunlight. Pascoe in the middle of it, his dark eyes on Gilchrist, only his quick breathing betraying his anger.

And Farquhar. He glanced at him and saw the look in his ice-blue stare. Farquhar had kept Gilchrist busy and obedient. Now it was out in the open again. He recalled his sudden anger. *What ails that damned fellow?*

Farquhar snapped his fingers. 'Bosun's mate! Fetch my sword!'

He walked to the lee gangway and leaned on the handrail, his eyes on Gilchrist below him and at the opposite side.

'Mr. Pascoe, dismiss those ragamuffins!' He reached without turning his head as a worried looking bosun's mate hurried towards him. 'I believe you lost your sword in some reckless scheme with the Dons, Mr. Pascoe.' He drew his own from its scabbard and held it against the sky, eyeing it critically. 'This is a fair blade. It was presented to me by my late uncle.' He looked up at Bolitho's grave features and added, 'Although I gather that Sir Henry preferred something heavier, sir?' He added sharply, 'With your permission, sir.' Then he flung the sword straight at Pascoe. '*Catch!*'

Bolitho tried not to flinch as the youth reached out and caught it in flight.

Farquhar sounded very relaxed and composed. 'And *now*, Mr. Gilchrist. If you will be so good as to cross swords with our junior lieutenant, maybe the midshipmen will learn something, eh?'

Gilchrist stared from him to Pascoe, his eyes wild.

'Fight a *duel*, sir?' He could barely get the words out.

'Not a duel, Mr. Gilchrist.' Farquhar returned to the quarterdeck. 'An *instruction*, if you like.'

As he reached Bolitho's side he said quietly, 'Have no fears for Mr. Pascoe, sir.'

Gilchrist had been handed his sword by the wardroom servant and was holding it before him as if he had never set eyes on it in his life.

He said, 'At the first contact . . .'

He stared desperately at the midshipmen. Luce was grim-faced, and at the end of the line Saxby stood with his mouth wide open, his eyes like saucers.

Gilchrist seemed to realise the absurdity of his position and snapped, 'On your guard, Mr. Pascoe!'

The blades touched, wavered and flashed over the pale planking like steel tongues.

Bolitho watched, feeling the dryness in his throat as he saw Pascoe's slim figure moving around an eighteen-pounder's breech, his shoes feeling the way, his right leg forward to keep his balance. He wanted to tear his eyes away and look at

Farquhar. Was he really trying to demolish Gilchrist's arrogance, or was he using it and Pascoe's skill to remind Bolitho of his dead brother?

Perhaps Farquhar was remembering at this very moment. How they had been taken prisoner by Hugh Bolitho in his American privateer. He was not likely to forget it, or the fact that Hugh's downfall had begun when he had killed a brother officer when he had been in the King's service. *In a duel.*

He heard Gilchrist's sharp breathing, saw the concentrated stare of anger and hatred as he parried Pascoe's guard and forced him back a few paces before he could recover.

Farquhar said quietly, 'See how his skill with a sword gives way to anger.' He was speaking almost to himself. 'Watch him. Pushing on, using up his strength.' He nodded with silent appreciation. 'He has a longer reach, and is a harder man than Mr. Pascoe, but . . .'

Bolitho saw Pascoe's hilt dart up and under the other man's blade, twisting it aside and making it fly across the deck.

Gilchrist stepped back, his eyes fixed on the sword point which was motionless, in line with his chest.

'Good.' Farquhar sauntered to the rail. 'Well done.' He looked at Gilchrist. 'Both of you.' He turned to the spellbound midshipmen. 'I think that was quite a lesson, eh?'

Bolitho took a slow breath. A lesson indeed. For all of them.

The master's mate of the watch, who had been following the spectacle with the others, suddenly looked up, his hands cupped around his ears.

'Gunfire, sir!'

Bolitho wrenched his thoughts from the sword-play.

'Where away?'

He heard it then, like surf on a rocky shore. Muffled, but plain for what it was.

The master's mate said, 'To the east'rd, sir.' He pointed across the starboard bow. 'Sure of it.'

Farquhar hurried past him. 'That was well said, Mr. Bagley.' He reached the compass and peered at it for several seconds. 'I'd like permission to investigate, sir.' He watched Bolitho, his mouth half smiling. 'Before the wind leaves us with more time to 'er, *fill.*'

Bolitho nodded. 'Signal the squadron to make more sail. *Harebell*, too, if you can attract Commander Inch's attention.'

Farquhar strode to the rail as Gilchrist appeared on the larboard ladder.

'Pipe all hands!' His voice was crisp, indifferent to Gilchrist's confusion. 'Get the maincourse on her, and the stuns'ls, too, if need be.' He paused, his head cocked to listen to the shrill of calls between decks. 'We will let her fall off a couple of points.' He glanced at the master's mate. 'And let us all hope Mr. Bagley's estimate is correct.'

As the men poured to their stations at the braces and at the foot of each mast, Pascoe hurried across the quarterdeck to supervise Luce's signal party.

Bolitho barred his way. 'I am glad you are spared another cut, Adam.'

The youth's sunburned features split in a smile. 'It was easy, Uncle.'

Bolitho snapped, 'That time perhaps. It was not of your making, I know that, too.'

The smile vanished. 'I am sorry, er, sir.'

'If you want to cross swords again, then please ask *me*, Adam.'

Pascoe hesitated and then smiled awkwardly. 'Yes, sir.'

'Now be off with you. I want our ships to see the signals today.'

Farquhar joined him by the rail. 'A fine young man, sir.'

Their eyes met.

Then Bolitho said calmly, 'And I'd be obliged, Captain Farquhar, if we can keep him that way.'

Farquhar smiled and walked forward to watch the men dashing aloft to the yards.

Major Leroux appeared by the poop ladder and touched his hat.

'It sounds like a *pair* of ships, sir. Probably *Nicator* or *Buzzard* getting to grips with a Frenchman.'

Bolitho looked up as the great mainsail billowed free from its yard, the thunder of canvas drowning the distant sound of gunfire.

'I hope you may be right, Major.'

Leroux was watching his own men at the mizzen braces. In an almost conversational tone he said, 'My Corporal Cuttler is an excellent marksman, sir. If he earned his living in a fairground he would doubtless be a man of wealth and property by now.'

He walked away as Lieutenant Nepean hurried to him to make his report.

Allday had come on deck and said, 'He's a dark one is Major Leroux, sir.'

Bolitho looked at him. 'In what way?'

Allday gave a lazy smile. 'He had that Corporal Cuttler down in the wardroom lobby. With his long musket he's so proud of.'

'D'you mean that he was ordering Cuttler to be ready to shoot?' He stared at Allday's smiling face.

The coxswain shook his head. 'Not exactly, sir. He asked him if he *could* shoot a sword out of a man's hand, if necessary like.'

Bolitho walked to the nettings. 'I do not know about you, Allday.'

He saw Leroux watching him, his features expressionless. For that brief moment he felt quite sorry for Gilchrist.

*

Bolitho leaned back to watch *Lysander*'s towering spread of canvas. Ship of the line perhaps, but Farquhar was driving her with the fanatical demand of a frigate captain.

With the wind coming almost directly astern the ship was forging ahead well, her yards and shrouds creaking and vibrating under the tall pyramids of sails. Every so often her bow would dip and the forecastle would then be drenched in great showers of spray, like slivers of glass in the bright glare.

Bolitho stood halfway up a poop ladder, feeling his hair blowing wildly as he peered ahead of the lifting and plunging bowsprit. The gunfire had ceased, and he could see dark brown smoke drifting along the horizon, the uncertain silhouette of a large ship under reduced sails.

From the mainmast crosstrees he heard Luce yell, 'She's *Nicator*, sir!'

Farquhar, who had sent Luce aloft with his big signals telescope, paused in his restless pacing and snapped, 'I should damn well hope so!' He glared at Fitz-Clarence. 'What the hell is she firing at?'

Luce called again, his voice excited, and totally unaware of the tensions far below his dizzy perch. ' 'Nother vessel on her lee side, sir! I think they're grappling!'

Farquhar swung round. 'Mr. Pascoe. If you think it not too undignified for a lieutenant to swarm up the ratlines like a damn monkey, I'd be obliged for a more rational report.'

Pascoe grinned and threw off his coat before hurrying to the main shrouds.

Farquhar saw Bolitho watching and shrugged. 'Luce comes of a good family, but I fear his powers of description would be better suited to poetry than to a man o' war.'

Bolitho raised his eyes to see Pascoe hanging out and down as he pulled himself around the futtock shrouds and up beyond the maintop. How easy he made it look. He turned his attention to the distant ships, unable to torture himself with his hatred of heights.

'A glass, please.'

He felt one handed to him and trained it through the angled rigging. Yes, it was easy to recognise *Nicator*'s bluff outline, the dull yellow paint of her figurehead. Beyond her hull he could see three masts, only one of which was square-rigged, as far as he could tell.

He heard Pascoe shout, 'Barquentine, sir! I can see her flag!' A pause while Farquhar stared up at the swaying masthead until his eyes watered. 'A Yankee, sir!'

Farquhar turned and looked at Bolitho. He said sourly, 'As if we haven't troubles enough!'

Bolitho tried to hide his disappointment from those who were watching his reactions. An American merchantman. Going about her affairs. There was nothing they could do about that, even if she was trading with the enemy. Blockade was one thing, but to provoke another war with the new United States would receive no praise from King and Parliament.

Bolitho said, 'Signal the rest of our ships to remain in the patrol area.' He watched an out-thrust spur of land, almost hidden in mist and haze. 'We have enough risk as it is, to be standing so close to the Isles of Hyères, without leading the whole squadron ashore.'

Farquhar nodded. 'Bosun's mate! Call Mr. Luce to the deck!'

Minutes later, in response to Luce's signals, *Osiris* and the prize tacked heavily away from their leader to begin the long beat back to more open waters.

Bolitho said, 'Make to *Nicator* that we are joining her directly.'

What was Probyn doing? It was natural enough to feel resentment at the sight of an American flag, especially to those, like Probyn, who had been taken prisoner during the revolution. But it was over and done with, and time for it to become a part of history. If a war was provoked by some act of stupidity, England would be worse off than ever. Fighting France and Spain, and an America which was now far more powerful than she had been those fifteen years back.

'*Nicator* has acknowledged, sir.' Luce sounded breathless from his hasty descent down a backstay.

'Very well.'

It took another half-hour to manoeuvre close enough to heave-to. By that time *Nicator* had ungrappled the American vessel, but as she had drifted downwind Bolitho had seen her poop spotted with the scarlet coats of Probyn's marines.

He snapped, 'Call away my barge.' He looked at Farquhar. 'It'll save time, if nothing else.'

The barge was swayed up and over the lee gangway, the crew tumbling into her almost before she had touched the water alongside. Allday's voice pursued the bargemen like a trumpet, and by the time *Lysander* was hove-to and Bolitho had reached the entry port, all was ready.

He said quietly, 'Keep a weather-eye open for *Buzzard*. She should be beating round from the east'rd shortly.' He looked grimly at Farquhar's handsome features. 'I will send her to the admiral with my despatches.'

Farquhar shrugged. 'I am sorry. I'd hoped for something of value.'

But Bolitho was already climbing down the entry port stairs, trying not to lower his head to watch the sea sluicing along the rounded hull and lifting the barge towards his legs.

He paused, counting seconds, and then as the barge swam up beneath him he jumped out and down, Allday's order to cast off coming before he had taken a proper breath.

He sat in the sternsheets with as much dignity as he could manage and said, 'To *Nicator*, Allday.'

He watched the other seventy-four's crossed yards towering above him, the slackness of some of her running-rigging. Like the man, he thought, untidy.

Allday steered the barge around the ship's great counter and towards her entry port. Bolitho was too busy watching the barquentine to care for Probyn's feelings or the inconvenience of a visit from his commodore.

She was a lean, graceful vessel, and her name, *Santa Paula*, stood out in rich gold against a completely black hull.

'Toss your oars!' Allday swung the tiller as the bowman hooked on to *Nicator*'s main chains.

Bolitho said, 'Return to the ship, Allday.' He saw the sudden doubt. 'It is all right this time. *Nicator* is still an English vessel, I trust!'

Allday touched his forehead and grinned. 'I'll watch for your signal, sir.'

Bolitho scrambled up to the entry port, noticing how scarred were the wooden stairs, while the chain plates of the main shrouds were badly dappled with red rust.

He found Probyn waiting with the side-party, his portly figure doused with spray.

He said, 'I fear the reception is short-handed, sir, but my marines are aboard the Yankee.'

'So I see.' Bolitho began to walk aft, away from the curious faces by the port. 'Now tell me. What happened?'

Probyn stared at him. 'We ran down on the barquentine at noon, sir. I guessed she was a runner trying to pass through our patrol, so I signalled her to heave-to.' He nodded, sensing Bolitho's mood. 'I know we are not supposed to get involved with American neutrality, but – '

'There is no *but* about it.'

Bolitho glanced at the ship's two helmsmen. They looked as if they were dressed in the same clothes as when they had been caught by the press. All the captains knew his opinion about that. He had put it in his written orders to ensure that every man, pressed or volunteer, should begin life aboard ship in a proper issue of slop clothing. It was such a cheap but vital thing that he was amazed at the stupidity of some captains who were so miserly they issued nothing until their wretched seamen were almost in rags. Probyn knew it well enough, and had outwardly complied. But out of sight, out of mind, apparently. He would deal with that later.

He added, 'What was your true reason?'

Probyn led the way aft to his quarters. 'I am badly short of hands, sir. I had to sail from England before I was given a fair chance of recruitment, otherwise . . .'

Bolitho stared at him. 'And you sent a party into an American ship to *press* some of her people?'

Probyn paused and regarded him resentfully. 'It is well known that hundreds, *many* hundreds, of our seamen desert to the American flag each year.'

Bolitho did know it, and it was a very sore point indeed on both sides of the Atlantic. The British Government had stated that they considered any seamen to be fair game for a short-handed naval vessel, unless the American captains in question carried certificates of citizenship for all their people who were so entitled.

The American President, on the other hand, was equally firm. He had demanded that once a man was signed into an American ship that was evidence enough the man *was* American. Documents could be destroyed or ignored. The American flag could not.

He said, 'We heard gunfire, too.'

Probyn thrust past a marine sentry and answered, 'The Yankee refused to heave-to even after a warning shot. I'll not take that from anyone.' He hesitated in the small lobby to the cabin. 'I have her master aboard, under guard, sir.' He sounded suddenly apprehensive. 'Now that you are here, I suppose I had best hand him over to you?'

Bolitho watched him coldly. 'Take me to him.'

The barquentine's master was seated in the stern cabin with one of Probyn's senior midshipmen for company. He stood up and eyed Bolitho with obvious surprise.

'So there *is* some higher authority, eh?' He had a soft accent, but it failed to conceal his anger.

'I am Richard Bolitho, Commodore of this British squadron.' He walked to the windows, adding, 'I have been hearing about your refusal to heave-to.'

The American retorted hotly, 'Heave-to be damned! I've a hard enough living to earn without being fired on by a bloody Englishman!'

Bolitho sat down and looked at him. A sturdy man with a neat brown beard, the *Santa Paula*'s master was about his own age.

'And your name?'

'Cap'n John Thurgood.' He glared at him. 'Of New Bedford.'

'Well, Captain Thurgood.' He smiled. 'Of New Bedford. The shortage of seamen is a constant worry for a King's officer in time of war.'

Thurgood sat down, ignoring Probyn completely.

'That will have to remain your problem, Commodore. I am not at war, and my hands are not for King George.' He relaxed slightly. 'My government will make the strongest protest and take all the action needed once I have laid my complaint.'

Bolitho nodded. 'That is your privilege, Captain. But you know as well as I that some of your crew will be no more American than Westminster Abbey.' He held up one hand. 'And I know what you will say to that. No matter. You are obviously a shrewd man, and I see no value in our arguing.' He stood up. 'I shall have you returned to your fine barquentine, Captain, and I will send you a gift of some excellent cheese which I brought from England. I hope it will ease if not remove the hurt we have done you.'

Thurgood was on his feet. 'You mean I can go?' He stared from Bolitho to Probyn's fuming face with amazement. 'Well, I'll be . . .'

Bolitho added evenly, 'Your cargo, Captain? May I enquire what it is?'

Thurgood replied, 'Cheap red wine. A full hold of the stuff. In my home port they'd use it for paint!' He chuckled, his eyes vanishing into crow's feet. 'By God, you sure know how to scatter a man's anger!'

Probyn exclaimed, 'I must protest!'

Bolitho said calmly, 'Please leave us, Captain Probyn. And tell your midshipman to go away. I am not in danger of my life.' He smiled at the American. 'Am I?'

Thurgood grinned after the retreating Probyn. 'By God, I'm glad you came, Commodore. I think he'd have liked me kicking at his mainyard.'

'He was a prisoner in the last war.'

Thurgood shrugged. 'So was I.'

Bolitho picked up his hat. 'There is one thing, Captain. You sailed from Marseilles, no doubt.' He shook his head. 'It is not a trap. But it is unlikely you would have taken on a cargo like yours elsewhere. And you are bound for?'

Thurgood watched him with amusement. 'Corfu. Then I'm off and away, back home to New Bedford. I've a wife and three boys there.'

'I envy you.' Bolitho did not see the look of warmth on the other man's face. 'I have a Spanish prize in company. We took her a while back.' He looked Thurgood in the eye. 'Now, if you were to exchange some of your seamen for, say, double the number of Spaniards.'' He watched the man's mind working busily. 'Well, I'd have thought you could drop them off when you return westward after you have delivered your cargo? I am certain the Spanish authorities would be very glad to reward you.'

Thurgood sounded doubtful. 'I ain't sure.'

Bolitho smiled. 'And they would not have to be paid. Nor would you have to share your profit with a larger crew than you need for the homeward voyage.'

Thurgood thrust out his hand. 'If ever you need employment, Commodore, and I mean *ever*, just come asking for me.' He shook his hand warmly. 'I've got a few bully-boys you can have. Trained seamen, but I will not miss them.'

Bolitho smiled. 'I dare say they will settle down.'

On deck it was oppressively hot, and the wind was rising and falling in gusts, making the ships lurch and stagger in a sickening motion.

Bolitho beckoned to Probyn. 'Make a signal to *Lysander*. I want the prize, *Segura*, to close with us. After that, send a good officer across to the *Santa Paula* with Captain Thurgood. He will explain what is needed.'

Probyn looked as if he would burst. 'If you say so, sir!'

Bolitho smiled at the American. 'When they are ready, I will hail for my coxswain to bring a good ripe cheese across to you. It might make even cheap wine palatable.'

Thurgood watched a boat being lowered from the quarter davits.

'I'll be off then, Commodore.' He studied him curiously. 'Bolitho, eh? We had a privateersman of that name in the war.'

'My brother.' Bolitho looked away. 'But he is dead now.'

Thurgood held out his hand. 'Good luck with whatever you intend. I shall tell my wife and sons about this meeting.' He grinned. 'An' the cheese.'

A lieutenant strode across the quarterdeck and touched his hat.

'Jolly boat's at the chains, sir.'

Thurgood made to leave but hung back, his face set in a frown.

'I want no part of this, or any other war. I've had a bellyful.' He dropped one eyelid in a wink. 'But if I was in charge of a force as weak as yours I'd be thinking very seriously of hauling off.'

Bolitho tried to conceal his excitement. His anxiety.

'You would?'

Thurgood grinned. 'I'm told there's a fleet at Toulon, and *three hundred* transports for good measure.'

'Thank you, Captain.' Bolitho walked with him to the rail. 'And a safe voyage to you also.'

He waited until Thurgood was in the boat and then said, 'Send for my barge.'

A fleet and three hundred transports. It was an armada.

Probyn's voice cut into his racing thoughts. 'I must lodge the strongest protest! I was humiliated in front of that Yankee!'

Bolitho swung on him, his eyes blazing. 'Humiliated, were you? And how do you imagine I felt to see a ship of the line firing on an unarmed vessel? To know that one of my captains was prepared to risk unnecessary killing, a war if necessary, just to get what he wants for himself?' He kept his voice low. 'And all because you knew that I would take any blame, was that it?'

'That was unjust, sir!' Some of the bluster had gone.

'I dare say.' Bolitho regarded him evenly. 'But do not take me for a fool. That I *do* find humiliating.'

He strode to the entry port, seeing his barge curtsying across the blue water towards him.

'You'll get your men, Captain. You would have probably been given them anyway, had you used common sense instead of a broadside.' He nodded towards some seamen at the boat tackles. 'Look at them, Captain. Would you fight for anyone who kept you in worse comfort than a dog?' He did not wait for an answer. 'Care for them. Or they'll not fight for *you*.'

He leaned over the rail and cupped his hands. 'Take your bundle to the barquentine, Allday! Then return for me!'

Allday waved one arm and steered the barge clear of the side.

An hour later Bolitho was back aboard his own ship, with Farquhar barely able to hide his curiosity.

Bolitho said, 'Make a signal to *Harebell* to close with us immediately. I cannot wait for Javal. Commander Inch can carry my despatches to the admiral.'

He waited while Farquhar shouted for Luce, and the barge was hoisted, dripping, on to the boat tier.

Farquhar came back and asked, 'May I enquire the nature of your plan, sir?' He pointed to the *Segura* which had almost reached the other ships. 'And what is *she* doing?'

'I am sending some of the Spanish seamen to Captain Thurgood in exchange for the barquentine's, er, non-Americans.'

Farquhar pouted. 'It will leave *us* short-handed, sir.'

'But it has provided us with *information*.' He could hide his relief no longer. 'The French have a great fleet here. *Harebell* must sail with all speed, before dusk if possible.'

Farquhar nodded. 'Captain Probyn will be happy about his good fortune.'

'Perhaps.' Bolitho recalled the captain's face. He had made an enemy there. Maybe he had always been one. All those years.

He said, 'Tomorrow, if nothing is changed, we will have a conference.'

He unbuckled his sword and handed it to Allday. He discovered that he was suddenly ravenously hungry. For the first time in many days.

As he made to walk aft he turned and looked at Farquhar again. 'If you were a French general, and did not wish your transports to be involved in a battle before your main objective. And if that objective was North Africa, and beyond that to India perhaps.' He watched Farquhar's eyes. 'Where would you go to prepare for the final assault?'

Farquhar rested both hands on the main bitts and frowned. 'To avoid a battle?' He looked up. 'Sicily might be too dangerous. A point on the coast of Africa which was far enough away from my objective to avoid suspicion would equally be too far for men and horses to travel and be fit to fight at the end of it.' He nodded slowly. 'I think I would choose an island already under my country's control.' He paused. 'Does that sound sensible, sir?'

Bolitho smiled. 'Do you know of such an island?'

Farquhar looked surprised. 'Yes, sir. Corfu.'

'Exactly.' He walked past the helmsmen and nodded to Grubb.

Farquhar crossed to the master's side and said, 'The commodore believes that the French may be gathering at Corfu.'

Grubb watched him warily. 'Aye, sir. But if you'll pardon the liberty, I thought it was *your* suggestion!'

Farquhar stared at him and then at the poop. 'The devil, you say!' He smiled tightly. 'That was cleverly done!'

10

Committed

FOR a further two frustrating weeks Bolitho's ships tacked back and forth, keeping to the south-west of Toulon's approaches, an area which would give them maximum advantage should the enemy emerge. With *Harebell* making all possible speed to Gibraltar, the work of inshore patrol fell to Captain Javal's frigate. While the seventy-fours and their prize wallowed unhappily under reduced canvas, Javal's topsails were usually to be seen sneaking around a distant headland, or standing hove-to in direct view of the enemy.

But even Javal's taunting manoeuvres had no effect. The French stayed where they were, and did nothing.

And then, on a hot, sultry evening, as *Buzzard* fetched off the land for the fortieth time, Javal took it upon himself to lower a cutter in the charge of his first lieutenant, Mr. Mears. It was more to ease the boredom than anything, for the French had showed no sign of sending out a frigate or corvette to chase the prowling *Buzzard* away.

On that particular night a French fisherman reacted in much the same way. Ignoring the instructions of the port admiral and garrison commander, he put to sea in his small boat, with his son and cousin for crew.

The first that Bolitho learned of these coincidences was when *Buzzard*'s cutter, complete with Captain Javal and three French fishermen, arrived alongside on the following morning.

The fisherman was elderly but defiant. He showed little concern for his life, and probably considered that as the English had rammed and sunk his little boat he had nothing left to live for.

Bolitho listened to Javal's report before having the three Frenchmen brought to his cabin. It was strangely moving. The old, grey-bearded fisherman, his cousin, as red as a lobster with a belly like a puncheon of rum, and the son, straight-backed, angry. Afraid.

Bolitho explained through Farquhar, whose French was excellent, the he wanted information about Toulon. Not unnaturally, the fisherman told him to rot in hell. The son shouted '*Death to the English!*' before being cuffed into a flood of tears by Sergeant Gritton.

The cousin, on the other hand, was more than practical. He explained that the boat had been all they owned. All they had to feed their families and eke out a poor living in a town where the military enjoyed the best of everything. It was very likely true.

Despite his great girth and his red, cunning face, the cousin was obviously the thinking member of the crew.

He suggested, warily at first, that if Bolitho provided another boat, and perhaps a little money or food, he would be prepared to tell him what he wanted to know.

Javal snapped, 'I'll have the varmint seized up and flogged, sir! I'll give him *boat!*'

'That way we will learn nothing useful.' Bolitho walked to the windows and watched some low banks of pale cloud. A change in the weather perhaps. 'Tell him, Captain Farquhar, that he can have the boat and some food. You can signal for a boat to be sent from the *Segura*.' To Javal he added, 'Those fishermen will be unable to confide what they have seen to their authorities. The fact they disobeyed a port-order by putting to sea *and* return with a strange boat is proof enough of treachery.'

Javal swallowed hard. 'Then you intend to *release* them, sir?'

'We may come this way again, Captain.' Javal's astonishment settled it. 'You cannot choose your friends in war.'

And so, while the fisherman and his son were taken to examine the Spanish longboat, the fat cousin described what he had seen every day in Toulon.

The *Santa Paula*'s master had given Bolitho a fair description, but if anything it was a conservative estimate. A well-found fleet, consisting of ships of the line a'plenty, and one of which, according to the fisherman, was of one hundred and twenty guns or more. She, it appeared, wore the flag of Vice Admiral de Brueys, and another that of Rear Admiral Villeneuve. Bolitho had heard of them both many times, and respected them. Preparations went on daily to provision and service this great assembly of ships, and the local victualling officers were making a special effort to purchase every available kind of food. Which had been the main reason for the fishermen putting to sea. Even their meagre catch would have brought ready money from the navy.

Farquhar asked the man one careful question. Bolitho watched his reaction, his gestures above his head and towards the sea.

Farquhar explained softly, 'The fleet is not yet ready to sail. It is said to be waiting for the right time. The leader of the expedition, too.' His eyebrows lifted very slightly. 'It could be so.'

Bolitho nodded. He did not speak much French, but knew enough to recognise the name Bonaparte.

Farquhar said, 'He insists that one portion is ready to weigh, sir. Several storeships, and some kind of escort.' He glanced meaningly at the man's red features. 'He is too much of a coward to lie, I think. He says that the ships will not sail because of our presence. Their cargo is probably very valuable.'

'*And* their destination.' Bolitho made his decision. 'Send them off in their boat. Then signal the squadron to close on *Lysander*. We will stand further to the south'rd.'

'Will they risk it, sir?'

'I would.' Bolitho looked at Javal. 'I will report your first lieutenant's part in all this. He did well. As did you.'

Risk, luck, coincidence, all had shared in this first real piece of vital intelligence. With his three seventy-fours staying well out to sea, and only *Buzzard*'s lookouts watching for the enemy's dash from port, Bolitho was in the best position to act as the situation dictated.

And when *Harebell* reached the admiral, it would be just a matter of time before a fleet, and not a mere squadron, came to complete what they had begun.

On the day that he watched the fishermen put over the side to begin their long haul back to the coast, Bolitho ordered his ships to their new position, some twenty miles south-west of Toulon. He wrote his orders and had them passed to each captain. He discussed the final details with Farquhar and Grubb, and when dusk finally descended he went to his cabin and enjoyed a filling meal of boiled pork from the cask, and the last of his cheese which he had carried from England.

As he sat at his table drinking a cup of coffee and listening to the creak and rattle of ship's gear, he thought of Falmouth and the empty house there. He thought, too, of the American captain, and the wife who was waiting for him in New Bedford. What a homecoming it would be. He could almost see it in his mind. How long would it be, he wondered, before he saw Falmouth again? He had been in *Lysander* for two months, and already it felt ten times as long. Perhaps now that luck was with them again time would pass more swiftly.

With that thought uppermost in his mind he went to his cot, and within minutes was in a deep, dreamless sleep.

It seemed as if his head had been on the pillow but a short while when he felt a hand on his shoulder. He awoke, staring into Allday's anxious face which shone yellow in a lantern above the cot.

'What is it?'

His senses returned and he struggled over the side of the cot. He had no further need to ask, and he cursed himself for sleeping so deeply. The night was alive with noise and violent motion, so that he almost fell as he groped his way to his chest.

Allday said, 'It's come on to blow, sir! Getting worse by the minute!'

Bolitho dragged on his breeches, staggering as the deck plunged and threw him against Allday.

'In the name of heaven, why wasn't I told of this?'

Allday said nothing, but turned as Ozzard appeared blinking in the door, another lantern above his head.

'Get the commodore's things, man!'

But Bolitho snapped, 'Just a coat. I must go on deck!'

Even before he reached the quarterdeck he knew it was no mere gale. It was a full-scale storm, and as he ducked beneath the poop deck beams he saw that the wheel was doubly manned, the seamen clinging to the spokes while the deck heaved violently to leeward.

It took several more moments to accustom his eyes to the dark, to pitch his hearing above the moan of wind, the boom and thunder of canvas overhead.

Figures darted past him, crouching and groping for hand-holds as spray lifted above the nettings and doused them violently before gurgling away through the scuppers. Every stay and shroud seemed to be vibrating and humming, and he found time to pity the awakened watch below, who even now must be fighting out along the yards to fist and reef the treacherous canvas.

He saw Farquhar, his slim figure very pale against the sea and sky, his hands cupped as he yelled to one of the lieutenants. He noticed Bolitho and lurched towards him, his fair hair streaming from his head. He was dressed only in shirt and breeches, and his feet were bare.

If any other evidence was needed to show the height of the emergency, Bolitho could not think of it.

Farquhar shouted, 'Wind's veered to the nor'-west, sir! I've ordered the hands to reef tops'ls and take in the forecourse!'

He swung round as a sound like a musket shot came from forward, and then changed to a great rippling tear as the foresail exploded into a mass of flapping fragments.

'They will be spared *that*!'

Bolitho clawed his way to the rail and peered along the slanting deck. To one side the sea was as black as pitch. To the other it lifted and surged in tremendous banks of foam, building up beneath the quarter until the lee gunports were awash. Of the other ships there was no sign, and he guessed that each captain would be too preoccupied to care much about *Lysander*'s plight.

He heard Grubb's deep voice rising like a bellow. 'Ease off, lads! You'll 'ave the sticks out of 'er else!'

A man slipped beneath the weather gangway and fell kicking and yelling in a flood of swirling water. He came up against an eighteen-pounder, and Bolitho could almost imagine that he heard his ribs stove in.

'In heaven's name, Captain, why so late? The squadron will be driven for miles in this!'

A broken halliard fell from aloft, writhing about the upper deck like a live thing. More would follow unless Farquhar acted, and immediately.

Farquhar spat out spray and replied, 'That *fool* Gilchrist! He left it too long! By God, where is that man, I'll have him – '

Bolitho gripped his arm. 'There is no time now! We must lie-to and make the best of it.'

Farquhar stared at him, nodding. 'Yes, sir. At once!' He sounded desperate.

Bolitho did not release his arm. 'Bring her about as soon as you've shortened sail!' He had to shout to make himself heard. 'We will lie-to under the main tops'ls!' He ducked, closing his eyes tightly as a wall of spray tumbled over the empty nettings and swept mercilessly across the deck and down to the one below. 'But have the main stays'l manned and ready to set in case the other carries away!'

He heard Farquhar's voice receding as he struggled along the rail, hand over hand, saw the blurred shapes of seamen hurrying to obey. Above in the darkness he could see the wildly flapping sails where the topmen were still fighting to obey the last order. Voices, too, caught up in the deafening chorus of wind and sea, of straining rigging and spars.

Grubb shouted harshly, 'Pass the word! Stand by to come about!' He blinked at Bolitho. 'I'll bet those damned Frogs are laughin', sir!'

Bolitho did not answer. But it was uppermost in his thoughts. A strong north-westerly was a curse to his squadron. To any French commander trying to gauge the right time to quit Toulon it would be merciful, a chance he could not possibly ignore.

He watched as Gilchrist's beanpole figure emerged above the quarterdeck ladder, shining dully in his long tarpaulin coat. Gilchrist had probably been more frightened of his captain than he had of the first storm signs. Or so eager to prove that he could manage any eventuality he had left it far too late for anything but submission.

He wiped his streaming face with one sleeve, feeling the sting of salt in his eyes and mouth. When he peered aloft again he saw that much of the canvas had vanished, although the fore topsail was only lashed to its yard at one end. At the other a great balloon of canvas filled and puffed as if it contained a living, savage monster. Something passed across the scudding cloud formations, and he ran to the rail as it struck the forecastle with a sickening thud.

A voice called hoarsely, 'Get that man below to the sickbay!' Then Lieutenant Veitch. 'Belay that order. There's nought the surgeon can do for him!'

Poor wretch, he thought. Fighting the lashing sail, with only his feet to support his body as he craned over the great, swaying yard. His messmates on either side of him, all cursing and yelling into the darkness, punching the wet, hard canvas until their nails were torn out, their knuckles raw. One slip, an extra gust of wind, and he had fallen.

'Man the braces there! Stand by on the quarterdeck!'

Grubb snarled, '*Ease* the spoke when I gives the word! Treat 'em like they was babies!'

'Helm a'lee!'

More figures staggered through the dismal gloom, a midshipman bleeding from the head, a seaman holding his arm to his side, teeth bared with agony.

'Lee braces! *Heave!*'

The *Lysander* dipped her seventeen-hundred tons of oak and artillery heavily into a maelstrom of bursting spray. Above, in a shortened, iron-hard rectangle, the reefed topsail seemed to swing independent of their muscle and bone, every mast groaning to the strain of wind and sea.

Bolitho saw it all, heard his ship and seamen fighting to bring the bows round and into the wind, to hold her under command. If the rudder failed, or the topsail was ripped to ribbons like the forecourse, it might be too late for them to set the staysail. And that could carry away just as easily.

But with the wheel hard over, the helmsmen's bare feet treading wet planking as if they were walking uphill, the two-decker responded. Bolitho watched the sea boiling inboard from the weather gangway to the beakhead, saw it surging across and down to the opposite bulwark, taking men and loose gear in its path. Much of it would find its way deep into the hull. The pumps must be going now, but in the din he could not hear them. Stores would be spoiled, fresh water, as precious as gunpowder, polluted and rendered useless.

He released the nettings and allowed the wind to thrust him along the tilting deck until he fought his way aft to the compass.

Grubb shouted, 'Ship's 'ead is almost due north, sir!' He turned to watch as a whimpering man was carried past. 'She might be able to 'old it!'

'*She must!*' Bolitho saw his words go home. 'If we run before this winu we'll never beat back in time!'

Grubb watched him go and then said to a master's mate, 'How say you, Mr. Plowman?'

Plowman gripped the binnacle for support, his coat shining like sodden silk in the feeble lamp. 'I *told* Mr. Gilchrist to call

all 'ands!' He added angrily, 'God rot 'im, 'e might 'ave been the death of us all!'

Grubb grimaced. 'Still time for *that*!'

Bolitho was on his way forward to the rail again when he heard a yell.

'Heads below! Fore t'gallant's coming adrift!'

Before anyone could move or act the uppermost spar on the foremast tilted violently to leeward, hung for a few agonising seconds and then plunged down like a tree. Stays and shrouds all followed it in a great mass of rasping cordage and blocks, until with a jarring crash it came to rest below the starboard bow, the furled topgallant sail showing through the darkness like some nightmare tusk.

Grubb shouted, 'She's payin' off, sir!' He threw his considerable weight on the wheel. 'It's like a bloody anchor up forrard!'

Bolitho saw Farquhar staggering along the weather gangway, drenched to the skin, one shoulder bare and bloodied by some fallen object from above. It was all plain to see. As if he were studying a diagram instead of watching a ship fighting for survival.

Had Herrick been in command at this moment none of it would have happened. No lieutenant would be too frightened to call him, and no matter what Herrick was like as a strategist and the squadron's second-in-command, he was a superb seaman.

Bolitho shouted, 'Get a strong party up forrard!' He strode past Farquhar, knowing that Allday was close on his heels. 'We don't have time to waste!'

Calls shrilled, and voices responded. Bolitho saw marines and seamen, some fully dressed, some naked, fighting through the torrential spray to where the boatswain and a handful of older men from the forecastle party were busy amidst the tangle of rigging.

Bolitho felt the ship lift and then dip heavily into a long trough, and heard several cries of alarm as the trapped topgallant mast and yard crashed against the hull.

He realised that Pascoe was already there and shouted, 'Are you in charge?'

Pascoe shook his head. 'Mr. Yeo is cutting some of the rigging adrift, sir!' He ducked like a prize-fighter, his arms bent, as a great wall of water surged amongst the gasping men. 'And Mr. Gilchrist is leading the main party outboard by the cathead!'

Bolitho nodded. 'Good.' To Allday he said, 'We'll add our weight. There's nothing more we can do aft.'

He groped his way down and through the huge coils of tarred rope, his shins and hands scarred within seconds.

A voice said 'Gawd, it's the commodore, lads!' Another muttered, 'Then we must be in a bad way!'

Bolitho peered over the side, seeing the frothy undertow beneath the bows, the broken mast surging and veering into the hull like a battering ram. In the darkness the jagged wood gleamed as if to mock their efforts. To put a seal on their hopes.

He saw Gilchrist waving his arms through the tangle, like a man seized by a terrible sea-creature.

'Axes, Mr. Yeo! Save the yard, but hack the mast away as soon as you can!'

A man tried to claw his way back from his precarious perch on the cathead, but Gilchrist seized him and forced him to look down past the massive anchor-stock, to the surging water below him.

'We save the ship, or go under together! Now catch a turn with that line, or I'll see your backbones tomorrow!'

Gilchrist's fury, his unintentional hint that there was indeed going to be a tomorrow, seemed to have an effect. Grunting and swearing they threw themselves into battle with the fallen spars, using their anger to hold fear at bay and drown the wail of the wind.

Bolitho worked alongside the anonymous figures, using the back-breaking work to steady his thoughts. The topgallant mast could be replaced. Herrick had made certain of a good stock of spare spars before leaving England. If the yard could be saved, the ship's sail-power should be normal again in a few days, once they enjoyed calmer weather. But it would take time. Time when they should have been on their station, the one he had so carefully selected to snare the enemy supply ships.

Gilchrist yelled, 'Mr. Pascoe! Take some men aft along the starboard gangway and grapple the spar!'

Pascoe nodded and touched the nearest men on shoulders or arms. 'Aye, sir!'

Gilchrist peered up at him. 'If you cannot save it, then at least make sure it causes no further harm to the hull!' He broke off, choking as spray leapt up and over the bowsprit.

When the water subsided in a great hissing torrent Bolitho saw that the man Gilchrist had been threatening had vanished. He was probably somewhere in the darkness, watching his ship moving away, his cries lost in the angry wave crests. More likely he had gone straight down. It was a sad fact that few sailors could swim. Bolitho found himself praying that the man had died quickly and had been spared the agony of being left out there alone.

Thud, thud, thud, the axes hacked savagely at the rigging, while other hands worked at hastily rigged tackles to sway the undamaged yard up and around the foremast.

'There she goes!'

The cry was taken up as with a grinding clatter of severed gear and cordage the released topgallant mast plunged freely down the lee side. Bolitho watched Pascoe's men struggling along the gangway trying to control the still-dangerous spar, and then caught his breath as a line parted and another went bar-taut, scraping along the gangway rail and catching Pascoe around the shoulders.

'*Belay those lines!*'

Midshipman Luce dashed down the gangway, heedless of the bursting spray.

'Cut him free!'

Another line snapped, and Bolitho felt his blood chill as Pascoe appeared to bow over the rail, dragged helplessly towards the sea by the surging mass of rigging.

But Luce was beside him now, his slim frame bent under the black ropes as he hacked upwards with an axe.

Yeo strode along the forecastle, his quick eye and twenty years at sea telling him instantly of the midshipman's danger.

'Avast there, Mr. Luce!'

But it was too late. As the keen blade slashed away one of the broken stays another tightened automatically, so that as Pascoe fell gasping into the arms of two seamen, Luce was pinned against the side, his arm taking the full weight. When the ship lifted sluggishly to the wind he cried out once, 'Oh God, help me!' Then as Yeo and the others reached him and cut the rigging free once and for all he fell senseless at their feet.

Bolitho said, 'Quick, Allday, take him below!'

Then he hurried along the gangway and helped Pascoe to his feet.

'How does it feel?'

Pascoe felt his spine and grimaced. 'That was near –' He stared along the deck. 'Where is Bill Luce, sir?' He struggled against the rail. 'Is he –'

'He was injured.' Bolitho felt the ship responding slowly to her freedom, indifferent perhaps to those who had suffered in the process. 'I have had him taken to the surgeon.'

Pascoe stared at him. 'Oh no, not after he saved my life!'

Bolitho sensed his distress, could see the grief despite the enclosing darkness.

He added, 'I will go below, Adam. You remain here.' It hurt him to continue, 'Others need you now.'

He walked aft, seeing Farquhar by the quarterdeck rail. As if he had never moved.

Farquhar blurted out, 'Thank you, sir! Seeing you there helped the men to rally.'

Bolitho looked at him. 'I doubt that. But one captain aft is enough!'

He peered up at the reefed topsail. Still iron-hard, but holding well, in spite of the enormous pressure.

He said, 'I am going to the sickbay.'

'Are you hurt, sir?'

'Call me instantly if anything changes.' He walked to the companion. 'No. Not physically, that is.'

As he made his way down and down by one ladder to the next he was conscious of the sea noises becoming muted, the new sounds of straining timbers, the smells of bilge and tar rising to greet him. Lanterns swayed and cast leaning shadows as he continued through the lower gun deck and below *Lysander*'s waterline, where natural light was unknown the year round.

Outside this small sickbay he found several seamen resting after treatment, some bandaged, some lying in an escape of sleep and rum. The air was thick with the combined smells of pain and blood.

He entered the sickbay where Henry Shacklock, the surgeon, was talking to some of his assistants as they arranged two more lanterns above his table.

Shacklock glanced up and saw Bolitho. '*Sir?*'

He was a tired-looking man with thin hair. In the swaying yellow light he appeared almost bald, although he was not yet thirty. Bolitho had found him to be a good doctor, which was unfortunately rare in King's ships.

'How is Mr. Luce?'

The men stood aside, and Bolitho realised that the midshipman was already lying on the table. He was naked, and his face was set in a frown, the skin very pale. Shacklock lifted a rough dressing from his shoulder.

Bolitho guessed that the rope had cut through the flesh and muscle like wire through cheese. The lower arm lay at an unnatural angle, the fingers unclenched and relaxed.

Shacklock held his own hand above the midshipman's arm, the palm open like a ruler. It was less than six inches below the point of his shoulder.

He said, 'It must come off, sir.' He pursed his lips. 'Even then . . .'

Bolitho looked down at Luce's pale face. Seventeen years of age. No age at all.

'Are you certain?'

What was the point? He had heard it asked so often.

'Yes.' Shacklock nodded to his assistants. 'The sooner the better. He might not come to his senses before it is done.'

At that moment Luce's eyes opened. They stayed fixed on Bolitho's face, unmoving, and yet in those few seconds they seemed to understand everything which had happened, and what was to come.

He made to move, but Bolitho gripped his uninjured shoulder. His skin was like ice, and his hair still wet with the spray from that other howling world three decks above.

He said, 'You saved Mr. Pascoe's life.' He kept his voice steady. 'Adam will come as soon as he can.'

Beyond the boy's head he saw Shacklock taking two knives from a case. One short, the other long and thin. An assistant was wiping something below a lantern, and as the deck tilted and the man lurched sideways he realised it was a saw.

Luce whispered quietly, 'My arm, sir?' He was starting to weep. '*Please*, sir!'

Bolitho reached out and took a cup of rum from a loblolly boy. 'Drink this.' He forced it to his lips. 'As much as you *can*.'

He saw it slopping out of his mouth, could feel his body
trembling as if in a terrible fever. It was all they had. Rum,
with opium to follow the operation as a sedative.

He heard footsteps and then Pascoe's voice, taut and barely
recognisable.

'The captain sends his respects, sir. We have just sighted
Nicator.'

Bolitho straightened his back but kept his hand on Luce's
shoulder.

'Thank you.' Around him the shadows loomed nearer, like
angels of death, as Shacklock's men waited to begin. 'Stay
with him, Adam.'

He made himself look at the midshipman. He was staring
up at him, the rum and tears mingling on his throat. Only his
mouth moved as he whispered again, *'Please.'*

He waited until Pascoe was by the boy's head and then said
to Shacklock, 'Do your best.'

The surgeon nodded. 'I have had the blades warmed to
lessen the shock, sir.'

As Bolitho made to leave he saw the surgeon give a signal,
heard Luce cry out as the assistants gripped his legs and held
his head back on the table.

Bolitho had reached the upper deck when Luce screamed.
The sound seemed to follow him up and into the wind, where
it ended abruptly.

*

Bolitho rested both hands on his chart and studied it for
several more seconds. The storm had blown itself out in two
long days and nights, so that the warm sunlight and the
gentle breeze in the sails made it feel as if the ship was all but
becalmed.

Around his table the other captains sat watching him, each
wrapped in his own thoughts, all weary from the storm's anger
and the battle for survival.

Throughout the scattered squadron seventeen men had
been killed. By falls from aloft, or being swept overboard.
Some had vanished without trace. As if they had never
been.

It was mid-afternoon, and with the ships sailing in a loose
formation once again Bolitho had ordered all his captains to
gather for a conference.

He looked at Javal's dark features. His news had been expected, and yet perhaps even to the last he had still hoped. But as they had sighted *Buzzard*'s topsails shortly after dawn the signal had been shouted down from the maintop. The French had put to sea. A dozen ships, maybe more, had sailed with the stiff north-west wind under their coat-tails, while Javal and his men had watched helplessly while they fought to keep the enemy in view. The French commander had even allowed for such an eventuality. Two frigates had swept out of the storm and had raked *Buzzard*'s rigging before standing off to follow the convoy into the darkness.

For a fighter like Javal it must have been terrible. With his rigging slashed and the storm mounting every minute, he had been forced to watch the French slipping away. He had tried to make contact with the squadron by firing signal guns and loosing off a flare. But while Gilchrist had waited too late and the ships of the line had steered comfortably along their allotted course the storm had made even that contact impossible.

Bolitho said slowly, 'The admiral should have examined the despatches sent in *Harebell*. He will assume that we are capable of standing watch over Toulon, or of shadowing any vessels which try to elude us.'

Overhead he heard the stamp of feet as Leroux's marines completed another drill. Hammers and adzes added their own sounds to show that the carpenter's crew were also busy completing storm repairs.

He looked at Herrick, wondering what he was thinking.

Probyn said heavily, 'Now that the French have avoided your er, ambush, it must leave us all in some doubt. Perhaps we placed too much value in hearsay, in rumour. Who knows where those French ships may be now?' He looked slowly round the table. 'Let alone what we can hope to do without information?'

Bolitho watched him impassively. Probyn had been careful to use 'we'. He had meant 'you'.

Javal shrugged and yawned. 'I could detach from the squadron, sir. I might be able to find some if not all of the Frenchmen. After all, the storm will not have made their passage an easy one.'

Bolitho felt them looking at him. Some would understand, perhaps share his dilemma.

If he sent the *Buzzard* in pursuit he would be without 'eyes'. The two-deckers and the prize ship would have their visibility reduced to the vision of the best masthead lookout. So, with little agility or speed to investigate, he had to hold on to his one and only frigate.

Probyn added, 'Of course, we could return to Gibraltar, sir. Better to add our strength to any fleet which may be assembling than to wander blindly to no purpose.'

Herrick spoke for the first time. 'That would be an admission of failure! It would be the wrong decision, in my opinion.' He looked at Bolitho, his eyes level. 'We know how you must feel, sir.'

Farquhar snapped abruptly, 'It is the devil's own luck!'

Javal said, 'It's the devil's own *choice*.' He looked at Bolitho curiously. 'For you, sir.'

'Yes.'

Bolitho let his gaze move along and down across the chart of the Mediterranean. All those miles. Even if he were right in his guesswork, and it was no more than that as Probyn had stated, he might still fail to make contact with the enemy. Ships could pass one another in the night or in foul weather and be none the wiser. An empire could fall because of a wrong choice, a hasty decision.

He said, 'This is what we will do.' It had come out as if it had been there in his mind from the beginning. 'Our present position, as far as we can estimate, is about sixty miles west of Corsica's north coast.' He tapped the chart with his dividers. 'Cape Corse. The storm carried us too far to the east'rd to make another passage profitable.' He saw them crane forward above the table. 'So we will continue, and once around the north cape of Corsica we will steer south-east.' He watched his dividers moving remorselessly further and further down the Italian coastline. 'We will put into Syracuse to take on water and land our badly injured people. The Sicilians may have news for us. They are at peace with the French, but have little love for them.'

He looked up sharply. 'While we are at anchor, *Buzzard* will sail independently, around the eastern side of Sicily, by way of the Messina Strait, and make a rendezvous with the squadron off Malta. I will be able to give you better information, Captain Javal, once we have made some progress.' He eyed them separately. He was committed. And he had committed each one of them, and every man-jack in the squadron.

Herrick cleared his throat. 'And then, sir?'

'*Then*, Captain Herrick.' He held his gaze, seeing the worry building up on his face. 'We will know what to expect.' He smiled briefly. 'I hope.'

Probyn spread his heavy hands on the table. They were like pink crabs. 'If we fail there also, sir, I'd not be happy to face the admiral.'

Bolitho faced him calmly. 'It is support I want, Captain Probyn. Not sympathy.'

Spray pattered against the stern windows, and he added, 'I think it best if you return to your ships. The wind is freshening, by the feel of it.'

The chairs scraped back from the table and they looked at each other like strangers.

Probyn gathered up his hat and sword and said, 'I trust that new orders will be passed to us, sir?' He did not look at him as he spoke.

Herrick snapped, 'There is no need for that, surely?'

'I think there is.' Probyn fiddled with his sword belt. 'I would not wish to insist upon it.'

Bolitho nodded. 'It will be done.'

Farquhar rapped on the screen door with his knuckles, and when the sentry appeared he said, 'Signal for the boats. Tell the first lieutenant to assemble the side party.'

Probyn asked, 'How is your first lieutenant, by the way?'

'Adequate.' Farquhar watched him coldly.

Bolitho turned away. 'You know him then?'

Probyn coughed. 'Not really, sir. Perhaps a passing acquaintance.'

They took their leave, as boat by boat they were pulled back to their various commands.

Herrick was the last. He said simply, 'The fore t'gallant mast, sir. When I knew of *Lysander*'s difficulties in the storm, I got to thinking. Maybe she took a ball through the fore-rigging and the rope woolding around the mast hid the damage. It is not unknown.'

Bolitho smiled. 'Perhaps. But it was none of your doing.'

Bolitho saw him looking around the decks and tried to read his mind. Loss, anxiety, or merely curiosity?

'And you, Thomas. Is everything satisfactory?'

Herrick turned to watch his barge pulling for the main chains.

'*Osiris* is a smart ship, sir. I've no complaints. But she's no heart, no zest.'

Bolitho wanted to reach out for him. To make him know that the sense of loss went both ways. But it was not yet time, and he knew it.

He said, 'Take care, Thomas.'

The marine guard shuffled to attention and the bosun's mates raised their silver calls in preparation to see Herrick over the side. But he hung back, his face lined with emotions.

Then he said, 'If you take the squadron to the Turkish forts and beyond, you'll not find *me* far astern.' He faltered, his eyes pleading. 'I just wanted you to know. To *understand*.'

Bolitho held out his hand. 'I do, Thomas.' He gripped it tightly. 'Now.'

He watched Farquhar and Herrick exchange salutes, and then walked slowly across the quarterdeck to the weather side.

The sails were booming in confusion while the ship lay hove-to to rid herself of her visitors, and Bolitho did not hear the footsteps beside him.

It was Pascoe, his dark eyes heavy with strain. He had been standing watches and carrying out his duties throughout the storm, but at every available moment he had been below with his friend.

Bolitho asked, 'Is something wrong?'

Pascoe lifted his arms and let them fall again. 'Sir, I – ' He shook his head. 'He is gone. He died a minute ago.'

Bolitho watched him, seeing his distress. Sharing it.

'He was a fine boy.'

He touched his arm, turning him slightly so that some passing marines should not see his face.

'And it is often harder to accept that sailors give their lives to the sea as much as they do in battle.'

Pascoe shivered. 'He never complained. Not after that first terrible cut. I held his hand. And just today I thought he was a little better. And then – ' He broke off, unable to finish.

Farquhar strode to the rail and touched his hat. 'Permission to get the squadron under way, sir?' He glanced at Pascoe, his eyes without compassion. 'The wind is certainly freshening.'

'If you please. And signal *Buzzard* to take station to lee'rd and ahead of the squadron. He knows what to expect.' He stepped in front of Pascoe. 'I think this officer might be excused from duty for the present.'

Farquhar nodded. 'Very well.'

But Pascoe said, 'I'm all right now, sir.' He adjusted his hat and moved towards the ladder. 'I'd like to attend to my work, if I may.'

Farquhar's lips twisted in a smile. 'Then it is settled.'

Bolitho followed them to the rail, seeing the seamen manning the braces and halliards, waiting to execute the first part of his new orders.

Pascoe hesitated, his foot in the air above the gun deck. 'There is one thing, sir. When will we be burying him?'

'At dusk.' He watched the pain in Pascoe's eyes.

'I just thought. My sword. I'd like it to go over with him. I've not much else.'

Bolitho waited until Pascoe had joined his division and then returned to the poop ladder.

Grubb remarked quietly, 'A fine young officer 'e'll be one day, sir.'

Bolitho nodded. 'He suits me very well as he stands.'

'Aye.' The master shaded his red-rimmed eyes to watch the flapping pendant high above the deck. 'There's some 'oo can give orders, but never learn nuthin'. Thank God 'e's not one o' *them*.'

Bolitho continued up the ladder and walked right aft to the gilded taffrail.

Below the poop he heard the helmsman's cry, 'Course due east, sir! Steady as she goes!'

He watched the lithe frigate forging swiftly ahead of her bulky consorts, but for once felt no envy of her freedom. This was his place, and only the rights of his decisions would decide if he should hold it.

He thought of Pascoe and Herrick, and Allday who was moving about in the cabin below.

And this time he had to be right, if only for men such as these.

II

The Letter

'WILL that be all for now, sir?' Moffitt, the clerk, regarded Bolitho gloomily, his weedy frame angled to the deck.

'Yes. Thank you.' Bolitho leaned back in his chair and loosened his neckcloth. 'Tell Ozzard to light some lanterns.' He looked astern through the great windows at the fiery orange sunset.

One more dragging day. It was two weeks since he had committed his ships to the passage south, and to all intents they had the sea to themselves. Day after day, using the light winds to steer south-east along the Italian coastline, and then tacking around to the westward to follow the hazy shores of Sicily. Now they were heading east again, with the island of Sicily lying about thirty miles off the larboard bow. And apart from a few Arab craft with their strange lateen rig, they had been unable to make contact with another living soul. They had sighted some isolated sails, but they had made off before the slow-moving seventy-fours could draw near enough to examine them.

Bolitho stared at the empty desk, wondering why he bothered to dictate another empty day's report for Moffitt's benefit. It was unlikely to carry much weight, unless as additional evidence at his own court martial.

He wondered what the *Buzzard* was doing, and if she had had any luck in finding information about the vanished Frenchmen. Or if, once free of his commodore's eye, and his needs blurred by distance, Javal had gone off to seek gains of his own. He knew he was being unfair to Javal, just as he understood that it was his own desperation which was causing it.

He stood up and strode to the door. It had been his custom for as long as he could remember to find peace, if not answers to his doubts, while watching sunsets. He ran quickly up the ladder and on to the poop deck, allowing the north-westerly to play through his shirt, to ease away the heat and staleness of the day. He walked to the weather side and gripped the nettings, watching the vast spread of copper and gold strengthening as it hardened along the horizon. It was very beautiful, even awesome, and he was not surprised to find he was still moved by it. He had watched the sun's parting display from every sort of deck, from the chill wastes of the Atlantic, to the scorching magnificence of the Great South Sea.

Bolitho saw *Nicator*'s fore topsail flapping and then refilling as she changed course slightly astern of *Osiris*. How untroubled the three ships must appear. If there had been anyone to see them pass. Nothing to reveal the teeming life within their rounded hulls, or the work of repairing storm damage which even now was still going on. Changing watches, sail and gun drill, eating and sleeping. It was their world. His world.

And yet, even after a full day of it, probably a twin of the one before, and the next beyond it, these men could still find time to escape from each other in their own way. Bone carving, and scrimshaw work, intricate designs made out of rope and scraps of metal, it was difficult to understand how such delicate and finely made objects could come from the hands of British seamen. Snuff-boxes, too, much prized in the wardroom by less experienced officers, which had been worked and polished from chunks of salt beef. Such boxes were as hard and as brightly polished as mahogany, and said much for their maker's skill as well as for their digestion under normal circumstances.

'Deck there! Land on the lee bow!'

Bolitho walked to the opposite side and peered towards the other horizon, already deep purple as the sky followed the retreating sun like a curtain. That would be a part of Malta, he thought, Gozo most likely.

Below the poop rail he heard a master's mate bark, 'You, what's yer name? Larssen, is it?' A mumbled reply and then the same voice. 'I told yer, I told yer, an' I *told* yer! Watch the compass and watch the set of the sails. Don't just stand a'gawpin' until the ship pays off under yer! Jesus, you'll never rate quartermaster, not in a 'undred years!'

Another voice this time. Bolitho recognised the haughty
lilt of Lieutenant Fitz-Clarence. 'What's the fuss, Mr Bagley?'

The master's mate replied, 'Nuthin' much. Just that the
poor old ship is so full of furriners I 'ave to tell 'em everythin'
twice!'

Bolitho began to walk loosely back and forth across the
empty poop. Bagley was right of course. Like many King's
ships, *Lysander* had gathered a good portion of foreign seamen
into her belly. Swedes and Spaniards, Hanoverians and Danes.
There were eleven Negroes, and one Canadian who spoke
better French than Farquhar.

He thought suddenly of the American captain, John Thurgood. He would have dropped his cargo and be on his return
run by now. His would not be the only happy homecoming.
The Spanish sailors whom Bolitho had sent to the barquentine
from the prize ship *Segura* would make their wives and mothers
weep and laugh when Thurgood sent them ashore in their own
country.

He paused by the rail again and looked astern. But the
Segura was too well hidden by the other ships to be seen. He
sighed. He had sent some of her crew to an American barquentine, and one of her boats he had given to some French
fishermen in exchange for information. Information which he
had been unable to transform into results. Because of the
storm? Or because he had failed to grasp the situation completely, and by so doing had failed his squadron?

Feet clattered on a ladder and the midshipman of the watch
approached him warily.

'Well, Mr. Glasson?'

The midshipman touched his hat. 'Mr. Fitz-Clarence's
respects, sir. The masthead has reported sighting land to the
south-east. The master confirms it is Malta, sir.'

'Thank you.'

Bolitho looked at him gravely. Glasson was seventeen, and
had taken over as signals midshipman following Luce's death.
There was no other similarity. Glasson was hard and sharp-
featured, with a tongue and a sense of discipline to match.
He would make a bad lieutenant, if he lived that long. It was
strange and pitiful how many there were like Glasson. Who
never learned from the frightful stories of mutiny, when the
power of the quarterdeck became a small and isolated com-

munity in the twinkling of an eye. Between the wars there
has been Bligh's *Bounty*, which had captured the nation's
imagination. Civilians were ever eager to seek out the good or
evil of happenings in which they were not involved, and
where they suffered no threat or inconvenience. Then the
great uprisings at the Nore and Spithead, both caused by
grievances long-outstanding by the men of the fleet. And just
before he had sailed for Gibraltar to hoist his broad pendant
in *Lysander* Bolitho had listened, shocked and appalled, to the
latest evidence of what could happen when men and their
resources were pressed beyond limits. H.M. frigate *Hermione*
had sailed into the Spanish port of La Guaira and surrendered
herself to the enemy. Her officers had been butchered in the
most horrible manner, and some of her loyal hands had
suffered a similar fate. The mutineers had offered their ship
to an enemy in exchange for their own freedom. Bolitho did
not know much more of the mutiny, other than that the
frigate had been under the command of a tyrant. As he looked
at Glasson, much of whose confidence was fast departing
under his commodore's stare, he marvelled that the lesson
still went unheeded.

'What are your hopes for the future?'

Glasson drew himself up. 'To serve my King, sir, and to
gain my own command.'

'Very commendable.' Bolitho added dryly, 'Did you learn
anything from duties aboard our prize?'

The midshipman relaxed slightly. 'The Dons who man her
are dolts. They know nothing, and their vessel is in a filthy
state.'

Bolitho did not hear him, he was thinking of the letter, the
French agent named Yves Gorse. He could feel the blood
rushing through his brain like fire. Suppose the Frenchman
did not know which vessel should be bringing instructions
from Toulon? With communications so difficult, and the final
French intentions still a well-guarded secret, it was likely he
would know little about the form of delivery.

He turned to Glasson. 'My compliments to the flag captain.
I should like him to join me on the poop.'

Farquhar arrived five minutes later to find Bolitho striding
from side to side, hands clasped behind him, as if he were in
a state of trance.

Farquhar suggested, 'You have come upon a fresh idea, sir?'

Bolitho stopped and looked at him. 'I think maybe others gave it to me. I was too involved with my anxieties to heed the obvious.'

'Sir?'

'I heard the master's mate, Bagley, reprimanding one of the helmsmen. Because he did not understand him immediately.'

Farquhar frowned. 'That would be Larssen, sir. I can have him removed.'

'No, *no*.' Bolitho faced him. 'It was not that. And something Glasson said about the *Segura* just now.'

'I see, sir.' Farquhar was lost. 'At least, I think I do.'

Bolitho smiled. '*Segura*. We have been keeping her without knowing why. Vanity perhaps? Evidence that we did not fail at everything? And as time went on we forgot she was there.'

Farquhar watched him doubtfully, his eyes glowing in the sunset. 'She's too slow for scouting, sir. I thought we'd agreed on that.'

Bolitho nodded. 'Have a new prize crew detailed, and send the remaining Spaniards into the squadron. Tell a lieutenant of your choice that I want the prize crew to be as *foreign* as he can find!'

'Aye, sir.' There was not even surprise now. Farquhar probably believed the strain and responsibility had at last driven him mad.

'And I want it done *immediately*. Signal the squadron to heave-to before the light goes completely.'

Farquhar made to hurry away. 'What will the lieutenant be required to do, if I may venture to ask, sir?'

'*Do*, Captain?' He turned away to conceal his sudden excitement. 'He will sail the *Segura* into Malta under false colours, American, I think. And there he will deliver a letter for me.'

Farquhar exclaimed, 'The French agent?'

'Just so.' He started to pace. 'I suggest you start at once.'

Farquhar waited a moment longer. 'It's a great risk, sir.'

'You told me that before. As did Thomas Herrick. Have you never taken risks?'

Farquhar smiled. 'The men will most probably desert once they are in Malta. And the officer in charge will be seized and likely hanged. The Knights of Malta are only too aware of the danger in incurring France's displeasure. They have been friendly to us in the past.' He shrugged. 'But the French army and navy are much nearer than they were then.'

'I agree. Nor would I expect a junior lieutenant to be used in this way.'

Farquhar watched him with new interest. 'You intend to go with *Segura*?'

'Under all circumstances. Yes.'

*

Midshipman Glasson had been right about one thing, Bolitho decided. The prize ship *Segura* was not only dirty, but also contained so many smells of varying ages and strength that it was hard not to retch when between decks.

It was pitch-dark by the time the new prize crew were ferried across in exchange for the remaining Spaniards, and with two good hands on the wheel and canvas reduced to a minimum for the night *Segura* was left to her own devices.

Bolitho sat in the tiny cabin and munched some salt pork and iron-hard biscuits which he tried to dissolve in the ship's plentiful supply of red wine.

Farquhar had picked Lieutenant Matthew Veitch to accompany him, and he had already proved that he was as good aboard an unfamiliar vessel as he had been directing *Lysander*'s eighteen-pounders during their fight against the two Frenchmen. In his middle-twenties, Veitch appeared a good deal older and more experienced than his age suggested. He came from the north of England, from Tynemouth, and his hard accent, added to his normally stern features, made him seem too advanced for his years. But he could wipe it away with a ready smile, and Bolitho had noticed that his seamen liked and respected him.

Plowman, the senior master's mate, was again selected to join the expedition, and Mr. Midshipman Arthur Breen, a carrot-headed sixteen-year-old whose face was a mass of freckles, completed the vessel's senior authority.

They had been so busy settling into their new ship that the shadowy topsails of the three seventy-fours had vanished into the gathering darkness before anyone had found time to comment.

Bolitho looked up as Veitch entered the cramped cabin.

'Watch yourself!'

But it was too late. Veitch gave a gasp as his head cracked violently against a deck beam.

Bolitho pointed to a chest. 'Sit down and save your skull.' He pushed a wine bottle towards him. 'Is everything secure?'

'Aye, sir.' Veitch threw back his head and drained a metal goblet. 'I've got 'em standing watch and watch. It keeps 'em busy, and makes sure we don't get pounced on by some enemy patrol.'

Bolitho listened to the vessel's unfamiliar sounds, the rattle of rigging, the very near movements of the rudder. *Segura* was roundly-built, probably Dutch originally, whenever *originally* had been. Her holds were spacious for her size, and packed to the seams with cargo and gunpowder. Her sail plan was austere, and manageable with the minimum amount of hands. Again, it made her almost certain to be Dutch-built. Profitable, both in space and size of crew, she had doubtless worked every coastline from the Baltic to the African shores. But she was old, and her Spanish masters had let her go badly. Plowman had already reported on the poor quality of her standing rigging and topping lifts, some of which he described as being 'as thin as a sailor's wallet'.

But Plowman was Grubb's right-hand man. Like the master, he was not content with unreliable workmanship.

Bolitho smiled to himself. If Plowman was bothered, the seamen selected for the prize crew appeared quite the opposite. Even aboard the *Lysander,* as he had spoken to them briefly before they had clambered into the boats, he had noticed their grins and nudges, the cheerful acceptance of their surprise role. Escape from boredom, something to do to break the daily routine, or maybe the fact that each was hand-picked helped to extend this carefree atmosphere. The notion they had been chosen mostly for their foreign tongues had not apparently arisen.

He could hear someone singing a strange, lilting song, and a regular chorus of voices as the watch below joined in. There was an unusual smell of cooking in the damp air between decks, too, further evidence of their new identity.

Veitch grinned. 'They've settled in well, sir. That's Larssen singing, and the one detailed to cook is a Dane, so God knows what we'll be eating tonight!'

Bolitho looked round as Plowman entered the cabin. He

said, 'I've left Mr. Breen with the watch, sir.' He took the wine and regarded it gratefully. 'Well, thankee, sir.'

Bolitho glanced at them approvingly. Each, including himself, wore a plain blue coat, and a scruffier trio it would be hard to find. Typical, he hoped, of the countless hundreds of trading captains who sailed under every flag and carried any cargo they could find for a profit.

'Tomorrow we'll run for Malta.' Bolitho watched as Plowman tamped black tobacco in a long clay pipe. 'I am Captain,' he smiled gravely, 'Richard Pascoe. You can keep your own names. Mr. Veitch will be first mate. Mr. Plowman, second. My cox'n, Allday, will be filling the part of boatswain.'

Plowman hesitated and then thrust a great pot of tobacco across the rickety table.

'If you'd care to try it, sir? It's, well, it's *fair*.'

Bolitho took a pipe from a sandalwood box above the small chart table and handed another to Veitch.

'Anything once, Mr. Plowman!'

He became serious. 'I will go ashore with Allday and a boat's crew. You will appear to be preparing to open hatches. But be ready to cut the cable and put to sea if anything goes wrong. If this should happen, you can stand inshore for a further two nights. Where I have marked on the chart. If there is still no signal from me, you must rejoin the squadron at Syracuse. Captain Farquhar will act accordingly.'

The air thickened visibly with smoke, and Bolitho said, 'Fetch some more wine from the locker. Like our people up forrard, I feel strangely at peace. Tonight anyway.'

Shoes clicked overhead and Veitch smiled. 'Young Mr. Breen is alone up there. He is feeling like a post-captain, no doubt!'

Bolitho let the drowsiness move over him. He thought of Pascoe, his dark eyes eager and pleading as he had asked to be allowed to join him. He touched the old sword which lay against the table. Perhaps he should have left it in *Lysander*. If anything happened to him, the sword would probably disappear forever. And it was important in some strange way that Pascoe should have it. One day.

He did not see Veitch give a wink to Plowman, who rose and said, 'I'd better go an' relieve Mr. Breen, sir.'

Veitch nodded. 'And I must go forrard and see that all is well.'

He stood up and cracked his head again.

'Damn these stingy shipbuilders, sir!' He grinned ruefully. 'A ship of the line maybe is crowded, but she keeps a man's head on his shoulders!'

Alone once more, Bolitho leaned over his chart and studied it beneath a spiralling lantern. He removed his blue coat and loosened his neckcloth, feeling the sweat running freely down his spine. It was stiflingly hot, and the wine had not slaked his thirst.

Allday entered the cabin. 'I'm bringing something to eat in a minute, sir.' He wrinkled his nose. 'This hull stinks like Exeter market!'

'The heat is no help to us.' Bolitho threw down his dividers. 'I will go on deck for a breath of air directly.'

'As you will, sir.' Allday watched him pass. 'I will send word when your meal is ready.'

He looked round the untidy cabin and shrugged. Damp, dirty and smelly it certainly was. But after the oppressive heat of the day it felt almost cool. He saw the empty wine bottles and chuckled. The commodore's heat was probably an inner one.

*

'Brail up the fores'l.'

Bolitho shaded his eyes to examine the untidy sprawl of sand-coloured fortifications which protected every entrance to Valletta harbour. As they had made their slow approach, and had watched the sun rise behind Malta's weather-worn defences, it had been hard for some of the seamen to see it for anything but a fortress.

'Steady as you go.' Plowman shifted his sturdy frame around the helmsmen, a pipe jutting from his jaw.

Bolitho knew that he, like most of the others, was finding it difficult to act in this casual and slack fashion after the rigid discipline of a King's ship. And at no other time was there anything more important about a ship's appearance than when entering harbour.

Bolitho ran his eye along the littered deck. Seamen lounged against either bulwark, pointing at landmarks, some with genuine interest, others with elaborate pretence.

Midshipman Breen said, 'I've heard of this island many times, sir. I never thought I'd ever see it.'

Plowman grinned. 'Aye. Valletta was so named after the Grand Master of the Knights in honour of 'is defence of it against the Turks.'

'Were you here then?' Breen watched the master's mate with undisguised awe.

' 'Ardly, Mr. Breen. That was over two 'undred years back!' He looked at Veitch and shook his head. 'Was I 'ere indeed!'

The nearest fortress was gliding abeam now, its upper rampart crowded with colourful figures. It was apparently used as much as a thoroughfare as a bastion. Beyond it, Bolitho saw the glittering water opening up to receive the *Segura*. The harbour was busy with shipping and tiny oared boats which scurried back and forth from vessels to jetties like water-beetles. There were a few schooners, gaunt Arab dhows, and the more common feluccas with their huge lateen sails. Two painted and gilt-encrusted galliasses lay beside a flight of stone steps. Like things from the past. They might have looked not too much out of place when the Romans had conquered England, Bolitho thought. The Knights of Malta had used them very successfully over the centuries for harrying Turkish ports and shipping, and had done much to drive the Turks' influence away from the West, it was hoped for good.

But now, Malta's role had changed again. It had withdrawn on to its own resources, combing revenue and trade from ships which came to the harbour, or anchored out of sheer necessity through storm or attack by corsairs.

'Stand by the anchor.'

Bolitho strode to the foot of the mainmast and watched for any sign of a challenge. In fact, there was little interest, so he guessed that *Segura* was not the first vessel to enter wearing the American flag.

Allday whispered, 'By God, it will take Mr. Gilchrist a year to get these lads to jump like seamen again.' He grinned as one of the men spat deliberately on the deck and then grinned somewhat sheepishly at his companions. Such an act would have cost him a dozen lashes in *Lysander*.

Veitch called, 'Hands wear ship!'

Bolitho took a brass telescope and trained it on the longest stone jetty. Boats were already shoving off, laden to their gunwales with fruit, basketware and probably women as well. For despite the original Christian standards and guidance within these stout walls, the core had long since deteriorated, and it was hinted that even the Knights themselves looked more to personal enjoyments than to heaven.

'Helm a'lee!'

The *Segura* tilted above her shadow, the patched sails barely moving as she headed into the wind, and her rusting anchor splashed into clear water.

'Mr. Veitch. If you allow these bumboats alongside, I suggest you make certain their occupants stay in them. You can let a few aboard at a time. They'll get out of control otherwise.'

Veitch gave a rare smile. 'Aye, sir. It'd be a powerful combination, eh? A hold full of wine, some British tars and whatever mischief these traders are about to offer!'

Allday was already mustering a small but fearsome-looking anchor watch. Each man was armed with a cutlass, and in addition a heavy wooden stave.

'Lower the boat.'

Bolitho wiped his face and throat. It was more stifling in the harbour than below decks.

The first craft were already alongside, the merchants and boatmen standing upright to display their wares, and vieing with each other in a variety of tongues.

Veitch came aft again. 'All done, sir. I've got two swivels loaded with canister, and a stand of muskets hidden under the fo'c'sle. I noticed that the harbour batteries face seaward, so we'll be all right for the present.'

Bolitho nodded. 'People who build fortresses often make that mistake. They never expect an attack from the rear.'

He thought of the charge down a Spanish hillside, the crackle of musket fire, and the marines cheering like fiends as they went in with their bayonets fixed.

'Just as well.'

'Boat's lowered, sir.'

Allday strode to the bulwark by the main shrouds as a dark-skinned little man wearing a turban and hung about with beads, bottles and gaudy daggers tried to climb on to the deck. 'Wait for the order, *Mustapha*!' Allday cupped his hand under the man's chin and sent him pitching back into the water. It raised a chorus of laughter and jeers from the unfortunate bumboatman's companions, who probably considered that this vessel's master, if hard-hearted, was at least going to be fair to all.

Veitch followed Bolitho to the rail. 'If an official comes aboard, sir, shall I bluff it out?'

Bolitho had been in Malta before. He smiled grimly. 'Be guided by Mr. Plowman. I suspect he has visited here on *other* unorthodox missions. The port officers may decide to wait until you show signs of unloading. But if they come and ask for your papers, tell them what I told you to say. That we had to throw them overboard when chased by an unknown ship. You will find a bag of gold coins in the cabin to grease the hawse for you.'

Plowman grinned at the lieutenant's uncertainty. 'Love you, Mr. Veitch! Port officials are the same everywhere, an' with more an' more Yankee ships finding their ways into the Mediterranean they'll not want to lose a new sort of trade!'

Bolitho threw one leg over the rail. 'And watch our people. There may be French spies amongst these bumboatmen. It'll do no harm to spread the notion anyway!'

He clambered down into the *Segura*'s remaining longboat. 'Shove off.'

As the boat pulled away he saw one of the traders tap smartly on a pile of rugs, and from beneath it he also saw a smooth, rounded arm pushing the covering aside. It was no man's arm. With *Segura*'s captain out of the way, the real trading was about to begin.

Allday murmured, 'Top of the stairs, sir. Two officers of some kind.'

But the officers paid them little attention, other than a courteous nod, and continued to watch the anchored newcomer, possibly judging the right moment to board her.

Bolitho stood on the hot stonework and waited for Allday and one other to climb up beside him. The seaman was the Swede, Larssen. He had a cheerful, trusting expression, and one of the broadest pairs of shoulders Bolitho had seen.

Allday remarked, 'In case we run into a spot of trouble.' He paused and looked at him. 'You all right, sir?'

Bolitho replied, 'Of course. Don't fuss.' He turned away.

'Send the boat away. We will attract as little attention as possible.'

He heard Allday speaking to the boat's crew and tried not to keep plucking the shirt away from his body. It was wringing with sweat, and he felt strangely light-headed. The wine? Some of the food he had eaten last night? Inwardly, another more likely reason was already forming and it was all he could do to conceal his sudden anxiety.

It was improbable, surely. He gritted his teeth, willing Allday to finish with the boat and follow him into some shadow. *But it was not impossible.* Nearly nine years ago, in the Great South Sea. The fever had all but killed him. He had had a few bouts of it since, but not for a year or so. He almost cursed aloud. It could not be. It must not happen now of all times.

Allday said, 'Ready, sir.'

'Good. Now let us find that address and finish the matter.' He swayed and touched Allday's shoulder. '*Damn!*'

As he pushed his way through a group of chattering traders, Allday watched him with sudden alarm.

Larssen asked, 'The *capitan*? Is he not well?'

Allday gripped his arm tightly. 'Listen, and listen good. If it's what I think it is, he's going to be all aback within the hour. Stay with me and do whatever I do, see?'

The Swede shrugged. 'Yes, sir, Mr. All-Day!'

Mercifully the address was not far from the harbour stairs. In fact, the whitewalled building was attached to one of the smaller fortresses as if for support, and from a broad balcony Bolitho could see the end of a large telescope trained across the anchorage like a gun.

He felt beneath his coat to make sure his pistol was loose and ready to draw. He was taking a great gamble. Perhaps this French agent already knew of the vessel's fate which had been entrusted with this letter. The convoy which *Buzzard* had chased, and with which the ship had been sailing, might have been into Malta, left word and gone on to its intended destination.

But he still believed it unlikely. A letter of such importance, if such it was, would have been carried by one of the French escorting frigates and then sent ashore by boat, probably at night.

He said shortly, 'Come along. We shall have to make haste.'

The lower part of the building was filled with wine casks and mounds of straw for packing bottles. A few Maltese labourers were rolling empty barrels down a ramp to a cellar, and a bored-looking man with a ruffled shirt and mustard-coloured breeches was writing in a ledger on the top of another cask.

He looked up, his eyes wary. '*Si?*' He could have been almost anything, from Greek to Dutchman.

Bolitho said, 'I only speak English. I'm master of the American ship which has just anchored.'

The man did not reply at once, but there was no doubt in his eyes, no lack of understanding.

Then he said, 'American. Yes. I understand.'

Bolitho cleared his throat and tried to keep his voice steady. 'I wish to see *M'sieu* Gorse.'

Again the unwavering stare. But no cry of alarm, no rush of feet from this man's assistants.

He replied eventually, 'I am not *certain* that I can arrange it.'

Allday stepped forward, his face bleak. 'If the cap'n says he wants to see him, that's it, matey! We ain't come all this way with a goddamn letter just to be kept waiting!'

The man gave a tight smile. 'I 'ave to be careful.' He looked meaningly at the harbour. 'So do you.'

He closed the ledger and beckoned them to some narrow stone steps.

Bolitho looked at Allday. 'Stay here with Larssen.' His mouth was completely dry, and the roof of it was burning like hot sand. He shook his head with sudden impatience. 'No arguments! If things go wrong now, one will have as much of a chance as three!' He tried to smile, to reassure him. 'I'll call soon enough if need be.'

He turned his back and followed the man up the steps. Through a door and into a long room, one side of which was open to the harbour and the spread of ships and buildings which shimmered in the sunlight like a great tapestry.

'Ah, *Capitaine*!' A white figure moved from the balcony. 'I 'alf expected it would be you.'

Yves Gorse was short and rotund. He had a thick black beard, as if to compensate for his complete baldness, and small, delicate hands which were never still.

Bolitho eyed him calmly. 'I would have been here sooner, but I ran foul of a British frigate. Had to throw my papers overboard, but managed to shake the bastard off in a storm.'

'I see.' Gorse pointed one delicate hand to a chair. 'Please be seated. You look unwell, *Capitaine*?'

'I'm well enough.'

'Per'aps.' Gorse walked to the window and stared down at the water. 'And you are called?'

'Pascoe. It's a Cornish name.'

'I am aware of that, *Capitaine*.' He turned with remarkable lightness. 'But I am not aware of any *Capitaine* Pascoe?'

Bolitho shrugged. 'In this game we must learn to trust each other, surely?'

'*Game*?' Gorse moved around the room. 'It was never that. Although your country is still too young to appreciate the dangers.'

Bolitho retorted angrily, 'Have you forgotten about *our* Revolution? I seem to recall it came a goodly few years before yours!'

'*Touché*!' Gorse smiled, showing small but perfect teeth. 'I meant no offence. Now this letter. May I 'ave it?'

Bolitho pulled it from his pocket. 'You see, *M'sieu*, I trust *you*.'

Gorse opened the letter and held it in a patch of sunlight. Bolitho tried not to watch him, to search for some sign that Gorse had noticed how the letter had been re-sealed. Gorse, however, seemed satisfied. No, relieved was more the word for it.

He said, 'Good. Now per'aps you will take some wine. Better than the muck you will be carrying toer, *where* are you bound?'

Bolitho clenched his fingers in his pockets to control his limbs. They felt as if they were shaking so badly that Gorse must surely have noticed. This was the moment. If he tried to fence with Gorse, or attempted to trick him further, the man would know immediately. Gorse was a trusted enemy agent. His outward cover of wine merchant and chandler would have been built up carefully over many years. Which meant he would have no wish to return to France, a country very different from the one he must have left a long while ago. Many of his fellow merchants had breathed their last while staring down into a bloodied basket and waiting for the blade to drop.

Malta stood like an awkward sentinel in the gateway between the western and eastern Mediterranean. His work in gathering intelligence for France would stand him in good stead, especially when that fleet sailed from Toulon, as sail it must.

He replied casually, 'Corfu of course. There's no change. I'd have thought my friend John Thurgood would have anchored here in his *Santa Paula*. He had the same destination, as I expect you well know.'

Gorse smiled modestly. 'I know many things.'

Bolitho tried to relax, to find comfort that his lie was accepted. But he was feeling much worse, and he knew his breathing was getting faster. Visions flashed across his mind like parts of a nightmare. The pale beaches and waving palms at Tahiti, and beyond to other islands. Pictures at odds with men dying horribly of fever, and the remainder drawing together in terror and despair.

He heard himself ask, 'The letter, was it good news?'

'It was, *Capitaine*. Although the Maltese people may think otherwise when the time comes.' He appeared concerned. 'Really, I must insist that you rest. You do not seem well at all.'

Bolitho said, 'Fever. Long time ago. Coming back again.' He had to speak in short sentences. 'But I will be ready to sail.'

'But there is no 'urry. You can rest –' A look of alarm crossed his face. 'Unless it is dangerous to others?'

Bolitho stood up and steadied himself against the chairback. 'No. Call my men. I will feel better aboard the ship.'

'As you wish.' He snapped his fingers to someone outside the door.

Even through his dizziness Bolitho was able to grasp that Gorse had been prepared to kill him, had posted men out of sight for the purpose, if he had failed to convince him.

He managed to ask, 'Do you wish me to carry any letters to Corfu, *M'sieu*?'

'No.' Gorse regarded him worriedly. 'My next letters will come by more direct means.'

Allday loomed into the room, the Swede at his back.

Gorse snapped, 'Your captain is ill.'

Bolitho felt Allday gripping his arm. 'Easy, sir! We'll soon have you safe!'

Down the steep steps and out into the merciless sunlight again. He was more carried than aided, and he was dimly aware of passing Maltese grinning at the three sailors who had emerged so unsteadily from a wine store.

Allday barked, 'Go on ahead, Larssen, an' signal for the boat!' He added harshly, 'If you're not at the jetty when we gets there, I'll find you if it takes a lifetime!'

Bolitho felt himself being helped into some shade. His body was streaming with sweat, but unlike the previous time it was ice-cold, so that he could not stop shivering.

He gasped, 'Must . . . get . . . on.' It was no use. His strength was fading fast. '*Must . . . tell . . . the . . . squadron.*' Then he collapsed completely.

Four seamen, led by Larssen, came running up from the harbour and stared at Allday with surprise.

Allday rapped, 'Lively, carry him to the boat!' He pulled off his coat and wrapped it round Bolitho. 'And don't stop for anyone!'

It seemed an endless stretch of water between jetty and ship, and every foot of the way Allday held Bolitho against his body, his eyes on the *Segura*'s loosely furled sails, willing them closer.

As far as he was concerned, the squadron, the French and the whole bloody world could go their own way. If anything happened to Bolitho, nothing else would matter.

12

Divided Loyalties

ALMOST identical in a relentless heat-haze, the three ships of
the line lay quietly at anchor within a cable's length of the land.

Captain Thomas Herrick crossed to the larboard side of
Osiris's quarterdeck and stared at the unfamiliar hills, the lush
greens and the hostile crags where some of the headland had
fallen into the sea below. Syracuse, remote, even unfriendly,
so that their powerful presence anchored amongst the un-
hurried movements of small coastal craft made the impression
doubly vivid in Herrick's mind.

He bit his lip and toyed with the idea of going below again.
But the great stern cabin always seemed to be waiting, lying
there like a trap. Part of Farquhar. He shifted his gaze to
Lysander and felt the old longing and despair welling up to
join his other constant anxiety.

They had been at anchor for over two weeks. The Syracuse
garrison commandant had been aboard *Lysander* several times,
accompanied on each occasion by a rotund, worried-looking
Englishman, John Manning, who was, as Herrick understood
it, one of His Brittanic Majesty's last *official* representatives in
the island. For even if Sicily showed no sign of helping France,
she was equally determined not to display open friendship to
King George.

Herrick moved restlessly about the deck, only partly aware
of the blazing heat across his shoulders whenever he showed
himself beyond one of the awnings.

When he had first heard of Bolitho's intention to find and
contact a French agent in Malta, it had already been too late to
protest. *Segura* had been swallowed up in the darkness, and
from that moment on Herrick had fretted and worried con-
tinuously. And now it was all of three weeks since *Segura* had
parted company. Not a sign of the prize ship, nor any word

from the British representative in Syracuse that she had entered
or left Valletta harbour.

John Manning was more concerned about finding reasons
for the three seventy-fours to stay at anchor in a port which
was officially neutral. Repairs, taking on food and water, all
the usual reasons had been sent ashore. And still no word came.

Bolitho must have been seized by the Maltese authorities.
They were even more frightened of the French than the
Sicilians, if half Herrick had heard was true. Or the enemy
agent might have caught and killed him. Herrick looked
towards the open sea until his eyes watered. Bolitho's place
was *here*, in a world he understood. Where he was known by
name, if not by personal contact, by most of the men in the
fleet.

He thought suddenly of Javal, and found himself hating
him. He had not come into Syracuse at all. After his own
passage through the Messina Strait he had been ordered to
rendezvous with the squadron off Malta. Failing that, and
Bolitho had always given them plenty of alternatives, he would
anchor here and await developments. Perhaps he, too, had run
foul of an enemy force?

But if only he would come. Farquhar would have no choice then
but to send *Buzzard* in search of *Segura* and her small crew.

Herrick had visited *Lysander* several times, without being
invited, to discover what Farquhar intended to do. As always,
he was met by a blank wall, a manner and attitude which
rarely failed to rouse and confuse him. Farquhar was imperturbable. If he was troubled at Bolitho's absence, he was
certainly hiding it very well.

His visits to his old ship had been made more painful by the
obvious pleasure of those who had hurried to greet him.
Leroux, and old Grubb, and Yeo, the boatswain. In Gilchrist
he had seen the biggest change of all since Farquhar's taking
command. Like a man on a razor's edge, someone who rarely
found time to rest or be at ease, he was almost a stranger.

Quite unlike *Osiris*'s first lieutenant, he thought bitterly.
Lieutenant Cecil Outhwaite, a bland young man in his middle
twenties, was very like a frog in appearance. Low forehead,
wide mouth, and eyes which were very dark and limpid. He
had a slight lisp, and went about his duties as if bored by the
whole business. Outhwaite, like Farquhar, came of a powerful

family, and why he ever became a sea officer was beyond
Herrick completely.

But then the two ships were totally unlike each other also.
Off watch in *Lysander*, the seamen had skylarked and found
time to joke about their lot under all but the most harsh
circumstances. In this ship there was no such feeling. Like
Outhwaite, the sailors went about their work cat-footed, and
when below were as silent as monks.

Herrick had tried to ease this unnerving tension aside, but
as with *Osiris*'s last captain, he was met at every level by an
unbreachable wall. Farquhar had run the ship to the highest
point of efficiency, cleanliness and appearance. For the people
who made all that possible he had allowed nothing.

And yet some, especially Outhwaite, showed a ready respect
for him. 'He don't tolerate fools, y'know.' The froglike face
had watched him curiously. 'An' he's a damn quick temper
for the scoundrels, too!'

The officer of the watch snapped, 'Ship rounding the point!'
He saw Herrick and added harshly, 'Take the lookout's name
for not reporting sooner!'

Herrick snatched a glass and hurried to the nettings. For
a while longer the newcomer's topsails were riding lifelessly
above a drifting curtain of haze, and then as her jib boom and
beakhead thrust into view Herrick knew she was the sloop of
war *Harebell*.

He pounded one fist into the other, his eyes misting with
strain. *At last.* Her commander, Francis Inch, would do
anything for Bolitho. And his little sloop was even better
suited for looking for him.

'Ah, sir, I see you have sighted her.' Outhwaite joined him
by the rail, his hat tilted rakishly over his eyes.

He was an odd bird, Herrick thought. He wore his dull
brown hair in a queue so long that the end of it was level with
his sword belt. When most sea officers followed the new army
custom of wearing their hair shorter, Outhwaite apparently
intended to retain his grip on the past.

'*Harebell*.'

Herrick watched the sudden activity aboard *Lysander*, the
signal flapping listlessly from her yards. Farquhar would want
to know what was happening elsewhere, and as quickly as it
took Inch's gig to cross the water.

'*Harebell*'s dropped her hook, sir.' Outhwaite showed only mild interest. 'She's too soon back from her mission to have visited England. So we'll not know how things are in London, eh?'

Herrick did not know what *things* in London were, nor did he care.

'I'm going below, Mr. Outhwaite. Call me the moment that *Lysander* signals for captains to repair aboard.'

'Aye, sir.'

Outhwaite smiled and touched his hat. He felt an unusual admiration for Captain Herrick. Rather like his father did for a rustic gamekeeper or groom. *Reliable but quaint.* The way he was so obviously worried about the commodore's disappearance, for instance. Outhwaite could not imagine what sort of experiences and dangers they must have shared in the past to create such a bond. A bond which even Bolitho's action about a change of commands had not diminished.

He watched the boat pulling away from *Harebell* towards the flagship, Inch's gold-laced hat in the sternsheets. Somewhat different from Charles Farquhar, he thought. He looked on one man's loss as an opening for his own gain. Outhwaite nodded. *As it should be.*

But for most of the afternoon, while Herrick sat or paced restlessly in Farquhar's beautifully equipped cabin, no signal came, nor any rumour of what *Harebell* had carried with her to Syracuse.

With a telescope he had examined the sloop more than once through the quarter gallery, and had seen the great scars of bared woodwork where the sea had done its best to hamper her, the patches in her loosely furled sails as evidence of Inch's determination to lose no time with his despatches.

He glared at the skylight as someone stamped overhead. *Damn Farquhar to hell!* Even this moment he was unwilling to share with his fellow captains.

There was a sharp rap at the door and a midshipman stared in at him. 'Beg pardon, sir, but Mr. Outhwaite sends his respects and –'

Herrick stood up. 'The flagship has signalled for me at last?' He did not bother to hide his sarcasm.

'N-no, sir.' The midshipman stared at him warily. 'Captain Farquhar is coming to *us*.'

Herrick snatched his hat. 'I will come up.'

He tried to imagine what was happening. Whatever it was had moved Farquhar to act swiftly at last.

Later, as the calls trilled and the marines banged their muskets to the present, Herrick watched Farquhar's handsome face for some indication. But there was nothing, beyond a slight smile at the corners of his mouth.

He snapped, 'Cabin.' And strode past Herrick with barely a glance at the assembled marines.

In the cabin he turned and faced Herrick.

'*Harebell* has brought despatches from Gibraltar.'' He darted a glance around the cabin. 'Some wine would not come amiss.'

Herrick asked, 'Then there is no news of the commodore?'

Farquhar stared at him. 'Did I say there was?' He shrugged. 'Really, Thomas, you are the most stubborn of men!'

'I thought perhaps that *Harebell* might have sighted . . .'

'Commander Inch has brought news of more pressing matters.' He sounded irritated at Herrick's interruption. 'Admiral Lord St. Vincent has been kept fully informed. Those heavy guns which we captured must have convinced him. He has appointed Rear Admiral Sir Horatio Nelson to command a fleet which will be powerful and ready enough to enter the Mediterranean and seek out the French, *once and for all.*'

Herrick looked away. It was good news of course, or should have been. Bolitho had been given the trust he needed to bring this plan into being. But now that an idea was fast becoming a reality, Bolitho was not here to share in the rewards he deserved.

Farquhar eyed him coldly. 'I have written my despatch for the admiral. *Harebell* will be making sail as soon as she has taken on water.'

Herrick faced him, his eyes filling with astonishment. 'But you will not release the sloop without sending her first to Malta?'

'You are wrong.'

'But – but – '

Farquhar snapped, 'When you were flag captain you had your opportunity to put your ideals into operation. It is too late now for misgivings. So do not blame me, Captain Herrick. If anyone failed the commodore, it was *you*!'

Herrick stared at the deck and at the bulkhead, seeing neither. It was true what Farquhar had said. All of it.

Farquhar added quietly, 'The squadron will remain here until we receive new orders. I have persuaded Mr. Manning that further "repairs" are vital to our survival.'

Herrick heard the words but their meaning did not reach him for several long seconds.

He exclaimed, 'But, you mustn't *ignore* all that the commodore has discovered. The prizes we've taken, the information we've gathered. It all points to Corfu.' He heard his voice pleading, but no longer cared. 'You can't just stay here and do nothing!'

Farquhar shrugged. 'Rumours. I cannot afford to squander the squadron to the points of the compass. When the first supporting ships arrive I intend – '

Herrick stared at him, disgusted. 'You will be ready to meet them. To visit Nelson in person, is that it?'

Farquhar frowned. 'Do not press me too far! I only came to you because I intend to give you back *Lysander*.'

Herrick looked around the beautiful cabin. Far more suited to a flagship than *Lysander* could ever be.

Farquhar added, '*Harebell* brought other, less rousing news. My father, Sir Edward, died two days after I left England.'

Herrick could only stare at him, his mind clearing and sharpening the pain. Farquhar had everything now. There was no remorse on his face, no sense of loss.

He had the title at last, and all the land and property which went with it. And when Nelson came to the Mediterranean he would appoint a new commodore for this squadron. Sir Charles Farquhar.

He asked huskily, 'Have you told Captain Probyn yet?'

'All in good time.' Farquhar was far away, his eyes reaching beyond Sicily and beyond again. 'Probyn behaves as if stupidity was a virtue. You should know that.' He walked to the stern windows. 'I have ordered my servant to bring my things across before dusk. You may transfer back to *Lysander* as soon as you receive my written appointment. That pleases you, surely?'

'I've small room for pleasure at present, *Sir* Charles.'

He watched for some reaction, but Farquhar had already accepted and grown into the title within hours of hearing the news. He looked away in case Farquhar should see his sudden anxiety.

'I have a favour to ask. And I don't find it an easy task.'

'Well?'

'I believe that the commodore was right.'

'Perhaps. We shall see, one day.'

Herrick persisted, 'You could detach a ship. If you are remaining here under Sicilian protection, one ship less would aid the deception.'

'Continue.' Farquhar watched him calmly. 'And where would this *one ship* be heading, might I ask?'

'You know that, too, Sir Charles. Corfu. To discover what the French are doing there.'

'I see.'

Farquhar walked a few paces to the table and looked with distaste at Herrick's chart and the mass of scribbled calculations.

'*Please.*' Herrick watched him desperately. 'I've never asked you for anything before.' He hesitated. 'I'm asking now.'

'Very well. Your orders would be such that you would act on your *own initiative.*'

'Thank you.'

Farquhar's eyebrows lifted. 'You thank me? It is your own ruin you are demanding. Corfu is of no consequence. The big fight will be outside Toulon, or on the shores of Egypt.' He shook his head sadly. 'When I was a midshipman in the *Phalarope*, and you her first lieutenant, *eventually*, I used to listen to the men talking about you. How you would always speak up for them.' He turned away. 'I hope there will be someone to speak up for you when the time comes. But I doubt it.'

He became impatient and banged sharply on the door. '*Sentry!* Pass the word for the first lieutenant!'

Then he looked at Herrick again. 'Return to your precious *Lysander* now. Before I change my mind. I'll send you your orders at once.'

Herrick nodded. 'And if you get the chance, sir . . .'

'Yes. I'll try to discover what happened to the commodore, although –' He did not finish it.

Outhwaite appeared in the door. 'Sir?'

'Captain Herrick is returning to his own ship.'

The frogface was expressionless. 'By whose order, sir?'

Farquhar smiled tightly. 'Mine.'

As Herrick made to leave he added, 'One thing. I'll need a good signals officer. I will keep your sixth lieutenant.'

'Yes, sir.'

Herrick sighed. At least Pascoe would be spared. Although he suspected that Farquhar's was no mere gesture of confidence. More one to advertise his humanity in saving Pascoe from a wasted death.

He strode out beneath the poop and into the sunlight. The news of his leaving was already making itself shown. Glum faces, curious stares followed him as he strode towards the entry port. Perhaps they would miss him after all.

Outhwaite hurried along with him. 'I'll have all your gear and chests sent across, sir. Your cox'n is already in the barge.' He held out his hand. 'I doubt we'll meet again, sir. But I'd not have missed it.'

Herrick studied him, suddenly very calm. 'Nor I. It taught me a great deal. Which was intended.'

'It *did*, sir?' Outhwaite was surprised.

'Yes. About people. Mostly about myself.'

He touched his hat abruptly and walked to the open port.

Outhwaite waited until the boat had thrust away from the side and then snapped, 'Turn the hands to, Mr. Guthrie. We'll have no slackness.'

He thought of Herrick's face in those last few moments. He had half-expected to see humility but had found only pity. For him perhaps. When he glanced across the wide quarterdeck he was strangely troubled. It no longer seemed like the same place.

*

Herrick stood motionless by the open stern windows looking down into the swirling water below the counter. He could see the stars reflected there, and by leaning slightly over the sill he could also see the solitary lantern by his head and the line of bright windows from the wardroom below his feet. The ship was unusually quiet, as if holding her breath. There had only been one break in the stillness, and that had been when he had returned aboard, some two hours ago.

An unknown voice had begun it, and then, as if at a signal, and despite Gilchrist's anger, the ship had burst alive with cheering. The noise had drowned out the calls and the marine drummers completely, and even old Grubb had removed his hat and had waved it in the air, his ruined face scarlet with his, ' 'Uzza, lads! The cap'n's come back!'

He walked away from the windows and glanced momentarily at the empty sword-rack on the bulkhead. Bolitho had been unwilling to take the sword with him. Ozzard had told him that. Perhaps he had foreseen something. A warning.

He sighed. Farquhar had kept his word, and the wording of *Lysander*'s orders made it perfectly clear where the blame would lie if Herrick acted wrongly. Herrick told himself that Farquhar was correct. That he would have done the same. But the doubt was there.

There was an uncertain tap on the door. It was Pascoe, his hat under his arm. Even in the light of a solitary lantern Herrick could see the strain on his face, the brightness in his eyes.

'Yes?'

Pascoe said, 'Mr. Manning is come aboard, sir. He has a lady with him. They came to say goodbye to Captain Farquhar, as they are leaving for Gibraltar in *Harebell* as soon as a wind returns.'

Herrick nodded. There was no wind at all. And it added to the sense of brooding despair.

He said quietly, 'Tell Ozzard to bring more lanterns. Then show the visitors aft. I'll explain about Captain Farquhar.'

He thought of his orders again. Signed *Acting-Commodore*.

Pascoe said, 'I'd like to stay in *Lysander*, sir.'

'I know.' He faced him. 'But you must transfer to *Osiris* at first light tomorrow. It is probably for the best. I'd like to think you at least were here if . . .'

Pascoe asked, 'Are you going to Corfu just to show that you believe he is right, sir?'

'Yes. It is all I *can* do now.'

He crossed to his side and added, 'Take care, Adam. A lot may depend on you now.'

Pascoe's eyes were wide. 'You speak as if he were already dead?'

'I'm not sure. Not any more.' Herrick looked around the quiet cabin. 'But I am certain of one thing. People in England who do not understand as we do will try to smear his name.

It is a common custom with our country's heroes, and hero your uncle is, and never forget it!' His voice was loud but he could not bottle his thoughts any longer. 'I met his father once, did you know that? Your grandfather. A fine man, from a proud tradition. You'll have a lot to live up to, and many will try to splinter your defences with envy and hate. So just you remember this day, Adam, and treasure it.'

He swung away. 'Now bring those damned visitors aft.'

He heard Pascoe's footsteps retreating, and felt the pounding of his own heart matching them.

Light flooded around him as Ozzard hung fresh lanterns, and with a start he realised that Manning was in the cabin door, a lady in a dark boat cloak and hood at his side.

Manning said stiffly, 'I regret the intrusion, Captain. It now seems I have wasted time and effort and will have to take a boat to the *Osiris.*'

Herrick tried to smile. But his face felt numb. 'I am sorry, Mr. Manning.' It was typical of Farquhar of course. 'I expect you would have been told of the new arrangements in the morning.'

Manning searched his face and replied dryly, 'Indeed, I would like to think so.'

To the lady, who had remained silent, he said, 'We will go over to *Osiris* right away. I have some matters to discuss with Captain Farquhar before you leave.'

Herrick said, 'There'll be no wind before dawn. You can rest assured of that.'

'I see.' Manning seemed irritated. 'This is my sister, by the way, Mrs. Boswell.'

She threw back the hood of her cloak and gave a quick smile.

Manning continued, 'Better be off then.'

She said, '*I* am sailing in the *Harebell,* Captain Herrick, but my brother is remaining in Sicily for the present.' She looked sadly at Manning. 'Though how the poor dear will manage, I cannot imagine.'

He glared at her and then snapped, 'Are you coming, Dulcie?'

'No.' She walked further into the cabin, her boat cloak swishing behind her. 'I will have enough of cramped quarters and boats before I reach England again. And I have seen enough of Captain Farquhar anyway.' She gave Herrick a smile. 'I should like to remain here until you have finished your business, John. If the captain has no objections?'

Herrick shook his head. 'No, Ma'am. My pleasure.'

She was a very pleasant looking woman, with the fresh cheeks and bright eyes of someone raised in the country. He wondered what she was doing out here. Perhaps her husband was like Manning, a man who served the King without wearing his coat.

Manning tutted and grunted and then said, 'Oh, very well. I'll be back in an hour.'

The silence closed in again, and Herrick felt as if he was too large to be in the cabin.

She watched him thoughtfully and then loosened her cloak before sitting easily in one of the chairs.

'So you are Captain Herrick. I have been hearing about you. One of your men told me you are sailing soon. I hope you have a safe voyage.'

Herrick looked at her, wanting to be left alone. Needing her to stay.

'Aye, Ma'am. There's plenty of talk in ships.' He changed the subject. 'I gather you are bound for England?'

'Yes. We live in – ' She dropped her eyes. 'That is, my husband died two years ago. So I am returning to Canterbury. I have been dreading it in many ways. I came out to live with John. He has never married, poor lamb. But he insists that the war is getting closer each day.' She sighed. 'So home I must go.'

Herrick sat down opposite her. 'But, Ma'am, I come from Kent, too. My home is in Rochester.' He smiled awkwardly. 'Though I fear not as fine as yours will be.'

She watched him, her skin very pale under the lamplight. 'That young officer who brought us to the cabin.' She lowered her eyes. 'I couldn't help hearing what you said to him.'

Herrick flushed. 'Ma'am, I do apologise.' He recalled his anger. *Bring these damned visitors aft.* 'Had I realised.'

'No, Captain. Before that. You were deeply upset, as I believe that good-looking boy was, too.'

Herrick nodded slowly. 'He is the commodore's nephew. A fine young man.'

She said quietly, 'I've heard about your commodore. I was very distressed. I understand he was greatly liked.'

'Aye, Ma'am. None better. None braver.'

'There's no hope?'

'Not much. Your brother would have heard something by now.'

'Tell me about *yourself*, Captain. Do you have a family in England?'

And that was how it all began. Herrick speaking his thoughts and memories aloud, while she sat quietly listening.

When someone cried a challenge and a boat surged alongside, Herrick could hardly believe an hour had passed so fast. He stood up anxiously.

'If I have bored you, Ma'am . . .'

She patted his sleeve and smiled at him. 'I should like to call upon your sister, if I may, Captain. It will help to keep us both cheerful until – ' She fastened her cloak. 'Until you return to Kent again.' She looked up at his face, her gaze level. 'I hope you'll not forget us.'

Herrick grasped her hand. It was small and firm and made him feel all the clumsier.

'I'll not forget your kindness to me, Ma'am.' He heard Manning's voice drawing closer. 'I'd like to think we might meet again, but – '

'No buts, Captain.' She moved back from him. 'I can now understand why your commodore is sadly missed. With friends such as you, he must have been a man indeed.'

Herrick followed her on to the quarterdeck where her brother was speaking with Major Leroux.

Pascoe called, 'Boat's ready, sir!'

Herrick said roughly, 'Go with this lady in the boat, Mr. Pascoe. My compliments to Commander Inch. Tell him to take good care of his passenger.'

She touched his arm. 'Inch? Another friend?'

'Aye.' Herrick guided her around the projecting humps of gun trucks and ring-bolts. 'You'll be in good hands.'

She moved her elbow gently in his grip. 'No better than now, I think.'

*

The nightmare was rising to another great climax. Leaping patterns of dark red, like solid flame, interspersed with cruder shapes, sometimes human, other times obscure and all the more frightening.

Bolitho wanted to get to his feet, to cry out, to escape the surging movement and encirclement. Once, against the molten banks of fire he saw a woman, deathly white, her arms beckoning him, her mouth calling silent words. When he had tried to reach her he realised that both his legs had gone, and a ship's surgeon was laughing at his rising terror.

All at once it was gone. Silence, and a darkness too unreal to accept, so that Bolitho felt himself drawing in his muscles and limbs to resist another terrible nightmare.

It was then that he realised he could feel his legs, his arms and the sweat which ran across his neck and thighs. Slowly, fearfully, like a man climbing back from the dead, he tried to assemble his thoughts, to separate reality from that which he had been enduring since . . . he struggled on to his elbows, staring at the darkness. *Since when?*

As his senses returned he noticed a sluggish movement beneath him, the shudder and tilt of a vessel under way. Blocks and rigging creaked, and he felt a new sensation, that of dread. He remembered the return of the fever, the signs he had known were there but had refused to recognise. Allday's face above him, lined and anxious, hands carrying him, the enfolding darkness.

He groped up to his eyes and winced as his fingers touched them. He had gone completely blind.

A great slackness came over his limbs, so that he fell back on the bunk exhausted. *Better to have died.* To have sunk deeper into the haunting nightmares of fever until it had ended completely. He thought of the naked woman. Catherine Pareja. Trying to sustain him as she had done before when he had all but lost his life.

With a gasp he struggled up in a sitting position as a thin yellow line opened the opposite darkness like thread. Wider still, and then a face, unfamiliar against a lantern in the passageway beyond the door.

The face vanished and he heard someone yell, 'He's awake! He's going to be all right!'

The next few minutes were the worst in some ways. Allday cradling him against the vessel's motion, Lieutenant Veitch peering down at him, his face split into a wider grin than he had ever seen. Midshipman Breen's carrot head bobbing about in a sort of jig, and others crowding into the small cabin and giving vent to what sounded like a dozen different tongues.

Veitch ordered, 'Clear the cabin, lads.'

Allday made Bolitho lie back, and said, 'Good to have you back with us, sir. God, you've had a bad time, and that's no error.'

Bolitho tried to speak but his tongue felt twice its proper size. He managed to croak, 'H-how long?' He saw Veitch and Allday exchange quick glances and added, *'Must know!'*

Veitch said quietly, 'All but three weeks, sir, since you – '

Bolitho tried to push Allday aside but was helpless. No wonder he felt weak and empty. *Three weeks.*

He whispered, 'What happened?'

Veitch said, 'After we got you back aboard we thought it better to stay at anchor in Valletta. It seemed safe enough, and I was troubled, fearful, if you like, of taking you to sea as you were.'

Allday stood up slowly, his head bowed between the beams. 'I've never seen you so bad, sir.' He sounded exhausted. 'We was at our wits' ends as to what to do.'

Bolitho looked from one to the other, some of his anxiety giving way to warmth. For three weeks, while he had been helpless and confined in his own private torment, these others had fended as best they could. Had nursed him, without caring for themselves, or what delay might cost them. As his eyes grew accustomed to the yellow light he saw the deep shadows around Allday's face, the stubble on his chin. Veitch, too, looked worn out, like a prisoner from the hulks.

He said, 'I was thinking only of myself.' He reached out. 'Take my hands, Both of you.'

Allday's teeth were white in his tanned face. 'Bless him, Mr. Veitch, he *must* be feeling a mite better.' But he had to look away, at a rare loss for words.

Bolitho said, 'Tell me again. I will try to be patient and not interrupt.'

It was a strange tale which Veitch and Allday shared. Strange because it represented part of his life which he had missed. Which now he could never regain.

Within a day of his return aboard an official had come

alongside and ordered them to remain at anchor until all risk of fever had gone. Veitch had been worried at Bolitho's desperate condition, but had not missed the fact that two of his seamen had deserted. A coincidence? He could not be sure. But from that moment he had made plans for leaving harbour before some unbreakable restriction was placed upon them. For several days the *Segura* had remained apparently unheeded, a warning yellow flag at her masthead, while the morale of her small company had crumbled and stores had run lower and lower.

As he listened to their story, Bolitho wondered if the French agent, Yves Gorse, had received some word that *Segura*'s crew were impostors. By having them held at anchor he may have done his best to delay them while he sent word elsewhere that the enemies of France were no longer at Gibraltar or off Toulon, but inside Malta. He could, after all, do little else without revealing his own role as a foreign spy.

Allday took up the story. 'Two sentries came aboard next. Mr. Plowman suggested that it was the best time to leave. Others on shore would drop their guard once responsibility was shifted.'

Bolitho managed to smile. Plowman, if he was an ex-slaver, would certainly know about such matters.

'There was a squall one night. Sharp and fierce, an' not too much in our favour. But it was then or not at all, Mr. Plowman said, so we cuts the cable and makes sail.'

'The sentries?'

Allday grinned. 'We met with a Genoese trader two days later and we put 'em aboard her.' He became serious again. 'It was a good thing. By speaking with the trader we heard that a French man o' war was nearby. A corvette, by the description. Looking for us, waiting to contact the agent in Malta, we don't know.' He patted the crumpled bunk and added quietly, 'We had more important things to attend to.'

Bolitho ran his fingers through his hair. 'Bring more light. I must get up. But why three weeks?'

'We've been lying up in a little bay to the south'rd of Sicily. The squall, which damn near flung us back into Valletta, was a hard one, but it was gone again in no time.' Veitch could not suppress a great yawn. 'So we anchored and did what we could. I think you nearly died, sir.'

Breen entered the cabin with another lantern. Unlike the others, he was able to walk upright.

Bolitho swung his legs to the deck and allowed Allday to help him to a broken mirror on the bulkhead. He studied the hollows in his cheeks, the feverish stare, the filthy stains on his shirt.

He said, 'I'll not tell you what you *should* have done.'

Veitch shrugged. 'We did not know what had passed between you and the Frenchman, sir.' He added grimly, 'But in any case, I'd have made the same decision. Your life would have come first.'

Bolitho studied Veitch in the mirror. 'Thank you for that.'

Allday said, 'We sighted the corvette a couple of times, but she didn't come near our little anchorage.' He watched Bolitho's worn features and explained, 'As it is, sir, we're now under way and steering north for Syracuse. Mr. Veitch said that with all the calms we've been having, it was best to sail at night. This old barrico is no match for a Frog corvette!'

'I see.'

He rubbed his chin and despised himself for his sudden thought. A shave and a bath seemed more precious than anything.

Allday continued, 'Yesterday morning it was. I was forcing some brandy into your mouth and you spoke to me. I think we knew then that we must quit the bay. A proper surgeon is what you need now.'

Bolitho grimaced. 'The squadron will have sailed long since. Even without my new information, Farquhar will have weighed.'

Veitch asked, 'You were right then, sir?'

'I think we all knew, Mr. Veitch.' He recalled the cool wine store, the sweat on his back changing from fire to ice. 'Gorse hinted that the French will seize Malta on their way to Egypt.'

'I'm not surprised, sir.' Veitch sounded weary. 'From what I saw in Malta, most of the defences have been allowed to fall into ruin.'

'With Malta taken, and a goodly supply of weapons and stores for a full scale invasion building up in Corfu, the French have nothing to stop them.' He gave a tired smile. 'So we must send word to the admiral. In this wretched vessel, if necessary.'

Veitch walked to the door. 'It will be dawn in an hour, sir.

With luck, and provided that this whisper of a wind does not desert us, we will reach Syracuse during the afternoon watch.'

He paused by the door. 'I must relieve Mr. Plowman, sir.'

Allday waited until the door was closed and then said, 'He has the makings of a good officer, sir.'

'You think that?'

'Aye.' Allday helped him to a chair. 'He is better tempered than *some*.'

Bolitho watched him, content to remain where he was, despite all the urgency at the back of his mind. He could tell merely by watching Allday what the days and the weeks had cost him. He could not have slept for more than minutes at a time.

Allday said brightly, 'I washed a Don shirt that I found in a locker, and Larssen cleaned up your breeches.' He turned into the lantern light, a razor in his hand. 'So now, sir, we'll make you a bit more presentable, shall we?'

Later, as a pink glow showed itself through the filthy cabin skylight, Bolitho stood up in his Spanish shirt and examined himself in the mirror.

Allday was wiping his razor on part of a flag. '*You* know, sir, and *I* know, but the lads will think you're just as you were.'

The razor froze in mid-air as a voice called, 'Deck thar! Sail on th' weather bow!'

Allday reached out and gripped his arm. 'Easy now, sir! Mr. Veitch is able to manage!'

Bolitho looked at him gravely. 'Mr. Veitch has been made to *manage* for too long. And so have you.' He fought against the ringing in his ears. 'Help me on deck.'

For such a small vessel it seemed a vast distance to the poop.

The sea looked very calm, and the hint of sunrise gave the water a strange pink hue, beyond which the vague humps of land seemed ugly. Bolitho seized the rail and sucked in great gulps of air. After the cabin it was like wine. He looked up at the loosely flapping sails. Barely enough wind to hold them on course. He nodded to Veitch and Plowman, not daring to trust his voice or his breath. When the sun showed itself in earnest he would see the Sicilian coastline across the larboard bulwark more clearly, be able to fix their position.

He stiffened as the pink light touched a small square of sail, far away across the larboard bow. The uncertain light made it seem a great distance off, but soon she would cut the range down as if by magic.

He turned and looked at Veitch. 'One of ours perhaps?'

Veitch closed his glass with a snap. 'No, sir. It's that same damned corvette again!'

Bolitho sensed the bitter despair in his voice. After all he and the others had done, the corvette was still with them. Standing like a pike between a helpless duckling and the nearest reeds.

He thought of *Segura*'s armament and dismissed it. Two or three swivels and the men's own muskets. It only made the comparison more cruel.

He snapped, 'How far from the land are we?' He was surprised by the strength in his voice.

'Two leagues, sir. No more by my reckonin'.' Plowman regarded him doubtfully. 'The water's very deep hereabouts, and I'd hoped to run closer inshore, but for the bloody wind, beggin' your pardon, sir!'

He wished he could pace up and down and gather his thoughts, but knew his strength would fail instantly.

Six miles out. It might as well be six hundred.

He heard Breen say shakily, 'With all that powder stored below, we'll blow to dust at the first shot!'

Bolitho turned and looked at him. 'Well said, Mr. Breen!' He lurched to the wheel and held on to it. 'Allday, have the boat lowered.'

'It *is*, sir.' Allday peered at him anxiously through the pink gloom. 'Towing below the counter.'

'Good, good.' He had to keep talking, to stop the dizziness returning. 'Rig a mast and sails in her and warp her around to the lee side, so that the Frenchman won't see her.'

Veitch exclaimed, 'We'd never outrun a *corvette*, sir.'

'Don't intend to.' He bared his teeth, pretending to grin. 'Make up a long fuse and set it to the powder hold.' He saw Veitch's disbelief but hurried on, 'We'll let the corvette grapple us, and then bear away in the longboat.'

Plowman cleared his throat. 'But suppose the Frogs don't grapple, sir? They might send a boardin' party instead.' He looked meaningly at Veitch, as if to indicate that he thought the fever was still controlling Bolitho as before.

Bolitho took the glass from his hand and trained it across the rail. The French corvette was much sharper already. She had the wind-gage and was setting her topgallants to take full advantage of it.

He returned the glass and said slowly, 'We shall have to wait and see, Mr. Plowman. Now get that fuse, and be sharp about it.'

As Allday made to leave he caught his arm and asked, 'When I called out during the fever. Did I ask for anyone?'

'Yes, sir.' Allday looked towards the sunrise. 'You called for Cheney, sir. Your wife.'

Bolitho nodded. 'Thank you.'

Midshipman Breen hurried after Allday and whispered nervously, 'But is not the commodore's wife dead?'

'Aye.' He paused above the bobbing longboat and looked towards Bolitho by the wheel. 'An' more's the pity for it.'

13

Pursuit

BOLITHO crouched over the *Segura*'s flaking companion hatch
and scribbled hastily on a small piece of paper. He was aware
of the strengthening light, a hint of warmth after the first
dawn air, but forced his mind to concentrate. Every so often
he had to pause and gather his strength for fear that the fever
was returning.

Once, when he half rose to peer above the larboard bulwark
he saw the French corvette's yards and sails edging round, her
slender jib boom displaying her intention to run down her
quarry on a simple converging tack.

Not much more than a mile separated the smart man-of-war
and the badly-used *Segura*.

Bolitho folded the paper carefully and moved to Veitch's
side. 'Take this with you.' He slipped it into the lieutenant's
pocket. 'It tells all I know.' *Suspect* was more the word. 'So,
if I fall, you must get this message to higher authority as best
you can.'

Plowman called hoarsely, 'The Frenchie's shortenin' sail, sir.'

Veitch nodded. 'He'll be up to us very soon now.'

Bolitho ran his eye along the deck. It was tilting even less
now, and with the light airs barely able to fill each sail, his
plan was decided. If there had ever been any choice, he thought
grimly.

Allday came aft. 'Fuse set and ready, sir. Should give us a
quarter-hour.'

Bolitho trained a telescope on the corvette. 'Too long. Cut
it as close as you dare. Five minutes.'

He heard them gasp but watched the French ship drawing
nearer, her sails braced round to retain the wind, showing her
bilge in the strengthening sunlight as she heeled jauntily on
her new tack.

Plowman remarked, 'Look at 'er copper. She's not long out of port!'

Bolitho felt a shiver of excitement. One of de Brueys's vessels perhaps? Part of a scattered line of scouts which in turn would lead the admiral's mighty fleet into open seas and to Egypt. He thought of all the information, certain and hearsay, and knew it represented far more than the solitary corvette which was blocking their path to safety. Like a great colossus, de Brueys's fleet of transports and ships of the line would stride via Malta, using it as a stepping-stone, before setting down again on the Egyptian shore. And thence to India, and all the trade and possessions which England had so nearly lost in that other war.

He said, 'Get the hands into the boat, if you please.'

He waited, expecting further argument from Veitch or Plowman.

The lieutenant merely said, 'I'll not cast off without you, sir. And that's my last word on it.'

Bolitho smiled. 'You'd disobey your commodore, Mr. Veitch? In time of war it could hang you!'

They both laughed, and Veitch answered, 'A risk I'll take, sir.'

The seamen were already scrambling over the lee bulwark, and Bolitho hoped that nobody aboard the French ship had noticed anything unusual. After all, there was little point in trying to outpace a man-of-war as lively as a corvette. And to attempt an escape in a longboat, with the Mediterranean and not dry land across the bows, was a measure of madness.

Allday came aft again, breathing heavily. 'Fuse ready, sir.' He squinted at the other vessel. Three guns had been run out. Small six-pounders, they would be enough for the elderly *Segura*, even without her lethal cargo. He added, 'There's just us left.' He gestured to the wheel. 'And this mad Swede.'

Larssen grinned, his face as devoid of fear as a child's. 'Aye, so I am, sir!'

There was a sharp crack, and as they turned to see a puff of smoke from the corvette's side, a single ball ripped through the fore-rigging and threw up a thin waterspout, away on the starboard quarter.

Bolitho gave a quiet smile. 'Signal received and understood.' He nodded to Allday. 'Get forrard, and start shouting at your invisible crew.'

He knew that the French captain must be watching *Segura* and probably himself. He darted a quick glance at the longboat, as the bows and then the rest of it slewed awkwardly away from the lee side, every inch of it filled with men and oars, and the jumble of mast and canvas which Veitch was preparing to raise.

Bolitho took the spokes and said, 'Hoist the flag, Larssen.'

The Swede grinned, and moments later the American colours broke once again from the gaff.

It brought an instant response in another sharp explosion, and this time the six-pound ball smashed into *Segura*'s hull, shaking her violently like a great hammer.

Bolitho had not expected the corvette to be fooled. But it all took time, and from one corner of his eye he saw Veitch waving his hat back and forth to show that he was ready.

There was a thump from forward, and he watched Allday jump clear with an axe as the tanned jib sail came crashing down around him in a flailing heap. It seemed to satisfy the Frenchman, for her captain was already bringing her round to run almost parallel, keeping *Segura* to leeward, while her men shortened sail yet again in readiness to drive alongside. Sailors were clambering into the shrouds with grapnels, and there was a glint of metal as a boarding party ran smartly towards the forecastle for the first contact.

Bolitho felt the wheel bucking in his hands, as deprived of her jib, *Segura* idled heavily, her sails in trembling agitation.

'Light the fuse!'

He heard Allday dash below, and then handed the wheel back to the Swede. He saw a seaman on the corvette's mainyard pointing and gesticulating, and guessed he had seen the longboat and was trying to yell his information to the poop above the din of sails and blocks, of shouting men, eager for a fight, even a one-sided one.

Bolitho made himself remain beside the wheel. If he ran too soon, the Frenchman would still be able to sheer away. He thought of the hissing fuse below decks, and hoped Allday had not been too exhausted to estimate the proper length.

'Fuse burning!'

Allday was covered in wisps of hay, as if he had just fought his way out of a farmyard stack. He had probably taken the fuse clear of the stored fodder in the other hold to avoid a premature explosion.

'Stand by the boat's sternrope!' He waited until Allday was at the bulwark with his axe. 'You, too, Larssen, move smartly now!' He saw a shadow by his feet and then looked up at the American flag. He grimaced and said, 'I've dirtied that flag enough for one day, I'll cut it down.' But when he groped for his sword he realised that in all the excitement and his return from feverish oblivion he had forgotten to bring it on deck.

A musket barked across the fast-narrowing strip of water, and he heard the ball smack into the opposite bulwark. The French boarders were all yelling now, baying like enraged hounds at the thought of their enemy trying to escape.

Allday saw Bolitho's expression and thrust his axe into the seaman's hand. 'Hold this! I'm going for the sword!'

Bolitho yelled, '*Leave it!*'

Another ball zipped past him, and then a whole fusilade of shots which threw splinters from the deck like darts and ricocheted in every direction.

Bolitho heard Larssen cry out, and saw him sag to his knees, his eyes tightly closed as he tried to stem the blood which ran freely from his thigh.

Bolitho controlled his racing thoughts, tried not to see the fuse in his mind. *Five minutes.* It must have been burning that long already.

He dragged the seaman against the bulwark and heard Allday panting across the deck to join him.

He gasped, 'Hold him! We'll jump together!'

Then they were up on the bulwark, the wood still misty from the night air, and as Allday cut the boat's long line the three of them fell like untidy bundles into the water, the severed rope wrapped around them.

Down and down, the sunlight fading through a pink mist, which Bolitho's reeling mind told him must be Larssen's blood, and all the while he could feel the rope dragging like a snare, and knew Veitch's crew were pulling at their oars like madmen. Despite all which was happening, he found he was thinking of the two men who had deserted at Malta. They would never know how fortunate their crime was at this moment. Had they remained aboard, it was doubtful if there would have been room for them in the one remaining boat, nor space to pull an oar.

He saw the water brightening over his head, and as he broke surface, shaking hair from his eyes and gasping for breath, he caught sight of the longboat, its sail hoisted, and several figures waving and maybe cheering towards him.

Larssen had fainted, and it was all he and Allday could do to hold his face above water, and at the same time cling to the boat's sternrope which was being hauled hand-over-hand against the pressure of oars, sail and the drag of undertow around their legs.

Allday gasped, 'By God, I'd not want to do this very often!'

Bolitho turned his head to speak and then felt his ears cringe as a deafening explosion tore the morning apart. He felt the shock-wave surge against his legs and chest, knocking the wind from his lungs and twisting the three of them round in the trailing rope like helpless puppets.

Fragments of wood and cordage, huge yellow-coloured bundles of hay rained around them. A whole section of timber plunged straight down beside Allday, only to shoot up again like a jagged battering-ram, missing him by inches.

Allday croaked, 'Jesus! That was a near thing!'

Bolitho managed to pivot himself, treading water as the deluge of shattered pieces subsided, and peered back at the two ships. In fact, there was only one, *Segura* having vanished completely, leaving a great widening circle of froth and bubbles, flotsam and scattered fodder, which would never feed French cavalry now.

It was as if the *Segura* had bled to death even as she plunged to the bottom, for the froth which continued to swirl around in confusion was tinged with red. Every cask of wine must have burst apart with the gunpowder.

The corvette was in a bad way. At first glance he had imagined that she had escaped the worst of the explosion, but as she swung unsteadily across the disturbed water he saw the weak sunlight play over a deep rent in her hull where her copper had been slit open like the belly of a shark. Her rigging and sails were in shreds, swaying like creeper as the hull tilted more steeply, hiding the hole in the side as the sea surged into her. Why she had not caught fire was a miracle, but Bolitho knew her captain would be hard put to save his surviving men, let alone prevent his command from following *Segura*.

A shadow loomed above him, and he felt hands under his armpits, others reaching down to lift the inert Swede to safety.

Veitch watched him, grinning, as he was hauled unceremoniously inboard with Allday.

'You see, sir, I waited!'

Bolitho lay back and stared at the sky. 'It was close.'

Allday was wringing out his shirt across the gunwale. 'I gave the fuse *ten* minutes, sir. Otherwise . . .' He said no more.

Bolitho turned to look at him, his chest heaving painfully. He saw the weals across Allday's back where the mounted trooper had used his whip. They were still very red, and would never vanish completely. He felt strangely sad about that. Allday had served at sea for most of his life and had avoided the lash throughout that time. In the Navy it was no mean feat. And now, because of his courage and unwavering loyalty, he would wear those stripes to the end of his days.

Impetuously, he reached out and touched Allday's shoulder. 'It was well done. And I am sorry about these.'

Allday twisted round on the thwart and looked at him. 'Still a long way to go to catch up with you, sir.' He grinned, the tiredness, or some of it, fading. 'I reckon you've got more scars than a cat's got lives!'

Bolitho smiled, sharing the moment only with Allday. 'But none more honourable, my friend.'

Veitch cleared his throat. 'Where now, sir?'

Bolitho struggled against the gunwale, watching the listless sail, and then turning to study the corvette. Someone fired a musket, and a seaman in the boat stood up to jeer.

Bolitho said quietly, 'Easy, lads. I know how you feel. But it was not fired at us that time. The corvette's people are trying to rush the boats.'

He looked at Veitch, seeing the slow understanding. A few officers, a terrified crew. It had happened to Bolitho, it was something which Veitch might never experience, if he was lucky.

'She's goin'!'

The little corvette was beginning to turn turtle, her decks bared as she tilted towards the silent watchers. White feathers of spray showed where fragments from the explosion were falling from her masts, and a six-pounder cannon tore loose from the upended side and charged through the other bulwark, taking a handful of struggling figures with it.

Across the blue water they could hear the faint cries and screams, the jubilant roar of inrushing water. The masts hit the surface almost together, smashing amongst some swimmers and cutting the one successfully launched boat in halves.

Plowman said roughly, 'Nuthin' *we* can do for 'em, sir.'

Bolitho did not answer. The master's mate was right of course. The boat would be swamped, or at best his men would be taken prisoner by the overwhelming number of French survivors. To know it was one thing. To merely accept it was another.

He heard Midshipman Breen sniffing loudly, and when he glanced along the boat he saw he was perched on a cask, the Swedish seaman, Larssen, cradled against his lap.

Plowman climbed across the other men and asked, 'What is it?'

The boy stared aft at Bolitho and murmured, 'He's dead, sir.'

Allday said, 'Poor fellow.' He sighed. 'Put him over, lads.'

But the midshipman clung to the man's body, his eyes still on Bolitho. 'B – but, sir, couldn't, shouldn't we say something for him?' His freckled face was streaming with tears, and in the boat he alone seemed totally unaware of the sinking ship nearby, of anything but the man who just died beside him.

Bolitho nodded slowly. 'You do it, Mr. Breen.'

He turned to watch Veitch, hearing Breen's high-pitched, wavering words as he stumbled through a prayer he had learned, probably from his mother. Nearby, he noticed that one of the seamen, a tough, experienced gun captain, had removed his neckerchief which he had been wearing over his head in readiness for the sun.

He said quietly, 'It is a hard lesson, Mr. Veitch.'

'Aye.' The lieutenant touched his arm, but gently, as if afraid of disturbing Breen's words. 'There she goes!'

The corvette was slipping beneath the water, and already some of the survivors still afloat were swimming purposefully towards *Segura*'s longboat.

There was a splash, and Bolitho saw Larssen's face, very

pale and misty below the surface as his body drifted clear of the side.

'Out oars! Stand by!'

A man in the bow yelled, 'God damn them! Here comes another!'

Out of the land's shadow and morning mist, a small rectangle of pale canvas showed itself with sudden brightness in the sunlight. Some of the Frenchmen who were clinging to pieces of wreckage and broken spars raised a cheer, while in the longboat there was no sound at all.

Bolitho snatched the brass telescope from the bottom-boards and trained it on the other vessel. She might stop to pick up survivors. A wind might rise in time to save them.

He felt his mouth go dry. Then he said, 'Rest easy, lads! She's the *Harebell*!'

With what wind remained held firmly under his coat tails, Inch brought the sloop steadily towards them, his boats already swayed out ready for launching.

The corvette had practically gone now, and only her stern section, complete with its tricolour, was still visible.

Bolitho watched *Harebell* turning into the wind, the boats dropping alongside as she idled close to the nearest cluster of swimmers. A jolly boat was speeding towards them now, and a young lieutenant stood up to hail, his face red with anger.

'God damn you for a coward, *M'sieu*! Leaving your people to drown while you have a boat!'

The boat surged closer, and Allday cupped his hands, barely able to restrain his huge grin.

'Is that the way you always greet your commodore? *Attention* in that boat, I say!'

While hands reached out to draw the two hulls together, and Bolitho clambered across to join the blushing lieutenant, he said calmly, 'A few moments ago, I had a *ship*, too, Mr. McLean.' He patted his arm. 'But I can understand how it looked.'

By the time they had reached the sloop's side, Bolitho could see what excitement his appearance had caused. The embarrassed Lieutenant McLean had already explained that *Harebell* was on her way to Gibraltar with despatches for the admiral. Commander Inch, it appeared, was making a longer

passage than he should have done, just in case he might have
sighted the *Segura*. McLean left Bolitho in no doubt that it was
just a brave gesture, and that hope had long since been given
up.

Bolitho hauled himself up the side and was greeted by a
beaming Inch, whose voice was completely drowned by
cheering sailors. He wrung Bolitho's hand, his long horseface
shining with pleasure and relief, while others pushed forward
to pound their returned commodore on the shoulders.

Veitch said harshly, 'The commodore was near dead with
fever. I fear he'll die of bruises in a minute, sir!'

Inch led Bolitho aft, bobbing with excitement. Bolitho
realised with surprise that there was a woman in the small
cabin, and she, too, seemed as overcome as Inch.

Inch said, 'This is Mrs. Boswell, sir. On passage for England.
I am to take her to Gibraltar with me.'

Bolitho nodded to her. 'I must apologise for all this, Ma'am.'
He looked meaningly at Inch. 'We will return to Syracuse with
all speed.'

'Yes, of *course* I understand.' She dabbed at her eyes.

Bolitho asked, 'Well, Commander Inch, tell me everything.
Is all the squadron still at anchor then?'

Some of Inch's pleasure seemed to fade. 'All but *Lysander*
and *Buzzard*, sir. Javal is away on his own mission, but
Lysander has gone, I am told, to Corfu.'

Bolitho sat down and plucked at his frilled Spanish shirt.
'So Captain Farquhar intends to use his own initiative, eh?'

Inch looked uncomfortable, even wretched. 'No, sir.
Captain Herrick has been given *Lysander*. Sir Charles Farquhar,
as he now is, commands the squadron in Syracuse. He intends
to wait there.' He wavered under Bolitho's grim stare. 'Until
a fleet comes under the flag of Sir Horatio Nelson.'

Bolitho stood up, ducking beneath the beams, until he had
reached the open stern windows.

Herrick had gone. Alone. The rest was as clear as the water
below the transom.

He heard the woman say, 'He is a good man, I met him
before he sailed.'

Bolitho turned towards her. 'He is, Ma'am.'

Inch said, 'When we heard the explosion we thought some
great vessel had blown up.'

'*Segura*'s cargo. We had to rejoin the squadron. That corvette thought otherwise.'

He recalled the midshipman's face, the Swede's cheerful acceptance of orders he sometimes did not even understand. Allday's scarred back.

He added harshly, 'So rejoin it we will, and as fast as you can manage!'

The *Harebell*'s first lieutenant appeared in the doorway, his eyes avoiding Bolitho as he reported, 'We have picked up thirty Frenchmen, sir. The captain was not one of them.'

He said as an afterthought, 'The master says that the wind is a piece stronger and has backed further to the sou'-west.'

Inch nodded, his long face set in a frown. To Bolitho he said, 'I believe you have met Mr. McLean, my senior, sir?'

Bolitho smiled gravely. 'Indeed. I had met him before when he came aboard *Lysander* with you on one occasion. It seems that the Navy is unchanged. Whereas lieutenants never remember their superiors, even commodores can recognise their lieutenants!'

Inch glared at the lieutenant. 'Call all hands and make sail. It will be hard work, but I want *Harebell* at her anchor by mid-afternoon!'

Bolitho sat down again, his limbs suddenly weak.

Inch said, 'I will go on deck, if I may.' He hesitated. 'I am indeed glad to be the one to find you, sir. Captain Herrick would have been pleased if –' He hurried from the cabin.

The woman said quietly, 'We spoke for a long time. I found Captain Herrick's story, his life, quite fascinating.'

Bolitho studied her for the first time. She was a pleasant looking woman, probably in her early thirties. She had a nice skin, and dark brown eyes to match her hair. It was all there in the way she had spoken of Herrick. Love denied. Love still to offer, perhaps.

He replied, 'I intend to find him, Ma'am. When I have spoken with Captain Farquhar I hope to know a great deal more than I do now!'

He had spoken with unusual sharpness, and she said, 'I think that Captain Farquhar is a man with great ambition.'

He smiled, liking her and her quick appreciation.

'Superior ambition does not necessarily breed superior

ability, Ma'am. I should have known that earlier. Much earlier. I pray to God I've not learned the lesson too late.'

Her hand moved to her neck. 'For Captain Herrick?'

'For Thomas, and a whole lot more, Ma'am.'

Allday peered through the door. 'Could you get him to lay down, Ma'am? He's done enough for a regiment today.'

She nodded. 'I will.' As Allday withdrew she asked, 'Is he one of your contemporaries?'

Bolitho lay back in the chair and shook his head, feeling the strain fading with his strength.

'No. He is my coxswain, and a good friend. But as a contemporary I fear he would soon be my superior. And that would be too much.'

She watched his eyelids droop, his head loll to the sloop's easy motion.

Bolitho was not quite as she had expected from what Herrick had told her. He seemed younger, for one who had carried so many, and who had experienced so much. Sensitive, too, something he obviously regarded as a flaw, and tried to hide with sternness.

She smiled. She was quite wrong. He was *exactly* as Herrick had described.

*

Farquhar stood quite still by the cabin screen, watching while Bolitho read carefully through the admiral's despatches.

Bolitho sat on the bench seat, the papers spread on the deck between his feet while he leaned above them, his elbows resting on his knees. On the seat beside him was a piece of fresh bread and a crock of butter which Manning had sent aboard that morning. Bolitho had eaten almost a whole loaf, liberally smeared with butter, and had washed it down with, to Farquhar's estimation, seven cups of coffee.

Bolitho looked up, his eyes searching. 'And you were going to remain here, were you?' He tapped the scattered papers. 'Did this mean nothing to you?'

Farquhar faced him calmly. 'If my assessment of the situation was different from yours, sir, then – '

Bolitho stood up, his eyes blazing. 'Don't make speeches

to me, *Captain* Farquhar! You read these despatches, the findings in the report on the artillery we captured, yet you saw *nothing*!' He stooped and snatched up two sheets of paper and thrust them on the table in a single movement. 'Read it! These cannon are forty-five-pounders. The military tested one, although to them it was probably unnecessary.' He tapped the table in time to his words. 'It can fire a forty-five-pound ball over *five thousand yards*. If you rate that unimportant, then you must be a fool! How far does the biggest gun in the fleet fire?' He strode to the quarter windows, his voice bitter. 'Let me refresh your memory. A thirty-two-pounder can reach three thousand yards. With luck, *and* a good gun captain.'

Farquhar retorted angrily, 'I do not see what that has to do with us, sir.'

'No, that is quite obvious.' He turned to face him. 'The French people expect a great victory. After their bloody revolution they may well *demand* such matters. And so to conquer Egypt, and reach far beyond, their fleet must first command the sea. Once safely beneath the protection of artillery such as these great cannon, the French could anchor an armada, several armadas, and know that there was not an English ship which could not be pounded to boxwood before she could grapple with them!'

Farquhar bit his lip. 'Coastal batteries.'

'At *last*, Captain.' Bolitho looked at him coldly. 'The pieces begin to fit for you also.'

There was a tap at the door and the sentry bawled, 'Officer of the watch, sir!'

Farquhar said, 'Pass him in.' He was probably relieved at the interruption.

The lieutenant stood just inside the door. 'We have just sighted *Buzzard*, sir. Coming from the north.'

'Thank you, Mr. Guthrie.'

Bolitho sat down and massaged his eyes. 'Get my clerk. I will dictate a despatch for Inch to carry to Gibraltar.' He could not hide his anger. 'Somewhat different from yours.'

Farquhar was expressionless. 'I will send for *my* clerk, sir. I am afraid yours is still in *Lysander*.'

'He will suffice for the present.' He walked to the door. 'I will get mine back when I recover my flagship.'

Farquhar stared after him. 'But I have had your broad pendant hoisted aboard *Osiris*, sir!'

'So I see.' He smiled gravely. 'Yours or mine? Were you *that* sure I was dead?'

He walked to the companion without waiting for an answer.

He found Mrs. Boswell on the poop talking with Pascoe. Seeing his nephew had brought home to him how desperately he needed to find Herrick, how much they needed each other.

If he understood Herrick too well, it was his own fault. Probably more so than Herrick's. He had been searching for something different in Farquhar, when Herrick's real value was so obvious that neither of them had seen it.

The woman turned and smiled shyly. 'I came over in the boat to say goodbye, Commodore.' She slipped her hand through Pascoe's arm. '*We* have been getting along very well.'

Bolitho nodded. 'I'm certain of it.' He saw through her cheerful tone and added, 'As soon as I have met with *Buzzard*'s captain I will order the squadron, or what is left of it, to weigh.'

She understood and walked with him to the poop ladder. 'I will leave you now. I am glad you are recovered. I know something of medicine, as fever killed my late husband. It is always hotter in these climates aboard ship than on the shore. In Sicily it has been quite cool until these last weeks.' She faced him sadly. 'If your men had left you in Malta, or worse, taken you ashore where you anchored, I fear you would have perished.'

A boat was waiting at the chains, and Bolitho saw the *Osiris*'s froglike first lieutenant peering impatiently from the entry port.

He said quietly, 'I have one piece of advice, Mrs. Boswell.' He guided her across the sun-warmed deck, oblivious to watching eyes and his own strange appearance. 'If you feel something for Thomas Herrick, I beg you to speak it.' He felt her tense as if to pull away from his hand.

But instead she asked, 'Is it *so* obvious?'

'There is nothing wrong in that.' He looked away towards the green slopes of land. 'My own love was too short, and I begrudge every second of it which was wasted. Also,' he forced a smile, 'I know that if you say naught, Thomas will remain as tongue-tied as a nun in a room full of sailors!'

'I shall remember.'

She looked at Pascoe. 'Take care of yourselves. I have the strangest feeling that something great is about to happen.' She shivered. 'I am not sure I like it.'

Bolitho watched her being lowered into the boat by boat-swain's chair, and then strode aft to watch *Buzzard*'s topsails edging slowly, so painfully slowly, around the northern headland.

Pascoe said, 'A nice lady, sir. A bit like Aunt Nancy.'

'Aye.' Bolitho thought of his sister in Falmouth, and her pompous husband. He had always been very close to Nancy, who, though younger than he, had always tried to 'mother' him.

Pascoe continued, 'They say that Nelson is coming to the Mediterranean, sir?'

'I'm thankful that somebody at last believes there is a real threat here. The battle, and battle there will be, may be decisive. Which is why we have work to do before that day dawns.'

He saw Pascoe's face and smiled. 'What's the matter, Adam? Don't you want Nelson to come? He is the best we have, and the youngest. That alone should please *you*!'

Pascoe dropped his gaze and smiled. 'One of the fore-topmen said it for me. We've got our *own* Nelson already.'

'I never heard such nonsense!' Bolitho made for the ladder, adding, 'You're getting as bad as that cox'n of mine!'

That night as Bolitho sat in *Osiris*'s unfamiliar cabin, writing his report on his conclusions, he listened to the creak and mutter of the hull around him. The wind was rising slightly, and had already veered more to the north-west. The sloop *Harebell*, which had set sail just before darkness, would be making heavy going, tacking back and forth, back and forth, merely to stay in the same place.

He thought of Javal's swarthy face as he had come aboard, surprised at seeing the broad pendant above *Osiris*, relieved to discover that Farquhar was not yet the commodore.

He had explained bluntly that after failing to discover the ships at the pre-arranged rendezvous, and hearing from a fisherman that they were at anchor in Syracuse, he had made a second patrol of the Messina Strait, and with the wind backing, had gone farther north in search of news. He had explained, 'I make no excuses, sir. I'm used to independence, but I don't *abuse* it. I put into Naples and visited the British Minister there. I had to come back with *something*.' His hard face had eased slightly. 'Had I known that you were off on your own, er, *expedition*, sir, I'd have sailed right into Valletta and brought you out, Knights or not!'

Javal knew his weak spot. As an ex-frigate captain, Bolitho had acted rashly by going to see Yves Gorse, but in keeping with his old calling. Perhaps Javal had used the point to dilute his own guilt.

Javal had explained, 'Sir William Hamilton may be old, sir, but he has a vast knowledge of affairs, *and* the communications to inform him.'

Bolitho signed his report and stared at the opposite bulkhead. His tarnished sword looked out of place against the ornate panelling.

Javal had delivered only one piece of news. To be more precise, he had brought a name.

Sir William had been informed through his chain of associates and spies that the one man who could determine the next weeks and months was known to be making for Toulon. That man would not be prepared to waste time on empty gestures.

His name was Bonaparte.

14

Run to Earth

ANY hopes of a quick passage to Corfu, or of Javal's lookouts sighting *Lysander* far ahead of the depleted squadron, were dashed within days of weighing anchor. The wind veered violently to the north, and as all hands worked feverishly to shorten sail, even *Osiris*'s master expressed his surprise at the intensity and speed of the change. Swooping down from the Adriatic, the wind transformed the gentle blue swell into a waste of steep, savage crests, while above the staggering mastheads the sky became one unbroken cloud bank.

Day after day, the two ships of the line used their bulk and strength to ride out the storm, while behind shuttered gun ports their companies fought their own battles against the sickening motion, and waited for the call, 'All hands! Hands aloft and reef tops'ls!' Then to a more perilous contest against the wind, clinging to dizzily swaying yards and fighting each murderous foot of canvas.

Buzzard, unable to withstand such a battering, had been made to run ahead of the storm, so that to the remaining ships it seemed as if the whole world was confined to this small arena of noise and drenching seas. For the visibility dropped with the hours, and it was hard to tell spray from rain, or from which direction the wind would attack next.

For Bolitho, the endless days made him feel remote from *Osiris*'s own struggle. The faces he met whenever he went on deck were unfamiliar, shouted opinions as yet carried no weight. He saw Farquhar in a different light as well. Several times he had given way to displays of anger which had made even the urbane Outhwaite quail, and once he had reprimanded a bosun's mate for not striking a man hard enough when he protested at being sent aloft in a full gale. The bosun's mate had tried to explain that the culprit was not a proper seaman, but a cooper's assistant. So many hands had been hurt in the storm that, like the officers, the bosun's mate was trying to gather as much extra muscle as he could.

Farquhar had shouted, 'Don't you *dare* argue! You've had to flog men! You know what it will feel like if you cross words with me again!'

The man had been driven aloft, and had fallen outboard without even a cry as he had lost his hold in the futtock shrouds.

Bolitho wondered how Herrick was managing to ride out the storm, and where he was during each sickening day.

Farquhar had said, 'But for this bloody weather, I'd have caught up with *Lysander*!'

'I doubt it.' Bolitho had reached beyond empty agreement. '*Lysander* is a faster ship. And she is well handled.'

It was unfair on Farquhar, but he had shown such indifference to Herrick's possible fate that it was all he could do to restrain some more biting comment. Like a nagging conscience, a small voice seemed to repeat, *It was your decision. You drove Herrick too hard, too soon. It was your fault.*

And then, a week after leaving Syracuse, the gale eased and backed to the north-west, but as the sky cleared and the sea regained its deep blue, Bolitho knew it would take several more days to recover lost ground. To beat back through time and distance which they had surrendered to the storm.

Whenever he went on deck he was aware that the officers on duty were careful to avoid his eye, and stayed well clear of his lonely pacing on the poop. His chosen solitude gave him time to think, although without fresh information it was like re-ploughing old land with nothing to sow.

During the forenoon on the ninth day he was in the cabin, studying his chart and drinking a tankard of ginger beer, something which Farquhar had stored in some quantity for his personal use.

How Farquhar would laugh, if after all there was nothing in Corfu to sustain his theories. He would not show it, of course, but it would be there just the same. It would not merely prove Farquhar correct in his actions, but also that he was far more suited to hold this or some other command.

Sir Charles Farquhar. It was strange that he should be so irritated by the man's title. He was getting like Herrick perhaps. No, it went deeper than that. It was because Farquhar had not earned it, and now would never want for anything again. You only had to look at the Navy List to see where the promotion went. He thought of Pascoe's words and smiled. The 'Nelsons' of this world gained their rewards and even titles on the battlefield, or facing an enemy's broadside. Their precarious advancement was often admired but rarely envied by those more fortunate ashore.

Bolitho walked restlessly around the cabin, hearing the seamen working on deck and in the yards above it. Splicing and re-rigging. After a storm each job was doubly essential. He smiled again. *Those more fortunate ashore.* In his heart he knew he would fight with all his means to avoid a post at the Admiralty or in some busy naval port.

He returned to the chart and stared at it once more. Corfu, a long, spindly island which seemed about to lock itself snugly to the Greek mainland. A narrow approach from the south, about ten miles across for a ship under sail. From the north, much less. Inviting self-destruction if the French had shore batteries along the high ground. Although the island was separated from the mainland by what was to all intents a small, private sea, some twenty by ten miles in size, the two real hazards were the narrow channels north and south. Also, the one good anchorage was on the eastern shore, so any sort of surprise there was out of the question. Herrick would know it, too. He was stubborn and determined, but he was no fool, and never had been.

He thought suddenly of the young widow, Mrs. Boswell. Strange he had never pictured Herrick being married. But she was exactly right for him. She would not stand by and let others step on his good nature. She would never have allowed him to admit that he could not sustain the posting of flag captain.

Bolitho straightened his back and marvelled that he could even consider such things. He had two ships, and might never find *Lysander* at all. But whatever happened, he was about to penetrate the enemy's defences in a sea area which was almost unknown to him beyond his charts and available hints on navigation.

There was a tap at the door and the sentry called cautiously, 'Midshipman of the watch, sir!'

It was the red-headed Breen.

'Well, Mr. Breen?' Bolitho smiled at him. It was the first time he had spoken with him since being rescued by *Harebell*.

'The captain sends his respects, sir. The lookout has reported a sail to the nor'-west. Too far off to recognise.'

'I see.'

Bolitho glanced at the chart. Even allowing for their drift and loss of way during the storm, they could not be that far out in their calculations. *Osiris*'s beakhead was pointing approximately north-east, and with luck they would sight the highest range of hills to the southernmost end of Corfu before nightfall. *Buzzard* had run with the storm, and although Javal would be quick to rejoin the squadron, and might appear even today, he would come from the south and not the north-west where this newcomer had shown herself.

He asked, 'How d'you like being temporarily attached to *Osiris*'s gunroom?'

The boy looked past him towards *Nicator*'s tall outline some three cables astern.

'N-not much, sir. They treat me well enough, but . . .'

Bolitho watched him gravely. Like the lieutenants, most of the midshipmen in this ship were of good family stock. Farquhar had evidently planned his wardroom and his midshipmen with great care. It was quite common for a captain to take a boy to sea as midshipman, the son of an old friend perhaps, or as some special favour. Farquhar appeared to have taken the custom right through his command.

Breen seemed to think he was expected to add something. 'I keep thinking about the seaman, sir, Larssen. But I'm all right now. I-I'm sorry about the way I acted.'

'Don't be. A sword must bend. If it is made too hard it will snap when it is most needed.'

He wondered why he was trying to save Breen from the inevitable. It came to all of them sooner or later. He recalled his own feelings after a sea fight when he had been a young lieutenant. The guns working so hard and the battle so fierce that there had been no time to treat the dead, even the wounded, with care or respect. The corpses had been pushed overboard from friend and enemy alike, and the wounded had added their cries to the thunder of battle. When the firing had ceased, and the ships had drifted apart, too damaged and hurt to claim victory or offer defeat, the sea had been covered with drifting corpses. Because the wind had dropped during the battle, as if cowed by its savagery, they were made to watch them for two whole days. It was something he often thought about and could never forget.

He said quietly, 'Have some ginger beer.'

Poor Breen, with his rough, scrubbed hands and grubby shirt, he was more a schoolboy than a King's officer. But who in his town or village had seen Malta? Had been in a sea fight? And how many would ever know the full extent of naval power as it really was, and the men and timbers which made it?

Farquhar appeared in the door and stared coldly at the boy with a glass in his fist.

To Bolitho he said, 'That sail has sheered off, sir.'

'Not *Lysander*?'

'Too small.' Farquhar nodded curtly to Breen as he hurried away. 'Brig, according to the masthead lookout. A good man. He's usually right.'

Farquhar seemed much more controlled now that the storm had gone. A waiting game perhaps. Standing aside to see what Bolitho would do.

Bolitho walked to the open stern windows and leaned out above the small bubbling wash around the rudder. A good clear sky, and the horizon astern of *Nicator*'s fat hull was hard and empty. The brig would see more of these two ships than they would of her.

'Tell the lookouts to take extra care. Send telescopes aloft, too.'

'You think the brig was French, sir?' Farquhar sounded curious. 'She can do *us* little harm.'

'Maybe. In Falmouth my sister's husband owns a large farm and estate.' He looked impassively at Farquhar. 'He also has a dog. Whenever a poacher or vagrant comes near his land, the dog tracks him, but never attacks or barks.' He smiled. 'Until the stranger is within range of a fowling-piece!'

Farquhar stared at the chart, as if he expected to see something there.

'Following us, sir?'

'It is possible. The French have many friends here. They

would be willing and eager to pass information which might ease their lot once the tricolour has extended its "estates".'

Farquhar said uneasily, 'But supposing that is so, the French cannot know our full strength.'

'They will see we have no frigates. If I were a French admiral, that would be very valuable news indeed.' He walked to the door, an idea emerging from the back of his mind. 'Fetch your sailmaker, will you?'

On the quarterdeck, several hands paused to watch him before returning to their work with added vigour. They probably thought him unhinged by the fever. Bolitho allowed the light wind to cool him and smiled to himself. He was still wearing his Spanish shirt, and had declined any of Farquhar's spare clothing. His own was still aboard *Lysander*. He would get it when he found Herrick. *And find him he would.*

'Sir?' The sailmaker was at his side, watching him with a mixture of caution and interest.

'How much spare canvas do you have? That which is useless for making new sails and the like?'

The man glanced nervously at Farquhar, who snapped, '*Tell* him, Parker!'

The sailmaker launched into a long list of stores and frag-ments, item by item, and Bolitho was impressed that he retained so much in his memory.

'Thank you, er, Parker.' He moved to the starboard gangway and stared along it towards the forecastle. 'I want a strip of canvas sewn and lashed along the gangway nettings on either side of the ship. Hammock cloths, unwanted scraps which you may have been keeping for repairing awnings and winds'ls.' He faced him calmly. 'Can you do that?'

'Well, that is, sir, I expect I could manage if . . .' He looked at his captain for support.

Farquhar asked, 'For what purpose, sir? I think if this fellow knew what you required, and I, too, for that matter, it would help him.'

Bolitho smiled at them. 'If we join fo'c'sle to quarterdeck in this manner, then paint the canvas the same as the hull, with black squares at regular intervals,' he leaned over the rail to gesture at the eighteen-pounder gun ports, 'we can transform *Osiris* into a *three-decker*, eh?'

Farquhar shook his head. 'Damn me, sir, it would do the

trick. At any sort of distance we'd look like a first-rate, and no mistake! The Frogs will begin to wonder just how many of us there are.'

Bolitho nodded. 'Inshore we may stand a chance. But we cannot afford a pitched battle in open waters until we have discovered the enemy's real strength. I doubt that the French will have many ships of the line here. De Brueys will save them for the fleet and for protecting his transports. But I must know.'

'Deck there! Sail on the larboard quarter!'

Bolitho said, 'Our will-o'-the-wisp again. As soon as it is dusk we will begin the disguise. We can change tack during the night and maybe give our inquisitive friend the slip.'

Another hail made them look up. 'Deck there! Sail on the *lee* bow!'

'Company?' Bolitho prodded the sailmaker with his fist. 'Get your mates to work, Parker. You may be the first man in history to build a King's ship out of canvas scraps!'

He saw Pascoe hurrying up the weather shrouds to join the lookout who had made the last report. He was hampered by a large telescope slung over his shoulder, but ran up the ratlines with the ease of a cat.

Moments later he shouted, 'She's the *Buzzard*, sir!'

Farquhar muttered, 'About time, too.'

Bolitho said, 'Make a signal to *Buzzard*. Take station ahead of the squadron.'

Farquhar replied, 'She'll not be in signalling distance for quite a time, sir. She'll have to claw every inch of the way against the wind.'

'She cannot see the signal, Captain. But the other vessel *will*. Her master will know there is another, maybe several ships close by. It may give him something to chew on.'

Bolitho thrust his hands behind him, seeing the boatswain and some seamen already broaching the paint, while others dragged the canvas across the upper deck.

He began to pace slowly along the weather side, willing *Buzzard*'s topsails to show themselves to him above the horizon.

Three ships now instead of two. He thanked God for Javal's determination to find him. Weak they may be. But they were no longer blind as well.

While *Osiris* and her consort continued at a snail's pace to the north-east, and Javal worked the frigate through countless zigzags to join them, the small blur of canvas which betrayed their follower was rarely out of sight.

All afternoon, as the sailmaker and his mates sat cross-legged on every spare piece of deck, heads bent, needles and palms flashing in the sunlight, Bolitho prowled about the poop or visited the cabin in a state of near exhaustion.

In the last dog watch, when the lookout shouted, 'Land ho!', he guessed that the pursuing brig would be satisfied that the squadron, large or small, was indeed making for Corfu.

Bolitho examined the purple shadow of land through the rigging and shrouds, and pictured the island in his mind. The brig's master had been too faithful to his orders. Now, with night closing in more rapidly, he would have to bide his time and hold the information to himself. Under similar circumstances, Bolitho thought that he would have taken the risk of his admiral's displeasure and called off the chase long ago. He would have been more use to his admiral alongside the flagship than riding out a long night off this dangerous coast. Curiosity had been the brig's weakness. It was not much, but it might be vital.

He returned to the cabin and found Farquhar waiting for him with Veitch and Plowman.

Farquhar said, 'You wanted these two, I believe, sir.' He sounded disdainful.

Bolitho waited as a servant hung another lantern above the chart.

'Now, Mr. Plowman. I need a good volunteer to spy out the land for me.'

The master's mate looked at the chart and the marks which denoted cliffs and deep soundings along the western shore.

He gave a slow grin. 'Aye, sir. I take your meanin'!'

Farquhar asked sharply, 'Are you sending men ashore *at night*, sir?'

Bolitho did not reply directly. He looked at Plowman and asked simply, 'Can you do it? If it was not important I would not ask.'

'I've tackled worse. Once in West Africa . . .' He sighed. 'But that's another story, sir.'

'Good.'

Bolitho studied him gravely. He was probably asking far

too much. Sending Plowman and others to their deaths. He toyed with the idea of going himself but knew it would be pointless either way. Conceit, desperation, anxiety, none came into it. He would be needed *here*, and very soon.

To Farquhar he said, 'They will want a cutter and a good stout crew.' He turned to Veitch. 'I'm putting you in charge of the landing party. Choose your men carefully. Men used to the countryside, who'll not fall headlong down a cliff.'

He saw the gravity on the lieutenant's face giving way to something else. Satisfaction. Pride perhaps at being offered such a demanding task without restriction. If Bolitho had doubts they were in himself. Veitch had already proved his worth and his ability.

Plowman was still examining the chart. 'This looks a likely place.' He jabbed it with a thick finger. 'An' there'll be a good moon tonight. We can run under sail till we're close in, then pull the rest of the way.'

Bolitho said, 'You can take all night. But tomorrow, try to discover what is happening. The island is about five miles across at the point you have selected, Mr. Plowman. The hills rise to a thousand feet or more. From there you should see enough for our purposes.'

Veitch said slowly, 'It may be difficult to hide the cutter, sir.'

'Do what you can.' He looked at each of them. 'Otherwise, you will have to sink it where you land. I will send another to take you off later.'

Farquhar coughed. 'There is a fact to be faced, sir. The whole party may be taken prisoner within minutes of getting ashore.'

Bolitho nodded grimly. So even Farquhar was now accepting the reality of their situation. The enemy was fact, not shadows.

'*We* will attack from the south'rd at dawn, the day after tomorrow. If Mr. Veitch can discover the whereabouts of shore batteries, and their strength, it will make our task less demanding.' He smiled at their tense expressions. 'Although I fear our arrival will not be welcome.'

Veitch breathed out noisily. 'We'll do our best, sir. Let us hope that the French have none of their new guns along the coast.'

'That I doubt.' Bolitho pictured the great cannon smashing his little force into submission before they had even got to grips. 'They are being saved for something more important to Bonaparte.'

Veitch and Plowman left the cabin to gather their men and weapons, and he said, 'I would like to see my signals officer. Tomorrow we will head northwards under our new guise, but hold *Buzzard* well to windward. Javal may get a chance to catch that brig or any other spy, if he's in the right place. One more vessel under our flag would be welcome.'

He suddenly saw himself at Spithead, awaiting the boat which would carry him out to the frigate. To Gibraltar, to *Lysander*, and all those countless hours and miles sailed since. *To here.* A small cross on the chart. He shivered, despite the heavy air. It was almost symbolic. And this was when he needed Herrick most. His loyalty and devotion. He wondered what Farquhar thought about it. Really thought. Did he see this as his chance to add fame to his new status? Or did he see it only as an end to all his hopes?

They made light of risk. They always did beforehand. But he was asking much of every single man. Far too much. When battle was joined, causes and grand ideals counted for very little. It was the speed you could fire and reload. The strength you held to withstand the awful sights and sounds.

He shook himself from the lingering depression.

'Well, Captain Farquhar.' He saw him come out of his own thoughts. 'We will do this together, or if one of us falls, the other will carry on with it. Either way, *it must be done.*'

'Yes.' Farquhar looked around the quiet cabin. 'I can see that now.'

*

Within hours of full daylight the brig's topsails appeared again, tipping the horizon, but taking care to stand off well to windward. Either her master had managed to send word ashore by boat during the night, or he was eager to learn more about Bolitho's ships.

Bolitho made certain that their attendant spy had plenty to hold his attention. Pascoe's signal party hoisted several meaningless flags, which were acknowledged with equal vigour by *Nicator* and *Buzzard*. Then, when Bolitho made a genuine signal, to call the other captains aboard for a discussion of their position, he played his other card. With sails aback, *Osiris* came round into the wind, displaying her broadside to the distant vessel, and her impressive new height above water.

When Javal arrived in his gig he exclaimed admiringly, 'I thought I was seeing things, sir. Or that St. Vincent had arrived in his flagship. From my gig she looks every inch a first-rate!'

Probyn was less enthusiastic. 'A novel idea, I agree. But we can't shoot with painted canvas!'

Once more in the great cabin Bolitho looked at his captains. Javal seemed strained after his long fight against the sea and wind, but otherwise unworried. Farquhar, tight-lipped and pale, but neither a hair nor a gilt button out of place. Probyn was as untidy and as brooding as ever. He looked heavy-eyed, and his cheeks were redder than one would expect from wind alone. Drinking more than usual. It was strange, but Bolitho found he had forgotten how Probyn had used to drink when they had been lieutenants together. More than once he had stood a watch or a duty for him, when the first lieutenant had drawled, 'See to it, Dick. Poor old George is in his cups again.'

He waited until each of them had a glass of Farquhar's claret in his hand, then said calmly, 'Tomorrow, gentlemen, we will make our play. I hope to pick up Mr. Veitch and his party tonight. What he tells me may alter our tactics, but cannot postpone an attack.'

Probyn kept his eyes on his lap. 'What if he doesn't come back?'

'It will keep us in the dark.'

He thought of Veitch out there on Corfu. The villagers, if he was unlucky enough to stumble on them, might take them as Frenchmen. He was not sure if that was good or bad. Veitch had shown himself to be a quick-thinking and intelligent man. Bolitho would make certain his name went forward for early promotion if he survived another night on the island. He had toyed with the idea of telling him beforehand, but had decided against it. Such a promise could make an ambitious man too careful, an eager one too reckless.

'We have shown ourselves as preparing to attack. The enemy will still not know our full strength, but as they may now believe we have a three-decker supporting us, they must decide on their own plan of defence. Or attack.'

Probyn slammed his empty glass on the table and looked meaningly at the cabin servant.

Then he asked, 'Why not wait, sir? Watch and wait, until we get more support.' He looked from the corners of his eyes at Farquhar. 'If *Lysander* had been here, then I might have said otherwise.'

Bolitho watched Probyn emptying another glass of claret.

'We do not know enough to wait. At any day, the enemy might try to sail out of Corfu, and if their numbers are what I believe, we could not hope to contain them.' He saw Probyn was unconvinced, and added, 'Besides which, the French fleet may even now be steering in *this* direction to escort their precious supply ships elsewhere.' He tapped the chart with his glass. 'Caught on a lee shore, or worse, bottled up on the eastern side of the island, what chance would we have then?'

He kept his gaze on Probyn, willing him to accept, if not condone, the reasoning. For Captain George Probyn's part could be the most important of all. Tomorrow, hours not days now, and his *Nicator* might be the sole survivor.

He said quietly, '*Osiris* will force the southern channel at dawn. The supply ships will be anchored anywhere from fifteen to twenty miles up the coast, and once amongst them it will be a busy time for us all.' He saw Javal's hard face break into a smile. 'The French, I believe, see themselves in a strong position. They will know we are coming, and move what guns they have ashore to command our approach.'

Javal nodded. 'Aye, it makes sense. A three-decker would be seen as the real threat.'

Bolitho thought of Grubb and wished he was here. *Osiris*'s sailing master seemed capable enough, but lacked Grubb's knowledge and philosophy on the weather's habits. He had been a mate in an Indiaman before joining a King's ship, and his early service had been spent weighing the value of a fast passage against goods lost by poor navigation.

If so much depended on what his ships could do tomorrow, the wind was almost equal in importance.

He shut it behind him and said to Probyn, 'You will leave us at dusk. Steer to the north'rd. When the time is ready you will enter the top channel, I am hoping, unopposed. The defenders should think the real menace is from us in the south. If "lady luck",' he hesitated, seeing Herrick's blue eyes crinkling to his favourite talisman, 'blesses us, and the wind holds, we will hit the enemy hard, and where it will do our cause most good.'

They all stood up, knowing it was over.

Bolitho added, 'God be with you.'

They filed out in silence, then Bolitho heard Farquhar shouting for someone to recall the captains' boats.

Allday entered the cabin by the other door and asked, 'Can't I get you a uniform coat from somewhere, sir?' He sounded more worried by Bolitho's appearance than the prospect of battle.

Bolitho walked to the quarter windows and saw Probyn's barge pulling strongly away. He thought of this ship, *Osiris*, the men who would work her up that channel. Would fight and, if need be, die. It was not a happy ship. He frowned. Nicator. *Judge of the Dead*. He felt suddenly chilled.

He answered, 'No matter, Allday. Tomorrow they may look aft, as you insist they do in action.' He saw him nod. 'I want them to see me. More like one of themselves than as one more oppressive uniform. This ship has no *warmth* about her. She carries all the marks of discipline and efficiency, but . . .' He shrugged.

Allday said, 'They'll fight well enough, sir. You'll see.'

But Bolitho could not shake off his feeling of foreboding. 'If anything should happen.' He did not turn from the windows but heard Allday tense. 'I have made provision for you in Falmouth. You will always have a home there, and want for nothing.'

Allday could not restrain himself. He strode aft to the gallery and exclaimed, 'I'll hear none of it, sir! Nothing will happen, nothing can.'

Bolitho turned and looked at him. 'You will prevent it?'

Allday stared at him wretchedly. 'If I can.'

'I know.' He sighed. 'Perhaps, like Thomas Herrick, I am here too soon after that other time.'

Allday insisted, 'The surgeon was right, sir. Your wound is not properly healed yet, your health more set back by the

fever than you'll allow for.' He added meaningly, 'Cap'n
Farquhar's surgeon is no butcher. He's a *proper* doctor.
Cap'n Farquhar took good care of that!'

Bolitho smiled gravely. *He would.* 'Ask Mr. Pascoe to lay
aft. I have some signals to prepare.'

Alone again, he sat down at the table and stared unseeingly
at his chart. He thought of Catherine Pareja, and wondered
what she was doing now in London.

Twice a widow, yet with more life in her than most young
girls just free of their mother's arms. Never once had she
mentioned marriage. Not even a hint. Something seemed to
hold it back. An unspoken agreement.

He opened the front of his Spanish shirt and examined the
tiny locket which hung around his neck. Kate had never
even shown resentment for that. He opened it carefully and
examined the small lock of chestnut-coloured hair. It caught
the sunlight from the stern windows and shone as brightly
as the day he had met her. An admiral's bride-to-be. Cheney
Seton. The girl he had won and had married. He closed the
locket and rebuttoned his shirt. It never changed. No wonder
he had cried her name.

Pascoe entered the cabin, his hat beneath his arm, a signal
book in one hand.

Bolitho faced him, concealing his sudden despair as best
he could.

'Now, Adam, let us see what other ideas we can invent,
shall we?'

*

'Course nor'-east by north, sir! Full an' bye!'

Bolitho heard the master whispering with his helmsmen
but hurried to the nettings, now packed with neatly stowed
hammocks and starkly pale in the moonlight.

Farquhar joined him and reported, 'Wind's steady, sir. We are
about twenty miles south-west of the island. *Buzzard*'s to windward, you can just make out her tops'ls in the moon's path.'

'No sign of a boat?'

'None. I sent the other cutter away under sail three hours
back. If Veitch saw it he made no signal with either lantern
or pistol-shot.'

'Very well. How long does the master think we can remain on this tack?'

'An hour more at the most, sir. Then I'll have to recall my cutter, and by that time I'll be ready to come about. Otherwise, we'll be too close to lie-to, and if we continue round in another great circle we'll be further away from the southern channel than I care for when dawn comes.'

'I agree.' Bolitho added reluctantly, 'Another hour then.'

Farquhar asked, 'Are you certain you did right by sending *Nicator* to the northern channel, sir? It will be a disaster if Probyn fails to engage in time.'

'The channel is narrow, I know, but with favourable winds *Nicator* will be able to manage.'

'I was not referring to the channel or the danger, sir.' Farquhar's face was in the moon's shadow, his epaulettes very bright against his coat. 'I have to admit, I feel no faith in *Nicator*'s captain.'

'When he sees our dependence on his support, Captain Farquhar, he will do his duty.'

He recalled Probyn's reddened features, his indirect manner. His caution. But what could he do? If things happened as he had predicted, *Osiris* would take the worst of it, and would need the most tenacity. He could not ask Javal to thrust his frail ship into the teeth of a bombardment, although his part in the attack was bad enough anyway. Without *Lysander*'s support, the surprise would have to be left to *Nicator*. There was no other way. He wondered if Farquhar was cursing himself now for letting Herrick go unaided, for failing to act as a squadron against the enemy when he believed himself in overall command.

'Deck there! Light on th' weather bow!'

Bolitho ran to the larboard gangway and peered above the painted canvas.

He heard Farquhar snap, 'The signal, by God! Mr. Outhwaite! Heave-to, if you please, and prepare to hoist boats inboard!'

The ship came alive, the hurrying seamen like phantoms in the eerie moonlight as they ran without hesitation to halliards and braces.

Someone raised a cheer as first one and then the second cutter bumped alongside, and men scrambled down to them to bear a hand.

Sailing and pulling at the oars, it must have been an
unnerving job for the crews, Bolitho thought.

He waited by the quarterdeck rail, gripping his hands
behind him to prevent his impatience from sending him down
to the entry port with the others.

He saw a sturdy figure limping aft and recognised him
instantly.

'Mr. Plowman! Come over here!'

The master's mate leaned against the hammock nettings and
tried to regain his breath.

'Glad to be 'ere, sir.'

He waved his arm towards the invisible land, and Bolitho
saw that his hand was wrapped in a stained bandage, the
blood soaking through it like black oil.

' 'Ad to lie low, even when we saw t'other boat standin'
inshore. Place was alive with pickets. We run into one of 'em.
Bit of a fight.' He examined his bandaged fist. 'But we done
for 'em.'

'And Mr. Veitch?' He waited for the inevitable.

But Plowman said, ' 'E's fine, sir. I left 'im ashore. 'E
ordered me to find you an' report.'

Even the cabin lanterns seemed too bright after the strange
moonscape on deck, and Bolitho saw that Plowman was filthy
from head to toe, his face and arms scarred from rock and gorse.

'Have a drink.' Bolitho saw Farquhar and his first lieutenant,
and behind them Pascoe, coming into the cabin. 'Anything
you like.'

Plowman sighed gratefully. 'Then I'd like a measure o'
brandy, if I may dare ask, sir.'

Bolitho smiled. 'You deserve a cask.' He waited in silence,
watching Plowman's expression as he drank a complete
goblet of Farquhar's brandy. 'Now tell me the news.'

Plowman wiped his mouth with his wrist. 'It ain't good,
sir.' He shook his head. 'We did like you said, and Mr. Veitch
was fair amazed by what we saw. Just like you told us it
would be, only more so.'

Farquhar snapped, 'Ships?'

'Aye, sir. Thirty or more. Well-laden, too. An' there's a
ship o' the line at anchor offshore, a *seventy-four*. An' two or
three smaller ships. A frigate, an' a pair o' corvettes, like the
Frenchie we done for with *Segura*.'

Farquhar said softly, 'What a find! A small armada, no less!'

Plowman ignored him. 'But that ain't all, sir. They've hauled a pair o' them new guns to the 'eadland.' He leaned heavily across the chart and jabbed it with his thumb. 'There. We thought for a bit they was unloadin' all the ships, but they just ferried these two beauties ashore. We met up with a shepherd at dawn. One of the lads won 'is confidence like, speaks a bit of the language. The locals don't care for the Frogs. They've bled the island white. An' the women, too, by th' sound of it. Anyway, he said that the ships are preparin' to leave. Goin' to Crete or somewhere, to wait for more ships.'

'De Brueys.' Bolitho looked at him gravely. 'Why did Lieutenant Veitch stay behind?' He had already guessed the answer.

'Mr. Veitch told me that 'e thinks you'll attack, sir. Said you'd not let the *Nicator* go in on 'er own.' He scowled. 'But for this mangy fist I'd 'ave stayed there with 'im.'

Bolitho said, 'Your return is of greater value to me. And I thank you.'

Veitch had seen it, right from the beginning. That without more ships they could not keep in contact with *Nicator*, nor could they reach her before dawn and the moment of attack.

Plowman added wearily as Bolitho refilled the glass, 'Mr. Veitch said 'e would try to 'elp, sir. He got three volunteers with 'im.' He gave a sad grin. 'All as mad as 'im, if you'll pardon the liberty, sir, so I can't tell you no more.'

His head lolled with fatigue, and Bolitho said quietly, 'Tell Allday to help him to the sickbay and have his hand dressed. And see that both boat crews are rewarded in some way.'

He looked at their faces. Farquhar's set in a grim frown. Outhwaite's liquid eyes watching him with quiet fascination. And Pascoe, his black hair falling across one eye, as if he, too, had a scar to hide.

Bolitho asked, 'Well, Captain Farquhar, what is your opinion on this?'

He shrugged. 'But for *Nicator*'s safety, I'd advise you to withdraw, sir. There is no sense in putting your honour before the loss of a squadron. We gambled on the French keeping all their precious artillery stowed in their holds, and relying on more "conventional" weapons.' He glanced briefly at Plowman's sagging shoulder. He had fallen into an exhausted sleep. 'But if fellows like Plowman here, and Lieutenant Veitch, are prepared to throw their lives down the hawse, I suppose I will do the same!'

He looked calmly at his first lieutenant. 'Commodore's instructions, Mr. Outhwaite. One hot meal and a double ration of rum for all hands. After that, you may douse the galley fires, and then clear for action. Our people will sleep beside their guns tonight.' He looked at Bolitho. 'If sleep they can.'

Farquhar nodded curtly. 'Now, if you will excuse me, sir. I have some letters to write.'

Bolitho looked at Pascoe. 'I wish you were in almost any other ship, Adam. In any place but here.'

Pascoe regarded him searchingly. 'I am content, sir.'

Bolitho walked to the windows and stared at the silver glow across the water. Like rippling silk, the patterns changing endlessly. He thought of Farquhar writing his letters. To his mother? To the Admiralty?

He said, 'In my steward's keeping at Falmouth, Adam, there is a letter. For you.'

He felt Pascoe step beside him, and saw his reflection in the thick glass. Like brothers in the strange glow.

'Don't say anything.' He reached out and put his arm round his shoulder. 'The letter will tell you everything you must do. The rest you will decide for yourself.'

'But, Uncle.' Pascoe's voice sounded unsteady. 'You must not speak like that!'

'It must be said.' He turned and smiled at him. 'As it was once said to me. And now,' he forced the pain out of his thoughts, 'we must help Mr. Plowman below.'

But when they turned from the windows, Plowman had already gone.

15

Disaster

'STEER nor'-nor'-east.' Farquhar remained near the wheel, looking towards Bolitho. 'We will weather the headland as close as we dare.' He glared at the master. 'Do you *understand*, Mr. Bevan?'

'Aye, sir.' The master shifted under his stare. 'It's a bad entrance. Shoals below the headland. Some others offshore, but the charts can't fix them exactly.'

Farquhar walked down to the quarterdeck rail. 'No sign of life yet, sir.'

Bolitho raised a telescope and moved it slowly along the uneven summit of the headland. About a mile across the larboard bow. But it was still resting in deep shadow, with only the paling sky to give some indication of height and depth. But he could see the writhing movement at the bottom of the nearest point, to mark the sea breaking and sluicing over a steep, stony beach, and jagged reefs, too. He heard Farquhar's sudden impatience with the sailing master, and guessed it had been as much to relieve the tension as anything. But he had been wrong to vent his feelings on him. Bevan, the master, ex-mate of an Indiaman, needed all his wits about him now, and the complete confidence of his three helmsmen, without his captain throwing his temperament to all and sundry.

'I expect none.'

Bolitho stiffened as something passed above the nearest hump of land. For a moment he thought it was smoke, but it was a solitary feather of cloud, moving diagonally towards the water beyond the headland which was still in semi-darkness. He saw that the forepart of the cloud was pale gold, holding the sun which was still hidden to the men in both ships.

He strode to the nettings and climbed on the top of a nine-pounder to peer across the quarter. *Buzzard* was right on station. Two cables astern, with her mainsail and topgallants clewed up and her big forecourse braced round to contain the light south-westerly wind. She looked very slender and frail in the dim light, and he pictured Javal with his officers watching the same jutting land, and willing time to pass. To get on with it.

But it would be some while yet, he thought. The French would bide their time and not risk their enemy's escape by opening fire too early.

He stepped down from the gun and almost fell. Despite the liberal scattering of sand along every gun deck, the planks were damp with night dew and treacherous underfoot. A seaman caught his elbow and grinned at him.

'Easy sir! We'll not 'ave 'em sayin' it was our gun which downed the commodore!'

Bolitho smiled. As in every part of the ship, the guns were fully manned and loaded. All it needed to complete her preparedness was to open the ports and run out. But if there was some watcher on the land, there was no point in showing that *Osiris*'s upper line of gun ports was only black squares painted on canvas.

He said, 'Nor that I was too drunk to stand upright, eh?'

They laughed, as he knew they would. The air around the guns, even in the cool wind, was heavy with rum, and he guessed that far more than a double tot had found its way to each man. Or that some had used their issue to pay old debts, or to purchase something better. Most likely, some had held back their rum to cover bets. What had they bet on? Who would live or die? How much prize money they would receive? Which officer would hold his nerve the longest? He had no doubt that the bets would be many and varied.

He walked forward again to the rail and stared along the shadowed gun deck. Figures moved restlessly around each black barrel. Like slaves as they tested each piece of tackle and equipment for their trade. The gun captains had done their part. Had made certain that the first balls to be fired were perfect in shape and weight, that each charge was just right. After the opening shots, it was usually too desperate, too deafening to pause for such niceties.

He looked up and saw the marine marksmen in the tops, while right forward on the forecastle there were more of them, standing loosely beside their long muskets, or chatting with the carronade crews.

Bolitho heard Allday say, 'I've brought the sword, sir.'

He slipped off the boat cloak he had been wearing since three hours before dawn and allowed Allday to buckle on his sword.

Allday said softly, but with obvious disapproval, 'You look more like a buccaneer than a commodore, sir! I don't know what they'd say in Falmouth!'

Bolitho smiled. 'One of my ancestors *was* a pirate, Allday.' He tightened the belt buckle. He had lost some weight during his fever. 'When it was a respectable calling, of course.'

He turned as Farquhar hurried past. 'Have you extra hands on pumps and buckets?'

'Yes, sir.' Farquhar ran a finger around his neckcloth. 'If they use heated shot on us, I'm as ready as I can be.' He looked at the nets spread above the gun deck, at the looser ones draped along the shrouds to prevent a sudden rush of boarders. To the sentries at each hatch and companion, and the boatswain's party who waited to hack away fallen spars, or clear corpses from an upended gun.

Bolitho watched him, seeing his mind examining each part of his command for a flaw or a weak point. Under their feet, and beneath the crowded gun deck, the lower batteries of thirty-two-pounders would be ready and waiting. And below them, standing like ghouls in a circle of lanterns, the surgeon and his assistants, watching the empty table, the glittering knives and saws. Bolitho recalled Luce's pale face, his pleading. His one frantic scream. He looked across at Pascoe who stood on the lee side by the main shrouds, talking with a petty officer and a midshipman. Was he thinking about Luce, he wondered?

Aft, on the poop, the bulk of the marines waited by the nettings, in three lines, for if *Osiris* was to engage from her larboard side, they would have to fire rank by rank, like soldiers in a square.

Bolitho tried to pick out faces he knew, but there were hardly any. Anonymous, yet familiar. Typical, but unknown. Marines and seamen, lieutenants and midshipmen. He had seen them in a dozen ships, in as many fleets.

A marine lieutenant's silver shoulder-plate gleamed suddenly as if heated from within. As Bolitho turned his head to starboard he saw the sun's rim on the horizon, the rays filtering down across the ruffled water towards him like molten metal.

Allday remarked, 'Going to be a fine day.'

Lieutenant Outhwaite was standing by the main companion way, his eyes glowing like little stones as he stared towards the sunrise. Like his captain, he was impeccably dressed, his hat set exactly square on his head, his long queue straight down his spine.

Farquhar wore no hat, but a midshipman stood near him, carrying it, and his sword, as if for an actor waiting to begin his most difficult role. In fact, Bolitho saw that Farquhar's mouth was moving. Speaking to himself, or rehearsing a speech for his men, he did not know.

His hair was very fair, and he had it pulled back to the nape of his neck and tied with a neat black bow. Whatever happened in the next hours, Farquhar was dressed for it.

He seemed to sense Bolitho's scrutiny and turned towards him. He gave a slow smile. 'A new uniform, sir. But I recalled your own custom before a fight of consequence.' He gave a brief shake of the head. 'And as your tailor is elsewhere, I thought I would set the example.'

Bolitho replied, 'A kind thought.'

He peered along the deck again, seeing the land-mass growing and looming towards the bowsprit, as if they were touching.

'The enemy will not fire until he has a sure target. His gunners will have the sun in their eyes directly, but once we are standing well up the eastern shore it will not help us much. There is a dip behind the bay I have in mind. A good site for long-range guns.'

He strained his eyes beyond the bows as a voice yelled, 'Surf! Fine on the larboard bow!'

The master said tightly, 'That'll be the damned reef, sir.'

'Let her pay off a point, Mr. Bevan. Steer nor'-east by north.' Farquhar looked at his first lieutenant. 'D'you have a good leadsman in the chains?'

'Aye, sir.' The frogface watched him questioningly. 'I have stressed the importance of his task this morning.'

Bolitho found he could smile, in spite of the gnawing uncertainty of waiting. Farquhar and Outhwaite were well matched. So maybe Farquhar was right in his methods of selection. After all, they said of West Country ships that they were foreign to all but the Cornish and Devonians who manned them. The ways of St. James's and Mayfair were as hard to learn.

The light was spreading and filtering on to small beaches now and winkling out shadows from hillsides and coves. The sea's face, too, was clearer, the tiny white cat's-paws moving away to starboard to merge in the colourful horizon and the sun.

Maybe the real Lysander has seen such a sea, Bolitho thought. When the fleets of triremes and galliasses had smashed into each other and the sky had been dark with arrows and darts of fire.

From astern he heard the sudden squeak and rumble of guns being run out, and knew that Javal was getting ready.

Farquhar snapped, 'Alter course three points. Steer north.'

He craned over the nettings to watch a hump of sand or rock edging past the quarter. Some gulls rose squawking from their little islet, very white against the land's backdrop. They circled above the mastheads, hoping for food, noisy in their greed.

Bolitho looked up at his pendant as one gull dipped near it, screaming angrily. It was flapping less persistently, for the land was creeping past, dampening down the wind. He thought of Probyn. It was to be hoped he had worked his ship into position early, to allow for adverse winds, the treacherously narrow channel.

He pulled his watch from his breeches and examined it. He could see it well now, even the beautiful lettering on the face, *Mudge and Dutton of London*. He closed the guard with a snap and saw Midshipman Breen jump with alarm.

He said, 'Very well. We are past the headland.'

Outhwaite swung round, his speaking trumpet to his mouth. 'Mr. Guthrie! Pass the word! *Run out!*'

As the port lids squeaked open there was a brief pause, and down on the lower gun deck the seamen, stripped and ready, would be seeing the land for the first time. A whistle shrilled, and with a mounting tremble *Osiris* ran out her artillery.

'Brail up the forecourse!'

Farquhar watched the great sail being subdued and brailed to its yard, and snapped his fingers. The midshipman gave him his sword and then his hat. He adjusted his hat with care, and after a moment walked forward to the weather gangway.

The forecourse had completed the illusion. The stage was set. The actors were prepared.

Bolitho drew his sword and laid it flat on the rail, feeling the steel, cool under his palms.

'Run up the Colours.'

He heard the squeak of a block and saw the flag's great shadow rippling across the gangway and above the gentle bow wave.

'Now stand-to, lads, and make each ball count.'

He glanced quickly at the nearest gun crews. They could have been placed in any part of history. One seaman, standing by a sixteen-pounder immediately below the quarterdeck, was leaning on a rammer, his neckcloth tied around his ears to withstand the first deafening roar. Men like him had sailed with Drake aboard his *Revenge*, and had cheered as the Armada had been "drummed up the Channel". But this time there were no cheers, not even an isolated one. The men looked grim, watching the open gun ports, or standing close to one another as if for support. He saw Farquhar's fingers opening and closing repeatedly around his sword scabbard, his head very erect as he stared towards the wavering coastline, from where the enemy would open fire.

A light blinked from the nearest hilltop but did not re-appear. A broken bottle reflecting the first ray of sunrise. The window of some concealed dwelling. Bolitho shivered. Or a ray of light catching the lens of a telescope? He imagined the signal being carried over the hill to the waiting artillery. *The English are coming.* As expected and predicted. He frowned. No matter what happened, they had to hold the enemy's attention until Probyn swept down on the anchored ships from the northern channel. A few heavy broadsides amongst a crowded anchorage and the odds could change considerably.

He remembered suddenly what his father had once told him. *There is no such thing as a surprise attack. Surprise is only present when one captain or another has miscalculated what he has seen from the beginning.*

He glanced at Pascoe and smiled briefly. He now knew exactly what his father had meant.

*

Bolitho re-crossed the quarterdeck and trained a glass on an out-thrust shoulder of land. A few tiny dwellings were visible at the foot of a steep slope, nestling between some scrub and the nearest beach. Fishermen's homes. But their boats lay abandoned on the coarse shingle, and only a dog stood its ground by the water's edge, barking furiously at the slow-moving ships.

He heard Farquhar say sharply, 'The next bay will be the one.'

Outhwaite turned and called, 'Be ready! Hold your fire till the order, then shoot on the uproll!'

Allday muttered scornfully, '*Uproll!* Until we get clear of this headland and find some sort of wind again, there'll be no uproll!'

'Deck there!' The masthead lookout's voice seemed unusually loud. 'Ships at anchor around the point!'

Bolitho breathed out slowly. 'Signal the information to *Buzzard*.'

An acknowledgement broke from the frigate's yards within seconds. Javal was like the rest of them. On the last edge of tension.

He glanced at his watch. *Nicator* should be well through the other channel by now and setting more sail to begin her vital part. Even if French pickets had sighted her, it would be too late to move artillery to the other end of their defences.

The bang, when it came, was like an abbreviated thunder-clap. Bolitho saw neither smoke nor flash, but watched the ball's progress across the swirling current. It must have been fired from a low level, for he could see its path in a line of tiny wavelets, like an unnatural wind, or a shark charging to the attack.

The crash of the ball into the forepart of the hull brought a great chorus of shouts and yells, and Bolitho saw the second lieutenant hurrying from gun to gun, as if to reassure the crews.

'Look there, sir!' Allday pointed with his cutlass. 'Soldiers!'

Bolitho watched the tiny, blue-coated figures bursting from the trees and scurrying towards the point. Perhaps they believed that the second wave of attacking ships would attempt a landing, and were getting ready to repulse them. Bolitho licked his lips. If only there *was* a second wave.

He said, 'Bring her up a point, Captain. Give our upper battery a target.'

Farquhar protested, 'Eighteen-pounders against infantry, sir?'

Bolitho said quietly, 'It will give them something to keep their minds occupied. It may also shake the enemy's confidence up ahead. They are anticipating a squadron, remember!'

He winced as another bang echoed across the water, and he heard the ball hiss viciously overhead.

'Stand by to larboard!' Outhwaite pointed at the running soldiers. 'On the uproll!' He raised his speaking trumpet. '*Fire!*'

The long line of guns hurled themselves inboard on their tackles, the smoke rising and swirling above the packed hammock nettings. Bolitho held his glass on the land, seeing the balls whipping through trees and scrub, throwing up stones and clods of earth in haphazard confusion. The soldiers had obviously held the same ideas as Farquhar, for many were caught out in the open, and Bolitho saw bodies and muskets whirling through the air with the other fragments.

It was little enough, but it had given the gun crews some heart. He heard a few cheers, and yells of derision from the lower battery who had not been allowed to fire.

Outhwaite had caught some of the excitement. 'Move roundly, lads! Reload! Mr. Guthrie, a guinea for the first to run out!'

From a corner of his eye, Bolitho saw the headland dropping back, the first group of anchored ships glinting in frail sunlight, their sails furled, and their unmoving rigidity suggesting that each vessel was attached to the next, and so on, making them into an unbroken barrier. He had expected the French to anchor in this manner. It had been a favourite defence since long before a revolution had even been dreamed of.

Then he saw a flash. It came from a deep green saddle between two hills, and he knew the gunners had fired earlier to obtain a ranging shot.

It hit *Osiris* amidships, deep down and close to the waterline. The planks under Bolitho's feet rebounded, as if the ball had struck a few paces away instead of three decks down. He saw Farquhar's anxiety as he watched his boatswain dashing for a hatch with his seamen, and the wisps of dark smoke which eddied above the nettings as evidence of the gun's accuracy.

From astern he heard the controlled crash of cannon fire and knew that Javal was following his example and raking the nearest hillside in the hope of finding a target.

'Deck there! French ship o' the line at anchor beyond the transports!'

Bolitho swung the glass across the rail, seeing faces on *Osiris*'s forecastle looming like visions in the lens before he found and trained on the French seventy-four. Like the packed mass of transports, she was anchored. But her sails were only loosely brailed up, and her cable shortened home in readiness for weighing. And beyond her, gliding very slowly downwind, was a frigate, setting her foresail and shining momentarily as sunlight passed along her hull. The two smaller escorts, corvettes, Plowman had said, were hidden elsewhere. It was not surprising. For the assembled fleet of supply ships overlapped in what appeared to be a hopeless tangle of masts and yards. He watched them grimly through the glass. Deep-laden. Guns, powder and shot, tents, weapons and supplies for an army.

He felt the deck stagger as another ball smashed close alongside.

The only way to avoid being destroyed slowly by the hidden guns was to set more sail, to attack and close with the anchored vessels and make accuracy impossible.

He heard Farquhar say fervently, 'Where is *Nicator*? In God's name, she should be in sight by now!'

'French seventy-four's weighed, sir.'

Bolitho looked at Farquhar, but he had not heard the report. He said, 'Thank you. Tell your starboard gun crews to prepare, Mr. Outhwaite.'

Bolitho watched the boatswain emerging from beneath the quarterdeck and waited for him to come aft.

' 'Oled in two places, sir. But no damage below the waterline yet. She's sound enough, if it gets no worse.'

Farquhar nodded abruptly. 'Yes.'

Bolitho said, 'Set the fores'l, Captain. Make to *Buzzard*, *I am about to pass through the enemy's line.'*

Farquhar stared at him. 'We could get fouled in their moorings, sir. I'd advise – '

They ducked as another ball passed low above their heads, and Bolitho felt the breath of it across his shoulders like the wind of a cutlass blade.

Bolitho said, '*Nicator* should be in sight. At least from the masthead. Probyn must have met some opposition. If neither of us can get to grips, we are being destroyed for nothing!'

He strode to the lee side and watched a thin waterspout rise far abeam. The French were very good, as were their new guns. At this range they could hardly miss. And yet they were biding their time. Saving their aim for the rest of the squadron, or to decide on the English tactics.

No. It was wrong. No gunnery officer could be that confident.

He heard the wheel going over, the sudden flap and boom of canvas as the foresail was reset and its yard trimmed by the men at the braces. It made some difference. He could see the way one of the quarterdeck nine-pounders was tugging at its tackles as the deck tilted to leeward. The sudden increase of sail might make the French gunners show their hand.

He walked as slowly as he could to the other side, peering across the crowded gun deck towards the French two-decker. Under minimum canvas, she was standing off about two miles distant. Even that was wrong. Her captain commanded the most powerful ship present. His first duty was to defend the merchantmen and supply vessels, no matter what.

Half a mile to go, and through his glass he could see the tiny figures of seamen running about the decks of the nearest transport. They probably still believed *Osiris* was a three-decker, and that they would take the first overwhelming broadside.

'Bring her up a point, Captain.'

'Aye, sir. Nor' by west.'

Bolitho looked at Pascoe. 'Any sight of *Nicator*?'

'None, sir.' Pascoe gestured towards the massed shipping. 'She's missing a promising target!'

But Bolitho knew him well enough to see through his calm remark. He saw Midshipman Breen, who was helping Pascoe, stare at him, as if to seek confirmation that all was well.

The nearest transports, anchored at the head of two separate lines, opened fire with their bow guns, the balls whimpering overhead, one forcing a neat hole in the main topsail.

The master called suddenly, 'Lee bow, sir! Looks like shallows!'

Farquhar replied tersely, 'They're well clear, man! What do you want me to do? *Fly?*'

Bolitho heard nothing for the next few seconds. Like something from his feverish dreams, he saw the larboard bulwark burst apart, the deck planking torn diagonally in a gash of flying splinters, while wreckage and the complete barrel of a nine-pounder landed with a crash on the opposite side. The primed gun exploded, and its ball upended another gun on to some of its crew, the screams and sobs lost in the explosion.

When Bolitho stared aft he saw that the great ball, probably double-shotted, had smashed the wheel to fragments. Two helmsmen lay dead or stunned, and a third had been pulped to bloody gruel. Men and fragments of men lay scattered around the quarterdeck, and others tried to drag themselves away. Bolitho saw that Bevan, the master, had been all but cut in half by the exploding nine-pounder, and his blood was pouring across the splintered deck, while one of his hands still clawed at his exposed entrails, as if it alone still clung to life.

Plowman dashed out of the drifting smoke. 'I'll take over, sir!' He dragged a terrified seaman from behind some scattered hammocks. '*Up!* Come aft and we'll rig a tackle to the tiller head!'

Another crash, this time into the side of the poop. Several marines toppled down a ladder, and Bolitho heard the heavy balls smashing through the cabin and careering amongst the crowded gun deck.

He yelled, 'Shorten sail, Captain!' He raised his sword like a pointer. 'The French artillery judged it well.'

He felt neither fear nor bitterness. Just a sense of anger. *Osiris*, her steering gone, was falling heavily downwind. Bevan, the dead sailing master, had seen the danger without understanding what it meant. Now it was too late. The pressure of wind into her sails and against her hull was enough to guide *Osiris* into that one shoulder of hard sand.

The enemy had used their opening shots like goads on wayward cattle. A prod here, a tap there, to send the helpless beast into a carefully ranged and sited trap.

Both of the hidden guns renewed firing with sudden vigour, the shots crashing into the hull, or falling dangerously near the *Buzzard*, which alone still headed towards the anchored ships.

Pascoe yelled, 'The enemy frigate is making more sail, sir! And I see one of the corvettes breaking clear of the anchorage!'

Bolitho trained his glass through the drifting smoke. The frigate first. Long and lean. Thirty-eight guns against Javal's thirty-two. Provided he had managed to avoid the heavy artillery, he would stand a good chance. If he could hold off the corvette. *If, if, if*. It was like hearing a taunt in his brain.

Something made a dark flaw in the side of the lens, and he swung it further to hold the French seventy-four in view. She was still under minimum canvas, and was moving very slowly towards *Osiris* on a converging tack, her guns run out, but in shadow. He considered this fact. *In shadow*. So her captain had no intention of trying to hold the wind-gage. Even now she was steering across *Osiris*'s starboard bow, her reefed topsails braced hard round, her forecastle and even the beakhead alive with waving seamen and glittering weapons. He could see her name quite clearly, *Immortalité*.

Farquhar shouted hoarsely, 'How is the helm, Mr. Outhwaite? Have they rigged emergency steering?'

Bolitho watched the water rippling above the concealed sand-bar. Fifty yards. Less. Even if they anchored they would be unable to fight clear now, let alone do any damage to the transports.

He watched the two-decker, her tricolour very bright in the sunlight. He stiffened as he saw another flag at her mainmast. A dovetailed broad pendant.

Pascoe looked at him. 'A commodore, sir.' He tried to grin. 'It should have been a full admiral to do *us* honour!'

A ball thundered through a lower port, and Bolitho heard the attendant chorus of screams and cries for the surgeon's helpers.

He turned again to the French ship. Pascoe was wrong. It should have been Probyn, pouring his broadsides into the anchored transports, now completely undefended as the two-decker and her smaller consorts came down the coast to give battle. *Nicator* would have had nothing to oppose her. He felt the anger welling up like a burning flood.

The deck shuddered slightly, and with the sound of a pistol shot the fore topgallant mast plunged down and over the side, dragging broken rigging in its wake like black serpents.

Farquhar stared at him wildly. '*Aground!*' He moved a few paces to the side, his shoes slipping on blood. 'God's teeth!' He shielded his face with one arm as a ball slammed through the bulwark again, upending another gun and cutting down two men who were dragging a wounded comrade away from their port.

Farquhar asked flatly, 'What orders, sir?'

Bolitho kept his eyes towards the transports, they seemed to be moving now, edging across the bows in one vast mass. But it was only because *Osiris* was swinging very slowly to the pressure of wind, her stem and forepart of the hull firmly embedded on hard sand.

He said slowly, 'It is my belief that we will soon be able to use the starboard guns.'

He saw Farquhar nod, his face ashen as more explosions threw spray high above the nettings. The painted strip of canvas which had been their only deception had long since gone, torn away in the hot wind of those guns. He gripped his arm tightly, dragging his mind from the threat and damage all around.

'See the Frenchman, Captain? *Now* he is making more sail.'

Farquhar's eyes widened. 'In God's name!'

Slowly, inexorably, her bow pivoting on the bar, *Osiris* was swinging away from the land. No wonder the French commodore had stayed his hand. Within half an hour, when he passed to leeward of the sand-bar and the trapped ship, he would see only *Osiris*'s exposed stern. No commander could hope for a better, or a steadier target, and one broadside would sweep through the ship from stern to bow.

Farquhar said, 'Then we're done for.'

Bolitho walked past him. 'Pass the word. Engage with every gun that bears. We'll sink a round half-dozen of them with any luck.'

He heard the order being passed, the squeak of trucks as the gun captains brought their weapons round as far as they would move towards the supply ships.

They would see only the enemy, and even if they had guessed at their predicament, it was unlikely they understood its full meaning. Farquhar knew well enough.

'*Fire!*'

The long battery of thirty-two-pounders crashed out in a ragged broadside, and at full elevation Bolitho knew that many of the balls would find targets.

'*Fire!*'

The eighteen-pounders hurled themselves inboard, their crews working like madmen to sponge out and ram home new charges.

Bolitho darted a quick look at the captain. It showed on his face with each savage crash of a broadside. The recoil of so many guns was enough to edge *Osiris* still firmer aground. It told him that the ship was already finished, and that Bolitho was carrying on with the attack despite it.

Allday said hoarsely, 'The hillside seems to be afire, sir!'

Bolitho wiped his eyes with his sleeve and stared across the larboard bow. *Osiris* had pivoted right round now, and he could see the dense wall of smoke, darting tongues of flame, too, rolling towards the sea and adding to the scene of chaos and despair.

Allday said it for him. 'Must be Mr. Veitch. Set the hillside ablaze. It's probably like tinder.' He sighed. 'A brave man. One of those guns will be blinded by smoke. They'll not thank Mr. Veitch for *that*.'

A violent explosion thundered across the water, and through the thickening smoke Bolitho saw a vivid red heart.

Pascoe coughed in the smoke. 'We have hit one of the transports, sir! Must have been loaded with powder!'

Fragments splashed down lazily and bobbed around the embattled ship. Beyond the smoke Bolitho could hear sharper notes of gunfire, and knew Javal was there, fighting probably two enemies at once.

The masthead yelled above the din, 'Some of the French are making sail!'

Bolitho said, 'Cutting their cables.'

He did not blame them. With one or more of their number ablaze or badly crippled by *Osiris*'s broadsides, they had nothing to gain by remaining where they lay. He felt the deck under his feet. Lifeless, but for the guns' savage vibration. *And nobody could stop them.*

Something fanned past him, crashed against a nine-pounder in a shrieking wave of splinters. Men fell kicking and gasping, and Bolitho felt blood splashed across his breeches like paint.

He turned and saw Farquhar leaning back against the quarterdeck rail, his gaze fixed on the lower yards while he clutched his chest with both hands.

Bolitho ran to his side. 'Here! Let me help!'

Farquhar's eyes swivelled down towards him. He bared his teeth, spacing out each word to hold back the pain.

'No. Leave me. Must stay. Must.'

He had bunched the front of his new uniform coat into a tight ball. A ball which was already bright red.

Allday said, 'I'll take him below.'

The ship quivered again as the lower battery vented its anger on the anchorage. Several masts had fallen, and the two leading ships were listing towards each other, one almost awash, the other a blackened wreck in the path of that terrible explosion.

Farquhar tried to shake his head. 'Keep your damned hands off me!' He reeled against Bolitho. '*Mr. Outhwaite!*'

But the first lieutenant was sitting against one of the abandoned guns, his head lolling, and the deck around him spreading in blood.

Bolitho looked at Allday. 'Get Mr. Guthrie! Tell him I want all the wounded brought to the lower gun deck, larboard side, and be quick about it!'

He saw the smoke from the hillside mingling with that from the guns. At least Veitch's courage had given the wounded a chance. Without the smoke's screen, any attempt to get boats alongside would have been prevented by the two siege guns. As it was, the French were still firing blindly across the water, the great balls adding their strange notes to the screams of the dying and wounded men.

A small man darted through the smoke, and Bolitho saw it was the surgeon.

Despite Farquhar's protests, he ripped open the gold-laced coat, his hair blowing in the wind from another shot directly above the deck, and placed a heavy dressing above the bright stain.

Farquhar gasped, 'Get *below*, Andrews! See to our people!'

The surgeon looked despairingly at Bolitho. 'I'm getting

the wounded up, sir.' He peered dazedly at the shattered bulwarks and sprawled corpses. Even after the gruesome work he had to perform deep on the orlop deck, this must seem a worse horror. 'Will you strike, sir?'

Farquhar heard him and gasped, '*Strike?* Get below, you bloody fool! I'll see you in hell before I strike *my* colours!'

Bolitho beckoned to Pascoe. 'Attend the captain. You stay here, too, Allday.'

He ignored their anxiety and ran to the rail, straining his eyes through the smoke until he had found the boatswain. He could not remember his name, but shouted wildly until the man looked up at him, his face as black as any Negro's from powder-smoke and charred wreckage.

'Get the quarter boats alongside to larboard! A raft, too, if you can manage it!'

He turned as Pascoe called him and saw a pale square of canvas rising through the smoke, the ship beneath still hidden.

His sword blade touched the deck as his arms dropped to his sides. Time had run out. The Frenchman was here. Crossing their stern with the precision of a hunter stalking a wounded beast.

He saw, too, the enemy's broad pendant lifting and curling in the offshore wind, and wondered vaguely if its owner had seen his above the ruin and carnage.

The smoke seemed to fan upwards to a freak gust, but the ripple of red and orange tongues which spurted through it told Bolitho that this wind was man-made.

Deck by deck, pair by pair, the seventy-four's armament poured its broadside into *Osiris*'s stern.

It seemed to go on and on forever. The cringing, reeling men around him lost shape and meaning, their faces merely masks of pain and terror, their gaping mouths like soundless holes as they ran blindly before the onslaught.

Bolitho found that he was on his knees, and as his hearing started to return he groped for his sword, using it like a lever to prise himself from the deck.

Hardly daring to breathe, he staggered to the rail, or what was left of it, and saw that Pascoe and Allday stood as before, with the captain propped between them. Allday had a bad cut on one arm, and Pascoe had a dark weal on his forehead where he had been hit by a flying piece of timber. Bolitho could not get his breath to speak, but clung to them, nodding to each in turn.

Beyond the quarterdeck there was not a mast left standing, and the whole of the upper gun deck, forecastle and gangways were buried under a mountain of broken spars and rigging. Smoke billowed from everywhere, while beneath the heaped wreckage he heard voices calling for help, for each other, or cursing like men driven mad.

Allday gasped, 'Mizzen'll come down any minute, sir!' He sounded faint. 'Only the shrouds holding it, I'd say!'

Faintly through the din of shouts and splintering woodwork Bolitho heard cheering. Frenchmen cheering their victory.

Farquhar thrust Pascoe away and reeled towards the broken hammock nettings. His uniform was torn, and several wood splinters were embedded in his shoulders like darts. Blood ran unheeded down his chest and marked his passage towards the side, and when Bolitho caught him he had his eyes tightly shut.

He gasped, *'Did we strike,* sir?'

Bolitho held him firmly as Pascoe ran to help. The mast with his pendant, the halliards which had held the ensign, all had been blasted away in the enemy's broadside.

'No, we did not.'

Farquhar opened his eyes very wide and looked at him. 'That is good, sir. I-I'm sorry about – ' He closed his eyes against another searing pain, but exclaimed fiercely, 'I hope Probyn *rots in hell*! He's finished us this day.'

Bolitho supported him, knowing that Pascoe was watching his face as if for an answer to something.

Farquhar said quietly, 'Let me stand, sir. I will be all right now. Get that fool Outhwaite to – ' Some last understanding flashed across his eyes, and then froze there.

The second lieutenant staggered through the funnelling smoke, but stopped motionless as Bolitho said, 'Take your captain, Mr. Guthrie.' He watched a few men emerging from beneath the poop. 'Sir Charles Farquhar is dead.'

16

The Captain's Report

'ONLY the wounded into the boats!'

Bolitho was hoarse from shouting above the din of gunfire. Several transports were shooting through the smoke, and he knew that some of the shots would be hitting their consorts, as the packed anchorage changed from a prepared defence-line to a scene of indescribable panic. Three ships were blazing fiercely, and with their cables either cut or burned through, were already drifting amongst the others.

Bolitho could not tell how many guns were firing at *Osiris*, for with only a few of her lower battery still manned, it was impossible to distinguish between a thirty-two-pounder's recoil and an enemy ball crashing into the hull.

He peered over the gangway and saw the boats immediately below him, filled with wounded, while others clung to the gunwales or floated away, unable to swim, or without the strength to do so. Others were clambering down the rounded tumblehome, marines and seamen, coopers and sailmakers, while here and there the blue and white of an officer tried to restore order.

Pascoe ran to his side. 'What will happen now, sir?'

Bolitho did not reply immediately. 'Down there, Adam. That is what defeat is like. The way it looks. How it smells.' He turned away. 'Pass the word. Cease firing. This ship may take fire at any moment when one of those wrecks drifts against us.'

More violent crashes, and freed at last from its remaining shrouds, the mizzen mast plunged down alongside, bedding itself in the shallows like a great marker.

He walked a few paces across the deck, his shoes catching in splinters and the great diagonal rent where the French gunners had smashed down the helm and all around it.

A few men ran past him, not even giving him a glance. To where, and for what purpose, they probably did not know.

Smoke poured across the hull and eddied through holes in the deck. It was like walking in hell. Dead men were on every hand, weapons and small possessions where they had been dropped or had fallen in battle. A marine lay staring at the sky, his head and shoulders supported on the lap of a comrade. A best friend perhaps. But he, too, was dead. Killed by a metal splinter as he had watched his friend die.

There was no sign of Farquhar, and he imagined that they had carried him right aft, to the wrecked cabin with its once beautiful furniture and fittings.

A small figure emerged below the poop, and he realised it was Midshipman Breen.

'Go with Mr. Pascoe!' He watched the boy peering at him without a spark of recognition. 'And take care.'

Breen nodded, and then burst into tears. 'I ran away, sir! *I ran away!*'

Bolitho touched his shoulder. 'A lot of *men* did that today, Mr. Breen. There's nothing more they can do here.'

Pascoe came aft with the second lieutenant. The latter looked exhausted, white-faced with shock.

'The boats are full, sir.' He cringed as a ball ripped past him and struck something solid in the smoke. The smoke was so thick that the other ship was completely hidden.

'Very well.' Bolitho looked slowly along the deserted decks. There would still be some who were trapped under that great tangle of wreckage. Listening, or calling for help.

He said, 'Pass the word. Abandon ship. We will ferry the wounded ashore.' He looked at Pascoe. 'I am sorry for you, Adam. Twice a prisoner of war in so short a span.'

Pascoe shrugged. 'At least we're together this time, Uncle.'

Allday, who had been nursing his injured arm, levered himself from the rail and said, '*Listen!*'

They looked at him, and Bolitho put his arm round him, fearing that because of his own despair he had failed to help Allday.

Breen wiped his eyes with his fists and stared at Allday. 'I hear it!' He reached out for Allday's hand. 'I *do* hear it!'

Bolitho walked over the broken planks, listening to the swelling roar of cheers. It faltered only to a ragged crash of gunfire, which was followed instantly by an even louder, more violent broadside. Then the cheering resumed, stronger and fiercer, like one great voice.

Allday said huskily, 'That's no French cheer!'

'*Huzza! Huzza!*'

And again the smoke surged towards the stranded *Osiris*, stirred and blown by another massive broadside.

Pascoe said, '*Buzzard.*'

Allday leaned against him and looked at Bolitho. 'Bless him, sir, did you hear that?'

'Yes.' Bolitho sheathed his sword without knowing why he had done so. 'No frigate carries that number of men.'

The second lieutenant dropped his head and said brokenly, 'That damned *Nicator*. Here at last, too late to save our ship and all our men.'

Sunlight probed through the smoke, and Bolitho saw leaping flames and heard the crackle of burning timber. A mastless hulk, abandoned and well ablaze, was less than fifty yards away.

But as the smoke swirled high in the air, he stared at a ship which even now was firing another broadside downwind, at some other invisible target.

There was no mistaking her. *Lysander* was steering past the scattered transports, firing into individual vessels, or pouring a half-broadside into one isolated or apparently untouched. Her other side was obviously firing at the French seventy-four, which explained the first cheers and violent broadsides.

Bolitho saw and understood all of these things, but found they carried no meaning.

Only one thing counted. *Lysander*. Thomas Herrick had come for them, by some fantastic piece of luck and little less than a miracle, he had sailed down from the north channel and turned the anchorage into a shipbreaker's yard.

Pascoe said, 'I think that's *Buzzard* now, sir!' He was wild-eyed, his chest and throat moving with emotion. 'Yes, it is her! Her sails are so holed she is barely making way!'

Bolitho rubbed his eyes, seeing a corvette following close under *Lysander*'s stern. She was listing, but had less damage to her sails than Javal's victorious frigate. Also, above her flapping tricolour she was wearing a large Union Jack.

Bolitho wrenched his eyes away. 'They've got boats in the water. Tell our people that help is coming.'

He watched the drifting hulk and prayed she was not one of the ammunition ships.

Another gust of wind moved across the water, and he saw that many of the transports had sunk completely. If they were loaded with those great guns, it was not surprising.

Boats pulled below the *Osiris*'s shadow, and he heard voices shouting encouragement, while the oarsmen stared grim-faced at the battered, holed wreck which had once been Farquhar's command.

Plowman limped past carrying the ship's chronometer. He saw Bolitho and gave a tense grin. 'Pity to leave it in the wreck, sir. 'Er'll come in useful.' He hurried to the side adding, 'Glad you're safe, sir.'

Bolitho realised there were many boats nearby now, some with armed marines, and swivels mounted on their stems, while the others got on with the work of rescue.

That, too, became clear as he leaned on the rail to watch. Some boats were painted dark red, from *Nicator* then. So somewhere beyond the scattered transports and burning wrecks Probyn's ship was here to see the price of the battle.

A lieutenant crossed the deck and touched his hat to Pascoe. 'Nobody else survived but you?' He looked very clean against the horror and death.

Bolitho said, 'I survived.'

The lieutenant gaped at him and snapped, 'Beg pardon, sir! I did not recognise you in – '

Bolitho said wearily, 'No matter. It has become a custom.'

The officer blinked. 'I am from *Nicator*, sir. We did not think anyone had survived,' he waved his hand despairingly around the deck, 'all this!'

Guthrie, the *Osiris*'s second lieutenant, suddenly ran from the poop and seized the young officer by the coat.

'*You bloody coward! You damned, crawling toad!* Look what you did – '

As Pascoe pulled him away from the astonished lieutenant, Guthrie broke down completely, his body shaking violently to his sobs.

The lieutenant gasped, '*Nicator* ran aground, sir. But when *Lysander* appeared out of nowhere, we were able to kedge off fairly well. Without Captain Herrick's arrival I fear we would have been even later.'

Bolitho watched him gravely, seeing his despair, his shame at Guthrie's attack.

'Of that I am quite sure.'

He walked to the sagging gangway. 'Now we can clear the ship.'

He paused above the nearest launch, his eyes on the hull's bare outline. Without masts or sails, and with only the dead and a few trapped and crazed men to crew her, *Osiris* was already a wreck. He felt the hull shudder, as if in protest against his thoughts, and knew that the blazing hulk had drifted along the other side. He heard the crackle of flames, the jubilant roar as they spread along *Osiris*'s tarred rigging which lay in huge coils to receive them.

The French, or others, might salvage some of her seventy-four guns, and perhaps her bell as a souvenir. But the keel and ribs would lie in the sand long after the flames had been quenched, and until time and the sea completed the victory.

'Cast off.' He sat on the gunwale, surrounded by silent men, some wounded, some merely stunned by all they had witnessed and suffered. 'Give way all!'

Bolitho looked at the other boats. Every one crowded with survivors. But of *Osiris*'s original company of six hundred souls there were about half that number. He tightened his lips and felt his gaze smarting from strain. A very heavy price. It was to be hoped someone would appreciate their sacrifice.

He heard a voice calling, and then Allday croaked, 'God, look at that gig!'

It was Lieutenant Veitch, blackened from head to foot and almost naked, but waving towards him and grinning from ear to ear.

Plowman murmured, '*Said* 'e'd make it. That what 'e said. The mad bugger!'

Bolitho lost sense of time and distance, and as the boats were followed and surrounded by drifting smoke it was almost a surprise when he saw *Lysander*'s black and buff hull rising like a cliff to greet him, her gun ports crammed with cheering faces, her gangway thronged with seamen and marines.

He gripped the nearest stair below the entry port and pulled himself from the boat. He felt as if his arms would not hold him, or tear from their sockets.

There were hands gripping his, figures pushing around him, helping, staring.

Herrick took his arm and guided him aft.

He said softly, '*Thank God.*' He turned and studied Bolitho's face for some seconds. 'Thank God.'

Bolitho swung round as a searing column of flame shot above the smoke. *Osiris*'s pyre.

He said, 'See to her people, Thomas. They fought well. Better than I dared hope.' He shrugged heavily. 'But for your arrival, their efforts would have failed. Their losses too great when weighed against the gains.'

He nodded as Pascoe joined them. 'Adam, too, is unhurt.'

Herrick peered through the smoke. 'And the captain?'

Bolitho watched the leaping flames. 'He died in battle.' He turned to Herrick. 'Bravely.'

More cheering echoed through the din of gunfire, and someone called wildly, 'The Frenchie's struck, sir!'

Bolitho looked at Herrick questioningly. 'The seventy-four?'

'Aye. We shot her steering away, and raked her twice before she could fight clear. I think her captain was so taken with *Osiris*'s defiance he did not see us at all.' He reached out awkwardly. 'So you'll have another ship to replace the one lost.'

Lieutenant Kipling strode aft and touched his hat. 'Boarding party in command now, sir. Mr. Gilchrist has hailed us to say that the French commodore and most of his senior officers are wounded.'

Herrick nodded. 'Very well. Tell Mr. Gilchrist to arrange an exchange with the enemy. Their officers and seamen in return for any of *Osiris*'s people who managed to swim ashore. And *we* keep their ship.'

Bolitho watched him. What a change. Herrick had not even hesitated or asked his aid.

Herrick faced him again. 'I'd like to anchor, sir. I understand that the French will not pursue their bombardment for the present. Javal ran their frigate into the shallows and she is hard and fast. He took a sprightly corvette as a prize, and I think the surviving one fled south as fast as he could go.'

Bolitho replied, 'Yes, I agree. But it is your decision as flag captain.'

Herrick looked at him and then smiled sadly. 'About Captain Farquhar, sir.'

'It is over for him, Thomas. He died because he put facts before ideas. Because he put too much value in his own future perhaps. But when he did die, it was with courage.'

Herrick sighed. '*That* I never doubted.'

A figure hurried beneath the poop and said, 'You're back safe and sound!'

It was Ozzard, his sad features set in a rare smile.

'Please come aft, sir!'

Bolitho shook his head. 'Later. I want to watch.'

He looked at the ships which were already anchoring, their boats surging alongside with cargoes of rescued men. *Buzzard*, pockmarked from the French guns, with her neat prize close by. The other French ship, her broad pendant gone and British flags at every masthead. *Immortalité*. The name had served her well, he thought. She had survived, and with luck would make a valuable addition to his little squadron.

He heard a loud explosion and watched scattered fragments falling all around. *Osiris*'s powder store or a magazine had ignited at last. He saw her open gun ports glowing like lines of red eyes as the fire consumed her from within. Deck by deck, yard by yard.

His mind ached and he wanted to go to find seclusion, deep in the hull, beyond a man's voice or a sight of the sea.

But he stood by the nettings, watching *Lysander*'s preparations, the hurrying figures of so many familiar faces. Old Grubb, nodding and saying something to him about honour. Major Leroux striding to speak with him, but turning away at the last moment after seeing his expression.

Fitz-Clarence, and Kipling, little Midshipman Saxby with his gap-toothed grin, and Mariot, the old gun captain, who had served with his father.

He heard Herrick shout, 'Tell them to *make haste*, Mr. Steere! The wind is better placed, and I'd like to weigh before noon.'

Before noon? Had it taken so little time since dawn? Bolitho stared listlessly at the littered water, the corpses and charred timbers. Just hours since dawn. That was all it had been. Many had died, more would die later.

He gripped the nettings and took several deep breaths. And

he most of all had expected to be killed. That was the strangest part. He had often been near to death in his life at sea. Sometimes so close he had almost felt its presence like another being. This last time had been the worst yet.

Herrick came back to him again. 'I hate to leave you, sir. With most of the men at quarters, and the rest all wild with their victory, it is hard to seize a moment when you need it the most.'

'Thank you, Thomas.' He looked at the blazing *Osiris*. 'For them, and for me.'

Herrick said ruefully, 'Had I only *known*, sir.' He looked away. 'But I thought it useless to remain at anchor when you had done so much, had wanted so much for the squadron.'

Bolitho watched him gravely. 'So you just sailed away, Thomas. With a scrap of paper from your acting-commodore which if it had protected him from higher authority would most certainly have damned you. Your future would have been in ruins.'

He saw the lines on Herrick's homely face and guessed that he had thought him dead or captured. By sailing alone from Syracuse he had made his own gesture, just as Inch had described.

Some boats pulled abeam, being careful to keep well away from the burning two-decker in case there should be an even worse explosion.

Herrick said, 'There go the French, sir. They fought well, but were vanquished without the loss of a man to us. We took them in surprise. To us as much as them, I suppose.'

Bolitho craned over the side and watched the nearest boat. He saw a thin officer, one arm in a sling, and his uniform streaked with blood, staring up at him, his face dull with pain.

'Their commodore.' He raised one hand above his head and saw the French officer's companions return the salute. 'I know how it feels to lose. What he is thinking at this very moment.'

Herrick regarded him anxiously. 'He has his freedom, sir.'

'From his thoughts, Thomas? I think not.'

He turned abruptly inboard. 'Once we are clear of this place I want a full report from Captain Probyn.'

Herrick watched him, sensing his bitterness and anger. 'Aye, sir.'

Bolitho faced him again. 'But I'll not let anything more

spoil the pleasure of seeing you again, my friend!' He smiled, his exhaustion making him appear somehow defenceless. 'I had a message for you anyway, Thomas. From a delightful lady, who even now is planning a welcome for you in Kent!'

Herrick stammered, 'Hell, sir, I mean —' He grinned. 'Did you meet her then?'

'It is what I am saying, Thomas.' He took his arm. 'I hope I am there at your wedding, as you were at . . .' He stopped and looked away.

'I'd be honoured, sir, if it ever comes to it.'

Veitch hurried across the quarterdeck, grinning to the laughs and taunts which attended his wild entrance.

Herrick smiled. 'Another Lysander has got home, sir.' He looked at Bolitho and added, 'But if you've no objection, I'd like to make him my first lieutenant immediately. Mr. Fitz-Clarence can command the corvette and Mr. Gilchrist the French seventy-four. That is, until other appointments can be arranged.'

'As I said, Thomas, you are the flag captain. Your opinions are mine. I suppose always have been without either of us knowing. But have you asked Captain Javal about *his* officers?'

Herrick smiled. 'I hailed him in the battle. He escaped unscathed, but . . .' He looked Bolitho in the eyes. 'We have only one frigate. She needs to be better than all she meets. Anyway, Javal will be content with his prize money.'

He became serious again as Fitz-Clarence hurried aft, his face full of questions. 'I'll deal with him, if I may.'

Pascoe came to the side and said quietly, 'It feels strange to be back.'

Bolitho nodded. 'For you especially, Adam.'

'For me?' The dark eyes were surprised.

'With Gilchrist and Fitz-Clarence in temporary command of the prizes,' he saw Pascoe's face clear with understanding, 'you will step up two places to *Lysander*'s fourth lieutenant. And at eighteen that is fair gain!'

He thought suddenly of Guthrie, *Osiris*'s second lieutenant. At least Pascoe had not got his advancement by another's death, or a gap left by someone like Guthrie, his mind unhinged by the cruelty of battle. And he thought, too, of Probyn, seeing him again as a lieutenant. His excuses, his constant drunkenness.

If all these men had died today because of him, there was no influence or authority in the world to save him.

He saw Pascoe's expression and knew he must have shown his own anger as he thought of Probyn.

He said, 'You've earned it, and far more beside.' He turned to watch the white flag of parley being pulled past on one of *Lysander*'s boats. 'Your father would have been proud of you.'

Bolitho walked away to join Herrick by the gangway. He did not see Pascoe's face, but knew in his heart he had just given him a far greater reward than promotion.

*

Bolitho was writing in the cabin when Herrick came aft to see him. It was a full week since they had sailed from Corfu with its bitter sights and memories, and after steering south and east around the countless Greek islands they had discovered a safe anchorage where further repairs could be carried out.

For the time of year, the weather was surprisingly bad. If he hoped to return to Syracuse with his squadron intact, Bolitho knew he would have to make sure they could withstand the passage there.

Buzzard had been badly mauled, and had received several holes below her waterline. Once, in a heavy gust of wind as they had fought to shorten sail, he had thought that the frigate was about to founder. But Javal had kept *Buzzard* alive, working her and his men until the immediate danger had passed.

The captured two-decker, *Immortalité*, had also endured several hazards in the gales. With her company of spare hands taken from all the squadron, and the bulk comprising *Osiris*'s survivors, she had not found the time to settle into a single unit. Her jury steering had carried away twice before she had been brought under command, and Bolitho could do nothing but admire the determination of her temporary captain, Lieutenant Gilchrist. Herrick had certainly been right in his choice. In fact, with their resources stretched and reduced by battle, it was hard to know how they would have managed without him.

He looked up and smiled as Herrick entered the cabin. 'Sit down, Thomas. Have some wine.'

Herrick sat, and waited until Ozzard had brought him a goblet.

Bolitho said, 'I've been making my report. As soon as the weather eases I want Fitz-Clarence to sail for Syracuse and then on to Gibraltar.' He added, 'D'you think he can do that?'

Herrick grinned over his glass. 'I think he will find his way, sir.' He grimaced as a gust of wind brought spindrift splashing across the stern windows. 'But it may be a while yet. I'm grateful we found this little island. Major Leroux had his pickets ashore, but says it seems uninhabited. It will give us shelter at least, until Javal and Gilchrist have done some more repairs.'

Bolitho looked at his thick report. 'Mr. Gilchrist has shown up well, Thomas.' He glanced across the cabin, seeing faces in his imagination. 'I've recommended that he be made commander at the first opportunity and given a ship of his own. A brig, most likely. It should teach him the more human side of command. A small ship with a vast amount of work!'

'Thank you, sir. I'm glad. I know he got off badly with you, and I blame myself for it. But he's had a hard climb to get where he is, and I admire his tenacity.'

'Yes.'

Bolitho thought of the letters he had written for the despatch bag. To Farquhar's widowed mother, to others who would know before long that a husband or father would never come home.

Herrick hesitated and then said, 'Mr. Grubb fears that the adverse winds will not blow out for days, sir. Maybe weeks. We're snug enough here, and I was wondering if you'd wish the other business to be dealt with now.'

They looked at each other.

Bolitho replied, 'You were right to remind me.' Perhaps he had only been putting it off, avoiding a confrontation. 'I'll have Captain Probyn aboard tomorrow, unless there's a full gale again.'

Herrick seemed relieved. 'I read his account, sir. Straightforward grounding in a badly charted channel. When I reached *Nicator*, I saw she was on a bar. Not badly, but enough for us to need a kedge-anchor.'

Bolitho stood up and walked to the wine cabinet. Over and over again he had thought about Herrick's sudden and vital arrival at the scene of battle. With the aid of *Lysander's* log, the master's lengthy explanation and what he had managed to drag from Herrick himself, he had built up a picture of the ship's movements after leaving Syracuse.

Driven by that strange loyalty, Herrick had sailed not direct to Corfu, but much further south and to the coast of Africa. East and still further east, the lookouts scanning every mile for a ship, or better still, a fleet. When he recalled Herrick's early despair, his apparent inability to contain the work of flag captain, it was all the more incredible.

All those long, empty miles, until finally they had sighted the walls of Alexandria and the Bay of Aboukir which guided them to the mouth of the great Nile itself.

When he had praised Herrick for his stubborn determination, his inbuilt belief in Bolitho's conclusions, Herrick had said, 'You convinced *me*, sir. And when I told the people that, they seemed content to go where I wanted.' He had shown some embarrassment when Leroux had said, 'Captain Herrick made a speech to all hands which I think must have reached you, sir, *wherever* you were at the time!'

With no sign of a French fleet, Herrick had decided to make for Corfu. Confident that the supply ships would be there, and imagining the squadron still at anchor in Syracuse, he had sailed into the attack. From north to south, he had explained, was better for surprise, and left the wider channel as an escape route.

But he had run down on *Nicator*. Two ships meeting as if by plan, timed to the hour of attack.

The same storm which had scattered Bolitho's depleted squadron had sent the faster *Lysander* as far as the Nile and back across the sea to Corfu.

Bolitho refilled their goblets and returned to the table.

'Unless there has been a great change, Thomas, we can only believe that the French will soon move to attack. The corvette which escaped from Corfu may have returned there, but far more likely she will have headed for France.' He glanced at the streaked windows and listened to the moan of wind through the shrouds and furled sails. 'She may have a hard fight, but we must accept that she will get to a port before anyone else.'

Herrick nodded slowly. 'True. So the French admiral may

decide to come out at last. If he knows that his heavy artillery is on the sea bed, he'll anticipate a running battle. It makes good sense.'

Bolitho said, 'We are badly placed here. With these prevailing winds we need to be much further west again. Where we can be of use to our fleet when it comes.'

'*If* it comes.' Herrick sighed. 'But we've done what we can so far.'

'Yes.' He thought of the sea-burials which attended each day after the battle. 'And they'll not find us wanting.'

There was a tap at the door and Midshipman Saxby said anxiously, 'Mr. Glasson sends his respects, sir, and could you come on deck.'

Bolitho looked at Herrick and gave a quick wink. With two lieutenants short, the vacancies had gone to the senior midshipmen. Glasson, more sharp-faced and seemingly sourer than ever, was making the most of it. He rarely held a watch without calling Herrick or Veitch to attend one of his tantrums over duty or apparent incompetence of some seaman or other.

Herrick stood up. 'I'll come up.' In a quieter tone he said, 'I'll put this little prig over my knee in view of the whole ship's company if he tries my patience much more!'

Bolitho smiled gravely. 'Our wardroom gets younger every day, Thomas.'

'Or we get older.' Herrick shook his head. 'These youngsters! If I'd called down to my captain when I was commissioned lieutenant, I'd have been torn into small pieces unless the ship had been actually falling apart!'

Faintly above the wind and ship noises Bolitho heard the hail, 'Boat ahoy?' and the reply from somewhere near *Lysander*'s quarter, '*Nicator*!'

Herrick looked at him questioningly. 'Mr. Glasson is not troubling me for a trivial cause *this* time!' He reached for his hat. 'Captain Probyn is coming aboard without waiting for your summons.'

'So it seems.' He listened to the marines clattering towards the entry port. 'Bring him aft, Thomas. And we shall see.'

Captain George Probyn loomed into the cabin, his coat and breeches blotchy with spray from the hard pull to the ship. His face was even redder than before, and as he stared belligerently around the cabin he said, 'I trust you will see me, sir?'

'I *do* see you.' Bolitho gestured to a chair. 'Well?'

Probyn sank into the chair and glared at him. 'I'll not mince words, sir. I've been hearing things. About my ship, and what happened off Corfu. I'll not stand by and have my good name slandered, bandied about by rogues not fit to wear the King's coat!' He pointed at the papers on the table. 'I made a full and proper report. It will stand any scrutiny, a damned court of enquiry if need be!'

Bolitho said quietly, 'Some claret for the captain, Ozzard.' He added, 'Or brandy, perhaps?'

Probyn nodded. 'Brandy. Better for a man in these damned waters.' He almost snatched the goblet from Ozzard and downed the drink in one huge swallow. 'If I may, sir?' He thrust the glass to Ozzard for refilling.

Despite the persistent wind which swept across the little bay and sent countless white-horses amongst the anchored ships, the air in the sealed cabin was warm and humid. Bolitho had put on his coat to receive Probyn, but was wishing that he was still in his shirt. He watched the brandy moving into Probyn's eyes and voice, blurring and distorting as he repeated, almost word for word, how his sailing master and the officer of the watch, *a young booby if ever I saw one*, the leadsman in the chains, *I had him seized up and flogged double quick, I can tell you*, and several others had made the grounding inevitable.

Bolitho waited until there was a pause while Ozzard filled the goblet again. The servant's eyes were lowered, but he could not hide his interest. His experience as a lawyer's clerk was probably too much for his normal reserve.

Then Bolitho said calmly, 'So you were not actually there when it happened?'

'*There?*' The red-rimmed eyes fixed on him with obvious effort. 'Of course I was there!'

'I'll trouble you to keep a civil tongue in your head, Captain.' Bolitho kept his tone level, even gentle, but saw a warning show itself on Probyn's reddened features.

'Yes. Yes, I apologise. It's been troubling me, thinking you might blame me in some way for what –'

'Well, Captain, where *were* you in *Nicator* when she struck?'

'Let me see now.' He pouted heavily. 'Must be exact,

eh? Like we used to be in the old *Trojan* when we were lieutenants together.'

Bolitho remained very still, watching the emotions and blurred memories on Probyn's heavy features.

He said, 'That was a long time ago.'

Probyn leaned forward, his sleeve knocking over the empty goblet. 'Not so long, surely? It's like a dog watch ago to me. She was a fine old ship.'

'*Trojan*?' Bolitho nodded to Ozzard who brought a full goblet for the captain. 'She was hard and demanding, as I remember. A good school for those who wanted to learn, but hell on earth for the laggard. Captain Pears was never a one to tolerate fools.'

Probyn looked at him, his eyes glazed. 'Of course, I was that bit senior to you. Knew a bit more, so to speak. Saw through their little game.'

'Game?'

Probyn tapped the side of his nose. 'Y'see? You didn't even suspect. The first lieutenant was always on at me. The captain's lickspittle. And that other lieutenant, the one who got killed, he was a crawler.'

Bolitho stood up and walked to the wine cabinet, seeing Kate's face and hearing her infectious laugh when she had given it to him. She would laugh at him now, if she were here. How she despised the ways of true authority.

He said sharply, 'Apart from the very junior lieutenants then, that only left you and me.' He poured himself a glass of claret, waving Ozzard away as he continued, 'I remember that ship in many ways, but one of the things which I recall most clearly, and which has come back to me during this last week, was the way you drank.' He swung round, seeing the sudden alarm on Probyn's face. 'Several times that I knew of, men were flogged because of things which *you* had done wrong. Do you remember the night watches which others had to perform because you were too much in your cups to get on deck? That *lickspittle* you just mentioned saw to it that the captain knew nothing about it. But by God, Probyn, if I'd been your captain, I'd have made certain you never did it twice!'

Probyn lurched to his feet, his great shadow reaching towards Bolitho like a curtain.

'Indeed you would! Like the time we took two prizes! I was put in charge of the first. A rotten, worm-infested hulk, that's all *she* was! I never stood a chance when the enemy ship came after me!' He was squinting with fierce concentration, his face and throat wet with sweat. 'It was deliberate, to get rid of me!'

'You were senior to me. The prize was yours by right. What about a previous one? A little schooner? You were supposed to take her into New York, but a master's mate went in your place.'

He watched his words slamming home, the fuddled way which Probyn's eyes were swivelling around the cabin as if to discover answers.

Bolitho said harshly, 'You were drunk then. *Admit it, man.*'

Probyn sat down very slowly, his hands shaking as he supported himself on the arms of the chair.

'I'll admit nothing.' He looked up, his reddened eyes filled with hate. '*Sir.*'

'So you've nothing more to tell me about *Nicator*'s grounding?'

The question seemed to take him momentarily off guard. Then Probyn said, 'I have made a full and proper report.' He thrust his hands under the table. 'And I have taken sworn statements from those of the watch who were involved.' He leaned forward, his drink-sodden face crafty as he added, '*If* there is a court of enquiry, I will produce those statements. One of which may incriminate the officer of the watch, an admiral's nephew, by the way. And it may be thought that you were not unbiased, sir. That you were levelling old scores by having my reputation tarnished.'

He fell back, startled, as Bolitho stood up, his eyes blazing with contempt.

'Don't you bargain with me! A week back we struck a blow against the enemy, but the harm which was done to our people was more deeply felt! But for *Lysander*'s arrival, and *Buzzard*'s support, yours would be the only ship afloat today! Think on these things the next time you dare to talk of bias or honour!'

He called for Ozzard and added, 'You may return to your ship now. But remember, what cannot be proved is nevertheless between us. The squadron is undermanned, and officered for the most part by inexperienced youngsters. For that reason alone, I am not holding an official court of enquiry.'

Herrick appeared in the door with Ozzard, but stayed very still as Bolitho said, 'But hear me, Captain Probyn. If I ever discover that your failure to give support was deliberate, or that at any time in the future you act against the interests of this squadron, I will see you *hanged* for it!'

Probyn snatched his hat from Ozzard and lurched blindly from the cabin.

When Herrick returned he found Bolitho as before, staring at Probyn's empty chair with an expression of disgust.

He said, 'That was an ugly side of me, Thomas. But by God, I meant every word of it!'

17

Storm Clouds

IT was nearer to two weeks before Bolitho could hoist his signal to up anchor and leave their sheltering islet. Even then, the ships were plagued by fierce gusts of gale force, and it soon became apparent that *Buzzard*'s damage was worse than Javal had realised. His men worked through every watch on the pumps without a break, and with the limited resources he had aboard, he used all spare timber and canvas for the most severe hull damage.

After the savagery of battle, the elation at seeing *Lysander* thrusting her bows through smoke and falling spray, this renewed effort by the weather to delay their every move was all the more disheartening.

As the ships became scattered, and worked back and forth on varying tacks to gain headway into equally determined south-westerly winds, Bolitho was thankful they had not sighted an enemy squadron across their path. His crews were worn out by constant work, and with each ship left under-handed because of dead and wounded, he knew that any sort of a victory would fall to the opposing side.

Perle, the captured French corvette, had made off with his despatches, and he knew that Herrick was still worrying about Lieutenant Fitz-Clarence's ability to make the right landfall and pass his information to the admiral at Gibraltar.

Perhaps he should have directed *Perle* to sail directly to Gibraltar. But if his news was to reach all available sources of communication, he knew that Fitz-Clarence must first call at Syracuse.

He was pacing his cabin, his chin on his chest, his body angled to the ship's tilt, when he heard the cry, 'Deck there! Sail to the nor'-west!'

For once he was unable to restrain himself, and without

waiting for a message from the quarterdeck, he hurried from
the cabin to join Herrick and the other officers at the rail.

Herrick touched his hat. 'You heard then, sir?'

'Aye, Thomas.'

Bolitho ran his eyes quickly along the upper gun deck. Due
to the weather and the necessary delays while repairs were
carried out, it was a month since they had watched the French
supply vessels sinking and burning under their bombardment.
Since Farquhar had died with so many of his men. And
Nicator had gone aground.

The men who were by the bulwarks and gangways, or
standing in the shrouds in the hopes of sighting the newcomer, looked tougher, he thought. Herrick had done well.
It was not easy for common seamen to understand what was
happening beyond their own ship. Some captains did not
bother to tell them, but Herrick, as always, had tried to
explain whenever he could the reasons and the rewards.

Had Farquhar remained in *Lysander*, he would have benefited
from Herrick's example. These men, Bolitho knew, would have
given that bit extra as the ship had drifted towards the sand-
bars, her master dead, and the helm shot away.

He looked up sharply as a lookout yelled, ' 'Tis the *Harebell*,
sir!'

Herrick grinned, his face shedding some of the strain as he
said, 'Good old Inch! I was beginning to wonder what had
happened to him!'

They watched the sloop's sails growing out of the horizon,
the steep angle of her masts as she crammed on more canvas
to run down on the squadron.

Bolitho saw the changing shadows on the sloop's topsails,
and found himself pleading that the wind would not choose
this moment to desert them. The thought of being becalmed,
with Inch and his news too far away to contact, was almost
unbearable. And the wind had acted in that fashion several
times since they had sailed from the Greek islands. Strong to
gale force, and then breathing away to nothing, the sodden
decks and sails steaming in fierce sunlight, the ships motionless, like men beaten senseless in a brawl.

Herrick asked softly, 'What d'you think, sir? Good or bad
news?'

Bolitho bit his lip. Inch had been away a long while. As his little squadron had sifted information and news of the enemy's whereabouts and strength, almost anything might have happened.

He replied, 'My guess is that a blockade will now be built up around the French ports. Once de Brueys knows his supply fleet and siege artillery are destroyed at Corfu, he may think differently about invasion. Our people have worked hard, Thomas. I hope their efforts will have given the fleet *time*.'

The air was heavy with greasy smoke from the galley before *Harebell* had tacked close enough to lower a boat. Bolitho noticed that most of the off-watch seamen remained on deck, instead of going for their midday meal. To see Inch come aboard, to try and learn something of what was happening.

In the great cabin, Bolitho made Inch take a glass of wine, to give him a moment to regain his breath.

It was strange, he thought, that after all the battles and the pain, it often fell to men like Inch to carry really important news. You would hardly notice him in a street. Gangling, with his long horseface and excited manner, he did not seem the stuff of heroes as their public liked to imagine. But Bolitho knew differently, and would not have traded him for a dozen others.

Inch explained, 'I delivered the despatches, and,' he shot Herrick a quick glance, '*and* my passenger, sir. Then I was caught up in tremendous activity.' He frowned to gather his thoughts. 'Rear-Admiral Sir Horatio Nelson in his flagship *Vanguard* passed through Gibraltar Strait at the beginning of May and headed for Toulon.'

Herrick breathed out deeply. 'Thank the Lord for that.'

Inch stared at him. 'No, sir, I beg to differ. There was a great storm, and Nelson's ships were scattered, his own completely dismasted and almost run ashore. He had to make for shelter to effect repairs. To St. Peter's at Sardinia.'

Herrick groaned. 'That's bad!'

Inch shook his head. 'Well, in *some* ways, sir.'

Bolitho said, 'Come, man, *spit it out*!'

Inch grinned apologetically. 'Nelson's repairs delayed his plans, but allowed his other reinforcements to join him. He now commands fourteen sail of the line, but – ' He saw Herrick's face and added hurriedly, 'The truth is, sir, the same gale which dismasted *Vanguard* allowed the French to slip past.' He looked from one to the other. 'The French are out, sir.'

Herrick said bitterly, 'And they escaped much as *our* Frenchmen did. God damn the weather!'

'Is that all, Commander Inch?' Bolitho kept his tone level, but could feel the disappointment rising inside him.

Inch shrugged. 'The French have taken Malta without a fight, sir. Nelson's ships have been searching for de Brueys's fleet without success. He has followed their passage through the Ligurian Sea, and even looked into some ports where other French ships might have been sheltering until they were ready to move out.'

'You have done well, Inch.' Bolitho gestured to Ozzard for some more wine. 'And you have brought despatches?'

Inch nodded. 'I was ordered to Naples by the admiral, sir. There I met with the fleet at last.' He grinned awkwardly. 'And with Nelson.'

'The devil you have!' Herrick stared at him. 'That I should like to have seen!'

Bolitho said quietly, 'So you did not meet with *Perle*.'

He looked away as Herrick started to explain about the battle and the new prizes. But Bolitho's mind was elsewhere. By the time Fitz-Clarence had reached Gibraltar it would be too late for him to return and find Nelson. He blamed himself for not thinking that a fleet would be sent so quickly to act upon his own sketchy information and the captured siege guns.

Inch was asking excitedly, 'So where are the French? Nelson has been off Elba and Civita Vecchia and into Naples without sighting a one. And you have come west'rd without meeting them. I do not understand it.'

Bolitho faced them again. 'Did Nelson receive you well?'

'Indeed yes, sir.' Inch frowned. 'He was not *quite* as I expected, but I found him most compelling, in spite of his anxieties.'

Bolitho tried to imagine what might lie behind those simple words. Was Nelson blaming him for losing the French, too? For leading a British fleet which was sorely needed elsewhere to an empty trap?

Inch added, 'If and when I was able to find you, sir, I was to tell you to join the fleet with all speed off Alexandria.' He saw Bolitho's surprise and said, 'Oh yes, sir, Nelson has every faith in your conclusions. He still believes that the French are heading for, if not already in Egypt.' He seemed to expect a show of excitement.

Bolitho said, 'Captain Herrick took it upon himself to visit Alexandria. But for a few decrepit Turkish men o' war and the usual coastal craft, it was empty. As it will be when Nelson gets there.' He looked at Herrick. 'Are you agreed, Thomas?'

Herrick nodded. 'I fear so. From what we discovered and heard at Corfu, it seemed as if those supply ships were expecting to leave for another destination before they joined their main fleet.' He looked at the chart on Bolitho's table, his face grim. 'So when Nelson sails east he will miss de Brueys by a hundred miles or more. The French will rendezvous up *here*.' He tapped the chart with one finger. 'Most likely off Crete.' He looked at Bolitho. 'While we sheltered amongst those islands, the greatest force since the Spanish Armada probably steered just a few miles to the south'rd of us, and we knew nothing of it!'

Inch asked dubiously, 'What will de Brueys do, sir?'

Bolitho stared at the chart. 'In his shoes I'd gather up all the surviving transports, then wait for any others which may have been scattered amongst smaller islands and bays. Then I'd sail south-east. For *Egypt*.'

'Alexandria, sir.' Herrick watched him searchingly.

'Yes. But I think his fleet will remain outside the harbour. Somewhere where they can present their resistance to best advantage.'

Herrick nodded, understanding. 'The Bay of Aboukir. There could be none better.' He grimaced. 'For them.'

Bolitho walked to the stern windows, his legs braced as the ship swayed dizzily across some deep troughs.

'And Nelson will return to the west.' He was speaking almost to himself. 'He will imagine that de Brueys has tricked him, and has attacked some other place after all.'

He had often heard of Nelson's sudden depressions, his self-criticism when his bold ideas failed to show immediate results.

Something flashed across the windows, and he saw it was a gull, darting down to seize an unsuspecting fish below the counter.

A few hundred miles, and yet it meant the difference

between success and nothing at all. He knew where the
French would gather their combined strength, which with or
without siege guns could soon occupy the walls and batteries
of Alexandria. He knew it, but could not tell the rear-admiral
in time. If only he were like that gull and his news could be
carried as swiftly as a bird's flight. The gull would be sleeping
on some Greek or Italian shore tonight, and his ships would
have made little progress in any direction.

He said slowly, 'I want all commanding officers aboard at
once, Thomas. If we are to be of any use we must use our
independence.'

Inch bobbed. '*Not* join Nelson, sir?'

Bolitho smiled at his anxiety. '*Eventually*.'

Herrick jerked his head to Inch. 'Come with me while I
have the signal made.' He glanced at Bolitho's grave face. He
knew from experience when he needed to be alone with his
thoughts.

Two hours later they had all assembled in the cabin. Javal,
hollow-eyed from sleepless nights, fighting the sea and wind
with weakening resources. Probyn, his heavy face wary, and
avoiding Bolitho's glance as he found a chair in a patch of
shadow. Lieutenant Gilchrist, awkward amongst his superiors,
but more sure of himself than Bolitho had ever seen before.
Being in charge of a seventy-four could affect a man in several
ways. It appeared to have been good for him.

Herrick and Inch completed the gathering, while Moffitt,
the clerk, sat at a small table with his pad and pen, and Ozzard
stood curiously beside the polished wine cabinet.

Bolitho faced them. 'Gentlemen, I have to tell you that we
must go and search for the French again. De Brueys is out,
and so far has avoided the fleet which was sent to contain him.'
He saw Javal's tiredness slip away, the exchange of glances
between them. 'We, in this small force of ours, must do all we
can to delay the enemy's plans. You've done far more than
any orders dictated,' he smiled, 'or left unsaid!'

Herrick grinned ruefully and Inch nodded in silent agreement.

He continued, 'I will be honest with you. If we are called to
fight unaided, the odds will be great. Perhaps too great.' He
looked straight at Javal. 'And from you, Captain, I must have
complete honesty, too.'

Javal's narrow features were guarded. '*Sir?*'

'Your ship. Without a proper refit, and within a short space of time, what chance does she have?'

The others looked at the deck or the chart on the table. Anywhere but at Javal's face.

Javal half rose and then sat down heavily. 'I can fight another storm if it's no worse than those gone before, sir.' He looked into Bolitho's eyes. 'But that is not what you were really asking, is it?' He shook his head. 'I can't *fight* her, sir. She took a great hammering. A few more balls into her and I fear she'd founder.' He stared at some point above Bolitho's epaulette. 'She's a fine ship, sir, and I'd not ask –' His voice trailed away.

Bolitho watched his distress, the agony his words had cost him.

He said quietly, 'I was a frigate captain myself. I know what you are feeling. But I am grateful for your honesty, more so because I know what *Buzzard* means to you.'

He continued in the same quiet tone, '*Buzzard*'s main armament must be jettisoned at once. If that does not suffice she will have to be abandoned.' He kept his eyes on Javal's lowered head. 'I am giving you the French prize, *Immortalité*. The bulk of your people can be spread amongst the squadron at your discretion. We will need *every man jack* before long. I understand that your first lieutenant was wounded in the fight, Captain?'

He saw him nod, and then turned to Gilchrist.

'*You* will take charge of *Buzzard* and sail her to Gibraltar with a skeleton company. Avoid trouble, and you should make a safe passage. I will give you your orders, and also the recommendation that you be promoted to commander at the first opportunity.'

Gilchrist, who had been listening to his decisions with obvious dismay, jerked to his feet and exclaimed, '*Thank you*, sir! I'm only sorry that –' He sat down again without finishing what he had started.

Bolitho said, 'We have three ships of the line. They must be commanded by men of experience.' He glanced briefly at Probyn, but the man stared through him. 'And courage.'

Herrick asked, 'Shall I order the squadron's badly wounded to be transferred to *Buzzard*, sir?'

'If Captain Javal is satisfied she is seaworthy after the guns have been jettisoned, I think it should be done.' He raised his head to listen. 'The wind has eased, I think. So let us be about it directly.' He gave Inch a pat on the arm. 'And *you*, Commander Inch, will be able to carry the news of our discovery to your new friend, Sir Horatio Nelson!'

As they prepared to leave the cabin, Herrick said, 'Farquhar would have wished to be with us.'

'Aye, Thomas.' He saw Gilchrist waiting to say something. 'See the others into the boats and then tell Pascoe to signal the squadron on the matter of wounded.'

He turned to Gilchrist. 'What is wrong? I thought you were happy with your appointment, temporary though it will be.'

'I am, sir.' Gilchrist looked wretchedly at the deck. 'I am not a rich man, but I have had great hopes in the King's service. Now you have given me the first real chance – '. He sounded near breaking point. 'And I cannot accept it.'

Bolitho watched him impassively. 'Why? Because of Captain Probyn? The influence he has used on you to unsettle the flagship's affairs?' He saw the astonishment on his face and continued, 'I knew that something was wrong. No man who wished to better his position in the Navy, and wanted to marry his captain's sister, would have acted so foolishly, unless he was affeared of something.'

'Yes, sir. It was from a long while back. My father was sent to prison for debt. He was a sick man, and I knew he could not endure it. He was weak in many ways and had no one to sustain him.' He spoke fiercely, reliving his despair. 'I borrowed money from the wardroom funds which we had built up to pay for extra wine and fresh food whenever possible. I intended to return it when I could. The first lieutenant found out about it. Made me write a confession which he threatened to use if I ever failed in my duty again.'

'He did wrong, Mr. Gilchrist. As did you.'

Gilchrist did not seem to hear. 'When I came to *Lysander*, and eventually became senior lieutenant, I thought I was going to be safe. I admired Captain Herrick, and I found his sister, crippled though she is, a most gracious person. Then we joined the squadron under your flag, sir. And with it came the *Nicator* and Captain Probyn.'

'Your old first lieutenant from the past.'

'Aye, sir.'

So that was it. All the years since his capture by the enemy, Probyn had nursed his hatred for Bolitho, the one face in his memory which he could reach and hurt. And when he had found Gilchrist again, he had been prepared to use threats to make him force a breach between himself and Herrick.

The effect on Herrick had been for the good. But it had cost others dearly, and had indirectly put Farquhar to an early death.

Gilchrist said desperately, 'After your kindness, sir, I'd not allow myself to profit further at your expense.' He gave a short, bitter laugh. 'And my father died anyway. For nothing.'

Bolitho watched the other ships through the salt-caked windows. *Buzzard* would be safe now, he thought. Lighter without her guns, strong in the knowledge that she could avoid any sort of fight or manoeuvre beyond survival. She *would* survive.

He said quietly, 'I am giving you *Osiris*'s surgeon. They say he is a sound doctor. Take good care of our wounded. They have suffered enough. Do not allow them to be left stranded at Gibraltar.' He turned, seeing the surprise and gratitude on Gilchrist's face. 'I am counting on your vigilance, on their behalf.'

Gilchrist nodded dazedly. 'You have my word, sir.'

'Then get about your business.' Bolitho could not bear to watch his emotion. Like a man released from a great weight of worry. From the shadow of the gallows itself. 'You've a lot to do.'

Gilchrist walked towards the screen door, his long legs ungainly, his steps without their usual bounce. He turned aft, his face in shadow.

'I'll tell them when I get home, sir. About what we did . . .'

'Just tell them we *tried*, Mr. Gilchrist.'

He heard him walking very slowly towards the quarterdeck.

Allday came out of the sleeping cabin, his face grave.

'Let me pour you a glass of wine.' He glanced meaningly at the closed door. 'You were too easy on that one, sir, if you'll pardon the liberty.'

'He learned a hard lesson, Allday. I think others will profit from it one day.'

Allday watched him sipping the wine. 'What about Cap'n Probyn, sir?'

Bolitho smiled sadly. 'A good question. But he'll fight when he has to.' He looked at Allday. 'Three captains. It is all we have. Personal differences must wait their turn.'

Allday grinned. 'We *do* have a commodore, sir. And with all respect, he's not a bad one at that.'

Bolitho smiled at him. 'Go to hell, Allday.'

'Aye, sir. I don't doubt I will.' He made for the door. 'If there's any deck space with so many flag officers in residence!'

Bolitho walked to the windows and leaned against the warm timbers. All the weeks and delays, the hopes raised and dashed, and now he saw a point in it all.

He thought of Gilchrist. *Tell them we tried.* It sounded like an epitaph.

He stirred himself and put down the glass.

It would be dusk in five or six hours. He needed to be under way by then. The wind aiding instead of hampering, and this time the objective would be far too big to miss.

*

In the following days while the three ships sailed east and south, each watch passed much like the one before. Bolitho deployed his small force in line abreast, with *Lysander* to the north and the *Immortalité* to the south.

The wind became sluggish and uncertain but maintained its south-westerly direction, so that after losing station during each night, Bolitho worked through the longer hours of daylight to regain his extended line. In the centre, Probyn's *Nicator* was a constant reminder of what Gilchrist had admitted. The weak link, but still the only man with experience enough to handle his two-decker in battle. Nearly three miles separated each ship, and with carefully chosen lookouts, he hoped the area covered would betray some sign, or an outflung patrol of the enemy's strength.

He had sent Inch away ahead of the squadron, to use his agility and speed to reach Alexandria well ahead of his heavier consorts. Only after he had received Inch's report could he release him to carry his final information to the fleet.

Day by day, with the sun getting hotter, and the first sweeping wave of excitement giving way to a more realistic attitude of resignation. Gun drill was carried out whenever possible, as much to keep the hands occupied as to incorporate the newly-joined men into their team. Herrick had told him that the purser was opening some of the lower tiers of salt beef and pork. And there was no fruit, and barely enough water to drink, let alone use for personal comfort.

In *Lysander*, Herrick did his best to keep his men busy on watch, and involved in their own entertainment once the sun had departed at the end of each long day. Hornpipes, and wrestling, a prize of a double rum ration for the most original piece of ropework. In many ways it was harder to think of new ideas than to keep the hands at work and drills.

Bolitho hoped that Javal and Probyn were acting with equal vigour to sustain their own companies. For if they failed to find the enemy this time, there would still be no relief. Just a long, relentless haul back to Syracuse, or to some other mark on the chart which their commodore thought profitable.

Several times Bolitho received signals from Javal that he had sighted the northernmost coast of Africa, but otherwise it seemed as if they had the sea to themselves.

Arguments began to break out, and a knife fight ended in a man being badly gashed, and the other flogged senseless as a grim reminder of discipline.

Then, when Bolitho was starting to worry for *Harebell*'s safety, the masthead sighted the sloop beating up from the south-east. It took another full day for Inch to draw near, and when he eventually arrived on board, his news was like a slap in the face.

He had sighted the Pharos and had sailed as near as he could to Alexandria. As before, it was empty but for the elderly Turkish men-of-war. Perplexed as to what to do, Inch had gone about, and almost by accident had fallen on a small Genoese trading vessel. Her master had confirmed what Bolitho had believed from the start. After leaving Naples, Nelson had sailed direct to Alexandria, but finding it empty, had led his fleet back to the west again. How far, and to what purpose, Bolitho could only guess, but he could imagine the

little admiral searching out information from Syracuse or
Naples, and trying to determine what action to take.

The Genoese trader also told Inch's boarding party that
he had heard of heavy French ships of war off the Cretan
coast. That had been many days ago. Despite all the questions,
comparing of charts, even threats, the trader could not be
more definite.

It was almost dark by the time Inch had completed his
report, and Herrick and Grubb had noted his sparse facts on
the chart for future reference.

Tomorrow, Bolitho would send *Harebell* to search for the
fleet again. In his shoes, Bolitho would have been glad to go.
To get away from the ponderous manoeuvrings of the two-
deckers. But Inch protested, 'One more day cannot hurt, sir.
The French are to the north of us somewhere. It would be
better to remain with you and gather something definite for
Nelson. Rather than finding the fleet once more with little
but rumour to offer.'

Bolitho agreed with him in part. But for the weather, and
long delays left in the wake of battle, they might have had
better luck.

When he had confided his anxiety with Herrick, the latter
had protested as strongly as Inch.

'There is nothing more you could do, sir. Even Rear
Admiral Nelson was dismasted in a storm and allowed the
Frogs to escape from Toulon. It's like seeking a hare in a
burrow. With only one ferret, the odds of success are hard
against you.'

Bolitho looked at them and smiled. 'If I ordered you to
sail up the cliffs of Dover, I believe you would obey.'

Inch grinned. 'I'd need it in writing, sir.'

They went on deck together, and while Inch waited for
his boat to pull alongside, Bolitho watched the molten ball
of sunset spreading like stained glass in a church.

'Tomorrow then.'

He walked aft and peered at the compass, and nodded to
Plowman, the master's mate of the watch.

'How is the wind?'

'Steady 'nough, sir.' He squinted at the broad pendant,
curling lazily in the sunset. 'Tomorrow'll be another day
like this one.'

Bolitho waited as Herrick came from the entry port and said, 'Signal the ships to remain in close contact tonight, Thomas.' He shivered, and clasped his arms around his stomach.

Herrick peered at him, startled. 'Are you ill, sir? Is that damned fever returning?'

Bolitho looked at him and smiled. 'Rest easy. It's just a feeling.' He turned towards the poop. 'I have a letter to write. It can go with Inch and his despatches.'

Later, in the great, creaking cabin, with the shadows swaying and looming around his table, Bolitho rested his head on his hand and stared at the letter he was writing to his sister in Falmouth.

He could picture Nancy without difficulty. Dark-eyed, and unusually cheerful, she remained closer than his other sister, Felicity, whom he had not seen for six or seven years. She was in India, with her soldier husband, while Nancy remained in Falmouth, the wife of Lewis Roxby, landowner, magistrate, and as far as Bolitho was concerned, a pompous bore.

Once they had all lived together below Pendennis Castle walls. With Hugh, and then, years later, Nancy's two children, Helen and James. Now, Hugh was dead, and Felicity across the world, knowing nothing of the French army moving in a blue flood towards Egypt, and towards her.

Nancy's children were grown up, and nearly as old as Adam. It was another world. In Falmouth the air would be heavy with blossom and the sounds of cattle, horses and sheep. The taverns would be full of laughter, of relief that the farms and fishing grounds had once more been good to them.

He wrote – ' *and young Adam is keeping well and does his duty with a dash which would have pleased Father.*

It is not yet certain, dear Nancy, but I think Thomas may have met his lady at long last. Indeed I hope so, for there could be no better husband.'

He looked up as voices and feet crossed above the skylight. But they moved away, and he tried to think of something more to tell his sister. He could not write of the other side of things. The faces of *Lysander*'s company whenever you caught them in an unguarded moment. Thinking of their own families, as with each hour they fell further and further astern. Nor could he explain what they were doing, or the great odds against any sort of success.

Anyway, she would guess some of it. She was a captain's daughter, an admiral's grand-daughter. *She would know.*

He continued – '*you will remember Francis Inch? He has trebled in size and confidence since meeting with Sir Horatio Nelson. He was much impressed, although I suspect he thought "Our Nel" would be a giant, instead of a slight man with one arm and a temper to match that of any collier's master!*

'*I send my love to you and the children, as does Adam, who still thinks of you as a kind of angel. He does not know you as well as I.*'

He smiled, seeing her pleasure as she read that part and remembered. When he had been at sea, and Adam had walked unknown and unhelped out of nowhere, it had been to Nancy that he had gone. Until that moment in time, nobody in the family, not even Hugh, had realised Adam had existed. Born illegitimate, he had lived to his fourteenth year with his mother at Penzance, and when she had died he had set out on foot for the family to which he really belonged.

Yes, she would recall those days as she read his letter.

He finished – '*Think of us sometimes. Your loving brother, Dick.*'

Allday entered the cabin and looked at him curiously. 'Moffitt's finished copying your orders for *Harebell*, sir.' He watched as Bolitho sealed the letter and addressed it. 'Falmouth, sir?'

'Yes.' He leaned back in the chair and looked at the spiralling lantern overhead. 'I've told my sister that you are as difficult as ever.'

Allday turned as Ozzard came through the door. 'Well?'

Ozzard flinched. 'Will the commodore be requiring anything more to eat or drink, please?'

Bolitho stood up and walked uncertainly to the bulkhead and touched the sword.

'Lay out my best uniform coat and hat tomorrow, Ozzard.'

Allday turned towards him very slowly. 'Then you think . . .'

'Yes.' Bolitho looked past him. 'I *feel* it. It will be tomorrow or not at all.'

'I'll need a tot to make me sleep on *that* news, sir.' But he grinned. 'Several, most like.'

Bolitho roamed about the cabin for a full hour after midnight, thinking of faces, and things he had shared with them.

Then he turned into his cot, leaving orders with the watch on deck that he was to be called at dawn.

Surprisingly, he felt calmer than he had since the return of his fever, and within minutes of closing his eyes he was fast asleep.

He was awakened by a hand on his shoulder, and saw Herrick studying him in the light of a dimmed lantern. Beyond him, the cabin skylight showed a pink glow.

'What is it, Thomas?'

Then he heard it. Very faint, drifting across the sea like echoes on a beach. *Cheering.*

'*Harebell* hoisted a signal at first light, sir.' Herrick watched him grimly. '*Enemy in sight.*'

18

The Din of War

BOLITHO strode across the quarterdeck with Herrick beside him. Figures, mostly in shadow, cleared a path for him, and he heard Grubb say, 'Steady at east-by-north, sir.'

Veitch, who had the watch, came to meet him, and touched his hat.

'*Harebell* has just signalled again, sir. *Ships in sight to the nor'-west.*' He glared at the signal party. 'Mr. Glasson was somewhat slack with his men, and I fear we missed some of *Harebell*'s flags.'

Bolitho nodded. 'I've little doubt that the ships which Inch saw were patrols ahead of a larger force. Otherwise they'd have come closer.'

He peered up at his pendant. It was shining cleanly in the new daylight, but the lower yards and shrouds were still in deeper shadow.

He said, 'Very well. Make to the squadron. *Prepare for battle.*' He smiled at Veitch. 'Have our people had breakfast?'

'Aye, sir.' Veitch looked at Herrick and stammered, 'Someone told me of the commodore's feelings about today, sir. So I had all hands called an hour earlier.'

Bolitho rubbed his chin. 'I will shave now, and have some coffee, if there's any left.' He heard the squeak of halliards as the signal dashed up the yards and broke to the wind. 'I hope *Nicator* is awake and repeats the signal to Javal.'

He turned to look for *Harebell*'s lithe shape, but she was stern-on, her braced topsails very pale against the sky.

He said, 'We must deploy our ships to best advantage, Thomas. Alter course directly and steer due north on the larboard tack.'

Across the heaving water he heard the staccato beat of

drums, and pictured *Nicator*'s seamen and marines hurrying to quarters.

Herrick nodded. 'Aye, sir. It'll be more prudent. I'll have the signal bent on, once *Nicator* has acknowledged.'

'She *has*, sir!' Glasson's normally sharp voice was hushed.

Veitch snapped, 'Then *say* it, Mr. Glasson! Or your rank will never rise above "acting"!'

Bolitho did not even hear the exchange. He was thinking. Imagining the breadth of an enemy fleet. The control from one or several flagships.

He said, 'Send away the quarter boat, Captain Herrick. Have the despatch bag sent over to *Harebell*.' He hesitated. 'And any letters there may be for England.'

Shouts echoed along the deck and the boat's crew dashed aft, Yeo, the boatswain, urging them with his powerful voice.

Bolitho looked once more at his pendant. Brighter yet again, but there was not much of a wind. His new course and tack would aid their speed a little, but it would still feel like an age before they got to grips with the enemy.

Pascoe hurried towards him, the heavy bag under his arm.

'Boat's ready, sir!'

'Off you go, Adam. Don't delay, and tell Commander Inch to make all speed to rejoin the fleet.'

Herrick asked, 'Will we take the wind-gage, d'you think?'

'I am not certain.' He felt his stomach contract. *Hunger? Fear?* It was hard to tell. 'But if it is the force I imagine, it will be large enough to see.'

Veitch came aft again. 'Boat's away, sir. Pulling like the devil.'

'Thank you.' He pulled out his watch. 'You may clear for action in fifteen minutes, Mr. Veitch. In the meantime, make to the squadron, *Steer north*. When that is completed, make one other. To *Form line of battle*.'

He walked away as the calls started to shrill and men ran to their stations for altering course. He could leave all that and more to Herrick. Now.

He ducked his head automatically beneath the poop as Grubb yelled, 'Stand by at th' braces there!' The wheel was going over, the sails flapping and banging and spattering the men beneath with great droplets of moisture.

In the cabin it seemed very cool, and he sat almost unmoving while Allday gave him a speedy shave and Ozzard plied him with black coffee.

Ozzard said dolefully, 'That was the last of it, sir.'

He heard Allday mutter, 'Never mind. We'll take some off a Frenchie, eh?'

More stamping feet overhead, and the shriek of blocks and rigging.

Veitch's voice, hollow in his trumpet. 'Make fast there! Belay that brace, Bosun!'

With the lantern giving only a feeble light, the cabin became extra dark, and he imagined the ship heading due north, the others following in a line astern. *Soon now.*

There was sudden stillness, broken within seconds by the rattle of drums, sharp and nerve-racking, so that he knew Leroux's little drummer boys were just above the skylight.

The hull trembled, each deck giving its own sound and reaction as screens were torn down, chests and unwanted gear stowed below, and every gun captain bustled around his crew like a mother hen.

Allday stood back and wiped the razor. 'Eight minutes, sir. Mr. Veitch is learning your ways.'

Bolitho stood up and waited for Ozzard to bring his best coat.

He said, 'Captain Farquhar did the honours last time.' Their eyes met. 'I think that is all.' He smiled. 'But for the sword.'

Ozzard watched the pair of them and then darted forward to adjust the bow around Bolitho's black queue.

Bolitho recalled his feelings about Farquhar. *Like an actor.*

He heard more yells from the upper deck, a clatter of oars as the boat returned alongside.

He looked at Allday, wondering if he was thinking the same. All together. Herrick and Pascoe, Allday and himself.

Bolitho said, 'It's time.'

They walked through the screen door, where instead of a dining table and polished chairs there was only open deck, the dark shapes of the waiting guns and their crews stretching away beneath the poop and towards the strengthening daylight.

He strode past the mizzen mast's great trunk and tried not to recall the broadside which had ripped through *Osiris*'s stern like a bloody avalanche.

Some of the gun crews turned to watch him, their eyes glittering white in the gloom behind the sealed ports.

One man called, 'Yew'm a fair zight today, zur!' He was finding courage in the darkness and ignored the harsh threats of a petty officer. 'Bet there's no better lookin' sailor in the 'ole fleet!'

Bolitho smiled. He knew the accent well. A Cornishman like himself. Perhaps even a face he had seen as a youth, now brought close for this encounter.

He walked past the double wheel and the imperturbable helmsmen. The master and his mates, the midshipman of the watch, little Saxby. And further, to the centre of the quarter deck.

He saw Pascoe, his head and shoulders soaked in spray, speaking in a fierce whisper to Glasson, who had taken charge of the ship's signals.

Pascoe touched his hat to Bolitho and said, 'I will go below, sir.'

Bolitho nodded, knowing that some of the seamen nearby were watching them curiously. Pascoe's new station was down on the lower gun deck with the great thirty-two-pounders. He had Lieutenant Steere as his superior, and a midshipman to fetch and carry messages. Youth indeed for *Lysander*'s main batteries.

'God be with you, Adam.'

'And you,' he hesitated, 'Uncle.' He shot a smile towards Herrick and then hurried down the companion.

'Deck there! Sails in sight on the larboard bow!'

Bolitho snapped, 'Aloft with you, Mr. Veitch. I'd like a firm opinion this morning.'

He stared at the sky, now pale blue and devoid of cloud. The red blobs of the marine marksmen and swivel gunners in the tops, the great yards and black tarred rigging. A living, vital weapon of war. The most complex and harshly demanding creation of man. Yet in the weak sunlight *Lysander* had a true beauty, which even her bulk and tonnage could not spoil.

He crossed to the larboard side and clung to the neatly stacked hammock nettings. *Harebell* was already fighting round in a steep tack, her topsails flapping, her topgallants and maincourse being set even as he watched.

Astern he could see the black lines of *Nicator*'s weather shrouds and tumblehome, but her outline, and *Immortalité*'s, too, were hidden beyond the sloping poop.

Major Leroux ran lightly down a ladder and raised his drawn sword to his hat with a flourish.

'I have arranged my men as you ordered, sir. The best marksmen where they will be unhampered by those less accurate.' He smiled, his eyes far-away. 'Maybe the French will expect to meet with Nelson?'

Herrick heard him and laughed. 'Our gallant admiral must take his turn!'

Veitch returned to the deck by way of a backstay with as much ease as a twelve-year-old midshipman.

He wiped his hands on his coat and said, 'It *is* the enemy fleet, sir. They seem to be steering south-east, and the bulk of it lies well to windward.' He hesitated and then said, 'There is a *second* squadron directly across our bows on a converging tack, sir. I had a good look at it, and I am certain that one or more of the ships were at Corfu. One of 'em was painted in red and black. I saw her just now, as plain as day.'

Bolitho looked at Herrick and drove one fist into his palm.

'De Brueys is holding his main squadron to the west of us, Thomas! He must still expect a chance to meet with our fleet!'

Herrick nodded and said bitterly, 'If he only knew that they had already gone from here!'

Bolitho seized his arm. 'Mr. Veitch is not mistaken!' He looked at both of them, willing them to understand. 'De Brueys has kept his other supply ships to the east'rd, *protested* by his lines of battle!'

'Then I'll warrant our appearance is causing some cackling!' Herrick climbed into the weather shrouds with a telescope. 'I can just make out some sails on the horizon. But you may well be right, Mr. Veitch! Our Frenchmen are protecting their charges from the wrong direction!' He said in a duller voice, 'But the French have plenty of time to re-arrange their defences.'

Bolitho toyed with the idea of going up to the topgallant yard to see for himself.

'There are but three of us, Thomas. The French will have sighted *Harebell* and may assume she is about to relay our signals to the main fleet.'

Leroux said quietly, 'Then I'd not be in Commander Inch's boots.'

Some of the gun crews had left their weapons and stood on the gangways to watch the enemy's slow approach. Like plumed cavalry topping a hard blue rise, the masts and sails began to show themselves even to the men on the gun deck. More and still more, until the horizon seemed engulfed by their sails.

'A fleet indeed, Thomas.'

Bolitho tilted his hat to keep the light from his eyes. He could feel the sun on his right cheek, the clinging weight of his coat. It would be hotter than this soon. In more ways than one.

Hour ran into hour, and as the sunlight grew stronger and harsher, the enemy ships took on style and personality. The measured lines of French seventy-fours, and the whole dominated by one great first-rate, the largest ship Bolitho had ever seen. That would be de Brueys's flagship. He wondered what the French admiral was thinking, how the small line of British ships would look to him and his officers. He wondered, too, if Bonaparte was there with him, watching and despising their brave gesture. Bonaparte was their one real hope. De Brueys was a very experienced and courageous officer, and of all those present he probably understood his enemy's navy best. His intelligence and cunning were well known and respected. But would Bonaparte be willing to listen to advice now, with Egypt almost in sight and nothing but three ships in his way?

He said, 'Tell your marines to strike up a tune of some kind, Major. This waiting burrs the edge off a man's strength. I know it does off mine!'

Moments later the drums and fifes led off with *The Old East Indiaman*, the youthful marines marching up and down the quarterdeck, stumbling only occasionally over a gun tackle or a seaman's out-thrust leg.

After some hesitation, and the knowing grins from his mates, Grubb delved into his pocket and joined the fifes with his tin whistle, the one which had become something of a legend.

'Deck there! Enemy frigate steerin' due south, sir!'

'She's after *Harebell*, sir!'

Bolitho gripped his hands behind him, as with a growing pyramid of sails a powerful frigate tacked away from the unending line of ships and headed towards the sloop.

Inch had the edge on her. With this slow south-westerly it would be hard for the French captain to overreach him now, and unless he crippled *Harebell* with a long shot from a bow chaser, he should be safely clear.

A gun echoed dully across the glittering water, and a thin white fin spurted in the sunlight. It was well short, and brought a ripple of cheers from the watchers in the tops.

The deck tilted heavily, and one of the marching drummer boys almost pitched headlong.

Grubb thrust his whistle into his coat and growled, 'Wind's gettin' up, sir!' To his helmsmen he added, '*Watch it,* my beauties!'

Bolitho looked at Herrick. 'You may load and run out when you are ready.'

He felt the ship lifting and then dipping into a low swell, the spray darting through the beakhead like broken glass.

Herrick cupped his hands. 'Mr. Veitch! Pass the word! Load and run out!'

Leroux said to his lieutenant, 'Bless my soul, Peter, I do believe that the French are keeping their formations!'

Nepean peered at him vacantly. 'But that will surely take *us* right amongst the second group, sir? Those supply ships seem to be heavily protected also.' He swallowed hard and blinked the sweat from his eyes. ''Pon my word, sir, I think you're right!'

The major looked up at the poop. 'Sar'nt Gritton! Spread your sharpshooters to either side! At this rate I think we will be into the enemy's centre before he knows it!'

Bolitho heard all of it. The busy clatter of rammers and handspikes, the shrill of whistles as the guns were run out, one side gleaming like teeth, the other still in a purple shadow.

Bolitho thought of Pascoe and his great charges, three decks beneath his feet. He wanted him here with him, and yet knew that the lower deck was probably safer.

'Run out, sir!'

Bolitho took a glass from Midshipman Saxby and it almost dropped to the deck. The boy was shaking badly and trying not to show it. Bolitho ran up a poop ladder and trained the glass astern.

He said sharply, 'Signal to *Nicator*, Mr. Glasson. *Make more sail.*'

He returned to the quarterdeck and said, 'We want no great gap between us.'

The remark reminded him of Saxby and he said quietly, 'Take this glass, my lad, and go aft with the marines. Keep levelled on *Nicator* for me, until I say otherwise.'

Herrick dabbed his face with a handkerchief. 'Worried about young Saxby, sir?'

'No, Thomas.' He lowered his voice. 'About Probyn.'

'*Nicator*'s acknowledged, sir.' Glasson sounded very alert now.

Bolitho nodded and climbed on to a nine-pounder, one hand resting on a seaman's bare shoulder. Heading on a diagonal tack towards *Lysander*'s larboard bow he saw the French men-of-war reforming to protect their scattered convoy of supply ships.

He counted them carefully. Four ships of the line. Odds against his own strength, but not too much so. Beyond the overlapping straggle of supply vessels he saw the squared sails of a frigate, snapping at the heels of those vital ships like a Cornish sheepdog when a fox was after the lambs.

He looked past Veitch without seeing him. An hour more at the most. The French admiral would know by then that there were no more British ships close by. What then? Revenge and destruction of the little squadron? Or on to Alexandria in case there was one more trick to play?

Bolitho saw the gleam of red amongst the enemy's formation and knew it was the supply ship from Corfu. Veitch would remember. He'd had plenty of opportunity to watch her and her scattering consorts while he had set fire to the hillside to protect *Osiris* from the guns. And she would be carrying more of those great guns. Without the last of them, de Brueys would never dare to anchor inside Alexandria's narrow entrance. He would need their protection for his ships and the landing of so many soldiers and stores. Denied them, he would do it as Herrick had described, in Aboukir Bay.

And with any kind of luck, Nelson would find them there. After that, it would be up to him.

He looked along *Lysander*'s decks, his heart heavy. And what of us? *We did our best.*

He heard several bangs, and saw smoke drifting downwind from the leading French two-decker. Some of the balls whipped across the low waves like flying fish, but were well clear of *Lysander*.

It was a show of anger. A sign that the French were ready and eager for battle after so long preparing behind their booms and harbour batteries.

Herrick said, 'Bow chaser, Mr. Veitch! Try a ranging ball or two!'

The crash of the larboard bow chaser brought some cheers from those who were unable to see the enemy's show of strength.

Below the quarterdeck, other men were already wrapping their neckerchiefs around their ears, and placing their cutlasses and boarding axes in close reach.

Bolitho heard Glasson say, 'Half a cable short!' But nobody answered him.

The leading French ship was firm placed towards *Lysander*'s larboard bow, sailing as close to the wind as she could, every sail fully visible on her tightly braced yards.

Bolitho watched narrowly, gauging time and distance. Whether they would collide or break the enemy's line. They had to get amongst the supply ships.

A ripple of bright orange tongues from the leading ship, and this time the controlled broadside was better directed. He felt the hull jerk, and heard the searing whine of iron passing over the poop.

Up and down between the eighteen-pounders and their motionless crews, Kipling, the second lieutenant, walked unhurriedly, his drawn sword over his shoulder like a stick.

'*Easy*, my lads!' He was speaking almost softly. As if calming a horse. 'Stand-to and face your front!'

Bolitho saw the Frenchman's forecourse stretched and hard-bellied on its yard, and it looked for all the world as if it was spread on *Lysander*'s bowsprit and jib boom.

Bolitho snapped, 'Let her fall off two points!'

He nodded to Herrick as Grubb's men put up their helm.

'As you bear! *Fire!*'

*

From forward to aft, *Lysander*'s larboard guns fired, reloaded and fired again, smoke and fire belching from her ports, the trucks squealing as the crews trundled them back again for another broadside.

Bolitho gritted his teeth, feeling the deck shaking violently to the guns' recoil. His eyes smarted as he trained his glass beyond the bow, seeing the Frenchman's sails jerking and tearing under the barrage. Some of *Lysander*'s guns would not bear on the French leader, but he hoped that the heavier balls from the thirty-two-pounders might be finding targets over and beyond her stern.

Herrick shouted, 'The French captain's altered course, sir!' He cursed as the enemy ship fired, the broadside haphazard and ill-timed, but nevertheless deadly. Great thuds shook the hull, and two large holes appeared in the main topsail.

Bolitho watched the enemy's yards moving, narrowing the exposed sails as she turned slightly away. To give her gun crews a better chance to fire and to take advantage of the wind, which by being so close-hauled had been denied her.

Bolitho said sharply, 'Alter course to larboard again! Steer north by west!'

He had not wasted his first broadsides. It had unnerved the enemy captain enough to make him edge round to return fire. It would take him far too long to work his ship back so close to the wind.

Men hauled wildly at the braces, the yards creaking and allowing the sun to spill more light into smoke-hazed decks.

'*Fire!*'

The larboard guns came crashing inboard, one by one, the crews sponging out and yelling like madmen as they reloaded.

Bolitho saw the second French ship rising above the rolling smoke, and knew he had caught the leader unprepared. The second one was already probing towards the larboard bow, and ahead of her, hidden in *Lysander*'s own gunsmoke, was the gap between the ships, the hole in the line.

'Set the forecourse!' Bolitho heard balls whimpering overhead and saw tall waterspouts bracketing the ship on either side. The deck bucked sharply, and several lengths of broken cordage fell unheeded on the spread nets. 'Hold her, Mr. Grubb!'

Major Leroux yelled, 'Ready, Marines!' He had his sword above his head. 'By sections, *fire!*'

The sharper cracks of the muskets, the hollow bang of the maintop swivel, must have made the men at the lower battery on the starboard side realise for the first time just how near the Frenchman was. And as *Lysander*, holding the wind in her increased canvas, surged across the leader's stern, the crews cheered, blinking in the sunlight, then reeling aside as

Lieutenant Steere blew his whistle, and the whole line of thirty-two-pounders roared out at the enemy.

Painted scrollwork, glass and strips of timber flew above the smoke, and Bolitho pictured the terror amongst the supply ships as *Lysander*'s fierce-eyed figurehead thrust through the line towards them.

'Fire!'

The second Frenchman, another seventy-four, was changing course rapidly, swinging to larboard and firing as she followed *Lysander* round. Balls ripped into the hull and hissed above the sweating gun crews, while from the French leader came a less powerful challenge from a stern chaser and a few charges of canister. Several marines had dropped, but Sergeant Gritton was holding them together. The ramrods rising and falling, the balls rammed home, and then the scarlet line back up to the nettings to shoot once more.

Bolitho ran to the lee side and peered through the smoke. The French leader had lost her main topmast and was drifting heavily, with either her steering gone, or so badly hampered by dragging spars and canvas she was temporarily out of control.

'Again, Mr. Veitch! Full broadside!'

Gun captains yelled to restrain the din-crazed crews, even used their fists, as one by one the starboard guns were trundled to the ports and each captain held a blackened hand towards his officer.

Veitch yelled, 'Fire!'

Starting with the lower battery, up along the eighteen-pounders, and finally to the quarterdeck nine-pounders, every black muzzle added its havoc to the bombardment.

Bolitho watched the smoke rolling away, trying to see the enemy, his eyes streaming, his mouth like sand.

The sky had gone, even the sun, and the world was confined to a thundering nightmare of flame and earsplitting noise.

He felt the hull shiver, heard muffled screams from far below as enemy iron came through a port and sliced amongst the crowded gun deck. He tried not to think of Pascoe lying hurt or crippled, the horror that a great ball could do in such a confined place.

He saw a flag making a small patch of colour in the smoke, and realised there was no other mast near it. Some of the gun crews started to cheer, their voices strangely muffled after the din of a full broadside. He watched grimly as the other ship showed herself through the fog, her stern and quarter smashed and almost unrecognisable. Only her foremast remained, and some brave soul was risking death to climb aloft and fix a new tricolour to the foretop.

Herrick shouted incredulously, '*Nicator*'s *not following!*' He fell back as a man was hurled from a gun, his scream dying in his throat. Herrick lowered him to the deck, his hands spattered with blood. As he scrambled up again he said savagely, 'Probyn's not going to help!'

Bolitho glanced at him and ran to the larboard side, seeking the rest of the enemy line, and saw that the remaining two were holding on the same course, while the one which had swung round after *Lysander* was still trying to overhaul, her forward guns firing towards the quarter.

Bolitho shouted, 'Direct your fire on that one!'

He winced as men fell kicking from a pair of guns. Splinters and charred hammocks burst across the boat tier, and he saw a ship's boy smashed to the deck and almost decapitated by a jagged length of planking.

'Fire!' Lieutenant Kipling was still walking up and down, but his hat had gone, and his left arm hung useless at his side. 'Stop your vents! Sponge out! Load!' He stooped to drag a wounded man from the path of a gun. '*Run out!*'

Thuds along the gangway and decks made some duck away, and Bolitho saw bright darting flames from the enemy's tops as the sharpshooters tested their aim.

'*Fire!*'

There was a ragged cheer as the enemy's fore topgallant mast toppled, steadied and then plunged into her own gunsmoke. Some of her marksmen would have gone with it.

But she was still firing, and Bolitho could feel the balls slamming into the side and poop, the crash and whine of metal, the dreadful screams.

A midshipman ran across the deck, his eyes fixed on Bolitho. 'Sir! *Immor- Immor-*' He gave up. 'Captain Javal's ship is breaking through, sir! Mr. Yeo's respects, and he saw her thrusting across the third Frenchie's bowsprit!'

Bolitho gripped his shoulder, feeling him jump with alarm as a ball crashed through the quarterdeck rail and killed two men at a nine-pounder. They fell in a bloody heap at the midshipman's feet, and it was then that Bolitho realised it was Breen, his ginger hair almost black with smoke.

'Thank you, Mr. Breen.' He held his shoulder tightly until he could feel some of the terror ebbing away. 'My compliments to the boatswain.' As the midshipman started to run for the ladder he said, 'Take your time, Mr. Breen!' He saw his words holding him, steadying him. 'Our people are looking to their "young gentlemen" today!' He saw the boy grin.

Herrick called, 'I can see *Nicator*, sir! She's still disengaged!'

Bolitho looked at him. Probyn was well clear. He could apply his strength to the rearmost French seventy-fours which were now exchanging shots with *Immortalité*. Or he could set more sail and come after *Lysander*.

He said, 'General signal. *Close action*.'

He turned as Herrick hurried away and stared across the nettings. He saw *Nicator*'s topsails, her hoisted acknowledgement very bright against the smoke.

Bolitho coughed and retched as more smoke funnelled through the ports.

'Mr. Glasson! Tell your men to *keep that signal flying*, no matter what!'

Herrick shouted, 'Glasson's dead, sir.'

He stepped aside as some marines lifted the acting-lieutenant clear of the guns. His face was screwed into a petulant frown, his mouth open as if about to reprimand the marines who carried him.

'*I'll* attend to it, sir!'

Bolitho turned and saw Saxby staring up at him. He had forgotten all about him.

'Thank you.' He tried to smile, but his face felt stiff and unmoving. 'I want the signal, and our Colours to be seen. If you have to tie them to the bowsprit!'

He heard a chorus of groans, and then Major Leroux shouted from the poop, 'Captain Javal's having a hard fight, sir! His mizzen is gone, and he seems to be trying to grapple!'

Bolitho nodded. The French would have recognised Javal's ship as one of their own. They would try to recapture her first. It was a natural instinct.

He said, 'More sail, Thomas! Set the t'gallants! I want to get amongst the supply ships!'

A seaman fell from an upper yard and lay with an arm thrust through the net. The dead reaching for the living.

But others were responding to the orders, and under more sails *Lysander* forged ahead of the French two-decker.

Herrick wiped his grimy face with his sleeve and grinned. 'Always was a fast sailer, sir!' He waved his hat, the desperation of battle in his eyes. '*Huzza*, lads! *Hit 'em*, lads!'

Another line of long flashes burst from *Lysander*'s hull, and with full traverse on the lower battery Lieutenant Steere's gun captains got several more hits on the enemy. The other ship had lost all her topgallant masts, and her forecastle was a shambles of broken spars and cordage. Several of her ports were black and empty, like blind eyes, where guns had been overturned, their crews killed or wounded.

But she was still following, her jib boom overlapping *Lysander*'s larboard quarter like a tusk, and less than eighty yards clear.

Leroux's marksmen were firing without pause, their faces grim with concentration as their tall sergeant picked out what he considered the most important targets.

But the French were also busy, and the air above the poop was alive with musket balls. Splinters flew from planking and gangways, or thudded viciously into the packed hammock nettings. Here and there a man fell from a gun or the shrouds, and the roar of gunfire was becoming unbearable. For across *Lysander*'s path lay several supply ships, two locked together after colliding in their haste to get away. Kipling was up in the midst of his forward guns, yelling to the carronade crews and encouraging everyone around him. The most forward guns on both decks were already adding their weight to the din, and the entangled supply ships were raked and ablaze with the swiftness of a torch in dry grass.

Veitch yelled wildly through his trumpet, 'Mr. Kipling! Point your guns to starboard!'

He gestured with the trumpet as a seaman touched Kipling's arm to catch his attention. Through the dense smoke, displaying her distinctive red wales, was the heavy supply ship from Corfu, yards hard-braced and her foresail filling strongly as she tacked to avoid her burning consorts.

'As you bear! *Fire!*'

Bolitho walked as if in a trance. Calling out and encour-

aging, not knowing if they recognised him, let alone heard his
words. All around men were working their guns, firing, and
dying. Others lay moaning and holding their wounds. Some
merely sat staring at nothing, their minds shattered perhaps
forever.

All daylight seemed to have gone, although in his reeling
mind Bolitho knew it was no later than eight or nine in the
forenoon. It was painful to breathe, and what air there was
seemed to be spewed from the guns, as if heated by each
blistered muzzle before it reached his lungs.

A blast of canister scythed over the nettings, and he saw
Veitch spin round, seizing his arm at the elbow and grimacing
in agony as blood poured down his wrist and on to his leg.

A seaman tried to help him to the ladder, but Veitch snarled,
'Bind it, man! I'll not quit the deck for it!'

Lysander's guns were firing from both sides at once, seeking
out the blurred shapes which loomed and faded in the dense
smoke, and with the din of their broadsides Bolitho could hear
the crash of the shots hitting the targets and cutting down
masts, sails and men in a devastating onslaught.

Herrick shouted, 'There she goes!' He pointed abeam.

The red-striped supply ship was listing steeply, her hull
punctured by several heavy balls. The weight of her cargo did
the rest. The great siege guns began to tear adrift in her holds,
and although there was no sound to rise above the thunder of
cannon fire, Bolitho imagined he could hear the sea surging
into her, while her crew fought to reach the upper deck before
she dived to the bottom.

Hopelessly outgunned, the French frigate which had been
trying to herd the supply ships away from the fighting, came
out of the smoke, her guns blazing, her deck tilting to the
thrust of her canvas. She swept across *Lysander*'s bows, her
iron slamming through the beakhead and foresail, knocking a
carronade off its slide and killing Lieutenant Kipling where he
stood.

As she forged across the starboard bow, *Lysander*'s forward
gun crews crouched at their ports, eyes reddened and smarting,
bodies shining and streaked in sweat and powder smoke,
watching the frigate's progress and awaiting Kipling's whistle.

The boatswain, Harry Yeo, cupped his hands and bellowed,
'*Fire!*'

Then he, too, fell bleeding and dying, and like Kipling did not see the proud frigate changed into a dismasted shambles by the great guns.

A violent explosion stirred the sails like a hot wind, the smoke rising momentarily above the embattled ships and allowing sunlight to probe down like a misty lantern.

The first French ship was still drifting downwind, and the water around her was littered with flotsam and dead men. The second one was dropping astern of *Lysander* with only one bow chaser which would bear. But Bolitho saw *Immortalité* and knew it must have been a magazine which had exploded. Javal had managed to grapple one of the Frenchmen, and while the other had tried to cross his stern and rake him from end to end, a fire had started. A lamp blown from its hook, a man running in panic and igniting some powder by accident, nobody would ever know. Of the captured prize there was little to be seen. Her masts had gone, and she was a mass of flame which grew and spread with every second. It had blown to the ship alongside, and with her sails blasted away, her rigging and gangway well alight, she, too, was doomed.

Bolitho wiped his eyes, feeling the pain for Javal and his men.

Then as the smoke swirled down again he heard Grubb yell, 'Rudder, sir!'

He crossed the deck, ignoring the occasional thud of a ball by his feet as he stared at the helmsmen who were swinging the big wheel from side to side.

Grubb added thickly, 'That bugger's chaser 'as shot the rudder lines away!' He pointed at the fore topsail beyond the quarterdeck rail. 'She's payin' off!'

Bolitho shouted, 'Get some men aft! Rig new lines!' He saw Plowman call for seamen from the nearest guns. 'Fast as you can!'

Herrick stared despairingly at the flapping sails. 'We must shorten at once!'

'Aye, Thomas.'

He tried not to think of their following Frenchman. One lucky shot had hit *Lysander*'s steering gear, and now, as the wind turned her gently downwind, she was swinging her stern towards her enemy. It would be *Osiris* all over again. He tried not to curse aloud. Except that this time there was no *Lysander* coming to the rescue.

On every side he saw or heard the chaos caused amongst the supply ships. De Brueys might have soldiers and horse artillery in plenty with his main fleet, but he would never have a single siege gun like the one which had sent *Osiris* to her death.

Then, as now, *Nicator* had kept away. Held off by a man so embittered, so twisted by his hatred that he would see his own people die, and do nothing to help.

More crashes came from below, and there was a chorus of yells as *Lysander*'s main topgallant mast came splintering down through the smoke, taking men and sail with it into the water alongside with a mighty splash.

As more seamen ran with axes to hack it away, Bolitho saw Saxby hurrying to the shrouds, another broad pendant wrapped around his waist like a sash.

As he hauled at the halliards he shouted, 'Thought I might need an extra one, y'see, sir!' He was laughing and weeping, his fear gone in the horror which surrounded him. Later, if he survived, it would be harder to bear.

Bolitho looked past him towards the Frenchman's topsails and beakhead as they towered above the larboard quarter. Guns hammered back and forth between them, and he felt the deck lurching, heard some of his men still able to cheer as they saw their own shots slamming home.

But it was no use. *Lysander* was still swinging helplessly, her tattered sails streaming through the smoke, her guns barely able to keep firing for want of men to supply their need.

The smoke writhed and blossomed scarlet, and Bolitho reached out for support as the first of the enemy's iron smashed through the poop. Marines and seamen fell dead and dying in its path. Lieutenant Nepean dropped his sword and fell choking on blood, and when Leroux yelled for his sergeant, he, too, was unable to reply, but sat holding his stomach, his eyes glazing as he tried to respond to his major as he had always done.

Allday drew his cutlass and thrust his body behind Bolitho like a shield.

Through his teeth he said, 'One more broadside, an' I reckon they'll try to board us!' He pushed a dying marine away and pointed his cutlass through the smoke. 'Just one man I'd rather kill than any Frog today!'

Herrick walked past, hands behind him, his face very composed.

He said, 'Mr. Plowman says it will take all of ten minutes more, sir.'

It might as well be an hour, Bolitho thought.

Herrick looked at Allday. 'And *who* is that?'

'Cap'n bloody Probyn, that's who!'

The French ship was barely feet away from the quarter, although with so much smoke it could have been any distance. What guns would bear were pouring shots into *Lysander*'s poop and lower hull, and from the bowsprit and spritsail yard marksmen were shooting at *Lysander*'s quarterdeck as fast as they could aim.

Bolitho shouted to Herrick, 'How are the supply ships?'

Herrick bared his teeth. 'Six done for, and maybe the same number crippled!'

Bolitho turned to see a body dragged clear of the poop.

Moffitt, his clerk, his thin grey hair marked with a bright touch of scarlet where a splinter had cut him down. Like Gilchrist's father, he had known the misery of a debtor's prison, and now lay dead.

He had to force the words out. 'I am ordering you to haul down our Colours, Thomas.'

Herrick stared at him, his mouth tight with strain. '*Strike,* sir?'

Bolitho walked past him, feeling Allday close at his back. Protecting him as always.

'Aye. Strike.' He looked at the upended guns, the blood, some of which had splashed as high as the tattered forecourse. 'We did what we intended. I'll not see another man die to save my honour.'

'But, sir!'

Herrick hesitated as Veitch lurched over to join him, his arm wet with blood, his face like wax.

Veitch gasped, 'We'll fight 'em, sir! We've still got some good lads!'

Bolitho looked at them wearily. 'I know you'd fight.' He turned towards the enemy. 'But then our men would die for nothing.'

He looked for Saxby and saw him crouching by the bulwark.

'Haul down the Colours!' He shouted, 'That is an order!'

The guns fell silent, and above the crackle of a blazing supply ship and the mingled cries of the wounded they heard the beginning of a French cheer.

They're getting ready to board. Bolitho sheathed his sword and looked at those around him. At least their lives would be spared.

The smoke lifted again to a tremendous roar of cannon fire, and Bolitho imagined for an instant that the French were making certain of a victory with one last murderous broadside at point-blank range. He saw some of *Lysander*'s shrouds tearing away like weeds as balls shrieked above the deck, and then turned as Herrick shouted wildly, 'It's *Nicator*! She's firing into the Frenchman from t'other beam!'

Because of the smoke and the drifting supply ships, some of which were adding their own pyres to the surrounding fog, nobody had seen *Nicator*'s slow and careful approach. Every gun was firing on the Frenchman, which pivoting between the savage broadsides and *Lysander*'s starboard quarter, could do nothing to escape.

Bolitho said, 'Tell our people to stay off the gangways!'

He heard some of *Nictator*'s shots lashing through the rigging above him.

Herrick pointed at Saxby, who was capering around the halliards which held Bolitho's broad pendant. Neither it nor the ensign had been hauled down.

It was soon over, and as the cheering seamen and marines surged on to the French ship's deck, the tricolour vanished into the smoke.

One of *Nicator*'s lieutenants arrived aboard some fifteen minutes later, as grappled the three vessels drifted downwind, the victors and vanquished working together to help the wounded.

The lieutenant looked around *Lysander*'s decks and removed his hat.

'I – I am *deeply* sorry, sir. We were late again.' He watched the wounded marines being carried down from the poop. 'I have never *seen* a fight like yours, sir.'

Herrick said harshly, 'And Captain Probyn?'

'Dead, sir.' The lieutenant lifted his chin. 'Brought down by a marksman. He died instantly.'

A man cried out in terror as he was carried to the orlop, and Bolitho remembered Luce, and Farquhar, and Javal. And so many others.

He asked, 'Was that before or after you came to our aid?'

The lieutenant looked wretched. 'Before, sir. But I'm certain that . . .'

Bolitho looked at Herrick. *Nicator* had been too far off to be reached by any musket. At an enquiry it would be hard to explain, impossible to prove. But someone, driven by shame and anguish, had shot Probyn down as he had stood watching *Lysander* and *Immortalité* fighting unsupported.

He smiled gravely at the pale-faced lieutenant. 'Well, you came.'

The young officer turned as Pascoe appeared on the quarter-deck. 'We had to, sir.'

As Bolitho crossed the deck and clasped his nephew tightly, the unknown lieutenant looked up at a clearing patch of blue sky and at Bolitho's signal which was still flying.

He said quietly, 'We saw the signal. *Close action*. That was enough.'

Bolitho looked at him. To Herrick he said, 'Cast off the French ship as soon as Mr. Grubb's hands have repaired our steering. She fought well, and I've no use for another prize with De Brueys and his fleet so near.'

Herrick walked to the rail and repeated his order to Lieutenant Steere who had emerged from the lower gun deck.

Grubb shambled beneath the poop, his ruined face smudged in smoke and grime.

'She'll answer the 'elm now, sir! Ready to get under way!'

Herrick said quietly, 'He won't hear you, Mr. Grubb.' He looked sadly towards Bolitho. 'He's looking at the signal and thinking of those who *can't* see it, and never will now. I know him so well.'

As the sailing master moved away to his helmsmen, Herrick said to Pascoe, 'Go to him, Adam. I can manage without you for a while.' He watched Pascoe's face and was moved to add, 'Try and tell him. They didn't do it for any signal. It was for him.'

Epilogue

CAPTAIN THOMAS HERRICK entered the cabin and waited for Bolitho to look up from his table.

'The masthead has just sighted the Rock to the nor'-west, sir. With luck we should be anchored under Gibraltar's battery before sunset.'

'Thank you, Thomas. I did hear the hail.' He sounded distant. 'You had better prepare a gun salute for the admiral.'

Herrick watched him sadly. 'And then you'll be leaving *Lysander*, sir.'

Bolitho stood up and walked slowly to the windows. There was *Nicator* about half a mile astern, her topsails and jib very pale in the sunlight. Beyond her he could see the untidy formation of captured supply ships, and a French frigate which they had taken in tow until some of her damage could be put right.

Leaving Lysander. That was the very crux of it. All the weeks and months. The disappointments and moments of elation or pride. The heartbreaking work, the horrors of battle. Now it was behind him. Until the next time.

He heard the bang of hammers and the crisp sound of an adze, and pictured the work continuing about the ship. As it had from the moment that Grubb had reported the helm answering once more and they had cast off the French two-decker. It still seemed like some sort of miracle that the main French fleet had continued south-east towards Egypt. Perhaps de Brueys had still believed that Bolitho's little force had attacked his well-defended supply convoy as a further delaying tactic, and that some other fleet was already gathering across his path to Alexandria.

Battered and holed, her hull filling with water with each painful mile, *Lysander* had sailed with the wind, doing makeshift repairs, burying her dead, and tending the wounded, of whom there were many.

Then, with *Nicator* in company, they had sailed westward again, dreading another series of squalls almost as much as an enemy attack. But the French had other things on their minds, and days later when *Lysander*'s lookouts had sighted a small pyramid of sails, Bolitho and the companies of both ships had watched with a mixture of awe and emotion as *Harebell* had run down towards them. In her wake, black and buff in the bright sunshine, had followed not a squadron but a fleet.

It had been a coincidence, and yet it was hard to accept that miracles had played no part.

Lieutenant Gilchrist in the badly damaged frigate *Buzzard* had not sailed directly to Gibraltar as ordered. Instead, and for no reason which had yet come to light, he had broken his passage at Syracuse. And there, resting and disillusioned after its fruitless sweep to Alexandria, was the fleet, with Nelson's flagship *Vanguard* in its centre.

Nelson had apparently needed no more than a hazy report to set him going once again. To Alexandria, where he had discovered the remaining French transports sheltering in the harbour. But to the north-east, anchored with rigid and formidable precision, much as Herrick had predicted, lay the French fleet.

With half of her company dead or wounded, *Lysander* had remained on the fringe of the fight. The Battle of the Nile, as everyone was calling it. It began in the evening and raged all night, and when dawn came up there were so many wrecks, so many corpses, that Bolitho could only marvel at man's ferocity.

Undeterred by the French line, and the fact that many of the ships were held together with cables to prevent a breakthrough, Nelson sailed around the end of the French defences and attacked them from the shoreside. For there was no heavy siege guns on the land to prevent him, and he was able to concentrate his skill and his energy against an equally determined enemy.

Although the French fleet was the larger, by dawn all but two of de Brueys's ships had struck or been destroyed. The remaining two had slipped away in the night after witnessing the most horrific sight of the whole battle. *L'Orient,* de Brueys's great flagship of one hundred and twenty guns, had exploded, damaging several vessels nearby, and having such an effect on both sides that momentarily the firing ceased.

De Brueys went with her, but the memory of his courage and endurance were as proudly remembered in the British ships as anywhere. With both legs shot off, the stumps bound with tourniquets, de Brueys had ordered that he be propped upright in a chair, facing his old enemy, and commanding his defences until the end.

Bonaparte's dream was ended. He had lost his entire fleet and over five thousand men, six times as many as the British. And his army stood at the mouth of the Nile, undefended and marooned.

It had been a great victory, and as he had watched the closing stages of the battle, the angry red flashes across the sea and sky, Bolitho had felt justly proud of *Lysander*'s part in it.

Later, when he had sent his own report to the flagship, Bolitho had waited to discover the rear-admiral's reactions.

With his usual vigour, Nelson was preparing to put his fleet to sea again, but sent an officer by boat to *Lysander* with a short but warm reply.

You are a man after my own heart, Bolitho. The risk justifies the deed.

He had instructed Bolitho to escort the handful of prizes to Gibraltar and there take passage to England and report once more to the Admiralty. At no time did Nelson mention Captain Probyn's death. Which was just as well, as Herrick had pointed out.

He turned and looked at Herrick. 'It is a strange thing, Thomas, but Francis Inch is still the only one among us to have met "Our Nel".'

Herrick nodded. 'But his influence is here, nonetheless, sir. That letter from him and the fact that a broad pendant still flies above this ship, is far better than any handshake.'

Bolitho said, 'After all we've been through, I shall miss *Lysander,* Thomas.'

'Aye.' His round face saddened. 'Once at anchor, I will get the more serious work done. Although I fear she may never again stand in the line of battle.'

'When you arrive in England, Thomas.' He smiled. 'But

then, I don't have to remind you, do I? I will always need a loyal friend.'

'Never fear.' Herrick turned to watch a yawl surging past the quarter windows, its crew waving and cheering the battered seventy-four, their voices lost beyond the thick glass. 'If I can come, I'll come.'

Bolitho saw Ozzard locking his two large sea chests in readiness to be taken to a boat.

He said, 'I've made a lot of bad mistakes, Thomas. Too many.'

'But you found the answers, sir. That's all that matters.'

'Is it?' He smiled. 'I wonder. I've certainly learned that it's no easier to decide who lives or dies just because you fly your flag above the end result.'

He glanced at the polished wine cabinet as two seamen started to wrap it around with sailcloth. Would he see her in London? Would there be anything more between them?

Some hours later, after the drawn-out crash of the salutes, the anchoring, and the necessary business of signing documents, Bolitho went on deck for the last time.

In the sunset, Gibraltar looked like a vast slab of coral, and the ship's yards and furled sails had a similar tint.

He walked slowly along the line of assembled faces, trying to stay impassive as he shook a hand here, spoke a name there.

Major Leroux, his arm in a sling. Old Ben Grubb, as fierce as ever as he mumbled, 'Good luck to 'e, sir.' Mewse, the purser, Lieutenant Steere, the midshipmen, no longer so nervous, but tanned and somehow aged in the months at sea.

He paused by the entry port and glanced down. Allday was already in the barge, very upright in his blue coat and nankeen breeches, as he watched over the oarsmen. They, too, looked different. In neat checked shirts and tarred hats, they were making a special effort for him.

Also in the boat was Ozzard, a small bundle of belongings in his thin arms, his eyes upturned to the ship. When Bolitho had asked him if he would like to be his permanent servant, he had been unable to answer. He had merely nodded, unable to accept that his life of hiding in one ship after another was over.

He turned and looked at Pascoe. 'Goodbye, Adam. I hope

to see you again soon.' He gave the youth a quick handshake
and to Herrick added, 'Take care of each other, eh?'

Then he raised his hat to the side party and climbed down
into the barge. As it pulled strongly beneath *Lysander*'s great
shadow he turned to look at her again.

Allday watched him, saw his expression as he listened to the
cheering which burst from *Lysander*'s deck and shrouds.

Bolitho said, 'There were a lot of faces missing back there.'

Allday replied, 'Never you fret on it, sir. We *showed* 'em,
and that's no error!'

As the barge wended its way around another anchored
man of war, Herrick, who had watched it until it was hidden
from view, walked slowly aft to the poop deck, his shoes
catching on the many splinter holes yet to be repaired. He
turned as Pascoe came after him, the stained and torn broad
pendant draped over his shoulder.

Pascoe smiled, but the sadness remained in his dark eyes.

'I thought you would want it, sir?'

Herrick looked around his ship. Remembering.

'I've got all this, Adam.' He took the pendant. 'I'll send it
to Captain Farquhar's mother. She has nothing left now.'

Pascoe left him by the broken nettings and crossed to the
other side. But there was no sign of the barge and the Rock
was already in deep shadow.